CUBE
ROUTE

TOR BOOKS BY PIERS ANTHONY

THE XANTH SERIES
Vale of the Vole
Heaven Cent
Man from Mundania
Demons Don't Dream
Harpy Thyme
Geis of the Gargoyle
Roc and a Hard Place
Yon Ill Wind
Faun & Games
Zombie Lover
Xone of Contention
The Dastard
Swell Foop
Up in a Heaval
Cube Route
Currant Events
Pet Peeve
Stork Naked

THE GEODYSSEY SERIES
Isle of Woman
Shame of Man
Hope of Earth
Muse of Art

COLLECTIONS
Alien Plot
Anthonology

NONFICTION
How Precious Was That While
Letters to Jenny

OTHER NOVELS
But What of Earth?
Ghost
Hasan
Prostho Plus
Race Against Time
Shade of the Tree
Steppe
Triple Detente
DoOon Mode

WITH ROBERT E. MARGROFF
The Dragon's Gold Series

Dragon's Gold
Serpent's Silver
Chimaera's Copper
Orc's Opal
Mouvar's Magic

PIERS ANTHONY

CUBE
ROUTE

A TOM DOHERTY ASSOCIATES BOOK
NEW YORK

This is a work of fiction. All the characters and events portrayed in this book are either products of the author's imagination or are used fictitiously.

CUBE ROUTE

Copyright © 2003 by Piers Anthony Jacob

A Tor Book
Published by Tom Doherty Associates, LLC
175 Fifth Avenue
New York, NY 10010

www.tor.com

Tor® is a registered trademark of Tom Doherty Associates, LLC.

ISBN-13: 978-0-7653-4309-3
ISBN-10: 0-7653-4309-6

First Edition: October 2003
First Mass Market Edition: October 2004

Printed in the United States of America

0 9 8 7 6 5 4 3

CONTENTS

1

REAR VIEW

Looking back, as was natural in the circumstance, Cube concluded that it all started with the rear-view mirror. What a complicated route, from such a minor trigger.

She was out picking bubble gum from the bubble gum tree beyond the hay field when there was a swirl of smoke beside her. "What are you doing?" the smoke inquired.

Startled, Cube gazed at it. "Talking smoke?"

"That doesn't exactly answer my incertitude," the smoke said, forming a set of eyes.

"Your what?"

"Dubiousness, skepticism, suspicion, mistrust, uncertainty—"

"Question?"

"Whatever," the smoke agreed crossly.

"I don't see why I should answer you if I can't see you," Cube said. "Are you a refugee from the smoking section?"

The smoke formed a mouth. "Ha. Ha. Ha," it said. "Very funny. Not. Don't you recognize a lovely demoness when you see one?"

"A demon!" Cube sidled nervously away from the smoke. "I never did anything to you. Why are you harassing me?"

"Because that's what demons do." A head formed around the eyes and mouth, framed by smoky hair. "Demoness Metria, not at your ritual."

"Not at my what?"

"Observance, rite, liturgy, ceremony—"

"Service?"

"Whatever! So who are you?"

"I'm called Cube."

"Cube! What kind of a stupid name is that?"

"It's not my name."

The hair spread out and formed a question mark. "You just said it was."

"I said I was called that. I didn't say it was my name."

The smoky features swirled a moment, then coalesced back into the face, which was now pretty in a dusky way. "Score one for you, drab mortal. So what *is* your name?"

"Cue. But when other kids saw me, they nicknamed me Cube, because I'm just not with it. I tried to pry it off, but that nickname stuck fast."

"They do," Metria agreed. "That's part of the curse of being human. Now answer my first question and I'll give you something."

Cube decided that she should do that, before the demoness got angry and did her some harm. "I was just picking bubble gum for the boys."

"What use have you for boys?" the demoness asked.

"I like them. But they don't like me."

The smoke formed a vaguely human female body below the head. "Of course they don't! Look at you."

"No thanks. I know I'm not pretty."

"That's the understatement of the hour. You give plain a bad name. Whatever made you suppose that any boy anywhere would ever be interested in you?"

"Well, I do have a certain quality of character."

"Like what?"

"Gumption."

"What?"

"Initiative, courage, aggressiveness, resourcefulness, common sense—"

"Guts?"

"Whatever," Cube agreed, frowning. "I've got gumption galore, but that doesn't seem to be what boys want."

"Naturally not. Boys can see, not think. They don't much notice character."

"So I have learned. But I thought that maybe if I got them something nice, like fresh bubble gum, they might let me hang around, and maybe get to know me."

"Not without a better appearance. Look at this." A dusky hand extended toward her, holding something. "Use the mirror. It is my promised gift."

Cube took the mirror and held it up before her. But it did not show her homely face. It showed an unsightly posterior in a dull skirt. "It's not working."

"Yes it is. It's a rear-view mirror."

"Rear-view mirror?"

"It shows your rear, idiot."

"Ugh! That's worse than my face. Take it back." She pushed the mirror toward the demoness.

"Nuh-uh! That gift can only be given, not taken back."

"I don't regard it as a gift. I don't want it."

But the smoke was fading, and in half a moment it was gone. She was stuck with the mirror.

She set it on the ground and turned away. And found it back in her hand. She threw it at the trunk of the gum tree, but it returned to her hand before striking the tree. She tried to smash it against a stone, but it shied away.

"!!!!" she swore, absolutely disgusted. At age twenty she was old enough to use an ugly word if so motivated. The demoness had succeeded in making a dull day into a bad one. That must have been why D. Metria had bugged her in the first place: to get her to accept the mirror.

She looked at the next tree, which bore pretty colored gum drops. She was half tempted to eat some of those, but they would just make her teeth drop out of her gums. That would make it difficult to chew.

She jammed the mirror into a pocket and headed for home, disgruntled. Maybe she could find someone else to give it to, someone with a prettier rear than her own.

That reminded her of her condition. "I wish I were beautiful!" she exclaimed. "Then I could nab a good man and settle down and have a nice family. Or something."

The demoness reappeared. It seemed she hadn't gone far when she faded out. "Ha. Ha. Ha!" she laughed in a carefully measured cadence.

"What's so funny?"

"You think pulchritude would solve your dreary life?"

"What?"

"Beauty," the demoness said crossly. "Whatever."

"Do you have a problem with vocabulary?"

"However did you guess?"

"Sometimes I get lucky, if the subject isn't men."

"Answer the question."

"Yes, beauty would transform my existence. Pretty girls have great lives, even if they have no perceptible minds. Everybody knows that."

Metria's form firmed into sheer loveliness. "Like this?"

"Yes!"

"You're wrong."

"How would you know? You're a demoness. You can assume any form you wish. You can stun any village lout with your beauty."

At that point a village lout appeared, walking down the path toward the gum trees. Metria turned toward him, opened her blouse, and inhaled. The lout fell stunned, blindly smirking at the sky. "True. But who wants a lout?"

"You could do it to a good man too."

"Yes. I did. I'm married."

"So you see. That's what I want to do. Then I'd be happy."

"Maybe. Lovely women traditionally make poor choices in men."

"I wouldn't. I'd choose a good one to stun. Because I have

as much character as I don't have body." Then reality crashed in on her. "But what's the use? I'll never be beautiful, so I'll never nab a man."

"If that's what you want, why don't you do something about it?"

"What *can* I do about it?" Cube demanded. "I am the way I am."

"You can go see the Good Magician Humfrey, dummy, and ask him how to get beautiful."

Cube stood still for a good three quarters of a moment. "I never thought of that!"

"That's why you're a dummy."

Cube realized that in time, without a whole lot of effort, she could get annoyed at the demoness. But it was a good idea. "I'll do it."

"Of course he'll charge you a year's service, or the equivalent."

"I know that," Cube said, annoyed.

"And his Answer will be confusing, so you won't properly understand it until it's too late."

"I know that too. But his answers are always true."

"Also obvious in retrospect, making you feel even more like a dummy." The demoness faded out again.

It was true. But what other choice did she have? If there was any barely possible, remotely conceivable, faintest shadow of an obscure hint of half a chance that she could become even marginally pretty if you liked that type, she had to try for it. What was gumption for, if not to do something brave and foolish? Thus was her decision made.

"Ha. Ha. Ha," the voice of the demoness came, with just a wisp of swirling smoke.

Cube frowned. She hadn't even voiced her decision, but the infernal demoness knew. Still, she felt buoyed, because now at last she was setting out to do something about her plight. Even if the Good Magician couldn't tell her how to become beautiful, she would know she had done her best.

And if, just maybe, somehow, there was a way—what a change that would make in her life!

"That's what yooo think," the singsong voice of the demoness came.

"Oh, go soak your face."

"If you insist." There was a sound of sloshing water. "Glub. Glub. Glub."

Cube had to smile. Metria was some character.

"Thank you."

Cube ignored her. The demoness had to be guessing at her thoughts.

"No, your smile gave you away."

Oh.

The demoness reappeared, evidently about to speak some other incidental mischief. Her feet touched the ground.

"Hay!"

Metria jumped and puffed into smoke. "Who called?"

Cube laughed. "You touched the hay field. It always gets your attention, the first time."

"Bother!" the demoness said crossly, and faded. Cube was glad to have seen her get fouled up, for once, instead of doing the fouling.

"At least you didn't land on the romants hill," Cube said to the space Metria had faded from.

Sure enough, there was a response. "What kind of hill?"

"Romants. When the ants bite you, you fall in love. I think there's a small love spring under the hill."

"That's novel."

"A romants novel?" Cube could take or leave puns, but this did seem to be a good occasion for one.

"I'm gone." And maybe this time she was.

So when should she make the trek to the Good Magician's castle? Well, there was no time like the present. It wasn't as if she had anything worth returning home for. She lived alone, without even hope of male company.

She headed for the nearest enchanted path. Those paths were always best for traveling, because dragons and other noxious beasts couldn't get on them, and they had regular rest stops with pie trees and shelter. In fact she had always wanted to travel, but never had a reason to do it. Now she had the best one: her future happiness.

Cube walked swiftly. She was a good walker, having muscles in her legs and stamina in her torso. Of course that was part of the problem; she had muscles instead of feminine curves. So she could out-walk any girl she knew, but of course they didn't need to walk. Men came walking to *them*.

Soon she was out of familiar territory, but she wasn't concerned. She could defend herself if she needed to. Which was another part of the problem: her talent was an ugly, aggressive one, befitting her character, when she would have preferred an appealing, feminine one.

She approached a huge mound. It looked like an ant hill, except that water was flowing down its slopes. She didn't trust this, but the trail led right by it on the way to the enchanted path.

A huge insect came out to challenge her. It was larger than she was, and had about thirty heads, each of which had a snout looking rather like the nozzle of a hose. What in Xanth could it be?

Then she saw the sign: BEWARE THE HYDRA ANT. Oh, no—this was one of those water-spouting bugs.

She reversed course, backing away. She didn't want trouble. But the hydra ant followed. Then it squirted water from one of its nozzles. The jet missed, but soon it would get the range, and Cube would get soaked. It was looking for trouble.

There was no help for it. She had to defend herself, because this was the only access in this area to the enchanted path, and she had to reach that path. It wasn't as if she lacked gumption to do it, just that she preferred to try to seem halfway feminine if that was manageable. But this was the time for boldness.

She invoked her talent. In a moment a swarm of little silvery bugs appeared. They were nickelpedes, the scourge of caves and crevices. "Sic 'em," she said, pointing to the ant.

The nickelpedes charged the big ant. In a moment they were chomping its feet, gouging out nickel-sized chunks of flesh. The hydra danced away, but they pursued. It aimed jets of water at them, but though it was able to wash any one nickelpede away, or any thirty, there were over a hundred of them. Soon it gave up the fight and retreated into its hill.

"Enough," Cube called. "Thank you."

The nickelpedes left off the chase, and faded into the woods. Cube walked on by the ant hill and reached the enchanted path.

Now she was safe, but unsatisfied. She didn't like having to use her talent, because every time she did it reminded her how unladylike she was. Summoning and controlling nickelpedes—what delicate flower of a feminine girl would ever be caught with a talent like that? There were probably plenty of male roughnecks who would love it. But they hadn't gotten it; she had. She hated it.

Well, she shouldn't have to use it anymore, because the enchanted path had no threats. She wasn't even sure she would be able to use it here, since nickelpedes were monsters. Little ones, but no less deadly for all that. So they probably were barred.

The enchanted path was nice. No brambles overlapped it, no tangle trees lurked beside it, and of course there were no dragons, griffins, or other dangerous creatures. It occurred to her that life should be like this, with a clear path and no dangers. It would be nice to travel forever on such a path. Except that she didn't want to do it alone. She wanted to travel with a man—a man she loved, who loved her too. And that was impossible as long as she was not beautiful.

It kept coming back to that. What would she do if the Good Magician couldn't help her? Now that she had gotten up the gumption to try to do something about it, she just had to succeed. Somehow.

The path wound into valleys, around hills, through forests, and wherever else it thought of, being in no hurry to get where it was going. It finally came to a camp just as evening was approaching. That was part of the enchantment, of course; it was as if the path knew who would be walking on it, and arranged things to be convenient. Yet again, Cube wished that her life could be like that.

She entered the camp, and found a nice little stream cutting across a corner, with assorted pie plants growing by its bank. There was a curtained shelter made of soft cottonwood beside a pillow bush. She was about to pick a nice apple pie when she heard something. She paused, listening.

It was footsteps. Someone else was coming to the camp, from the other direction. Cube wasn't sure whether to be nervous; would it be a nice person, or not?

It turned out to be a handsome young man with blue hair. He spied her as he entered the camp, and waved. "Hi! I'm Ryver."

That was straightforward. "I'm Cue—Cube."

"I didn't know anyone would be here. Is it okay to share?"

What could she say? She was nervous about strangers, yet he seemed nice enough. If he was as nice as he looked, he was exactly the kind of company she wanted. "Of course."

Then he paused, glancing at her more closely. "You're a girl!"

He had been in doubt? "And you're a boy."

Ryver evidently realized that he had been clumsy. "Uh, I mean—"

"Never mind. Make yourself at home." But they had gotten off to an awkward start. Which was the way it usually was, with her, with men.

He looked at the shelter. "Share that too?"

"Of course." Staying the night with a young man—how nice it could have been, if only she were the kind of girl to make a boy get ideas.

Nevertheless, after they had eaten, they harvested pillows and settled in the cottonwood shelter. Each plank was full of soft cotton, and the pillows made it that much more comfortable. It was dark outside, but there was a faint glow from the walls so that they could see well enough. "Wanta talk or sleep?" Ryver asked. Then, realizing that sounded wrong, he tried to backtrack. "I mean—"

"Talk," she said quickly. "Tell me about yourself." Because then she could listen and pretend she was part of his life.

"Sure. I'm twenty-three years old and on my own. My name's Ryver because of my talent. I can work with water. You know—make water balls and things. What's your talent?"

She had to tell him. "Nickelpedes. I can summon and direct them."

"Say, that's great! Can you make them go away, if you have to go through a cave or something?"

"Yes."

"That must be fun. Everybody's afraid of nickelpedes."

"Yes." Which was the problem. So she changed the subject. "Where are you from? Where are you going?"

"I'm going nowhere in particular. I just like to travel. So I'm coming from home and going back there. Nothing much else to do. Last night I met a pretty girl with the talent of negativity; that was a frustration."

"She had a bad attitude?"

"Not at all. She was nice. She said she expected to have a hot night with me, and I liked that idea. But then we slept in separate cabins and had nothing to do with each other."

Cube wished he had a similar idea about her, but of course he didn't. "Why?"

"Her talent reversed her expectation. What she thinks of *won't* happen, and it didn't. I was just as annoyed as she was, but I couldn't get close to her."

If only he wanted to get close to Cube! "Why didn't she announce that the two of you would never get together?"

Ryver stared at her. "She never thought of that. Neither did I. What a waste!" He shook his head. "How about you?"

It kept coming back to her, and not in any way she liked, which was exactly where she didn't want it. But she had to answer. "I'm just a dull village girl. I'm going to see the Good Magician."

"That so? What's your Question?"

Ryver was a bit too open for her taste, being short on sensitivity in the masculine manner. Now she was stuck with the answer. "How can I be beautiful."

"That makes sense," he agreed. Then, yet again, he caught up to the awkwardness too late. "I mean—"

"I know."

There was another ungainly silence. Finally he broke it. "That's my problem. I keep saying the wrong thing."

"I'm used to it."

"I guess so. But you know, sometimes things work out anyway. They did for my folks."

"Oh?"

"My mother, Lacuna—she liked this man, but he didn't notice her, so nothing came of it. Then his life didn't work out, and hers didn't, and she wished it had happened differently, but it was too late. They had both ruined their lives by not getting together."

"But then she found your father," Cube said.

"Not exactly. He was the one she liked, who married someone else and made a mess of it."

"A mess? But in Xanth marriages always work out."

"Marriages last, yes. But she was a mean woman, so he was stuck, and probably wished he hadn't done it. Certainly my mother wished he hadn't. So she made it a Question to the Good Magician. He wasn't there, then, but Magician Grey was substituting, and he told her she should have proposed to Vernon."

"That wasn't much help! How long had it been?"

"Twelve years. And of course she couldn't go back. But then she got a wish, and she wished she *had* proposed to him, and then she discovered her change of life."

"Change of life?"

"Yes. When she got home, she was married to him, and I was her first male child. She calls it her retroactive marriage. I mean, she changed the past, with her wish, and then just sort of stepped into how her life would have been, and now really was. I get confused when I think about it too much."

"That's not surprising."

"But anyway, it all worked out well, for my folks and for

me. I had a good childhood, after having been alone for ten years. I mean, that change of life affected me too, so I had no longer lived alone, and that was great, but I remembered some of how it had been, so I was really grateful. Except for Lacky, my big sister who never existed; I still miss her. Does that make sense?"

Cube pondered it. Vernon must have had a daughter in the bad marriage, who was undone by the change, and Ryver retained some memory of her. Changes of life did have consequences. "I think so. If I could somehow change my past, and make myself be delivered beautiful, I'm sure I'd be grateful, if I remembered my present life."

"Right. That's how it is with me. I hope the Good Magician comes through for you."

He seemed sincere, and she realized that she liked him. He was sometimes socially clumsy, but he had a good heart. "I hope so too." Then she got bold, which often as not got her into trouble. That was the liability of gumption. "If—if he has an Answer for me, and I get beautiful, maybe after I work my year off—where will you be?"

He looked at her in the dim light. "I'm afraid I'll say something stupid. I do that often enough. Maybe I don't understand your question."

"I'm twenty years old and have always been, well, plain. I'd like to—to have a relationship with a good man. Just as your mother did. She changed her reality and got it after she thought she'd lost it. If I got beautiful—would you care to be the man?"

He considered for a full moment, which was the time required for the average man to make such a decision. "Sure."

"I mean, I'd have the same personality. The same talent. I'd be the same person. Only lovely."

"That's what makes the difference."

How unfortunately true. He didn't care about her character, just about her appearance. He really was a typical man. "So if it works out for me, as it did for your mother, maybe I'll come to your house."

"Sure. Just ask for Ryver. Everybody in my area knows the water boy."

This seemed too easy. Did it mean he thought she was joking, or that he didn't believe she'd ever be beautiful? Was he humoring her so as to get rid of her without making a scene? Had she just made a worse fool of herself than she thought? Maybe she should cancel it now. "Of course, if—"

"Let me give you something, so you can find me better. When you come, I mean."

He was taking it seriously! "Oh, you don't need to—"

"I'll fetch it from the river." He got up and stepped out of the shelter.

Bemused, she followed. Now she saw that the rest of the camp was outlined with glow, including its internal paths, for the convenience of travelers. What could he give her, that was from the water?

At the river, he leaned down and swooped one hand through the water. He shaped something with his other hand. Then he offered it to her. "Here."

She couldn't quite make it out in this light. It seemed to shimmer. "What is it?"

"A water ball." He put it into her hands.

She held it. It was indeed a ball, cool and soft, but it couldn't be water because it held its shape. Yet she had seen him swoop it from the river. "How—?"

"I told you: my talent is water. I can shape it into things, and it will keep. Show that to anyone in my neighborhood, and they'll know I gave it to you. If you get caught without water, you can drink some of it, but don't drink it all. If you get tired of it, return it to any river or pond. It deserves to be with its own substance."

"I won't get tired of it," she said, amazed. "This is — amazing."

He paused. "Maybe I'd better show you the rest."

"The rest?"

He faced away from her, then quickly got out of his clothing. She saw just the shadow of his lean bare backside. What was he up to? Then he jumped into the river and disappeared.

"Ryver!" she cried, bobbling the water ball. "Where are you?"

His head appeared, rising from the surface. "Here's my head."

She laughed nervously. "And the rest of you, I trust."

"Not at the moment, exactly. Feel."

"What?"

"Put your hand down in the water. Feel where I should be."

"I can't do that! You're naked!"

"Not exactly. Feel."

Bemused, she held the ball in one hand and put the other down to feel his neck under the surface.

There was no neck.

She felt further. There was no body. Just the head.

"What *is* this?" she asked, growing alarmed.

"It's me. I'm made of water."

"Made of water!" Realizing that this must be a trick or illusion, she put her hand under the head and lifted it up. It came out of the water, like a shaggy ball.

"At least, when I enter water," the head said.

"Oh!" She was so startled she dropped the head. It splashed into the river and dissolved.

Then she saw it form again, downstream. This time it came out of the river by itself. His body was under it. She turned her eyes away, lest she see something she shouldn't, even in the darkness. Actually she was old enough, and was a member of the Adult Conspiracy, not that it did her any good. But she lacked experience, because of her appearance.

In one or two moments—certainly no more than two and a half moments—Ryver had recovered his clothing. "So you see, I'm not a regular man. That is, not when I'm in the water. Originally I was all water, and I longed to become flesh. When I became Lacuna's son, I became flesh—except when I get too close to my origin. I thought maybe you should know that, when you're beautiful, before you come to—to—"

"To have a relationship," she finished for him.

"Yes. This—this has turned off other girls. So if you don't want to do it, I'll understand."

Cube looked at the water ball in her hand. He was indeed not a regular man. But was it worse than the way demons were? He just had a more serious relationship with water than she had realized. "I think I can handle it."

"That's great!"

They returned to the shelter. On the way, she thought of something else. "You gave me something. I should give you something. But all I have is—is something you might not want."

"What is it?"

"A rear-view mirror. But I have to tell you, it's not quite what you think, and you can't get rid of it unless you give it away to someone else."

"That's okay. Let's see it."

She fished the mirror from her pocket and gave it to him. "It's what it shows."

"Seems like a regular mirror to me." He held it up before his face. "Say—what's that?"

"Your derriere," she said delicately.

"Isn't that something!" He changed the position of the mirror, getting a better view in the dim light. "I like it. It reminds me of my early life."

"How does it do that?" she asked surprised.

"When I look back, to see how it was and how it became, it's a rear view. Not quite the same as the front view other folk see. The mirror's like that, maybe."

She was relieved. "It's yours, as long as you want it." She glanced at her ball. "Is it safe to set this down?"

"No, not exactly. Keep it with you, or with something that's yours, like your clothing. If it leaves you, it will revert. That's why folk will know I gave it to you; no one else can touch it."

"That's sweet."

"So are you. I hope you get beautiful."

On that nice note, they went to sleep. Maybe if she got

beautiful she would get to sleep in his arms. As it was, she was satisfied to have their agreement for the future. Maybe it wouldn't work out, but at least she'd be in the game. That would be far more than she had ever had before.

In the morning they took turns using the sanitary facilities, then had a breakfast of milk and honey pies. Then Ryver went his way, and Cube went her way. Her determination to get beautiful had been reinforced; now she knew exactly what to do with that beauty. Until then, she could dream.

Outside the camp was a warning sign: DO NOT LAUGH. Cube looked at it and shrugged; she hadn't been planning to laugh anyway.

As she set forth, a shape looked up beside the path. "Come here and I will really send you," it called.

Cube realized it was a male demon. She knew better than to leave the path. "Where will you send me?"

"To Mundania," he said, chortling. "I am Demon Port."

Demons generally had a simple translation code, except for Metria, who evidently hadn't gotten her word quite right. Demon reduced to D, and the name. That would abbreviate to D. Port, or deport. "No thanks." And suppose she had laughed? Would she have fallen into the demon's power despite the protection of the path? Now she appreciated the sign's warning.

Another figure appeared. "Come to me," he called. "I reduce things to simpler forms. I am Demon Volve."

Which would be D. Volve—devolve. Cube did not want him either, so she kept walking, with a straight face.

A third demon appeared. "I am Louse. I hate bugs."

That would be D. Louse—delouse. Cube did not find that funny at all, because of her talent. Bugs could be very beneficial on occasion.

A demoness appeared. She was absolutely lovely as she preened; she looked like a goddess. She sang a brief melody, and her voice was divine. Then she paused. "Well, aren't you going to applaud?"

That surprised Cube. "Applaud?"

"I am Demoness Va. I expect my due."

D. Va—Diva. A prima donna. Probably the only way to get rid of her was to give her the applause she craved. Cube clapped her hands together several times.

D. Va made a bow and faded out. Cube smiled, but refrained from laughing.

Another demoness appeared. It seemed there was a whole troupe of them. "Tell me your secrets, and I will spoil them," she said enticingly.

Cube couldn't figure that one out. "Who are you?"

"Demoness Mystify."

Demystify. "No thanks."

The next demon was different. It was a fat male in a big washtub. He was scrubbing his own back with a long-handled brush. "Rub-a-tub-tub!" he sang, well off-key. He sounded intoxicated. "Rub my tub, summon me. Rub my back, I'll grant you three." Sparkling water sloshed as he moved.

"Really? Three wishes?"

He looked at her. "Of course not. This stuff is alcoholic. I can't focus well enough to get myself out, let alone grant wishes. But it's a fine-sounding promise." He belched.

What was the pun? "Who are you?"

"I'm a bathtub jinn."

Cube, surprised by the change in the code, laughed before she caught herself. And a bucket of dirty water that smelled of gin drenched her. The demon laughed so hard he and the tub exploded into smoke and dissipated.

Well, she had been warned. Apparently the magic of the path couldn't protect her entirely from her own folly. She paused at the next stream, rinsed out her clothing and herself, put it back on wet, and let it dry on her. At least the demons hadn't stayed to laugh at her unsightly body as she rinsed.

Her hand brushed something on her damp clothing. It turned out to be several stick-hers. She must have overlooked the stick-her bush when she took off her clothes.

There were also a few stick-hims, as though the bushes hadn't been sure of her gender. Even plants rubbed in the fact that she was no lovely creature.

Later, a small boy was standing at the edge of the path. He was staring at her midsection. "What are you looking at?" she asked sharply.

"I see your pan-tees!" he said in a singsong voice.

Cube refused to be fooled; she knew they were completely covered by her skirt. "No you don't."

"Yes I do. They're ugly. And they're wet."

That got to her. Her outer clothing had dried, but her underwear remained damp. "How do you know?"

"It's my talent. I can see panties, covered or not."

It seemed he could. "But that's a violation of the Adult Conspiracy."

"Yeah," he agreed zestfully.

Cube was annoyed. Then she realized that when this obnoxious boy grew to manhood, his talent would cause him to be perpetually freaked out. So that situation would take care of itself. She walked on by him.

She walked well that day, and knew she was getting close to the Good Magician's Castle. That was because there were signs along the way, saying GOOD MAGICIAN'S CASTLE TWO AND A HALF DAYS' WALK, and ONE AND A HALF DAYS' WALK. So her third day's walk should be half a day, and she'd be there.

She felt something in her pocket. She brought it out. It was the rear-view mirror. How had that gotten there? She had given it to Ryver yesterday, and not taken it back. Had he returned it to her in the night? That seemed unlikely; she didn't think he would have done such a thing without telling her, and in any event she would have been aware if he had come close enough to do it.

She had not been able to get rid of it before; could this be another aspect of that? She could give it to a person, but then it quietly returned to her? Magic objects could have odd properties. She'd have to try again, and stay alert. Meanwhile, she put it from her mind. At least she still had the water ball Ryver had given her.

She passed another sign: HEADLINE. At this point she was taking signs seriously. But what did it mean?

Then she saw a line of balls along the side of the path. Only they turned out to be heads. A head line.

"Step over me so I can see the color of your panties and freak blissfully out," the first head said. Then it blinked, getting a better look at her. "Cancel that." The eyes squeezed closed.

Cube almost ground her teeth. Even her panties were not good enough!

Just at the right place there was another campsite. She entered it, and discovered someone else there: a winged centaur filly, with the large human breasts and handsome brown equine flanks and tail of her kind. She also wore a quiver and bow, the harness nicely framing her front. "Hello," Cube said, surprised.

"Hello. I am Karia Centaur. Please don't repeat my name."

"I am Cube Human. I'm on my way to see the Good Magician."

"I just came from there. It's less than an hour's flight from here."

"Half a day's walk," Cube agreed. "But why are you here, since you're not land-bound?"

"I am a winged monster," the filly agreed, though she hardly resembled a monster. "But I can't fly indefinitely, so I need a safe place to spend the night."

"I'm happy to share the night with you, if you're satisfied to share it with me."

"Of course. I don't have human company very often."

They handled the routine of harvesting supper and pillows for the night, then settled down in the shelter and talked. "You said you just came from the Good Magician's Castle," Cube said. "May I ask—"

"I'm a flying centaur, so my talent is flying. That is, flicking myself light enough to float. But I have an associated side effect that I would like to be rid of. So I went to ask the Good Magician."

"As I am doing. Did he help you?"

"No." Then before Cube could look surprised, she explained. "I didn't get to ask my Question. I did not make it through the three challenges. In fact I didn't pass the first challenge. So now I am returning to the herd with my tail between my legs, as it were."

"But I thought centaurs were smart." Then Cube realized that she was being just as awkward as Ryver had been. "I mean, it must have been a formidable challenge."

"It was a stupid challenge, but it stymied me. It was a path that forked. One side passed close by a sticker bush that stuck me when I got close, so I had to avoid it."

"A stick-her bush," Cube said. "It probably stuck only females. I encountered one of those today."

"Oh, a stupid pun. I hate puns!"

"But there are puns all over Xanth; you can't avoid them."

"Yes I can; I fly over them. I make sure to land on pun-free terrain. It's just too awful when I accidentally step in one and get it stuck to my hoof." The filly shuddered. "There is nothing more revolting than having to scrape squashed pun off your foot."

"So maybe the Good Magician was forcing you to face what you hated. That was the real nature of the challenge."

Karia frowned. "I suppose so. I think it was unkind of him."

It was apparent that the centaur had lacked the gumption to tackle something she found objectionable. That would never stop Cube, of course, but there was no point in pointing that out. "Where did the other side of the forked path go?"

"I couldn't make head or tail of that. It terminated at a door. I opened the door, but it became a jug in my hand, and there was just a blank wall beyond it. When I moved the jug forward it became the door again, closed. It was no help at all. I was most frustrated."

Cube laughed. "You opened the door and made it a jar!"

"I fail to see the humor."

"A jar. Ajar—open. Another pun."

"Oh," the centaur said somewhat sourly. "No wonder I didn't appreciate it. In any event, it was of no use to me. So I turned around and flew for home."

"I wonder," Cube said. "Couldn't you have used the jar to catch the stickers, so they couldn't stick you?"

"I suppose I could have, had I thought of it. But I was already pretty upset, and it seemed pointless to continue."

"I'm sorry," Cube said. "It must be a big disappointment."

"It is. I so much wanted to have a rousing good adventure, but I can't risk it as long as I have the complication."

"Complication?"

"The side effect. You see, I get carried away when anyone else speaks my name. That can be extremely awkward."

"Another pun!" Cube exclaimed. "Karia. Carry-a! You must really hate that!"

There was no answer. Then she saw that the centaur was floating out of the shelter. She wasn't flying; she wasn't even walking. Her four legs were folded under her as they had been in the shelter, only now she was drifting in the breeze. Her eyes were glazed, as if she were distracted and not paying attention to her surroundings.

In fact, she was being carried away. "Oh, I'm sorry!" Cube said. "I said your name!"

Karia continued to drift. Cube ran after her, catching at a leg. "Please, I'm sorry! Please come back!"

The centaur opened her eyes. "Oh, did it happen again?"

"Yes! I said your name, and you got carried away. I didn't mean to. I didn't realize—"

"That's all right. But now you appreciate my problem."

"Yes I do. I won't speak your name again."

Karia straightened her legs and touched the ground. She walked back to the shelter. "I would like to go where nobody knows my name. Then I'd be safe. But there's always the chance I would meet someone unexpectedly, who would say my name, and then I could be in trouble. So I suppose I'll just have to stay home, where folk know to call me 'hey, you.' Not that I like that much either."

"That side effect—it's another pun," Cube said. "No wonder you hate puns!"

"No wonder," Karia agreed wryly. "Why are you going to see the Good Magician?"

"I want to be beautiful."

Karia looked at her more closely. "I suppose you aren't. I hadn't noticed."

"If you were a man, you wouldn't notice me at all. I want to marry and have a loving husband and a nice family and live happily ever after, but it will never happen as long as I'm homely."

"Oh, I'm not sure of that."

"You're not homely. You have a pretty face and a bosom that would make men stare even if it weren't bare."

"Point taken. I have not suffered that particular problem of being unnoticed. Yet I would exchange a portion of my assets with you, if I could abate my side effect."

"And I would gladly have that portion! If I had your breasts, no one would notice my face."

"Oh, I don't know. Others do notice my face, and of course my rear."

"Your rear?"

"Like most centaurs, I have a handsomer posterior than face, and of course I am duly haughty about it." Karia reached back and gave her haunch a resounding slap. "I just wish I could see it better."

"I have just the thing for you," Cube said, fishing out the mirror. "Try this."

"I'm not certain how this relates," Karia said, accepting it.

"Try it and see."

The centaur held the mirror up before her face. "Oh, my! Can that be my rump?"

"Yes. It's a rear-view mirror."

"Delightful! It's even handsomer than I thought."

"Keep the mirror," Cube said.

"Oh, I couldn't! I like it, despite the pun, but I have no return gift for you."

"I will be glad if you can keep it. A demoness with a speech impediment gave it to me, and I didn't want it, but I can't be free of it unless I give it away. I gave it away yesterday, but today I had it again. So it may not stay with you anyway, though I hope it does."

Karia considered. "In that case, I will keep it, and hope that it remains with me. If not, I will understand." She paused. "The demoness—would that by any chance have been Metria?"

"Yes. How did you know?"

"She's just about the only one who interacts with humans more than briefly, usually mischievously. And she has trouble getting the right word. She doesn't hurt people, merely annoys them. This is the kind of trick one might expect of her."

"That's interesting." Actually Cube had encountered several other mischievous demons, but they had departed once they tricked her into laughing and getting drenched. "But I still hope you keep the mirror."

"We shall see." They composed themselves for sleep.

2

GOOD MAGICIAN

In the morning they prepared to go their separate ways. Karia still had the mirror; she checked. Then she looked into the sky, and quailed. "Oh, no."

"What's the matter?"

"The dragon's there. I had hoped it would be gone overnight."

"A dragon is after you?"

"I am afraid so. That's the real reason I came here for the night, instead of to a camp closer to the home range. I knew it could not pursue me along the enchanted path."

"Why didn't you tell me?"

"I did not wish to concern you. You are in no danger from it, as long as you remain on the path."

"But I *am* concerned. A dragon!"

"You are a nice person. But you must be on your way. I shall merely wait here until the dragon tires of the pursuit."

"But surely you want to get home. Can you follow the enchanted path instead?"

"I could hoof it, if the path went where I am going. But it

does not. I must fly, when I can. Once I get close to home, I have a friend whose talent is to make any animal friendly for half an hour, and that will enable me to get the rest of the way in peace."

"I have heard that all centaurs are excellent archers. Could you shoot it with an arrow?"

Karia glanced down at her harness. "Ordinarily I could. But it seems this dragon has somehow learned my name."

Cube saw the problem. "It would make you be carried away, and would pounce on you while you are helpless."

"Precisely."

"Maybe I can help you."

"There is no need. I have enjoyed your company, but do not wish to inconvenience you."

"No, I want to help, and I think I can. I'll give you some nickelpedes."

"Nickelpedes!"

"It's my talent: to summon and control them." Cube squatted and put down a hand, summoning a nickelpede, and one came to her from a nearby crevice. She lifted it. "You see, it doesn't gouge me."

"That's remarkable! I should have thought the enchantment would prevent them from coming here."

"I suppose it would, ordinarily. But this one means no harm, so must be all right." Cube set it on her head, and it nestled in her somewhat messy hair, contented. "I can tell them not to bother you. Then you can throw them at the dragon, and it will go away."

"That's an interesting ploy. But I fear I would hear my name and be carried away before I could get close enough to do that."

"Suppose I stay close to you, so I can snap you back?"

"That would do it. Of course if you were with me, you could throw the nickelpedes yourself."

"Yes I could. I'll do it."

"But this would take you off the path, and cost you time. I can't ask you to make that sacrifice."

"It's no sacrifice. I want to help."

"You're so nice. But—" Karia paused again. "There is one thing. There is a good-sized river. The enchanted path of course has a safe crossing, but that is some distance downstream. I could carry you across a shortcut, saving you as much time as I cost you, perhaps more."

"That's great."

"And the dragon would assume that we were vulnerable while over the river. So it would attack. I will drift, but slowly, and you can deal with it when it gets close enough."

"Done."

"Get on my back and I will take you to the river. Then we shall see."

Karia settled on the ground, and Cube climbed on her back. "I've never ridden a centaur before, or anything else. I hope I don't fall off."

"You will not." The centaur's tail flicked, and Cube suddenly felt very light. "I have made you light so I will be able to fly with you. If by some mischance you did fall off, you would merely drift slowly to the ground."

"Fabulous."

They set off along the enchanted path. Karia trotted competently; she did not need to use her wings. She had made herself light, using the winged-centaur magic, so was using very little energy. Her wings were folded against her back, looking like a feather cloak.

The dragon followed, watching them from the sky. Cube had not realized that dragons preyed on centaurs, but probably it was a matter of opportunity. A healthy alert centaur with bow and arrows was nobody's prey, but Karia had her liability, so she was vulnerable. That was all the dragon needed. Cube was disgusted, but realized that this was the way it was with predators. They got their prey any way they could.

They came to the river. It was far too wide to jump across; in fact it would be a fair swim. There were colored fins circling in the water: loan sharks, waiting to take an arm and a leg or two. No swimming there!

The path turned and followed the riverbank south. This

was the detour to the safe crossing. Most travelers would follow it, rather than risk the dangers of air and water.

"Are we ready?" Karia inquired in a murmur.

"I think we are."

But the centaur hesitated. "It just occurred to me: Can the nickelpedes come to you if you are in the air? They will have no crawling space."

"You're right!" Cube said. "I forgot that they need some way to reach me. I'll summon a bagful now."

She dismounted, went to the edge of the path, and held out a cloth bag. Immediately nickelpedes came and swarmed into the bag until it was bulging. Cube held it carefully and remounted. "Now I am ready."

"Hold on to my mane."

"Mane? I don't see one."

"My hair," Karia clarified. Now Cube saw the lustrous fair tresses lying across the wings.

"I don't want to pull your hair."

"It's tough. Don't be concerned."

Karia trotted toward the river. Cube grabbed a handful of flying hair, her other hand held the bag. The wind rushed past as the centaur broke into a canter, and then a gallop, achieving takeoff velocity. She spread her wings and launched into the air just as they reached the river. The wings became huge, spreading out to either side like great white fans.

Cube stared down, seeing the river so close below that the centaur could almost have galloped on it. The loan sharks saw it too, and quickly clustered, snapping at hoofs. But Karia was already gaining altitude, just out of their reach. Still, it was scary; any mistake, and the sharks would feed on four centaur legs and two human legs, and four arms as well. Cube wasn't sure whether they ate anything other than arms and legs, and didn't care to find out.

"Dragon at one o'clock," the centaur murmured.

Was it that late in the day already? Oh—she meant a direction. Cube looked forward, just right of the arrow quiver. There it was, swooping down, not firing fire. Instead it was shaping its mouth to form a word. In this case, a word was more deadly than fire.

"Kaarriaa!" the dragon roared.

It was distorted, but recognizable. The centaur went inert, gliding without control. The loan sharks congregated below, gazing hungrily up, and the dragon glided in for the kill.

Cube balanced so she could use both hands. She held the bag with one, and reached in with the other. She brought out a handful of nickelpedes. "Chomp 'em!" she whispered, and hurled the handful at the approaching snoot.

Her aim was good. Most of the nickelpedes landed on the dragon's nose. A few fell to the side and dropped to the water, where they landed on upturned shark noses. There was a pause of two to three fifths of a moment.

"Wake," Cube said to the centaur. "It's happening."

The centaur became alert, steadying her flight with her wings, just enough to hover in place. She did not want to attract attention.

Then the dragon yiped. Nickelpedes were gouging out nickel-sized disks of flesh from its snout. There was a scream from below as the other nickelpedes did similar work on the noses of the sharks. Then they moved on to the dragon's body, and to the fins. They were feasting on dragon skin and making a gory soup of shark fins.

Distracted, the dragon tried to burn them off its chest. It curved its neck and blasted out a formidable jet of fire—and squealed as its skin charred. It lost control and plunged into the water, smoking. There was a great splash. But the nickel-pedes did not relent; they were still gouging. The dragon sank out of sight, twisting and wriggling, trying to escape the chomping.

This might have been a feast for the loan sharks, but they had problems of their own. More nickelpedes were in the water now, scrambling for lodging, and more sharks were getting tagged. They lurched away, trying to escape, but they were carrying the nickelpedes with them.

"How absolutely horrible," Karia murmured ecstatically.

"Awful," Cube agreed, smiling.

Soon the carnage had sunk under the surface and the water was calm. Karia resumed flight, crossed the river, and landed on the enchanted path on the other side. "I believe this is where we part," she said. "I now have a clear flight path home. It has been a pleasure."

"A pleasure," Cube agreed.

They shook hands. Then the centaur took off again, flying back across the river and up, up, away, into the sky. Soon she was a mere lovely speck. Then she disappeared behind a cloud.

Cube was sad. She really liked the centaur, and was glad they had had this extra interaction. She had never flown before, and would treasure the experience.

Then she remembered to check for the mirror. Sure enough, it was back. It had waited until they weren't paying attention, and rejoined her. She had not gotten rid of it, again.

She faced east and marched on along the path. It wasn't long before she saw the spires of a castle. She had indeed gained time, and was arriving at the Good Magician's residence early. That was fine; she wanted to get inside and Ask her Question, and hoped he had a good Answer.

The castle looked ordinary. It had a moat around it, complete with a serpentine moat monster, and a stone wall inside the moat, and turrets inside the wall. There was a drawbridge, and it was down across the moat, so was the obvious place to enter. Of course there would be a Challenge there, but she would do her best to handle it. Because she really, truly, desperately wanted to be beautiful, and this was the only way.

As she approached the drawbridge, it wavered, and became something not quite the same. But it still was a route across the moat, so that was her choice.

There was a sign by it: BEWARE THE COMIC STRIP. She paused to consider that. What was a Comic Strip? She had never heard of it, but it didn't sound particularly dangerous. Yet it had to be something that would balk her from entry, if she didn't figure it out. Well, there was one way to fathom it: she would walk in and find out.

As she stepped onto the path that was the drawbridge, there was a raucous burst of laughter, startling her. She looked around, but all she saw was a long-stemmed plant. She took another step, and the laughter came again. This time she verified the source: it was that stem, vibrating. It didn't seem to be dangerous, just strident.

"What's so funny?" she asked it. But now it was silent.

She stepped forward again—and got another loud burst of laughter. Evidently it found her attempt to cross the moat hilarious. She tried to ignore it, but each step she took made it laugh louder, until the very drawbridge was shaking.

She was afraid it would be shaken apart if the noise got any louder, so she stepped back to address the plant. "What do you want?"

But now it was silent. She took another step forward, and got another big laugh. This was getting annoying.

Then she had an inspiration. "You're a laughing stalk!" she exclaimed. "A stupid pun!"

The plant wilted and shriveled and finally disappeared. She had named it, and thus nullified it. She was past the Challenge.

But she wasn't off the drawbridge. She took another step, but found her way blocked by a stick. She didn't think it had been there before, but couldn't be sure. She took hold of it, to move it out of her way. And received a slight shock.

"What a lovely piece of wood you are," she said with nasty irony, throwing it down.

Then she was sorry to have been so rough and rude, even to a stick. "I didn't mean to do that." She bent to pick it up, and got another little shock. "You did it again, you delightful emulation of a club!" she snapped, hurling it away.

Again she regretted it. Normally she tried to be reasonably polite to every person and every thing, because many things of Xanth had feelings too.

The stick had returned to its original place, blocking her way. She reached for it—and stopped. "When I touch you, I get sardonic," she said. "You're a sarcas-stick!"

The stick sank into the floor and disappeared. She had

identified it and defeated it. Had she handled the second Challenge? She was still on the drawbridge.

She took another step, and almost walked into a column of ashes. She actually touched it before stopping, and got ashes on her front. Then a shower of ashes fell on her head, making her sneeze. She looked up, and saw that it was a whole tree, all of it covered in ashes.

Then a little dim bulb flashed just over her head. "You're not covered in ashes—you're *made* of ashes," she said. "You're an ash tree!"

The tree collapsed into a mound of ashes and was gone. She had solved another one. That made three.

But she was still on the drawbridge. So could she now just go on across, her Challenges done?

She took a step, and found her way blocked by a large cabinet. Evidently she was not done here.

Then she realized that these were all puns lined up in a row. This was the Comic Strip! Now she knew what it was. And it was only the first Challenge.

How long would it continue? She suspected it would keep putting puns in her way until she figured out not just how to identify them, but how to stop them entirely. But it was hard enough figuring out the individual ones; how could she solve the whole thing?

First things first. What was the nature of this cabinet? She opened its door and found it filled with little curled bits of metal. "Metal filings," she said. "A filing cabinet!"

But it did not disappear. The filings arranged themselves along its walls, but that was all. It was tall and narrow and in her way.

Then she got the rest of it. "People have to go through this single file," she said. "Filing through the cabinet." She stepped into it, turning sidewise to fit, and through it. When she looked back, it was gone. She had gotten the rest of the pun.

And how many more to fathom? Sooner or later she would encounter one she couldn't figure out, and then she'd be balked. So rather than run that line, she should stop now and figure out the larger riddle: how to abolish the comic strip itself.

Comic Strip. A strip of supposedly funny things, comics. But could there be another interpretation, as with the filing cabinet? Not just something to name, but something to do? Comic Strip—strip comic?

Oh, no! She hated that. But it did fit. It was probably calculated to repel her, just as Karia had been repelled by the puns. So she probably had to do it.

She faced ahead without moving. "I am not pretty. It would be ludicrous for me to take off my clothes. In fact it would be comical. So here is my comic strip."

She gritted her teeth and took off her shirt. Then she took off her shoes. Then she grimaced and took hold of her skirt.

The closed-in Comic Strip faded out. She stood on the open drawbridge. No barriers remained between her and the inner bank of the moat. And she hadn't even needed to strip all the way. She had gone far enough to make her point, and that had been enough.

She breathed a silent sigh of relief and put her shirt back on, and her shoes. Then she walked on across the moat. She had won a small victory; still, she wished she could have a body that was stunning when bared, instead of comical.

The drawbridge ended at a large drooping tree. No, not exactly a tree; a portcullis whose metallic spikes resembled branches. Maybe a gate decorated to resemble a tree. Whatever it was, it blocked the way; she could see between the bars to a hall leading into the castle. This was obviously the second Challenge.

The portcullis looked too heavy to lift clear, but assumptions were risky, so she put her hands on two of the bars and heaved upward. They did not budge. "Darn!"

"You swore at me!" a female voice cried, and water dripped down the branches.

Startled, Cube stepped back and looked up. There was a face in the upper foliage, vaguely human, but much larger than any person. A woman's countenance, with flowing green hair and huge liquid eyes.

"You're a person!" Cube exclaimed, astonished.

"I'm a willow tree," the face replied. "Forced to remain here unhappily until I am able to smile. Only then will I be freed from this horrible bondage."

"You're not here by choice? That's awful."

"It's unbearably sad," the tree agreed, and tears fairly cascaded from her eyes, wetting the rest of her substance like falling rain. "It makes me so unhappy that I know I'll never be free."

"I wish I could make you happy," Cube said.

"Well, there is one way."

"What is that?"

"Take my place."

Cube recoiled. She was not about to fall into this trap! "You're here as a Challenge I have to pass. I'm not supposed to do your job, I'm supposed to get by you."

"Oooo!" the face wailed, and the tears flowed so copiously that they started to pool on the floor.

Cube felt sorry for the weeping willow, but her sympathy was tempered by her knowledge that the tree's fate was not permanent. She was surely serving her year for an Answer. The tears were probably fake.

Still, it was a Challenge. She had to find a way past this unhappy barrier. The tree had told her that she would be free once she was able to smile, so the challenge might be to make her smile. But how could she do that? The tree would probably meet her every effort with a further deluge of tears.

Well, she had to try. "Would you like a gift?"

The flow eased. "A gift? What?"

"A rear-view mirror." Maybe when the willow got the pun, she would laugh, or at least let a smile out. Then she would depart, and the way would be clear.

"But I look awful," the tree protested. "Almost as bad as you do."

Cube could have done without that last remark. But she ignored it and brought out the mirror. "It will surprise you. Hold it up and take a look."

A branch creaked forward, with twigs like fingers. It took

the mirror. The willow held it up before her expansive face. "But this is not my visage!"

"Yes it is. It's your other side."

"Oh, my trunk. Now I understand. This is very nice."

"Your rear view."

"Yes. Thank you. You are so kind, I really hate to stop you from entering the castle." The tears resumed.

So much for humor. The pun had fallen entirely flat.

Cube pondered. The first Challenge had been deceptive. There had been a seeming way through it, solving pun after pun, but that was not the real way. The real way was to comprehend its basic nature and address that.

So what was the basic nature of this one? It seemed she had to make the weeping willow smile, but that might be impossible. Was there some other avenue?

What about the opposite? Making her cry? That seemed cruel, but maybe it wasn't, since she was a weeper by nature. Maybe her true satisfaction lay in weeping.

Cube braced herself and tried. "I have to agree. Your fate is very sad. It must be terrible to be locked into this abysmal gate with no hope of release."

"Yes, it is very bad," the tree agreed, the tears flowing more copiously.

"Just on and on, crying endlessly, without hope."

"Yes," the tree sobbed. The tears were rushing down, forming a small river at the base that made its way to the moat.

"Nobody ever had a worse fate."

"Nobody," the willow agreed, streaming.

"I don't see how you can stand it."

"I *can't* stand it!" The water came from her eyes in virtual cataracts, splashing onto the floor in twin waterfalls.

Cataracts. That was an eye condition. Could that be the key?

Cube acted before she could change her mind. She dived into the nearest cataract, desperately swimming upstream. In a moment she found herself being carried along, topsy-turvy, tumbling in the fierce current. She was in a rushing river—and the portcullis was gone.

She had found a way through. Where she was going she didn't know, but she was past the second Challenge.

The river slowed. She looked around, and saw that it was flowing into a larger channel with steep cliffs on the sides. She couldn't get out. There was just one place where the ground was low enough for her to wade out. There was a green tree by it, blocking the way. Well, she would climb through its foliage if she had to.

She splashed up to the bank. Then she recognized the variety of tree. It was a tangle tree.

She stayed in the water, realizing that she had come up against the third Challenge. She had gotten by the weeping willow; now she had to get by a more tough-minded tree. She couldn't swim through *its* eye!

While she was hesitating, a green girl walked around the tree. "Get away!" Cube screamed. "That's a tangle tree!"

The girl looked at her, surprised. "You're telling *me*?"

"Yes! Get away before it grabs you with its tentacles!"

The girl laughed. "Why should it do that?" She caught hold of a trailing tentacle and wrapped it around her body like a scarf.

Cube stared. The tree was not attacking. In fact it was quiescent. Maybe it had just eaten, so was sated, and the girl knew it. In that case, Cube could simply walk by it. Maybe the Challenge was to figure that out, and get up the nerve to do it.

She waded forward.

"I wouldn't," the girl remarked pleasantly.

"But if it's harmless now, I shouldn't wait. It could be hungry again in an hour."

"It's hungry now."

"But—" Then Cube saw the tips of the tentacles quivering. They were orienting on her, waiting for her to come within reach so they could fling out and snare her. That was how tangle trees operated: they remained still until something came within reach, then they nabbed it and hauled it into the trunk-mouth for chomping.

Yet the girl still wore the tentacle, and it wasn't squeezing her at all. She was twice as delectable as Cube, with much nicer mounds of flesh and no awkward clothing. In fact she was a succulent nymph.

A nymph—or a dryad? Could it be?

"I didn't know tangle trees had dryads," Cube said in wonder.

"Now you do," the dryad said.

"But what do you do for the tree? It eats human flesh."

"Come within reach and I'll show you," the dryad said.

Cube knew better. "I'll wait, thanks."

"If you were a man, you wouldn't wait."

"Why not?"

The nymph did a little dance. Her full bare breasts and buttocks bounced, her silken green hair flung about, and she kicked one lovely leg high in the air. High enough to show her panties, if she had been wearing any.

Cube thought about how a man would react to that show. "Oh."

"I have lured many men in to my tree," the dryad confided. "Then I have buried their bones, so as not to alert others. In return my tree protects me and feeds me."

"Feeds you what?" Cube asked, horrified. "Leftovers?"

The girl laughed again, her whole luscious body shaking. "Tanglefruit." She reached up, and there was a bright red fruit of some kind, looking like a cross between an apple and a cherry. She plucked it, brought it to her dainty mouth, and bit into it. "Delicious. Of course I could have leftover meat if I wanted it."

"How can you betray your own kind like that?"

"What kind? The prey is human; I'm not."

"You look human."

"I need to, to lure in the prey." She did another little dance that was so suggestive that it almost made Cube's eyes glaze, and she was not partial to women in that manner. It would numb a man's dull brain in half an instant.

Here she was talking, when she needed to get past the tree. How could she do that? Then she had a bright idea.

"You have an idea," the dryad said. "I saw the bulb flash over your dull head."

Did *everyone* have to insult her appearance? "I have a gift for you."

The dryad clapped her hands with girlish glee. "I love gifts!"

"A rear-view mirror." Cube brought it out, as it had returned to her in the interim since the second Challenge. "I will toss it to you."

She tossed, but her aim was bad and it flew high. The tangle tree snapped out a tentacle and caught it, then gave it to the dryad. "Thank you," she said sweetly. Cube wasn't sure whether the nymph was addressing her or the tree.

The dryad held the mirror up to her face. "Oh what a divine derriere!"

"It's yours," Cube said.

"Why so it is. I love it." She switched her hips, making her cute bottom swing. There went another man, if he had been watching, Cube knew. If only *she* had a bottom like that! But of course that was why she was here: to get such a bottom, and all the rest.

The nymph gave the mirror to a tentacle. "Save this for me, dear," she said, and the tentacle carried it away to disappear in the foliage.

Then the nymph looked at Cube. "But this doesn't mean I'll let you pass by my tree."

"I didn't think it did," Cube said. But she was sure that the dryad was the key to passage, and that there was some kind of price that would persuade her. If the nymph told the tree to let a person pass, it surely would. But how could she persuade the nymph? What could such a creature want?

She pondered, and slowly a grudging idea came to her. "How are you fixed for companionship, aside from the tree?"

The dryad didn't answer. That might be significant, because she had had an answer for everything else.

"How is your social life? Do you have a boyfriend?"

Still no answer. That meant she was on the right track.

"You know you can't have a boyfriend if you feed all the good men to the tree. You're going to have to make an exception."

"I can make an exception," the dryad murmured. "For the right man."

Ha. "And who is the right man?"

"Conun," the dryad whispered.

"Conan? What would you want with a barbarian?"

"CoNUN, with the accent on the second syllable. He's no barbarian. He's a drummer. He has such a divine beat." She gazed dreamily upward. "But he won't even look at me; I could win him if he did. He is another person doing service for the Good Magician, and no girl can win him unless she solves his riddle. I'm not good at riddles."

Cube believed that. Nymphs were famous for their bodies, not their minds. "Suppose I solve his riddle, and tell you? Would that earn me safe passage by the tree?"

"Yes," the dryad whispered.

This seemed suspiciously easy. "What's the catch?"

"No catch. The Good Magician wants to know whether you can relate well to people, even if they make you look even uglier than you are, and you have found my weakness."

That was surely a good deal more than the nymph was supposed to say, but again, nymphs' assets were on their bottoms, not their heads. "Where is Conun?"

"Next station downstream."

"I'll be back." Cube let herself drift with the current. She was sure there would be no exit from the river there, but if she fathomed the man's riddle, she could pass the tree.

Sure enough, the cliffs confining the river returned. A short way down there was a ledge cut into a cliff, and on it sat a handsome man with a big bold drum. "Hello, Conun!" Cube called.

Conun eyed her appraisingly. "I am looking for a girlfriend, but you are not what I have in mind."

Of course not. No man had her in mind. "But if I fathom your riddle, and prove it, you'll be mine regardless."

Conun winced. "I hope you don't." Then he beat on his drum, the loud sound making ripples on the river.

Conun drumming. Suddenly she had it. Fortunately he wasn't looking her way—few men ever did—so didn't see the bulb flash over her head. She waded and swam back up to the tangle tree stop.

The dryad was waiting. "What's your news?"

"I fathomed it. Conun is a drummer. Conun drums. Conundrum. That's a riddle, a play on words, a pun. That's *the* pun: What is Conun drum? He is a conundrum. Tell him that, and he is yours. He has no choice."

"Oh, goody!" The nymph clapped her cute little hands again. "You wait here." She dived into the water.

"But—" But the nymph was gone. Cube hadn't realized that she could leave her tree.

She waited. In two and a half moments there was an exclamation downstream, followed by what sounded like a loud kiss. "Let her pass!" the dryad's voice came.

That must be an order to the tree. Cube waded out of the water and approached the tree somewhat nervously. If she had misunderstood—

But the tentacles were parting, revealing a path to the other side. Cube walked along it, passing through an arcade of green tentacles. The tree could grab her now, if it wanted to. But it didn't, and in barely over another moment she was out the other side. She heaved a silent sigh of relief. She had passed the third Challenge.

She discovered she was in the entrance hall of the castle, soaking wet. A somewhat drab woman was hurrying toward her. "Don't wet the floor!" the woman cried.

Cube stopped. "The Challenges—the river—"

"The ladies' room is right here," the woman said, showing her a door. "Clean up and change there."

Bemused, Cube opened the door and entered the room. There was a basin and sponge, and a dry dress hung beside them. There was also a set of sheer stockings, and a silken bra and panty. Much nicer things than she had worn before. So she got out of her sopping clothing, sponged herself clean, put on the nice clothing except for the stockings, and transferred her things to the new outfit. Her things included the rear-view mirror and the water ball, which had somehow survived the river without dissolving. She gazed at the stockings; she had never worn such things before, but they were evidently for her use, and maybe were part of the required apparel for meeting the Good Magician. So she pulled them on, and was pleasantly surprised when they made her legs look nice. Too bad she couldn't wear a stocking over her head! She combed her hair without trying to use the mirror, and stepped back out into the hall.

A young woman was waiting there. "Hello, Cube. I am Wira, the Good Magician's daughter-in-law. He will see you now."

"That's good. Uh, who was the other woman?"

"She is Sofia Socksorter, the Magician's Designated Wife of the Month. She is very careful about keeping clothing in order, especially socks."

"I noticed." Cube followed Wira down the hall, through a chamber or two, and up a winding flight of steps. "Would you like a mirror?"

"Thank you, no. I could not use it."

"Why not?"

"I am blind."

Cube was astonished. "But you're showing me the way!"

"I am familiar with the castle."

Oh. Cube wasn't sure what to say, so said nothing. She wished she could apologize for her offer of the mirror, but that would only make it worse.

They came to a dingy little study lined with books and potion bottles. Inside was a gnomish man hunched over a huge tome. "Good Magician, here is the querent Cube."

The man looked up. He almost smiled as he saw Wira, then remembered himself and resumed his etched frown. "Ask."

"How can I be beautiful?"

There was a long pause, at least two moments and a trice.

Cube was afraid he wouldn't answer, but then he did. "You must travel the Cube Route."

"Cube? That's my name!"

"Your name is Cue. Complete the Cube Route and you will be beautiful."

And there it was: the way to become beautiful! "Thank you, Good Magician! Now what is my Service?"

"That is it."

"To go where I will be beautiful? I don't understand."

The Magician sighed. "I see I must explain." It was clear that he disliked explaining. "Xanth recently came into some additional territory of the contra-terrene persuasion. There are those who wish to explore and colonize it, but they do not know a safe route there or how to handle its special nature. You will gather assistants and find that route and fathom that land's nature. Once you have established it, others will be able to follow, and you will be free to enjoy your considerable beauty. Limit your party to nine: no more, no less. Each person in your party will be appropriately rewarded, in due course. Now be on your way."

"But I have no idea where the route is!" Cube protested. "Or whom to recruit to help. I don't even have nine friends. I don't know who would be suitable."

"That is your Challenge." The Magician's gaze returned to his musty tome.

"But—"

"Do not pester him," Wira whispered urgently. "That only makes him grumpy. He has Answered you and given you your Service."

"But the answer is no good, and I can't do the Service if I don't know how to implement it!"

"You must find a way," Wira said, gently drawing her out of the study.

Find a way? This seemed impossible.

Sofia met them at the foot of the stairs. "You will need this," she said, presenting a small bag or pouch.

"This?" Cube asked blankly.

"He did not explain?"

"Not sufficiently."

The woman nodded. "That is why he needs wives. Someone has to clean up after his confusions."

"Wives?"

"Each month there is a new designated wife," Wira explained. "In the course of Magician Humfrey's generous century of life and adventure, he met and loved six women, and married five and a half of them. Then the Demon Xanth gave them all back to him at once, so he alternates."

"Five and a half?"

"He didn't marry his first love until after she returned. It was a small ceremony a baker's dozen years ago. So he has a half wife of thirteen years."

"Oh." That probably made all the sense it was going to.

"Your mission is secret until it is successful," Sofia said. "Therefore a group of people must not be seen to search it out, lest hostile forces take note. One person must do it—someone with gumption, that no one will notice."

A black bulb flashed over Cube's head, for an unwelcome realization. "No one ever notices me if they can avoid it."

"Precisely. You are ideal."

"But the Good Magician said I should have assistants. How can I travel alone if I have companions?"

"You must limit the size of your party to nine, because secrets become difficult to maintain beyond that. You will carry the others in the magic pouch I converted from one of Himself's socks."

"Himself?"

"His wives call him that," Wira murmured. "Not to his face. Because he is full of—"

"Himself," Sofia finished.

Cube was coming to appreciate that. Then she picked up on something else. "You made this purse from a sock?"

"I am not called Sofia Socksorter for nothing. I have a certain way with socks. That's why he married me; he can't keep track of them. He wore this sock for fifteen years before I joined him and made him put on a fresh one. As a result it absorbed some of his magic."

"Fifteen years?"

"It stank," Wira said. "Sofia washed it for ten days, and couldn't get the magic out, but at least the smell was reduced."

Cube looked at the pouch. "I don't think anyone would fit in this. Not more than one foot."

"They will all fit," Sofia assured her. "Each person must put a foot in, and the rest will follow. When you need to take one out, reach in with your hand and haul him out."

"This is weird! I can't believe—"

"Show her, Wira."

Sofia held the sock down, and Wira found it with her dainty foot. She pushed the foot in, then abruptly the rest of her slid into the sock, and she disappeared.

"Oh!" Cube exclaimed, amazed.

"Now fetch her out," Sofia said, handing her the sock.

Cube took the sock, and with her free hand reached into it. It looked as though there were room only for her hand to the wrist, but it turned out to have no bottom; she reached in to her elbow and still was not at the end. Her hand was floundering in emptiness. "There's nothing there."

"You must say her name."

Oh, again. "Wira."

A hand caught hers. Cube pulled, and in a quarter of a moment Wira was out. "I'm glad you didn't leave me there."

"Oh, I wouldn't—"

But the young woman was smiling. It was humor. Cube had muffed it again. She would gladly have traded some of her useless gumption for a bit more social sensitivity.

"Remember," Sofia said. "Once you have recruited an assistant, put him in the pouch, and bring him out only at need. It is attuned to you, and will work only in your presence. No one else must know that you are not traveling alone."

"I—I'll remember," Cube agreed weakly. She tucked the empty pouch into a pocket. "Um, suppose I should at some point need to enter the pouch myself. Could I do that?"

"Yes, though this is not recommended for casual use. For you, time will not be suspended, and no one else can bring you out. You will bring yourself out when you decide. The pouch will effectively shelter you from extreme conditions. But while you are in it, someone else would be able to carry it or throw it away; you would no longer have control."

"I think I would prefer to retain control."

"I have some travel supplies for you," Sofia continued, producing a huge package. "Box lunches, changes of clothing, tools, bedding, potable water—"

"What kind of water?"

"Good to drink," Wira clarified. She was not the demoness Metria, so did not have to hunt for words.

Cube eyed the package, which was almost as big as she was. "But how can I ever carry all that?"

"In the pouch, of course. Bring it out."

Cube brought it out. Sofia put the end of the package at the mouth of the sock, and the whole thing slid smoothly in and disappeared. "You won't need to take it all out together," the woman said. "Just say what item you want, as you put your hand in, and it will be there."

"Uh, thank you," Cube said, somewhat numbly.

Sofia smiled for the first time. "That's quite all right. We homely women have to stick together."

Cube tried to formulate a suitable response, but her tongue would not cooperate.

"You both look beautiful to me," Wira said diplomatically. But of course she was blind.

3

RECRUITING

Before she knew it, Cube was out of the Good Magician's Castle, thoroughly confused. What was she supposed to do?

Well, what did she know? That there was a new territory to be explored, and nobody knew the way there. She had to find it. She could choose others to help her do that. And if she succeeded, she would be beautiful.

This was not at all the kind of assignment she had expected, but she had to do it. Because she truly wanted to be beautiful.

Maybe if she got the right people, they would have good ideas on how to locate the territory. So her first job was to find those people. Who might they be? It was hard to think of one, let alone nine.

She would simply have to ask people, and accept any who agreed to help. Maybe this mission was fated to succeed, and the right people would appear along her route.

And maybe she was dreaming. She would have to help herself. She would have to seek people.

What about those she had already met on the way to the Good Magician's Castle? Ryver and Karia? She liked the winged centaur, and Karia could really help get across rough terrain. And Ryver—she would just like to be close to him, even if she wasn't beautiful, and he paid no attention to her. She knew she was foolish, but that was the way it was.

But both those folk had gone the other way, and were nowhere close now. She didn't know exactly where they had gone. How could she find them, without taking endless time?

A bulb flashed over her head. "Demoness Metria!" she whispered.

"Yes?" a puff of smoke answered.

Cube jumped. "I didn't know you were so close!"

The smoke expanded into the lovely semi-clad form of the demoness. "I wasn't. But you spoke my name. That alerted me. What is on your homely mortal mind?"

Cube realized that the demoness would not help her out of the goodness of her heart. She didn't have either goodness or a heart. What would persuade her? The question brought the answer: "I have something interesting for you."

"You have gotten your Answer!"

"Yes. But it is secret."

"I love secrets! What is it?"

"If I told you, it wouldn't be secret."

"Oh, come on, you're going to have to share it with your Companions anyway."

"How do you know that?"

"Because you are obviously on a Quest, and all Quests have Companions. It's in the Big Book of Rules."

So it seemed. "But you're not a Companion."

The demoness put on a canny look: she became a huge floating can. "Suppose I were, what would you tell me?"

Cube realized that she would have to feed Metria's interest to some degree in order to win her cooperation. "Suppose I had to go to a new territory and mark a safe route there. But first I needed nine Companions. Suppose you helped me find them, you could be the first demon to see this territory."

"Suppose I went to see it on my own?"

"Suppose you didn't know the way?"

That stymied the demoness. "So where is it?"

"I don't know. I have to find it—with the help of others. I could tell you about it if you became a Companion. The Good Magician said those who participated would be appropriately rewarded. Do you want to be part of this effort?"

Metria considered. "What is the nature of this dependency?"

"This what?"

"Province, colony, demesne, possession—"

"Territory?"

"Whatever," she agreed crossly.

Cube was pretty sure now that Metria was going to sign up, so she answered. "The Good Magician described it as 'contra-terrene.' "

"Oh, *that* territory! Our side won it from the Demoness Fornax one year ago. Counter Xanth."

"You know of it?" But obviously she did.

"Sure. But not where it is. It's the opposite of Xanth, inverted, or something. If someone touched it and Xanth at the same time, he'd detonate."

"He'd what?"

"Fire, burst, blow up, blast, explode—"

"I think you had it right the first time, after all."

"Whatever," the demoness agreed crossly. "So there has to be a way to get there without touching any part of Xanth. You don't want to grab both ends of the charge together."

Cube was coming to appreciate the problem. There would have to be a very special route there. "So do you want to help?"

"Of course not. Demons don't help mortals, they torment them."

"Even if they lose the reward?"

"What is the reward?"

"He didn't say. Just that there would be one. Is there anything you are in need of?"

"No." But Metria hovered thoughtfully. "I wonder what it could be?"

"You can find out by earning and receiving it."

The demoness exploded into a generous slew of smoky fragments. "You bleeping mortal! You have aroused my insatiable curiosity. I want to know what I'm missing." The voice came from a fragment that had been left behind.

"Then give me your word."

"Bleep!" The fragment puffed into smoke, which swirled and formed a word: BLEEP! It floated across to touch Cube's hand. "Here is my word, you conniving creature. I'll keep the secret."

Score one for the home team. But there was still a possible hurdle. "You will have to travel in this." She brought out the pouch.

"But I can't get out of that on my own! That's one of Humfrey's old magic socks."

"True." Actually Cube hadn't realized that it would hold demons in too. "You will truly be committed."

Metria sighed. The sound blew the word into tatters of smoke. "All right," a tatter said. "Put me in."

"Not yet. First I need to contact Karia Centaur. Find her and ask her whether she would like to join me in a search for that territory."

"That would blow the secret."

She was right. "Maybe then just whether she would like to join me in an adventure. But don't speak her name."

The fragment swelled into the form of the demoness. "Does she know how to find it?"

"Probably not. But she can help us search."

"You have got hold of my curiosity, and you are using it to make me cooperate," Metria accused her.

"I thought you understood that when you agreed to join me."

"You must have a bit of demon blood in you."

"Do demons have blood?"

"No." There was a pop as she disappeared.

Cube resumed walking along the enchanted path. She did not know where she was going, but she would get there faster if she kept moving.

In a moderate while—whiles were difficult to measure precisely—the demoness reappeared. "The centaur is on her way. She will meet you at the rest stop closest to the castle."

"Wonderful!" Just like that, she had recruited her first assistant, or maybe her second if Metria counted. "Now do the same with Ryver, if you can find him."

"Ryver? Isn't he the water boy?"

"Yes. He gave me a water ball." Cube brought it out.

The demoness popped off again.

Cube continued walking along the path, hoping she had done the right thing. She wasn't quite sure she could trust the demoness, because demons had no souls and therefore no consciences. But Metria's help could make a huge difference.

A wisp of smoke formed before her. "Back already, Metria?"

"He wants to know if you are beautiful yet."

Darn! She had forgotten about that. How could she recruit Ryver if he wanted her lovely first? "I guess that's a no," she said wearily.

The demoness formed, unconscionably lovely. "So it's like that. I'm sorry."

"You're sorry? You don't have human feelings!"

"Yes I do. Ever since I married and got half a soul."

"You have a soul? That means you can be trusted!"

"Half a soul. So you can trust me halfway. Actually a quarter soul now; my baby got half of it."

"You have a child?"

"Yes, after signaling the stork 750 times and serving a summons on it. It used to be that a half-mortal child of a demon with a soul got all of it, but the Time of No Magic must have shaken up the rules, and now it's just half. Too bad about your boyfriend."

"But if you're married, how can you join the quest? Don't you have to tend to your husband?"

"My alter ego Demoness Mentia is doing that, and keeping an eye on my seven-year-old son, Ted. So I'm free to adventure, for the nonce."

"How can a demon have an alter ego?"

"It's not easy. D. Mentia is a little crazy. So is Demon Ted. But my husband doesn't care as long as Mentia pretends to be me. In fact he likes a little craziness mixed in with his delirium. And Ted likes my child alter ego, Woe Betide. Those two little mischiefs are trying to figure out how to get around the Adult Conspiracy."

Cube decided not to question that further. What counted was the discovery that Metria could indeed be trusted, at least halfway. That made her feel better. Not enough to compensate for the loss of Ryver, but better than nothing.

"I could cover your face and body with a shroud of myself and make you look beautiful."

For half an instant Cube was obscenely tempted. But then she realized that it was unworkable because Ryver would know, and dishonest if he didn't know. "No. I'll just have to do without Ryver."

"Well then, I have nothing to do, so let's try your pouch."

Cube brought out the pouch and held it out. "Put your foot in it."

The demoness lifted a lovely leg indecently high, and poked an exquisite dainty foot in. Then she slid all the way into the sock and disappeared. All that was left behind was the sound of her voice: "Wheeee!"

Cube returned the pouch to her pocket. It wasn't any larger than before.

Another person passed. Traffic was not thick, but she was meeting more people than she had at home. Was this a prospect to be a Companion? "Hello. I'm Cube. My talent is summoning nickelpedes."

"I am Kate. Dupli Kate. I make twins or triplets."

"You mean you get the stork to deliver them?"

"No, I twin or triple grown folk. I could demonstrate on you, if you wish, but you might find it inconvenient to have a twin, and I can't undo them after they appear."

"Thanks, I'll pass that up," Cube agreed hastily. The thought of there being two of her was awful; one was plain enough. She decided not to mention the quest.

Some time later she saw something off to the side, beyond the enchanted path. It was a person sitting on the ground, not moving. Was something wrong?

Cube left the path and went to investigate. It was a woman with a pale yellow complexion and wild hair. She held something in her hand and was staring at it. Some kind of fruit, or—

It was a gourd. A hypno-gourd! The kind with a peephole that sucked a person's mind inside, locking her in the realm of bad dreams. The woman must have seen the gourd, picked it up, looked at it without realizing its nature, and gotten trapped. She would remain that way until someone else interrupted her line of sight to the peephole.

Cube put her hands on the gourd, blocking the peephole, and lifted it out of the woman's grasp. The woman blinked, looking around. "What happened?" she asked sourly.

"You were caught by a hypno-gourd," Cube explained. "You would have remained that way until your body died of thirst or starvation. I knew you wouldn't want that, so—"

"Who the $$$$ are you?" the woman demanded irritably.

"I'm Cube. I was walking along the enchanted path and saw—"

"And I'm Fluorine," the other said wrathfully. "Chlorine's sister. She got to be beautiful and marry a prince or something, but I got nothing. Her measly talent is poisoning water, while I can practically make water explode. Why don't you mind your own business?"

There was something corrosive about Fluorine's personality. "But as I said, you would have remained—"

"I was in a really wild party," Fluorine said angrily. "There was a pool there, with mermaids who had a special aisle leading to Mundania that only they could use, so they were teasing stray Mundane men mercilessly, flashing breasts and tails, and the stupid men were falling into the water trying to catch them, and almost drowning. Great sport! And you had to come and break it up, you ignorant meddler."

Cube saw that there was no reasoning with this irascible woman. She preferred her bad dream of tormenting men to the reality of her loss of health and life. She certainly was no prospect for the quest. "Sorry I bothered," Cube muttered, and walked away.

"Good riddance!" Fluorine yelled after her.

Only when Cube was back on the enchanted path did she realize that she still carried the gourd. She considered throwing it away, but that might just make mischief for someone else, so instead she put it into the pouch. She would dispose of it somewhere else, or use it to stun some dangerous creature if she had to.

Belatedly she wondered who Chlorine might be, who poisoned water. She had married a prince? That almost gave Cube hope for herself.

She passed another woman. She was beginning to lose faith in finding suitable Companions by sheer chance, but some hope remained. "Hello. I'm Cube. I can summon nickelpedes."

"I'm Amanda. I can change one kind of plant to another."

Now that might have promise. "You mean, change varieties?"

"Any type to any type." Amanda looked around. "See that cemetree? Now it's a pie plant."

Cube was impressed. The tree that looked like a gravestone had become a bush bearing blueberry pies. "I wonder if you would be interested—"

"Sorry, I have to get home now," Amanda said, and moved on. "Nice meeting you."

This just wasn't turning out to be easy.

In due course she reached the camp. Just as she did, there was a sound in the air. She looked, and saw Karia gliding down. That was nice timing.

"Thanks for coming!" she called to the centaur.

"I have not committed to anything," Karia said as she landed and folded her wings. "I hope you are not in trouble."

"You came because you feared I was in trouble? I may be, but not because of any immediate threat. I made it in to see the Good Magician, and he gave me a mission, but I don't know how to proceed with it."

"You made it in! I envy you."

"I think I have a stronger stomach for puns."

"That must be it," the centaur agreed, smiling. "Meanwhile I regret to say that I seem to have lost the mirror you gave me after all."

"I'm sorry. It seems I can't give it away."

"What is the mission?"

"That's awkward. You see, I can't tell you about it unless you join it, because it's supposed to be secret."

"I certainly won't join something blindly," Karia said. "Centaurs are known for logic, not gambling."

"Yes, and I need a logical mind, because I'm not sure mine is up to it. I also need nine Companions, and all I have so far is one."

"Nine! Have you any idea how to get them?"

"Very little. Except that he told me they would be suitably rewarded."

"Rewarded? In what manner?"

"He didn't say."

The centaur shook her head. "We appear to be at an impasse. You can't tell me about it unless I commit, and I can't commit until I know about it, if then."

Cube hadn't anticipated this problem. That of course showed why she needed a good mind along. She wished for the moment that she had the ability of one of the louts in her home village, who could see from any part of his body. He had many points of view. That might enable her to get a different perspective. Then a bulb flashed brightly over her head.

"I saw that," Karia said. "You just had a bright idea."

"Yes. A logical idea. Let me try it on you."

The centaur shrugged, her front moving in a fashion Cube envied. Her own front would never bounce or ripple like that. "Let me have it."

"You were probably the person going to see the Good Magician before me. The questioner."

"The querent."

"Querent?"

"A person who queries."

"Oh. Yes. You were the querent right before me, only you didn't get through, so then I was the next."

"True."

"So maybe there was just one mission, and whoever came with a Question would get it, in return for her Answer."

"That seems likely."

"The Good Magician told me that when I completed the mission, I would be beautiful. That I would get what I wanted."

"That is the normal course," the centaur agreed, not quite evincing impatience at this rehearsal of the obvious.

"But if you had made made it through, it would have been your mission."

"Agreed." Karia was polite, but her tail was switching restlessly, causing little clouds of lightened dust to rise.

"And maybe your problem would have been solved at the end of it."

"Perhaps."

"The Good Magician didn't tell me he would make me beautiful after I accomplished the mission. He told me I would *be* beautiful. My impression was that it would happen when I got there."

"The Good Magician's Services often do work out that way." Now her mane was wavering, as her impatience worked its way forward.

"So if you had done it, your problem would have been solved right there. Not because you had completed your Service, but because that is where the solution is."

Karia paused a third of a moment. "That is an arguable case."

"So if you go there now, you may after all have your Answer, despite not seeing the Good Magician. And that might be your reward for participating."

"That is by no means certain, but by no means uncertain. Perhaps there is an even chance." Then the centaur made her decision. "I will join you. If you are correct, I will have my desire, and if you are incorrect I will still have what may be an excellent adventure."

"Wonderful! Now I can tell you all about it." She proceeded to do that, and Karia listened and nodded.

"Counter Xanth. Things are surely different there, and perhaps the laws of magic differ, so that our liabilities differ too. That might indeed cure me. In any event, it should be a remarkable experience."

"Only it seems I have to go there alone," Cube said. "I wonder why I need Companions, when they aren't supposed to travel with me. That is, openly."

"I can answer that. In any trip there are likely to be occasions where a single traveler is balked or in danger. For example, you may encounter a crevasse you can't safely cross. Then you would bring me out of the pouch, and I would fly you across. You would do it when no one was observing, so my presence would not be advertised. Similarly, there may be tasks the others can perform at need, inconspicuously. We do not need to be traveling openly with you to be effective aids to your progress."

"That must be it. You make it so clear."

"I would be less than a proper centaur if I did not reason and express myself clearly."

"I am glad to have you along," Cube said. "That leaves me only seven more to find, to make up the nine."

"Nine? That's interesting. That's the square of three. It must have significance."

"It must," Cube agreed, seeing it. "Now if only—" She cut that off.

"If only?"

"No need to bother you with it."

"Is it relevant to the Quest?"

"Not really."

"Allow me to be the judge of that."

"All right. It's that I had hoped to recruit another person, a man I met just before I met you, but I can't."

"A man. You are attracted to him?"

"Does it show?"

"Yes. A faint little heart leaked from you when you mentioned him. But he lacks interest in you?"

"Yes. Because—"

"I understand. That is why you want to be beautiful."

"Yes. Actually I wanted to be beautiful before I met him, but he added to the desire."

"There are other qualities than physical appearance."

"That men notice?"

Karia nodded. "Point taken. Still, there are other reasons to undertake this Quest, as I have just learned. They should be sufficient to enlist him also."

"The demoness Metria asked him, and he asked if I was beautiful yet. That was answer enough."

"Perhaps not. It is true that men are governed mostly by appearance, but there is a mitigating factor here."

"There is?"

"If you succeed in the Quest, you will be beautiful. He might want to be present for the occasion."

"I hadn't thought of that! Maybe he would."

"So I suggest we make an effort to recruit him, and perhaps in due course you will have your beauty and your man."

"It's a dream."

"Where is he?"

"He said that everybody knew him in his area, but I'm not sure what his area is."

"The demoness Metria knows, however, since she spoke with him."

"That's right. I'll bring her out and ask her."

Cube brought out the pouch and reached in. "Metria."

A smoky-feeling hand caught hers. She drew it out, and in a fraction of a moment the demoness was with them. "But I just went in," she said. "Why did you bring me out immediately?"

"It has been several hours," Cube said.

"Impossible!"

"Consider the position of the sun," Karia suggested.

"What are you doing here, horse-rear?" But the demoness looked at the sun. "It's evening!"

"I joined Cube here, as agreed," Karia said. "The flight took some time, during which she walked to this campsite. I have joined the Quest."

Metria shrugged, her shoulders lifting briefly off her body, then settling back into place. "Time has passed," she agreed. "So that pouch is timeless. We aren't aware of it."

"Interesting point," the centaur agreed. "So we shall be traveling without effort or loss of time in our awareness. It will seem like instant transport."

"Which is fine with me." Metria faced Cube, her head rotating on her neck to an impossible extent. "So why did you haul me out?"

"To find Ryver. We're going to try to recruit him after all. Where is he?"

"I'll show you." The demoness formed into a butterfly and flew upward.

"Get on," Karia said. "I will follow."

Cube got on her back and held on as the centaur flicked them both with her tail, lightening them, and leaped into the air. She followed the winged quarter of butter as it flew southward. Soon they were high in the sky.

"You know, you lightened me before, when we crossed the river," Cube said. "But I don't remember recovering my weight."

"It happens gradually. If you had exercised vigorously immediately after that, you would have sailed off the path."

"I'll watch it, after this."

A cloud formed ahead of them. "Oh, no," Karia muttered. "That looks like Fracto."

"Like what?"

"Cumulo Fracto Nimbus, the worst of clouds. All of us flyers know him. Theoretically he's a good cloud now, but you wouldn't know it when you have to get somewhere."

The butterfly looped back. "Fracto's playing games," it said. "We'll have to dive under."

"But he'll wet on us," Karia protested.

"Not if we fly low enough, fast enough. It takes him time to get organized."

They dived down. Fracto saw them and darkened frantically, trying to work up a good rain in time to catch them. But all he could manage on such short notice was a light sprinkle.

The sun was still shining. This was weather rainbows liked, and sure enough, a long colored bow wriggled up from the forest below and formed into a multi-colored arch. They flew right under it.

Cube looked up as they passed. "Look! Fish!" Indeed, several pretty fish were swimming in the rainbow.

"Rainbow trout," Karia agreed sourly. "A pun."

Beyond the rainbow the rain was gone, but the wind was rising. Then more water fell from the cloud, as Fracto scrambled to catch up. "Oh, I don't like this," Karia said. "I'm reaching my limited tolerance for puns."

"What is it?"

"The winds of change."

"But we want a change, to get out of this weather."

"Not this way."

Then something struck Cube's shirt and dropped to the centaur's back. "That's a coin!" Cube exclaimed, surprised.

"Many coins," Karia agreed, as more struck them. Some were small, but some were large, and made brief painful dents. Some were silver, others copper or gold. "Ugh!"

"Change," Cube said, catching on. The centaur's exclamation wasn't entirely because the coins stung, but because of the pun. But she decided not to mention that, because puns could not be avoided. "Now I understand why you don't like them. Those sting as they strike."

"We had better land," Karia said.

"Not here," the butterfly protested.

"Why not?" Cube asked. "It looks like a nice quiet valley below."

"Because Demoness Pression hangs out there. You wouldn't like her."

"D. Pression?" Cube asked. "What's wrong with— oh, no! Depression!"

"She makes you very sad," the butterfly agreed.

"I'll swerve to the side," Karia said grimly. "So we won't land near her."

They avoided the hangout of the demoness and came to a wet landing in the forest.

Karia glanced around as she shook off a few more clinging coins. "I don't like this."

"We'll have to stay on foot until the storm passes," Cube said. "Where are we? I mean, apart from being on a rounded ridge in a thick forest."

"The winds of change did more than dump coins," Metria said from the air. "They changed our location. Even I don't recognize this neck of the woods."

"Neck!" the centaur exclaimed, leaping off the ridge. "Another egregious pun!"

Cube realized that the ridge did resemble a giant neck. Fortunately it wasn't moving, so whatever huge creature it might belong to was inactive. But there was swamp on either side, and it did not look healthy. "I think we had better stick to the ridge, regardless."

A gross bubble rose up through the muck and popped right before them, releasing ugly vapor. Karia had to step back to avoid it. "Ugh."

"I think Ryver is in this general direction, south," Metria said, assuming her normal human form. Her dainty feet did not touch the ground, though when she walked she moved as if they did.

They followed the ridge south. "Let me get off and walk," Cube said. "No need to burden you when we're not flying."

"I could flick you light again, so there is no burden," Karia said. "But it would help if you found a way through this thicket."

Cube jumped down and went ahead. It was indeed a thicket; there were a number of saplings growing close together. All of them oozed sap, so she avoided them and approached a larger trunk that radiated spoke-like branches. She put her hand on one and it came loose, to her surprise, becoming a suitable walking stick.

"That's a pole tree," Metria remarked. "It makes poles."

"Ugh," the centaur repeated. But Cube was intrigued. She looked up, and saw that the general shape of the tree was like a huge chicken. Poultry. Another pun. No wonder Karia disliked it.

They passed the pole tree and came to another. This one bore jugs on its branches. As Cube approached it swept its branches in what seemed almost like a courtly bow, and lowered a jug to her. It was full of what looked like cider. Surprised, she unscrewed the top and sniffed. It *was* cider! "Why thank you," she said, taking a sip. It was excellent.

"Ugh!" Karia said.

"A gallon tree," Metria said, her smirk extending somewhat beyond her face. "With gallons of liquid refreshment."

Cube finally caught the pun: gallantry. That was the way it had behaved toward her. She capped the jug and put it in the pouch; it would be good to have cider when she could relax.

The next tree on the ridge stood straight and tall like a guard. A branch extended to bar Cube's passage. On it were sprouting pennies. Cube was moved to pluck one. When she did, she was suddenly compelled to speak. "We are just traveling through, meaning no harm to any tree of this forest." It was a penny for her thoughts, and she had had to give them when she accepted it.

The branch lifted, letting her pass. "Ugh!" Karia said yet again.

"A cent tree," Metria murmured mischievously.

A sentry. No wonder again.

The following tree had leaves in the shape of the letters L,

M, and N. "Triple ugh!" the centaur said. "If only that con-founded cloud hadn't forced us to land here!"

"Elementary, my dear centaur," the demoness said.

Then Cube got it: an L, M, and N tree. El em en tree. Once again the centaur had caught on before she did. It did seem that Fracto Cloud had made her feel worse than she would have, had she merely got wetted on.

There were more trees, but Karia's sharp eyes noted one in particular. "Go past that one, pun and all," she said.

That one had leaves shaped like N, so seemed like only part of the tree they had seen before. But when they passed it, they were suddenly out of the neck of the woods and back in more familiar terrain. It was, Cube realized belatedly, an N-tree: entry. The way out as well as in.

The cloud had cleared. "Now we can resume flight," Karia said. "Not half an instant too soon. Those puns were awful, not to mention forced and superfluous."

Cube remembered the jug of cider, so politely presented to her, and thought the tree was nice, natural, and relevant. But she didn't argue the case. She mounted the centaur, and they were on their way again.

"We're out of the woods," Metria said, assuming the form of a paper airplane. "Too bad we didn't stay long enough to find the fruits of the man-go and woman-go trees."

"Ugh!"

"What kind of fruits are those?" Cube asked, unable to re-strain her curiosity.

"They are shaped like little men and women," the demon-ess explained. "But when a mortal eats one, he has to go."

"Go where?"

"Right where he is."

"Ugh!"

Cube pondered, and finally got it: not traveling, so much as a natural function. It was indeed another awful pun. The demoness was cruelly teasing the centaur.

"This way," the paper plane said, angling down. They

were crossing open country now, with fields and farmsteads. A river ran through it, and it looked nice.

Ryver's house turned out to be beside the river, and made of water. That made sense, Cube realized. He worked with water, so needed a good supply of it, and could disappear into the river when he chose. There were sparkling windows, and a flowing roof. They landed beside it, unobserved.

"I think this is your scene," Karia said diplomatically. "We should enter the pouch."

Cube had been hoping for the centaur's support, but had to agree. Outsiders weren't supposed to know she had company. Also, Ryver would never even look at Cube if the filly's fine bare breasts were in view. She held out the pouch, and Metria stepped into it, and then Karia put in a forehoof and slid inside. Cube was essentially alone.

She approached the house and knocked on the door. She thought it might squish, but it was as hard as ice without being cold.

The door opened. There stood Ryver. "But you're not beautiful!" he said.

Cube suppressed a wince. "But I may be, in due course," she said as evenly as she could manage. "I have a case to make. May I come in?"

"I suppose so," he said, not quite graciously. "At least your legs have improved."

"My legs?" Then she remembered that she was still wearing the sheer stockings Sofia had given her. The female members of her party had not noticed, but the man did. "Oh." She didn't care to explain.

"And your dress looks better."

Cube realized that the underclothing Sofia had given her was causing aspects of her front and back to be more evident, and the dress was cooperating. She was less unshapely than usual, though hardly shapely. "Thank you."

"I lost your mirror."

"It returned to me. It seems I can't give it away after all." She entered, and took a seat on the water bed inside. It was the only furniture; evidently there was no woman's touch.

Which meant there was no woman in his life. How wonderful if she could become that woman! When she got beautiful. Then she wouldn't just sit on the bed.

She cut off that thought, as it was premature if not downright unrealistic. "I am not beautiful now, but I will be if I complete the Service for the Good Magician."

Ryver touched a wall and drew a ribbon of water from it. "Come back then."

"I need help performing the Service. I need several assistants. I thought you might like to be one."

"Why?"

"It could be a good adventure."

"I suppose. But I could do that by myself."

How much was it safe to say? "This one might be special."

"How?"

It was not getting easier. "I am not supposed to tell you, unless you become part of the Quest."

He shook his head. "Look, the deal was that you would look me up when you were beautiful. You're only about a tenth of the way there. I don't want to go on a Quest with you."

Why had she bothered to come? But she was here, so she had to argue her case. Anyway, shallow as he might be, she liked him. "When the Quest is complete, I will be beautiful. If you are along, you will be the first man to see me that way. Does that intrigue you?"

He considered, his eyes now focused on her legs. "If you get beautiful all over, you should be able to get any man you want. Why go to the trouble of recruiting me?"

She had probably lost the case. So she had no reason to hold back. "Because I need nine Companions and I wouldn't want to reward any of the local yokels in my home village with my beauty, and you are the only other man I've met who seems halfway decent. Maybe it wouldn't work out with you, but I thought it would be nice to try."

"You know how I turn to water."

"That's your magic. It's a nice talent. I think it would be useful when we need water or have to deal with it."

"If you were beautiful, you wouldn't think so."

So that was it! He had been shunned by beautiful women, so distrusted their motives. "No matter how beautiful I may become, I'll always be plain old me inside. I'd still like you. I still have your water ball." She brought it out.

"It seems like a lot of work for a long shot."

"The Good Magician said my associates would be suitably rewarded. I don't know how, but does that help?"

He rolled the water ribbon into a ball, then bounced it on the clear floor, pondering. "Okay."

"You are committing to the Quest?"

"Sure. What is it?"

She told him.

"You know something?" he said as she concluded. "I like it. But don't expect me to pay any attention to you before you're beautiful."

Obviously he lacked the diplomatic touch of the centaur. But by similar token, he could be trusted, because he spoke his mind bluntly. He lacked subtlety. At such time as he got interested in her, it would be unfeigned. That counted for something. "No attention," she agreed, putting away her ball.

"And you say I have to ride in that bag?"

"The pouch, so no one will know I'm not alone. That will not be arduous; it seems that its occupants are not conscious of the passage of time."

"And that demoness is one, and there's a centaur filly?"

"Yes, D. Metria and Karia."

"Centaurs. They don't wear much."

There was no way around it. He would see Karia soon enough and often enough, on the Quest. "She is bare breasted, yes."

He licked his lips. "Who else is going?"

"Why, I don't know. I hadn't thought that far ahead."

"Let's discuss it. As a group."

So he wanted to see the bare-breasted filly right now. He was a typical man. Cube brought out the pouch and reached in. "Karia."

A hand caught hers. Then the centaur was there, her hoofs on the shiny floor, facing Ryver. His eyes were already beginning to glaze.

"You must be Ryver," she said.

He found his tongue. "And you must be Karia."

The centaur's feet left the floor. Oops—she was drifting off. "Hey!" Cube called. "Come back here."

Karia snapped out of it. "Did it happen again?"

"Yes. I forget to tell Ryver about it."

"About what?" His eyes remained fixed in place.

Cube realized that he hadn't noticed the way the centaur had been carried away by the mention of her name. He had been too distracted by her front.

"About my condition," Karia said. "When I hear my name spoken by someone else, I get carried away. So I must ask you not to speak it in my presence."

"Speak what?"

The centaur turned around, facing away from him. "Do not speak my name in my presence."

"Karia?"

"Snap out of it!" Cube cried.

Because the centaur's rear was in view, instead of her front, this time Ryver saw her hoofs leave the floor. "A bad spell," he said.

"A side effect, yes. I wish to be rid of it. That is why I am undertaking this mission."

Cube remembered to bring out the demoness. She put her hand back in the pouch and spoke her name, and in half a moment Metria was out. "What have I misfired?"

"Have you what?"

"Absence, confusion, miscarry, overlooked—"

"Missed?"

"Whatever," Metria agreed crossly.

"One freakout and one carry-away."

"What and what?"

"Ryver saw Ka—the centaur's bare front, and spoke her name."

The demoness's buxom front turned momentarily bare,

but she wasn't facing Ryver, so no damage was done. "Got it. So did he sign up?"

"Yes."

"So where are we going next?"

"We are about to decide."

Metria nodded, her head coming briefly loose from her neck. "Who else do you know who might be useful?"

Cube pondered briefly. "No one."

"The Good Magician didn't give you a list of names?"

"No list."

"Then let's go to Castle Roogna," Ryver said.

Metria glanced at him, her décolletage lowering just enough to catch his full attention. "Why there?"

"Because we have to go somewhere, and I've never been there, and this is a dandy reason to go."

Karia glanced back over her shoulder. "He may have a point. Castle Roogna is the human capital of Xanth, and the folk there surely would know of others who might be good for such a Quest."

"But we can't tell anyone about it," Cube protested.

"We can't tell the specifics, but we, or rather you, can speak generally of wanting company for a private adventure."

"But that's where the king lives! I wouldn't dare go near him."

"Just go to the castle," Karia recommended. "You don't have to approach the king."

Cube dreaded it, but realized that this was probably her best course. "I'll do it," she agreed.

4

PRINCESSES

They considered, and concluded that Karia should not carry Cube to Castle Roogna, because the royal folk there were all Magicians or Sorceresses and would be too apt to catch on that she had a secret mission if she traveled that way. So Cube walked along an enchanted path, taking another day. She really didn't mind, because it *was* her Quest and she had always liked doing things for herself. Demoness, centaur, and man were in the pouch, relaxing, or whatever it was for folk who had no passage of time. At least they weren't having a party while Cube did the work, she trusted.

The journey was uneventful, because she stayed strictly on the path and the only folk she passed paid her no attention. She realized that that was one big reason the Good Magician had approved her for this Quest, but still it rankled slightly. If Ryver walked along, juggling water balls, he would be noticed, and he was handsome enough so that girls would notice him. Just as Cube had noticed him, despite knowing that he was not the most intelligent or sophisticated man. If Karia trotted along that same path, every human and centaur male would notice her bouncing breasts, lovely face, and flowing mane. She might think that her rear was her prettiest aspect, but a human man would not see that at all if he were approaching her; his glazing eyes would be fixed on her front. And the demoness Metria—she was a conscious flirt and tease, compelling male attention whenever she wanted it, which seemed to be most of the time. Even if she traveled as a floating cloud of smoke, others would notice, especially if she spoke and confused a word.

So Cube was nice and safe, having no attributes to attract the notice of others. Her discontent was ameliorated somewhat by the fact that by the end of this quest, she would be beautiful. Then she would be the one impressing women and attracting men by her mere presence. The magic of a fair face would make people like her and trust her, and the magic of a luscious body would make men desire and love her. The content of her character would have no relevance. There was no power like beauty. Oh, how she ached to possess it!

The day's walk gave her time to ponder other things. She had three of the nine Companions she needed. Wherever was she going to find six more? It had been a challenge to recruit the first three from the people she had met, and now she would have to seek among strangers. There might be a reason for it to be nine—three squared—but it was one daunting task to achieve.

Two young men approached, traveling along the path the other way. Their eyes oriented on Cube's legs, flicked to her face, and promptly returned to her legs. They walked on by without comment.

That reminded her: those stockings made her legs nice. That made her part-way noticeable. She would have to remove them.

She sighed and sat on a conveniently placed bench. She lifted one leg and drew off one stocking, then the other. A squirrel was watching from a low branch, but he lost interest when the stockings were off. Now her legs were dull again, like the rest of her. The new underwear made her body a bit less objectionable, but far from interesting; that could stay on. She tied the stockings together and stuffed them into the pouch. Maybe the time would come when she could afford to wear them again. Or when she wouldn't even need them to make her legs sightworthy. There were women who could freak out men simply by changing their stockings as she had just done, and she would love to do that sometime.

She smiled briefly as she resumed walking. It had been nice having Ryver look at her legs as she sat on his bed, and the two who had just passed her. No man had ever done that before. It was just a hint of how things would be when she got beautiful. How she yearned for that day!

A sign said CASTLE ROOGNA—TOMORROW MORN-ING. She was just as glad, as she preferred to come to the castle fresh, and not have to worry about where and how to spend the night.

A woman was walking the other way on the path. She looked about sixty-two and had a grandmotherly aspect. She also looked a bit lost. Cube had sympathy for lost folk. "Hello. I'm Cube. Is there any way I can help you?"

"Yes, thank you, my dear," the woman said with a Mundane accent. That explained a lot. "I am Sally Graham, and I have been trying to find my way home. I was on my way home from work, there was a crash, and then I found myself here. Now I have no idea where home is."

Cube knew Sally was never going to return to her Mundane home. She would have to find her place here in Xanth. But she didn't want to say that directly. "What do you do?"

"Well, I work at the newspaper—"

That was no good. "I mean, what else? That you really like?"

Sally smiled. "I make cookies all the time and give them to people. In fact around home they call me the Cookie Lady."

Cube smiled. Now she knew the place for this person. "There's a river north of here. It's called the With a Cookee River. Cookies of all kinds grow along its banks. But I understand that sometimes it gets dry, and then the cookies wilt and aren't much good. But maybe if there were someone to take care of them—"

"I must go there," Sally said. "Where is it?"

"You're on an enchanted path. It seems to have signs identifying where you wish to go. Just follow those signs and you should find the river in due course."

"Thank you so much." Sally hesitated, then broached what she evidently took to be an awkward subject. "This region—it seems extremely odd to me. Some of the things I've seen—"

"This is Xanth. It's magic."

"Then I'm not losing my senses?"

"Not at all. Magic happens all the time. Most of it is frivolous, but some is serious. Maybe you will be able to make magic cookies."

"Magic cookies! Now there's an idea. Do you think it would be possible to make fortune cookies that always speak the truth?"

"I don't know, but it seems worthy to try. Maybe you can do it."

"I will find out. Thank you so much."

"You're welcome," Cube said as the woman walked on. She hoped she had directed her well. It was nice to be able to help a person in distress.

As dusk approached she came to a campsite. No one was there. She considered bringing the others out of the pouch, but decided it was best not to disturb them, since they were not aware of any delays. The dull parts of the route were for her to bear by herself. So she would spend the night alone. It wasn't as if the experience were new to her.

Then a man came by. "Hello," Cube said.

"Just stopped for a drink," he said, going to the stream and throwing himself down to take in the water.

"But it's getting dark."

"I live close by. My talent is commanding; I can make anyone do anything, within reason. But it works only once a day, and I've already used it today. So I want to get home." He moved on down the path.

So much for that. She kept meeting men, and kept being brushed off by them. She hadn't even had the chance to exchange introductions. If only she looked better!

Would the man have lingered longer if she had been wearing the stockings? She brought them out of the pouch and considered. If she donned these, and sat with her knees lifted . . . No, she was right for this Quest as she was, highly ignorable. She put the stockings back in the pouch.

She picked a potato pie from a pie tree, and an eye scream stick, which screamed faintly as she took it. But the milkweeds had no pods. Well, she could drink water from the streamlet that cut across one corner of the camp. She also had potable water Sofia had packed. She fetched a cup from the shelter shelf. Then she remembered the jug of cider, and reached into the pouch. "Cider," she murmured, and her finger found its eyelet. She drew it out and poured herself a cup. It was just beginning to turn, which gave it a pleasant tang. Of course it made her turn around several times as she drank it, but that was part of the fun of it.

Overall, it was a good meal. Still, it would have been better if there had been someone to share it with. Someday, she trusted, there would be.

She checked for pillows, but there were only green ones, not properly fluffy, and no proper bedding. This camp must get a lot of traffic, using up its facilities. But maybe Sofia Socksorter had anticipated this too. Cube reached into the pouch. "Pillow."

Something nudged her fingers. She hauled it out: a wonderfully big soft pillow, scented faintly of new-mown hay. She reached in again. "Blanket." She caught a corner and brought it out, similarly nice. She had not been overly impressed by Sofia at first, but her appreciation was growing. The woman surely made a very comfortable home for the Good Magician.

She brought out Ryver's water ball and stared into its liquid center. It made her feel closer to him. It didn't care that she was not yet beautiful.

She slept well. It was as if the path's enchantment extended to sleep itself, so that no bad dreams or restlessness intruded. She could really get to like such traveling, if only she had compatible company.

In the morning she set out for the castle, refreshed. The path curved pleasantly, and she found herself curious about what was beyond the next turn or hill, though of course all she had to do was keep walking and she would find it. Then she almost collided with a man going the other way. "Apology," she said.

"My fault," he said. "I was looking through things and not watching where I was going."

"Through things?"

"My talent," he explained. "I make solid things appear like quartz, so I can see through them. Like this." He gestured at a tree.

Cube looked. The tree was now transparent, and she could see right through it. "That's a marvelous talent!"

"Now all I need to do is find a nice woman who thinks so," he said, and moved on.

He hadn't recognized her as a woman. That dampened her outlook, though it was hardly the first time.

She walked on, and soon she saw the highest turrets and pennants of the castle. It was surrounded by a large orchard, which turned out to have an enormous variety of magical trees and bushes. One section seemed to be an extensive graveyard. She paused by it, wondering who was buried there.

The ground over the nearest grave stirred. An emaciated hand popped out of the earth, followed by a gruesome head and shoulders. It was a zombie! She was too taken aback to move. Her nickelpedes wouldn't have much effect against a thing like this, because zombies didn't feel pain and were always shedding bits of flesh anyway.

The head turned to gaze at her with hollow eye sockets. "Khhannn Iii hellpsh you?"

It was talking! "I was—I was just going to Castle Roogna."

"Thhash waayyy," the zombie said, pointing at the castle.

"Thank you." Cube got her legs moving. When she glanced behind, the zombie was sinking back into its grave. Now she remembered: zombies guarded the castle, rousing themselves only when it was under attack. She would never want to try to attack it.

The path led up to the moat. Was there going to be a Challenge to enter? Probably not. What was she going to say to anyone she met? Surely there would be a guard demanding her business. She needed to have something reasonable to tell him. What would be technically correct, but not give away her mission?

An elf appeared before her. No, it was a cute little girl, wearing a cute little crown. She wore a green dress, had green/blonde hair and blue eyes, and looked to be about seven years old. "Hi!"

"Hi," Cube replied. Was this really a little Princess, or merely a child in costume?

"I'm Melody."

"Hello, Melody. I am Cube."

The girl laughed. "No you aren't!"

Was she guessing? "It is what others call me. My real name is Cue."

A second child appeared beside the first. This one wore a nice brown dress, which matched her hair and eyes. She held a toy harmonica in one hand, and wore a matching crown. "I'm Harmony."

"I am—"

"I heard. Why are you here?"

Cube wasn't sure she should state her business to children. On the other hand, there was no harm in it. "I am looking for for a traveling Companion."

Both children burst out laughing. "No you aren't!" Harmony said.

What was going on here? Cube suppressed her irritation. "Or Companions."

A third child appeared. This one had a red dress, red hair, and green eyes, and carried a toy drum. She, too had a costume crown. "I'm Rhythm."

"Hello, Rhythm. I was just saying—"

"I heard. Why?"

"Are you twins?" Cube asked.

All three laughed. "No," Rhythm said.

"We're triplets," Melody explained.

Oh, of course. Cube had clumsily gotten the wrong term. "I don't want to travel alone, so I need Companions. I thought I might find some here at Castle Roogna."

"Okay," Harmony agreed.

"We'll show you around," Rhythm concluded.

Cube wasn't quite satisfied with this. It would be hard to scout for potential Companions if she had to humor children. "Thank you, but—"

"Right this way," Melody said. They seemed to take turns speaking. The three of them turned and skipped across the drawbridge.

Cube had little choice but to follow. Maybe an adult would take charge of the playing children inside, and she would be able to get on with her business.

A huge serpentine head rose up from the water of the moat. It was a sea serpent, looming over the children. "Nickelpedes," Cube whispered, and suddenly she was surrounded by them. She wasn't sure they could reach the monster in time to prevent it from gobbling a child, but she had to try.

Harmony turned back. "You don't need those," she said, evincing no fear of the nickelpedes.

"This is Soufflé," Rhythm said.

"Our pet moat monster," Melody said.

"And baby-sitter," Harmony said.

Soufflé brought his huge head down, and all three girls reached up to pet him on the snout.

"Uh, all right," Cube agreed, banishing the nickelpedes. She wasn't entirely easy with this, but surely the girls knew their moat monster.

The monster nodded, then slowly sank back into the water. Cube realized that he understood human talk. The wonders of this castle continued.

They entered the castle. The central hall was enormous, with many arched doors along its sides.

"This way to your room," Rhythm announced, running to a stone stairway.

"But I'm not staying here!"

"Yes you are," Melody said, running beside her sister.

"But I only—"

"Hurry up," Harmony said. "We have a lot of showing to do."

Cube came to a stop. "Look, girls, I appreciate your interest, but I'm just a passing traveler. I can't—"

The three burst into laughter again. "No you're not," Rhythm said.

Every time she told a half truth, they caught her. What was going on here?

"Children!" a woman called, approaching from down the main hall. "What mischief are you up to?"

"Awww, Mom, we're just showing Cube around," Melody said innocently, a bright little halo appearing over her head.

"She needs to see the sights," Harmony added.

"And get some Companions," Rhythm concluded.

The woman turned to Cube. "I apologize. The Princesses are so mischievous it's hard to keep track of them. I hope they haven't been bothering you too badly."

"Oh, not too bad," Cube said.

The three girls burst out laughing again.

Then something else caught up to her awareness. "Princesses?"

"Perhaps we should make a more formal introduction," the woman said. "I am Princess Ivy, and these are my children, Melody, Harmony, and Rhythm."

Now Cube saw that the woman also wore a crown. She recognized the name. "P-P-Princess Ivy?"

There was more laughter from the children. "She didn't know!" Melody said.

"We were having real fun," Harmony added.

"Waiting to see how long it took her to catch on," Rhythm concluded.

Princess Ivy shook her head. "They are endless mischief, but it's hard to stop, because they are Sorceresses."

"Sorceresses," Cube repeated numbly. She was standing before a Princess—four Princesses—and didn't know whether she should bow or faint.

"Any one of them is a Sorceress," Ivy clarified. "Any two of them square it, and the three together cube it."

"Cube it," Cube echoed, wondering whether this was pure coincidence. She kept encountering squares and cubes of three. Had the Good Magician known?

"Whatever they sing, play, and drum together becomes real. Beware when they start making music."

Melody began to hum. Harmony played a note on her harmonica. Rhythm beat her drum. Cube felt intense magic coalescing around them.

"Girls!" Ivy snapped warningly.

The music cut off in mid note, but the children did not look too abashed.

"They don't know their own power yet," Ivy confided.

"Yes we do!" Melody said.

"So it's better to humor them," Ivy continued.

"That's right," Harmony agreed.

"And hope there isn't serious trouble," Ivy concluded.

"So there!" Rhythm said.

"I suppose I can do that," Cube said cautiously.

"So now come on up to your room," Melody said victoriously.

Ivy made a slight roll of her eyes.

"We saw that!" Harmony said.

"I'll go to my room," Cube agreed quickly.

"Now!" Rhythm said in peremptory fashion, imitating an adult. The three giggled.

Cube went. If their mother couldn't entirely control them, Cube certainly couldn't.

The room turned out to be quite nice, with a soft bed, a table, chairs, and plenty of closet space. There was even a comprehensive lavatory. A girl could get to like a room like this. But there was one liability: it had a mirror.

"That's a magic mirror," Melody said.

Harmony faced it. "Wira," she said.

The image of the Good Magician's daughter-in-law appeared. "Hi, Wira!" Harmony called.

The blind young woman looked toward them. "Are you spying on me again, you little mischiefs?" she inquired with a smile.

"Sure," Rhythm said. "We've got Cube."

"Leave her alone," Wira said. "She has her own life to lead."

"Maybe," Melody said as the image faded.

"Come see the Magic Tapestry," Harmony told Cube.

The triplets led the way to their own room. On its wall was a large picture tapestry showing a scene of Castle Roogna and its orchard.

"Watch," Rhythm said.

Then the picture changed. Instead it showed a section of the enchanted path, and in a moment Cube herself came walking along it. "That's me!" she exclaimed. "Coming here!"

"We can tune it in to anything except the secrets of the Adult Conspiracy," Melody said.

"We know where you've been," Harmony agreed.

"We saw you coming," Rhythm concluded.

"You mean it wasn't just chance that you intercepted me?" Cube asked, knowing the answer.

"You're on a mission for the Good Magician," Melody said.

"Because you want to be beautiful," Harmony added.

"But we can make you beautiful right now," Rhythm finished.

Cube was halfway overwhelmed. "But I can't tell you what my assignment is."

"Mice!" Melody swore. As a child she wasn't supposed to know any bad words, like Rats.

"We can't see or hear into Humfrey's study," Harmony said.

"And his designated wives know how to fuzz out our snooping," Rhythm said.

So they truly didn't know. That was a relief.

"We don't like mysteries," Melody said grimly.

"Especially when they are excluding us," Harmony agreed.

"The Adult Conspiracy is bad enough," Rhythm concluded.

"I wish I could tell you, but I can't," Cube said. "It would ruin everything."

To her surprise, they relented. "Okay," Melody said.

"Now we'll show you the grounds," Harmony added.

"And maybe help you find some Companions," Rhythm concluded.

"That would be very nice of you," Cube said, not quite trusting this.

"Where shall we go?" Melody asked her sisters.

"Not the Good Magician's Castle," Harmony said. "Humfrey would threaten us with an Answer."

"Not the Nameless Castle," Rhythm said. "Nimby would take away our magic."

Cube was privately interested. There was a person who could overrule the power of three Sorceresses?

"Not Castle Zombie," Melody said. "Breanna would make us eat zombie pie."

Another person they were wary of? What was her secret?

"Not the realm of Mixed Metaphor," Harmony said.

"Because that puts all our eggs in one place in the sun," Rhythm said.

"And our kettle of fish in the farthest pasture," Melody said.

"You girls are teasing me again," Cube said, forcing a frown. The three looked suitably abashed. They might be Princesses and Sorceresses, but they were also children, who could be cowed by an adult rebuke. That helped.

"So it must be Castle MaiDragon," Harmony said.

"Becka's fun," Rhythm said.

"Who is Becka?" Cube asked.

The three little princesses exchanged a wicked triangular glance. "You'll find out," Melody said.

She surely would. While her search for suitable Companions waited. But what could she do?

The Princesses formed a circle around her, so that she was enclosed in a manner. Melody hummed, Harmony played her harmonica, and Rhythm beat on her drum. The music swelled; these were really not toys, it turned out, but full musical instruments. Cube felt the magic intensifying around them. The Princesses might be young, but there was nothing childish about their power of magic.

Then the room wavered and faded. There was a moment of vertigo. Then the room re-formed. What had happened?

Cube saw that it wasn't the same room. The Tapestry was gone, and the furniture was different, as was the color of the walls.

"We're here," Harmony said, putting away her harmonica.

"Let's go find Becka," Rhythm said, putting away her drum.

"This way," Melody said, running out the door.

The others followed, with Cube trailing. The room turned out to be in a high turret, with a long winding stairway down. She got halfway dizzy going around and around. But finally they reached the ground floor. They ran on through chamber after chamber, looking for Becka, but the castle was empty.

"She must be outside," Harmony cried breathlessly.

They ran out the front gate. There was no moat; instead the castle was surrounded by a beaten dirt track. "Not here," Rhythm said.

"We'll have to call her," Melody decided.

"Yes," Harmony agreed.

"I'll do it," Rhythm said. She brought out her little drum and beat a brisk cadence.

The sound of the drum was surprisingly strong. BOOM! BOOM! BOOM! It reverberated through the forest, and made two innocent clouds shake in the sky. In fact one of them was so shaken it wet on the forest below. Cube was reminded again: these children were not mere little girls, they were Sorceresses, with power of magic ordinary folk could only dream about.

In two and a half moments there was an answer from the sky. It sounded like the roar of a dragon. That made Cube nervous, because she was not on an enchanted path at the moment. But the little princesses did not seem alarmed.

Then the dragon appeared, flying swiftly toward them. It had bright green scales with purplish tinges. It looked dangerous.

"We had better get inside," Cube said apprehensively.

The three Princesses burst out laughing. Cube realized that she had made another mistake.

The dragon came to land before them. Then it changed form. It became a cute girl with blonde hair and brown eyes, about eighteen years old.

"Hi, Becka!" the three Princesses exclaimed together.

"Hi, Princesses," the young woman answered. "Who is your friend?"

"Cube," Melody answered.

"We're showing her around," Harmony added.

"And you're part of the sights," Rhythm concluded.

Becka laughed. "Hello, Cube. I'm Becka Dragongirl, caretaker of the Princesses' castle."

The Princesses' castle? There continued to be details those naughty little girls didn't tell her.

"I'm glad you were able to come so quickly," Becka said to the Princesses. "I was on my way to fetch you, but turned back when I heard your drumbeat."

The Princesses were surprised. "You wanted us?" Melody asked.

"Yes. I fear only you can solve my problem."

"Problem?" Harmony asked.

"Brusque Brassy, my boyfriend, opened the forbidden door. He's gone, and I don't know what to do." The girl wiped away a tear of grief and frustration.

"But doesn't he know better?" Rhythm asked.

"Well, I certainly thought he did. He must have gotten confused. I asked him to fetch a broom from the closet so I could sweep out a speck of dust, and he went, and then I heard a horrible sound, the Forbidden Chamber Door being slammed shut, and I rushed there and he was gone. He must have opened it, and the Random Factor got him, and oh, I don't know what to do!" She wiped away another tear.

"This is suspicious," Melody said.

"Also a mystery," Rhythm agreed.

"What do you think, Cube?" Rhythm asked.

Cube was startled. "I don't know enough to have an opinion. I don't know who Brusque is, or what the Forbidden Chamber is, or anything about the Rancid Factoid."

The three Princesses and Becka laughed together, for half a moment. Then they reverted to serious. "Brusque Brassy is the grandson of Smash Ogre and Tandy Nymph. He's nineteen, and my boyfriend."

"He makes things hard and heavy," Melody said with a third of a titter. "Like himself."

"Or soft and light," Harmony added with another third of a titter. "Like Becka in maid form."

"We have no idea what they do when they get together," Rhythm concluded, with the last of the titter.

"You'd better *not* have any idea," Becka said severely. "The Adult Conspiracy forbids."

"Awwww," the three said together. It was clear that they were very curious about what was in the Adult Conspiracy to Keep Interesting Things from Children, and had some peripheral knowledge of it, but their naughtiness had not quite conquered it. That was surely just as well.

Becka faced Cube again. "The Forbidden Chamber was here when the Princesses made this castle. Inside it is the Random Factor, who does something weird to whoever opens the door. So we don't open it unless it's an emergency."

"But if they made the castle, didn't they make the—Random Factor too? In which case—"

"No, he existed on his own; they merely brought him in to stay here," Becka explained. "They don't understand all the aspects of their magic. Their folks are worried that they have more power than they can control, which could make for real trouble someday."

The three Princesses nodded in silent agreement.

Now Cube had a better basis to form an opinion. "Brusque must have gotten confused," she said. "So he thought he was opening the closet door. It was a mistake."

"But he's not a confused type," Becka said. "Not at all careless. He always knows what he's doing."

"Especially when he gets alone with Becka," Melody said with her share of a snicker.

"Oh, stop it!" Becka said severely, turning dragon for a good third of an instant. "This is serious."

The three Princesses looked abashed. "We're sorry," Harmony said, looking woeful.

"But not mortified," Rhythm concluded with a hint of a smirk.

"Maybe something happened to mislead him," Cube suggested. "Is there any way to check on that?"

"Sure," Melody said.

"We'll check the Tapestry," Harmony said.

"And here it is," Rhythm concluded with a beat on her drum.

The three turned to face the wall—and there was the big Magic Tapestry Cube had seen in Castle Roogna. Its picture was fuzzing and changing. Then it settled on Castle MaiDragon, in a cutaway view so that Becka and a handsome young man were visible.

Becka kissed him. "OooOooOoo!" the three Princesses Oooed together. Becka shot them a dark look and they stopped.

The Tapestry showed Becka say something to Brusque. He nodded and went through the halls, obviously to the broom closet. "It's on the other side of the courtyard," Becka said.

But when the man entered the courtyard, something shifted. He crossed it at an angle.

"He's going the wrong way," Becka said. "He's going toward the hall that leads to the Forbidden Chamber."

"We'd better check closer," Melody said. The picture on the Tapestry froze.

"There's illusion," Harmony added. The scene magnified, so that just the courtyard showed, with two halls leading from the court.

"The Forbidden Chamber hall looks like the broom closet hall," Rhythm concluded. Indeed, there was a picture of a broom marking it.

"That's why he took the wrong hall," Becka said. "He doesn't know this castle well enough to know that it's wrong."

"So someone tricked him," Cube said, glad that her hunch had proved correct. "He didn't do it on purpose."

"But this only deepens the mystery," Becka said. "Who used magic illusion to send him wrong? Who would want to do such a thing?"

The Princesses looked baffled. "Nobody," Melody said. "He's nice. He always smiles at me."

"And gives me hard candy," Harmony agreed.

"And tickles me," Rhythm concluded.

Cube realized that this wasn't much help. "Maybe we had best focus first on how to get him back, then worry about who did this."

"Exactly," Becka agreed. "We must check the Forbidden Chamber."

"Is that safe?"

"No," Becka said. "But I must help Brusque. Who knows what kind of picklement he's in?"

The Princesses conjured the Magic Tapestry back to Castle Roogna. Then all five of them walked toward the Forbidden Chamber. "Just what does the Random Factor do that's weird?" Cube asked uneasily.

"Oh, anything," Becka said. "It's totally random. Once it switched souls between—"

"Nuh-uh," Princess Melody murmured.

Becka looked startled, but she made a smooth transition. "I forget whom. Another time it put the victim into a Comic Strip. Do you know what that is?"

"Comic Strips are fun," Harmony said.

Cube did not agree. "I think I encountered one at the Good Magician's Castle. One egregious pun after another."

"But discussing them is dull," Rhythm concluded. The three of them ran ahead, losing interest in the dialogue.

"That's it," Becka agreed. "The Comic Strips are mostly on Ptero, separating the regions of the different species. No wonder there's not much intermixing!"

"Ptero?" Cube asked.

Becka paused half a moment. She was evidently too polite to call a person ignorant. "I guess you're from the back woods."

"Very much so. The whole of Xanth is mostly new to me. I would never have traveled, if I hadn't wanted to be beautiful."

Becka paused the other half of the moment. She was also too polite to agree that a person was lacking that quality. "I see. So you went to the Good Magician, and he gave you a confusing Service."

"How did you know?"

"I've been there and done that. I can't say I liked all of it, but it did pay off in the end. I'm sure it will for you. But how did you connect with the Princesses?"

"They intercepted me as I approached the castle. I had been hoping to—to recruit some Companions for my mission, but that can wait until we rescue your friend."

"I do appreciate your help. But apart from that, you may not be wasting your time. The Princesses, like the Good Magician, have ways of coming through for a person. They set me up as caretaker of Castle MaiDragon, satisfying both my forms. I had no idea, until the very end of that adventure."

Cube doubted that she was making much progress in recruitment, but once they had rescued Brusque, maybe she could get on with it. The Princesses couldn't take her time forever. She hoped.

They came to the door to the Forbidden Chamber. It was unmarked; apparently the occupants of the castle normally knew its danger. Cube's toe brushed something on the floor, and she stooped to pick it up. It was a pen, the kind used to write letters. "Did someone lose this?" she asked.

"Maybe Brusque dropped it when he opened the door," Becka said. "Hang on to it for now."

Cube put it in her breast pocket. It had a convenient little clip to fasten it in place. Something bothered her about that, but she couldn't quite figure it out.

The Princesses were already addressing the problem. "He came here and opened the door," Melody said.

"And the Random Factor zapped him," Harmony added.

"And now he's gone," Rhythm concluded.

Cube could have figured out that much for herself, but kept her mouth shut.

"Maybe we should open the door," Melody said.

"Don't you dare!" Becka snapped.

"And find out what the Random Factor does with us," Harmony added.

"You don't want to know," Becka said.

"We've always wanted to have a really gross adventure, fraught with horror, terror, and revulsion," Rhythm concluded. "We're tired of being Miss Nice Girls."

Cube stepped on a smile. What ideas seven-year-old children had!

"If the Random Factor sent him to some strange world," Becka said, "could you three locate him and bring him back?"

"Sure," Melody said.

"We'll do a Find," Harmony agreed.

"I'll serve as pointer," Rhythm said.

The three put their heads together. Melody hummed, Harmony played her harmonica, and Rhythm beat on her drum. Cube felt magic focusing.

Then Rhythm spun in place. Suddenly she stopped, facing Cube. Cube, realizing that she was in the way, stepped aside.

And Rhythm turned to face her again.

"He's not beyond you, he's with you," Becka said, surprised.

"He can't be," Cube said. But then she thought of something. "Unless—" But she couldn't finish, because her idea was that the man had been sent into the pouch she carried. That would explain his disappearance. But how could she tell them that, without giving away the nature of her Quest?

Becka caught on. "You can't tell what the Good Magician is making you do—why you need Companions," she said.

"Companions," Melody said. "That's right—you need some."

"So maybe Brusque has been made into a Companion," Harmony said.

Becka's face froze. "I don't want to be a spoilsport, but—"

Cube understood why she didn't want her boyfriend going off on a Quest with another woman, even a plain one. He could be away for a long time. "Maybe not that, but just—just hidden with the others," she said.

"Others?" Rhythm asked alertly.

Too much was coming out. "I—have some, but need more."

Becka resolved the issue. "All Quests require Companions. Everybody knows that. I was once assigned to be a Companion. We don't need to know where you are going. Just whether Brusque is with you."

She was right. Cube brought out the pouch. "I keep them in here. So that I can seem to be traveling alone. If Brusque is in here, I can bring him out."

She put her hand in the pouch. "Brusque," she said.

No hand gripped hers.

Oh, no! Just when she thought they had it worked out, it wasn't. "He's not here."

Becka was not pleased. "If the Princesses say he's with you, he's with you. Where is he—inside you?"

This was awful. "Can—can you do a more specific search?" she asked the Princesses.

"Sure," Melody said.

"A detail Find," Harmony agreed.

"Like this," Rhythm concluded.

They hummed, played, and beat again, and this time Rhythm pointed right at Cube's chest. Her finger almost touched the pen in the pocket there.

"The pen!" Cube said, taking it out. As she did, Rhythm's finger moved to follow it. "He's in the pen!"

"That's why it was lying there by the door," Becka said. "He was transferred into it, so it dropped; he couldn't carry it and be in it at the same time."

Cube pulled off the cap, but there was nothing under it except pen. She screwed the pen open, but there was nothing but a sleeve of ink. "He doesn't seem to be in here, unless he is the ink."

"See if it works," Becka suggested.

Cube brought out her notepad and wrote on it: "Where are you, Brusque?"

The pen worked perfectly, except for one thing: it oinked as it wrote.

"It's a pig pen!" Becka said, disgusted. The three Princesses chortled, loving the pun.

"I should have known," Becka continued. "He always has these punny little things. He thinks they're funny."

"They're great," Melody said. "He gave me my pocket watch." She reached into a pocket of her dress and drew out a little creature with big eyes. "It watches everything from my pocket."

"He gave me my water moccasins," Harmony agreed. She stamped one little foot, and her slipper splashed.

"And he gave me my elbow," Rhythm concluded. She touched her hair, and there was a green bow, matching her eyes. It was in the shape of the letter L. An L-bow.

"That doesn't solve the problem of exactly where he is," Becka said, her voice sounding slightly strained.

"He—he must *be* the pen," Cube said.

"Transformation!" Melody cried.

"We can fix it," Harmony agreed.

"Right now," Rhythm concluded.

They hummed, played, and beat. The magic intensified.

The pen wiggled in Cube's hand, then expanded explosively. Suddenly a man was standing there. He eyed Becka. "What took you so long?" he asked with a smile.

"I thought it would do you good to oink a while," she replied.

Then they kissed. "OooOooOoo!" the Princesses Oooed.

"Oh, put a sock in it," Becka said as they disengaged.

"I'm glad it worked out well," Cube said. "Now maybe we should get out of your way."

"We'd like that," Becka agreed, squeezing Brusque's hand.

Melody nodded. "It's time."

"Since we have a mission of our own," Harmony agreed.

"Joining Cube's Quest," Rhythm concluded.

"That's nice," Cube said. "So let's return to Castle Roogna, and then I'll be on my own way."

Then it hit her. "You're doing what?"

The Princesses laughed together. "Put us in your pouch," Melody said.

"Then check with Mother," Harmony added.

"She'll insist on an adult Companion," Rhythm explained.

They didn't consider Cube to be adult? But she had an answer. She reached into the pouch, murmuring, "Karia."

Out came the winged centaur. "There's a problem?"

"These children need an adult Companion," Cube said. "They want to join the Quest, and they didn't even know about the reward."

Karia turned her gaze on the three. "Oh, my! The little Princesses."

"You'll do," Melody said.

"Centaurs are always good," Harmony agreed.

"Mother will approve," Rhythm concluded.

Becka shook her head. "I fear you are in for more of an adventure than you anticipated," she said to Cube.

That was Cube's thought.

5

DRAGON

Before you go back to Castle Roogna," Becka said, "There's something—maybe you won't want to consider it—" Cube, still giddy from the sudden enlistment of the Princesses, who would add phenomenal power to her Quest, and maybe mischief too, was ready to listen. "I'll consider anything."

"Your Companions—I'm sure the Princesses can handle any problem you encounter. But for straight protection without using special magic—would you consider a dragon?"

"Don't tell me you want to join!"

Becka laughed. "Not at all! I've had my Quest, and I'm satisfied with my role here. I just want to get alone with Brusque before something else happens to him. But I know another dragon who is really a nice person, but, well, he's sort of a pariah."

"A pariah? Dragons aren't usually popular in human society anyway."

"Among his kind. Other dragons won't associate with him, so he's lonely. He—I think he'd like to be part of a group that might accept him. And he could protect you. Very well. Maybe too well."

This was becoming intriguing. "A friendly dragon, protecting too well?"

"Well, I have some trouble relating to dragons, because I'm a halfbreed. Drek's a fullbreed, but they still don't like him. Because of his, well, breath."

"Bad breath?"

"When he's happy, it smells of perfume."

Cube laughed. "No fire, smoke, or steam?"

"You can see why other dragons don't respect him."

"Yes. But how can he even stand up for himself, let alone protect anyone else?"

"When he's angry or upset, he breathes an awful stench. No one can stand it."

Cube was coming to understand. "So he protects by driving other creatures away."

"Yes. It's very effective. You'd get used to it, but would never enjoy it. Maybe it's a bad idea."

"He's really an ugly dragon," Cube said.

"Yes, in the way that counts with dragons."

"I'll consider him. Where is he?"

"That's another problem. He's hiding, and I'm not sure exactly where he is now. But the Princesses should be able to locate him."

"Sure we can," Melody said.

"Same way we located Brusque," Harmony agreed.

"Just as soon's we get Mother's permission," Rhythm concluded.

"Then I think that's settled," Cube said. "Thank you, Becka. We'll ask Drek."

"I hope it works out," Becka said. "He's my friend, and he's a nice dragon. I'd like to know he is happy."

"Time for us to conjure us back to Castle Roogna," Melody said.

"Perhaps not," Karia said.

The three looked at her. "Why not?" Harmony asked.

"Because if you wish to present me as a suitable adult

Companion, which I am, and protect the secret of the Quest from the knowledge of others, I should arrive in an evident manner, rather than being drawn out of the magic pouch."

Cube realized that she had a valid point. "Then maybe it is time for me to ride in the pouch. You can fly to Castle Roogna, carrying the three Princesses."

"Oh, goody!" Rhythm exclaimed. "We'll love it."

"I thought you might," Karia said.

They went outside the castle, leaving Becka and Brusque inside. Then Cube handed the pouch to the centaur, and put her foot in. Suddenly she was sliding into it, as if her body were greased. She found herself inside, surrounded by cloth. She was able to see fuzzily between the threads.

Karia tucked the pouch into the top of her quiver. Then she lay down so the three Princesses could mount. When they were there, she flicked them with her tail to make them light, and flicked herself. She trotted along the ground, spread her wings, and took off. Cube was aware of all this as much by motion as sight, because she couldn't see much from the quiver, and that was looking back. So she closed her eyes and relaxed.

In a moment she felt the slight jolt as the winged centaur landed. It must be Castle Roogna. Cube had not been aware of the passage of time, and realized that though she could remain alert in the pouch, if she did not make a conscious effort to, she would lapse into oblivion. That must be the way it was with the others, only they had no choice. She was not aware of their presences, but knew that Ryver and Metria were in here with her, as well as the supplies. The pouch seemed to have no limit on capacity. It was impressive, both in its magic and in the fact that it was so ordinary looking, like a darned sock; Sofia Socksorter had not been trying to impress anyone. All this was merely incidental magic from the Good Magician's foot. If that was the true story of this pouch. After all, he was the Magician of Information, not transportation.

The Princesses dismounted and ran off. Then Karia reached back and took the pouch in her hand. She held it close to her face. "Cube, if you hear me—now is a good time to come out. No one is watching."

Cube reached up with her hand. It emerged from the pouch—and then the rest of her was sliding out. She landed on the ground beside the centaur. "Thank you. I was aware, but couldn't see far."

"The Princesses are going inside to find their mother. I think you should introduce me to her, as you have met her before."

"How did you know that? I thought you were unconscious until I brought you out."

Karia smiled. "I was. The Princesses told me as we traveled. And I gave them some information on the Quest, since they have now joined it."

"But they need Princess Ivy's approval first."

"Do you have any doubt that they will receive it?"

Cube had to smile. "No. They won't even have to wheedle very much."

"I agree. Shall we enter now, or await their summons?"

"We can start in; they will intercept us."

They started in—and the Princesses intercepted them just outside the moat. "This way," Melody said.

"Mom wants to meet the centaur," Rhythm added.

"She thinks we made her up," Rhythm concluded. All three giggled.

Princess Ivy met them in the hall, as before. "Hello again, Cube! I hope the little mischiefs haven't been too hard on you."

"They took me to Castle MaiDragon, where we were able to help solve a problem. Then the little Princesses said they wished to join my Quest."

"And you couldn't say no," Ivy said with a smile. "I know exactly how it is." She turned to Karia. "Hello, Centaur. I am Princess Ivy."

"I am Karia Centaur."

"I am glad to meet you, Karia. I feel so much better about there being a centaur along."

But Karia was beginning to drift. Cube quickly kicked her on a hoof. "Snap to," she whispered urgently.

The centaur recovered. "I am glad to meet you too," she said.

Cube realized that she couldn't say more, because she had tuned out after her name was spoken. "And she is glad to be that centaur," she said. "I know she will do a good job of minding the Princesses."

If Princess Ivy noticed the slight discontinuity of dialogue, she didn't say so. Cube knew she was a Sorceress herself, who surely had the ability to learn anything she wanted to. She had probably known what the Princesses were up to beforehand, and checked out the centaur. "That's nice. I hereby give my approval for this excursion. But if the Princesses turn out to be too much of a handful, bring them back here."

"Of course," Karia agreed.

"Awww," the three girls said together.

"But I should explain that they will travel in this pouch," Cube said. "The Good Magician's wife gave it to me."

Ivy glanced at the pouch. "Sofia's handiwork," she said. "I am familiar with the type. That's fine. Do you need anything else for your trip?"

"I suspect the Princesses can conjure anything they need."

"That is true. See that they don't conjure too many things they *don't* need. They can get wild ideas."

"I'm sure they can," Cube agreed.

"Do you understand the specifics of their magic?"

"Just that they seem to be able to do anything they put their minds to."

"It is that anything they imagine while they sing, play, and beat becomes real. As I mentioned, together their magic power cubes. So if magic becomes necessary, remember that they have, potentially, more power than any other mortal in Xanth. Much more than they have wisdom to control. That is one reason adult guidance is essential. They will answer to adult authority, and at times it is necessary. But if there is a crisis, they will be able to handle it. Just see that they don't create more crises than they resolve."

"We will try," Karia said.

"Time to go," Melody said.

"Put us in the bag," Harmony agreed.

"And go there," Rhythm concluded.

Ivy shook her head wistfully. "At times I regret having lost the innocence of childhood. May you have a wonderful adventure."

Then Cube held forth the pouch. "Just put your foot in," she told Melody.

The girl did—and slid out of sight. Harmony followed similarly, and then Rhythm.

"I suspect you will prefer to keep them in there much of the time," Ivy remarked.

Then Cube mounted Karia, and the centaur trotted briskly out of the castle. When they got outside, she spread her wings and launched into the sky.

Only when they were well clear of the castle did Karia speak again. "Before we bring the Princesses out and have them orient on the dragon, there is one matter I thought I would mention."

"By all means."

"The Princesses also mentioned a problem at Castle MaiDragon. They said that Brusque Brassy had been turned into a pig pen and had to be rescued. Fortunately they were able to restore him."

"That's true."

"Who enchanted him?"

"Oh, we forgot to run that down! We meant to, but then didn't."

"It occurs to me that this could be a suspicious coincidence. Is it possible that it was intended as a distraction, to interfere with your Quest?"

"I hardly see how. It was just chance that brought us to Castle Mai- Dragon at that time."

"Perhaps. And perhaps I am being paranoid. But I thought I should mention it, without alarming the Princesses."

"It was worth mentioning," Cube agreed. "But I don't think there is any connection."

"Then let's find that dragon." Karia glided down to a private glade and landed.

Cube dismounted and took out the pouch. She reached in her hand. "Princesses."

Three little hands touched her fingers. Then they were out together, standing before her. "That was fun," Melody said.

"We knew nothing," Harmony agreed.

"We just quit there and appeared here," Rhythm concluded.

"It was actually a short flight," Karia said. "Before we proceed further, I must ask you never to use my name in my presence."

"Oh, we know," Melody said.

"That was funny when you started floating away while Mom was talking," Harmony added.

"She noticed, but saw Cube was handling it," Rhythm concluded.

"I'm glad you understand," Karia said. "It is a matter of safety. It would be awkward if it happened while I was flying."

"Now the dragon," Cube said. "Where is he?"

The Princesses got together, and soon Rhythm pointed. "That direction," Melody said.

"Not far," Harmony added.

"But it's odd," Rhythm finished.

Cube exchanged a glance with the centaur. What would strike the Princesses as odd? "We'll see," she said.

The Princesses returned to the pouch. Cube remounted, and Karia took off.

Not far in the indicated direction they saw a pretty collection of tents. They were arranged in the form of a large tome. "Ugh!" Karia exclaimed.

Cube realized that there must be a pun in evidence. She marshaled her thoughts and managed to come up with it. "A book fair," she said. "A pretty book."

"Exactly," the centaur agreed crossly.

"It is on the line they pointed," Cube said.

"No dragons there."

"We should check anyway. They said it wasn't far."

Karia sighed agreement and glided down to a landing beside the big book. It turned out to be made of piles of books, each with a brilliant cover. People were walking along, examining particular editions. They were evidently available for those who wanted them.

"These are interesting," Cube said. "I wish I had time to read some of them."

"I understand. A book can be a portal to another world. Xanth gets so dull at times."

"But no dragon here."

"He must be farther along."

Cube picked up a book. It was titled *Phaze*. "That's a funny word."

"Nice picture, though. I feel as if I could almost step into that scene."

"We can't afford the distraction." Cube looked again at the cover, which showed a handsome young man and two lovely young women standing before a green plain. It looked extraordinarily realistic. Then with regret she set it down.

They walked to the edge of the book fair and took off. The jungle closed in. There were no further things of interest.

They reached the great Gap Chasm. The depth of it yawned at them, followed by a small burp.

"I don't think the dragon is here," Karia said, landing. "There's a dragon in the Gap, but that's Stanley Steamer, not Drek. The Princesses would have said if he were beyond the Gap."

"We must have missed him," Cube agreed. She dismounted so she could stretch her legs. She spied a pretty little flower, and smelled it.

"Cube! Cube!"

Cube looked dazedly around. "Oh, hello Ka—centaur. What are we doing here?"

"I think you smelled an, ugh, dazey."

"A what?"

"It is a flower whose smell puts you into a daze."

"Oh. I'm sorry."

"Certainly it's not what we're looking for."

Cube agreed, embarrassed. She had forgotten that they weren't on an enchanted path; innocent things could be dangerous.

They turned around and flew back along the line. There was nothing until they arrived back at the book fair.

"I wonder," Karia said. "Where would a person hide, if he truly did not want to be found?"

"Somewhere nobody would look."

"How about a book?"

"A dragon wouldn't fit in a book, unless he were ensorceled."

"I wonder. We all fit in your pouch."

"You are thinking a book could be like the pouch?"

"Perhaps in the sense of being a portal to another realm. We think it is figurative, but with magic it just might be literal."

"It just might," Cube agreed.

They walked back through the fair until they came to the book they had admired before, *Phaze*. Cube poked a finger at the picture on the cover.

It went into the picture. Then she was sliding after it. She was entering the book, just as she had the pouch.

She landed on green turf. The three people looked at her, startled. "Who be thee?" the man asked.

"I, uh—just dropped in," Cube answered.

Then Karia landed beside her. The three people stared. "What manner of creature art thou?" the man asked.

"I am a winged centaur," Karia said. "You haven't seen one before?"

"Never."

Then Cube caught on. "We entered the book! We are in the book's world. Phaze."

"True, this be Phaze," the man said. "Thy world is different?"

"We call it Xanth," Karia replied.

The man exchanged a blank glance with the two women. "We know it not."

"The book—it's a portal," Karia said. "Just as we guessed. We have entered another world."

"Could the dragon be here?"

"Here there be dragons," the man agreed. "Mostly in the Purple Mountains to the south, but some do wander."

Drek could have hidden in the world of a book! "We came here looking for a particular dragon," Cube said.

The man laughed. "Why wouldst thou desire a dragon?"

"We believe he can help us. But he is hiding. We need to locate him."

"Dragons ne'er help others," the man said. "They eat them."

"I think we had better get a new direction," Karia said.

Cube wanted to bring the Princesses out, but didn't want the strangers to see it happen. Then she had a bright notion. "I think the rest of our party is about to arrive."

"The same way we did," Karia agreed.

Cube put a hand into the concealed pouch. "Princesses," she whispered.

The three girls appeared. "Yes, here they are," Cube said.

"Whence come these?" the man asked.

"We are all from Xanth," Cube said quickly. "Just visiting Phaze. We just want to find the dragon."

The three Princesses huddled, then pointed the direction. "That away," Melody said.

"Far away," Harmony agreed.

"But a stronger signal," Rhythm concluded.

"Then we had better get going," Karia said.

The man exchanged another glance with his companions. "Phaze be not a land safe for strangers to travel," he said. "There be dangers on land and in air. Particularly for children."

"He is surely correct," Karia said. "This isn't Xanth. We should not take unnecessary risks."

Cube considered. "Maybe we can make a deal." She faced

the man. "We have—some magic. What might we do for you, in exchange for your help finding our dragon?"

"We were looking not for reward, but merely advising of danger. We like not to see children endangered." He smiled at the Princesses, who smiled back.

"Perhaps we should introduce ourselves," Karia said. "I am Karia Winged Centaur, and these are Melody, Harmony, and Rhythm." She had not identified the rank of the children.

"And I am called Cube," Cube said.

"So appealing to meet thee, mare," the man said, his eyes lingering for a long moment, perhaps a moment and a half, on her front. Then he turned to Cube. "And thee, woman," his eyes not lingering. Then to the three Princesses. "And you, girls. I am Stoturyso Wolf, Stu for brief, and these are my companions Viola Corn and Forili Vamp. We be competent travelers, for we return not to our own kind."

Karia nodded thoughtfully. "I mean no offense, but I suspect you are not fully human."

"Indeed we are not," Stu agreed. "And I think neither be thy children mere young folk nor this thy full party. Shall we exchange wider introductions?"

Cube struggled with propriety versus secrecy, and decided that since this was a different realm, they could afford to be open. "We will do this, if our full nature is not told elsewhere."

Stu glanced at the two women. "We agree to bruit it not about."

"The children are the Sorceresses Melody, Harmony, and Rhythm," Cube said. "Capable of performing considerable magic."

The three reacted. "Adepts?" Stu asked, alarmed.

"What is an Adept?"

"A person with much power o' magic, a likely ruler o' his demesnes."

"That's close," Cube said. "But they are not planning on doing any mischief here." Then she reached her hand into the pouch. "Ryver," she murmured.

The man appeared. His eyes oriented instantly on the two attractive Phaze women. "Hello!"

"Our salutation to thee," Stu said.

"And one more member of our party," Cube said. She reached in again, and brought out Metria. "The Demoness Metria."

Again the three reacted. "A demon!" Stu said. "They come not often this way."

The demoness swirled into smoke, then spied Stu and coalesced into her loveliest shape. "Well, now, mortal. Whatever can I do for you?" Her blouse tightened and her skirt shortened.

Stu took a good look, then turned to his own companions. "Now will we show our further natures. I am not a man but a werewolf." He abruptly changed form, becoming a formidable wolf.

"Oh, can we pet you?" Melody asked.

"We love wolves," Harmony added.

"Especially werewolves," Rhythm concluded.

Now one of the women, Viola, spoke for the first time. "Thou mayst pet him, Melody, as he be tame."

"But pet not any strange wolf," the other woman, Forili, cautioned. "They be not always tame."

The three Princesses grouped around Stu, petting him on head, neck, and back.

"And I be a unicorn," Viola said, changing into one.

That immediately distracted the children from the wolf. "Oh, may we ride on you?" Melody asked.

"We love unicorns," Harmony added.

"But we hardly ever see one," Rhythm concluded.

"Thou mayst ride her," Forili said. "She also be tame." She lifted the children up to the unicorn's back.

The unicorn took them for a brief ride and returned. Then Forili spoke again. "And I be a vampire." She changed into a large bat.

For some reason the Princesses did not clamor to experience her nature.

Stu returned to manform. "Normally packs, herds, and

flocks remain with their own kind," he said. "But we prefer each other's company. This makes us unwelcome at home, so we travel together, not completely satisfied. We cannot marry without the support o' our kind."

Cube caught on. "You want acceptance of your relationship."

He nodded. "And that we fear we can ne'er have."

"One male and two females?" Karia asked. "Does your society accept plural marriages?"

"Nay. We need also another male. That be another reason we travel, hoping to find one."

"But suppose we could do something partway equivalent for you? Such as make you a castle, a preserve, where you could associate without being condemned?"

He shook his head. "Castles be beyond the means o' regular folk."

"But not necessarily beyond our means," Cube said, glancing at the Princesses. "If there is a suitable place."

"We know a place in the Purple Mountains," Stu said. "But unless thy children be truly Adepts, it is not feasible."

"Perhaps a token demonstration would be in order," Karia suggested.

The Princesses were glad to cooperate. They hummed, played, and beat, and soon formed a one-quarter-scale replica of Castle MaiDragon on the ground. Impressed, the wolf sniffed it and the two females peered over its outer wall at the myriad turrets and byways.

"Canst put such an edifice on a mountain slope?" Stu asked.

"Sure," Melody said.

"Anywhere," Harmony agreed.

"Full size," Rhythm concluded.

"For such a structure o' our own, we would guide thy group anywhere," Stu said.

Thus the deal was made. Stu resumed wolf form, while Viola kept unicorn form, and Forili retained human form and rode on her back. Cube put the others back in the pouch and rode Karia. They followed the running wolf, while conversing side by side.

"How camest thou to these demesnes?" Forili asked. "It be apparent that thy folk are not o' our world."

"You may find this hard to believe. We entered by stepping into the cover of a book about Phaze. The three of you were pictured there."

"There be a book about us?"

"There seems to be. But in our land, it is just a story."

"It be more than a story to us."

There was a musical note of agreement. Startled, Cube looked at the unicorn. "That sounded like a violin!"

"Aye. That be Viola's instrument."

"But I see no violin."

"It be her horn. Each unicorn plays a different instrument. They be most versatile."

"They certainly are."

Viola played an ongoing melody, the beat provided by her trotting hooves. It was quite nice.

"I say it as shouldn't, not being their kind," Forili said. "But a herd o' 'corns marching in formation be a most melodious thing."

"I should think so!"

They continued to exchange information about their two worlds as they moved toward the Purple Mountains. It was a long trip, and night fell before they got there. They stopped for the night beside a clear river, and the Princesses conjured meat for Stu, oats for Viola, and blood for Forili to eat in their natural forms, and more familiar food for their own party. Most of them could have remained in the pouch, but they preferred to come out and experience the world of Phaze.

The Princesses conjured a little pavilion made of hard chocolate, half filled it with marshmallow pillows, and slept there: their way of roughing it. Ryver disappeared into the nearest river, interested in the water of this world. Metria disappeared into the air, determined to check out the demons here. That left Cube and Karia, neither of whom was willing to go into the pouch while the Princesses were at possible risk out of it. So they joined them in the pavilion, which the Princesses obligingly made larger.

Stu assumed his wolf form and curled up beside the pavilion. Viola assumed her unicorn form and grazed in the night; she could sleep while grazing, it turned out. Forili assumed her bat form and hung from the branch of a nearby tree for her sleep. It seemed that they had to revert to their natural forms when sleeping; it required conscious will to maintain their human emulations. Cube thought that was just as well, because she wasn't sure whether they might otherwise have been inclined to summon the stork, or whatever it was in this world, and that would have been awkward with the Princesses in the vicinity.

In the morning Ryver and Metria returned, having taken their measures of the world. They and the Princesses got in the pouch, and the journey resumed. "Thy friends are interesting," Forili remarked. "What manner of land is this Xanth?"

Cube explained as well as she could, but it was clear that Xanth was impossibly strange to the vampire. Puns hardly existed in Phaze, and its social structure was odd.

The Purple Mountains loomed, seeming to grow out of the ground as the unicorn and centaur approached. They were literally purple overall, but closer inspection revealed them to be otherwise normal.

Then the unicorn halted, playing a warning note on her horn. "We be entering troll demesnes," Forili explained. "Needs must we consult on direction, and prepare for attack."

"Attack," Cube said, not liking this.

"Trolls be not generally nice creatures. They kill, cook, and eat the flesh of other creatures. There be few ways to pass by them safely."

"What ways?" Cube asked tightly.

"Safest is to kill them. But they be doughty fighters, and there be many of them, and they become more aggressive when attacked. So we have avoided that. But the other way be not comfortable."

"We don't like killing," Cube said. "What other way?"

"They be vulnerable to prettiness. They understand it not, and try to fend it off or destroy it. Could a pretty girl get close enough to kiss a troll male, she will stun him for an hour and pacify him for a day. A handsome man can do the same to a troll female."

"You get past them by kissing them!" Cube said.

"It be finely timed," Forili agreed. "I will fly to one, assume human form, and kiss before he can wring my neck. But this would be not effective for thee."

"I'm not pretty," Cube said.

"For a troll, thou beist pretty enough. But thou couldst not get close enough, being confined to human form."

Oh. "Our demon companion could do it," Karia said.

"Aye. But if several come, more be needed."

"Let me consult." Cube drew out the others and explained the situation.

"No problem," Metria said. "I'll be smoke until I kiss."

"I can turn water until close enough," Ryver said.

"We can do it too," Melody said.

"With an invisible magic shield," Harmony agreed.

"Until we're in their faces," Rhythm concluded.

Cube remained wary. "I'm not sure about this. You three would be nice morsels for them. What would your mother say if they caught you?"

Melody looked serious. "If they cooked and ate us, she would be most annoyed," Melody said.

"Especially with you," Harmony added.

"She wouldn't speak to you for a week," Rhythm concluded. Then the three of them overflowed with titters.

"Girls, this is serious. We can't afford the risk."

Melody gave her a brief serious look. "We can take care of ourselves."

Harmony nodded agreement. "And we mean to do it."

Rhythm tapped her little drum. "Mother would not have let us go, otherwise."

"They seem very sure, for children," Forili remarked.

Cube hesitated a moment more, then decided. "We'll try it. I hope this isn't disaster."

"Where be thy dragon?" Forili asked. "Needs we must select the closest trail."

Wordlessly, Rhythm pointed southwest.

Forili assumed her bat form and hovered just above the group. The three Princesses mounted Viola. Ryver walked behind them, followed by Karia and Cube. Metria brought up the rear in the form of a small black cloud. Stu, in wolf form, led the way.

The trail climbed steeply through the crevice between mountain slopes, confined by closely growing foliage. There was no way to see danger ahead; there was no visibility. But the wolf was sniffing the air, tracking the trolls that way, and Viola's ears were twitching nervously. Scent and sound—these were effective senses in this situation.

Abruptly Stu turned back, the fur on his neck rising. That was warning enough. The Princesses slid off the unicorn and readied their instruments. Then the party resumed forward motion.

The attack was sudden and surprising. It came from the rear. Three grotesque manlike figures charged in, waving crude clubs. There was hardly time to turn around.

Metria's cloud floated into the face of the first troll. She materialized in her lovely form, her face in his face. There was a resounding smack, and he fell back like a chopped tree. That interfered with the progress of the second. A bat flitted over his head and struck the second, becoming Forili's human form. She kissed him, and he too fell as if clubbed.

The third was grossly female. "My turn," Ryver said. He dissolved into water, flowed down the slope to the troll's feet, and rose up again in human form. He kissed her, and she sank to the ground, duly stunned. Cube hadn't realized he could turn to water in the absence of a pond or river.

Something jostled Cube. She turned to discover a fourth troll emerging from the brush on the side. She screamed.

Then his gnarly arms wrapped around her and lifted her off her feet. He hauled her into the foliage and started running heavily through the forest, heedless of the slope.

"Let me go!" Cube cried, sounding stupid even to herself.

"Marry pretty maiden," he rasped.

That amazed her into non-resistance. He thought she was pretty? But compared to the female troll, maybe she was. But that didn't mean she wanted to marry a troll!

However, it gave her an idea. She twisted around within his grasp, found his ugly face, and kissed it.

He stopped running, his grip on her loosening. He wasn't stunned enough to fall, but he did stand there halfway dazed. She got free of his grasp and backed away, and he did not protest. Then she turned to plunge back to the path and her group.

The wolf surged out of the brush, almost colliding with her. He assumed manform. "Be thou whole?"

"Yes," she gasped. "I—I kissed him. He wanted to marry me."

"Thou wouldst not much enjoy life as a troll. Follow." He reverted to wolf form and led her up the slope. She struggled after, using her hands to beat away the restraining saplings and branches.

Soon they came to the trail. There were the others, on guard against further attack, but no trolls. She rejoined them gladly. "A troll carried me away," she explained. "He wanted to marry me."

"We know," Karia said. "We realized too late that the ambush was a diversion. You were their target. They hoped to get you away while the rest of us fought. Then we would not know where you were."

"You're pretty," Melody said.

"For a troll," Harmony added.

"Girls!" Karia snapped, cutting off Rhythm's conclusion.

"It's all right," Cube said. "I *am* pretty for a troll. I proved it when I vanquished him with a kiss."

"We apologize," Rhythm concluded belatedly.

"We must move on before more come," Ryver said.

They moved on. On the far slope of the pass another band of trolls did charge them, but this time the others formed a wedge around Cube so she could not be reached. The three Princesses disappeared, then reappeared before three trolls, jumping up to kiss them. They giggled as the trolls fell.

Then the party hurried down the trail and to the level land south of the mountains. They were beyond the troll demesnes—but now they were in dragon demesnes.

Forili became human. "Find thy dragon," she said urgently. "Before other dragons find us." Indeed, they could see a large figure in the southern sky that wasn't birdlike.

Rhythm pointed west. They moved that way, and came to a projecting foothill. In Xanth, Cube thought, that would be in the shape of a foot, but here it was merely an adjunct to the larger mountain beyond.

And there was a well-beaten trail into the wooded wilderness of the foothill. That would be the dragon's path.

It occurred to Cube, somewhat belatedly, that she had little idea how to communicate with the dragon. Did he speak in the human manner? That seemed doubtful. Did he understand human talk? That was more likely; many creatures did, and if he was Becka's friend, they might have had that in common. So she would have to talk to the dragon, and hope that he understood. And agreed.

Suddenly they were at the dragon's den: a cave in the slope. Cube was sure of it, because there was a pile of bones outside it. Was the dragon there?

"We can shield you from fire," Melody said.

"Or smoke," Harmony added.

"But we're not sure about stink," Rhythm concluded, and they snickered.

"This is my job," Cube said. She walked out to stand before the den. "Drek Dragon—are you there? We come to talk with you."

A large head poked out of the cave. It was typically dragon, with a long greenish snoot, myriad teeth, big eyes, and small ears. There was a faint odor of violets.

"I am Cube Human of Xanth," she continued boldly, because she was afraid that if she were not bold she would soon be terrified. "Your friend Becka Dragongirl sent me. She said you might be interested in my Quest. It is to find a—a new territory of Xanth that may not be like what we have known. The Good Magician told me I would be beautiful if I reached it. Maybe it would do something similarly good for you. I don't know and can't promise. But the Good Magician did say that my Companions would be rewarded. Are you interested?"

She paused. She wasn't sure the dragon even understood her. How could she tell? Then she noticed that though the rest of him was still, Drek's right ear was wiggling. That was all, but it was a start.

"I—I don't know how to talk with you," she said. "But I see your ear moving. Does that meaning anything?"

The ear continued to wiggle. Maybe it itched.

She tried again. "Does it mean nothing?"

The right ear stopped wiggling—and the left ear wiggled instead.

Had she been in Xanth, a bulb would have flashed over her head. "That means no, doesn't it! The right ear is yes, the left ear is no!"

The right ear wiggled again.

"I need nine Companions to achieve my Quest," she said, excited. "I would like you to be one of them. You could protect us."

The right ear wiggled. "Does that mean you are interested?"

The right ear wiggled again.

"Or not interested."

The left ear wiggled.

She had it. "Then let me tell you more about it, on the assumption that you will join our group. I will introduce the other Companions." She did so, and each of the others stepped up to be seen as she named them. "There are three others, but they are not from Xanth; they are helping us travel. They are a werewolf, a vampire, and a unicorn, and they mean you no harm. We have agreed to make them a suitable castle here in the Purple Mountains in exchange for their help."

The dragon wiggled both ears. Then he drew himself slowly out of the cave. He turned sinuously as he emerged, going to the right. He started down the path there. He paused, glancing back, wiggling his right ear.

"You want us to follow you!" Cube exclaimed.

They followed the dragon to a valley behind the foothill. The forest gave way to widely spaced larger trees leading down to a fair-sized river. The valley was ringed by mountains, hills, and foothills, with the river squeezing out by plunging underground. Overall it was about as nice and secluded a region as Cube had seen.

"I wish we could have our castle here," Stu murmured, assuming human form.

The dragon's right ear wiggled.

The werewolf turned to the dragon. "Art thou offering us this valley during thy absence, if thou joinst Cube's Quest?" The right ear wiggled. "Until thy return—and if thou dost not return, it be ours?" The ear continued to wiggle. "We be caretakers in thine absence, protecting the valley from intrusion by others." More wiggles.

"I believe we have a deal," Cube said, more than satisfied. "Girls?"

The three Princesses huddled, then produced their instruments and made their music. The very air around them seemed to crackle with invisible power as their magic gathered. Then a full-sized castle developed on the far slope beyond the river. At first it was tenuous, as if formed of fog, but gradually it firmed, until it seemed quite solid in every detail.

At last they stopped, and for the first time Cube saw them tired. This had been a significant feat of magic, requiring a great deal of power.

They went as a party to the castle. There was actually a drawbridge across the river, part of the conjuration. The castle itself was huge, with a front gate more than large enough for a unicorn or dragon to pass without being crowded. It was solid stone; Cube tapped on a wall to verify that. Inside were great halls and chambers, completely furnished. It was ready for occupancy, but completely empty except for them.

The folk of Phaze were plainly awed. "You three indeed be Adepts," Stu said.

Cube thought of something. "If Drek returns—the castle is his?"

"Sure," Melody said.

"That's the deal, isn't it?" Harmony asked.

"But maybe they could share it," Rhythm suggested.

The werewolf looked at the dragon. The right ear wiggled. They did have a deal.

6

SIDESTEPPING

The journey back to their starting point in Phaze did not seem as long or arduous as the one down. The three natives accompanied them, and so did Drek Dragon. No trolls attacked them as they followed the mountain trail; apparently they were wary of the dragon. Then Cube got an idea, and the others agreed, surprised. She put them all into the purse, including wolf, bat, unicorn, and dragon, then rode Karia, who flew there much faster than they could otherwise have traveled. She brought them all out at what she called the Cover Site, and they were surprised, having thought they had gone in and out immediately. But they soon verified that they were two days' travel away from the Purple Mountain Retreat.

Only then did Cube realize that she didn't know how to return to Xanth. They tried walking back and forth across the area, thinking there might be an invisible curtain leading back, but there was not. Even the Princesses had no idea; they could perform mighty magic when they tried, but they had no information on how to cross between worlds.

Karia put her fine centaur mind to it. "We entered via a picture of Phaze. Perhaps if we reproduced that picture, there would be effect." But though wolf, bat, and unicorn obligingly posed as they had been, there was no effect.

Drek Dragon wiggled his right ear. Did he have an idea? Then Cube suffered another bulbless realization: "You came here before us, Drek! You know the way!"

He did, but it took a while to convey, because they had to speak it while the dragon agreed or disagreed. So they played the game of Nineteen Questions, all of them making suggestions, and the dragon wiggling ears.

"Try some other site?" Karia asked. Drek's left ear wiggled: No.

"Try it at the same hour of the day we arrived?" Cube asked. No.

"The two of you came through a picture," Stu said.

The dragon's right ear wiggled, pointing at the werewolf.

"So a picture is needed," Stu continued.

"A picture of Xanth!" Cube exclaimed.

The right ear wiggled. Now they had it.

The Princesses conjured an easel with a painting of Castle Roogna. They set it up where Karia and Cube had come through before. Then Karia put out one hand to touch it— and suddenly slid through the painting.

Surprised by this success, Cube peered at the painting. There was Karia, standing before the castle, waving. She was indeed in Xanth.

"Then we must go," Cube said, finding herself suddenly regretful. "I am glad to have made your acquaintance, and hope to see you again someday, if that is possible."

"Welcome," Stu said, embracing her. Cube tried to conceal her pleasure at being hugged by a handsome male, but didn't quite succeed.

"Hey, if you hug strange men, I can hug strange women," Ryver said, and proceeded to embrace Viola and Forili in their human forms, while the Princesses tittered. Now Cube had to conceal her jealousy, for both Phaze females were quite attractive in their human forms. That was not surprising, since they had crafted those forms themselves. If Cube had been able to craft her own form, she'd be lovely too.

Then everyone except the dragon got into the pouch. Drek obviously knew how to cross between worlds himself.

"Is thy quest public in thy land?" Stu asked.

"No, it is private," Cube replied. "Secret, in fact." Then she got the gist of his point. "And if Drek shows up beside Castle Roogna, many people will know that something unusual is up."

The dragon agreed. He poked the tip of his hind foot into the pouch, and slid into it. That was an interesting maneuver, as he had a good length of tail beyond the foot, yet somehow did not straddle the mouth of the pouch.

Then Cube faced the painting. "You can keep the picture," she said with a smile, and put her hand into it.

"We dare not use it," Stu said, "lest—" But his remaining words were lost as she passed out of Phaze.

In half a moment she was standing beside Karia, outside Castle Roogna. Cube turned to look behind her, but there was only the orchard. Still, she waved, just in case the folk of Phaze could see her in their picture, just as she had seen Karia.

Then she turned to the centaur. "Let's not go into the castle," she said.

"Agreed. Let me take you away from here."

"Agreed." She mounted, and the centaur flicked them both, trotted, spread her wings, and took off.

Once they were away from the castle, Karia addressed the next question: "We have seven Companions. Who is next?"

"I have no idea."

"Perhaps it is time to get, if you will excuse the expression, scientific."

That was an unfamiliar word. "Beg pardon?"

"It is a Mundane method for finding things out. I am thinking of asking the Princesses to do a Find on the next Companion, just as they did on the last one."

"Would that work? Without a specific name?"

"I don't know. But it seems worth the effort."

Cube had to agree. So they landed in a private glade and brought out the Princesses. "Can you do a Find on our next Companion?"

"Sure," Melody said brightly.

"That's great!"

"Who is he?" Harmony asked curiously.

"We don't know."

"Oh," Rhythm said dully.

But they tried it, and got a direction. It seemed there was a potential Companion not far distant. The Princesses returned to the pouch.

They resumed flight, and soon came to a likely site: a cave set into a hillside. "Another dragon?" Karia asked.

"I hope not. It is nothing against dragons, but we already have one."

"Agreed." The centaur glided down for a landing.

The cave turned out to be a human dwelling with a door. There were curtains and flowers, and things were neat. A woman, by the look of it.

"I think this is your job, again," Karia said.

"Yes." Cube braced herself and knocked on the door.

There was no answer. She knocked again, with no better response. Then she tried the latch.

The door opened, revealing a nicely furnished interior. It was a cave, but also a tasteful residence. "Hello?"

Still no answer. "They must be out," Cube called back to the centaur.

"That must be the case. We did not have an appointment."

"I suppose we'll just have to wait for them to return."

Karia looked thoughtful. "I wonder. There was a complication before you enlisted the Princesses, and the search for the dragon was remarkable. It occurs to me that we are encountering more complications than might be routine. Do you think there might be interference?"

"I haven't been on a Quest before. I don't know what is routine. Do you think something has happened to the person who lives here?"

"Perhaps it is my imagination, but it does seem possible. If so, we should consult."

"That wouldn't hurt." Cube brought out the others and explained the situation.

"We can find out," Melody said eagerly.

"We'll do a magic tracer," Harmony agreed.

"That will tell us," Rhythm concluded.

The three put their heads together, then made their music. Magic intensified. The air above them turned dark.

"There's bad magic here," Melody announced.

"Very strong magic," Harmony agreed.

"Too strong for us," Rhythm concluded.

"Too strong!" Karia said, startled. "But together you are the strongest Sorceresses in Xanth."

"Sure," Melody agreed.

"But this is stronger," Harmony added.

"Which means it must be Demon magic," Rhythm concluded.

"We have a demon with us," Cube said.

"Didn't you hear the capital D?" Metria asked. "The difference between a Demon and a demon is like that between the king of Xanth and a squashed ant."

"I don't understand."

Ryver and Drek looked at Cube, puzzled.

"She's from the back woods," Karia explained. "So I will explain. Metria is an ordinary demon, but there is another class. The capital Demons have the power of whole worlds. All of the magic of Xanth derives from the incidental leakage from the body of the Demon Xanth. The magic of gravity that suffuses Mundania and Xanth is from similar leakage from the body of the Demon Earth. There are more distant Demons of equivalent power. They seldom meddle in the affairs of mortal creatures; in fact they are rarely even aware of them. That is surely just as well, for they have the power to obliterate all of us on a whim."

"Half a whim," Metria said. "Or less."

Cube was amazed. "I never knew! But why would one of

these—Demons—want to interfere with our quest? If we are so insignificant—wouldn't he either ignore us or squash us flat, like that ant?"

"That is a fair question," the centaur agreed. "I conjecture that a Demon contest may be occurring."

"Contest?"

"The Demons, being omniscient and omnipotent, are at times bored," Karia said. "So they engage in contests between themselves. An essential element of any contest is randomness; a game is no fun when one knows how it will turn out. One of the random factors—and I am not referring to the monster in Castle MaiDragon—is the activity of mortal beings. We are, as Metria pointed out, like ants to them, and rather silly in our minuscule mortal concerns. They may place a wager on our quirky actions, and watch without interfering. The winner is the one who correctly predicts the outcome of a particular situation. But sometimes, perhaps, they cheat."

"How could someone cheat, when everyone knows everything?"

"I gather that most Demons are not paying much attention. Or there might not be a contest at the moment. I understand that one Demon is not supposed to interfere in the business of another. That is, Demon Earth keeps his magic finger out of the affairs of Xanth, and Demon Xanth leaves Mundania alone. But if one does decide to interfere, he may do it surreptitiously, so as not to be caught."

"Now it's starting to make sense," Cube said. "If there is something about this Quest that a Demon doesn't like, but he's not supposed to mess in, then he might do something sneaky."

"This is my thought," the centaur agreed.

"I think you're on to something, Karia," Metria said. Then she paused as the centaur's eyes misted and she started drifting away. "Oops."

Cube snapped her fingers. "Centaur! Attend to us."

Karia's body dropped to the ground. "Did I do it again?"

"Metria spoke your name."

"I forgot," the demoness said, blushing. The blush spread across her face, then drifted off to the side, collided with a wall, and stained it dull red. "I said you're on to something. One year ago a Demon contest won Counter Xanth from the foreign Demoness Fornax. That is the land we're trying to make a safe route to, so it can be colonized. It figures that Fornax would like to leave it empty, so it's pristine in case she should win it back in some other contest. So she could try to stop us from making that route—but not openly."

"That makes sense to me," Cube agreed. "But it's a pretty big assumption, just because a prospective Companion is out of the house at the moment."

"Not so big," Karia said, "considering the trace of magic stronger than the Princesses can fathom. It may be that the Demoness reckoned without the presence of the Princesses, or our insight into the problem, so thought we would not detect her mischief."

"Not paying attention," Ryver agreed. "But if this is the case, do we want to continue? The next ploy may be deadly. We can't fight Demon magic."

That drew Cube up short. "Of course you others don't have to take such a risk. I'll carry on alone."

Ryver looked at her. "Despite the risk?"

"It's my job. I don't know whether I can do it without Companions, but at least I can try."

"I doubt there would be much risk to us," Karia said. "The Demoness would not want to be obvious, and a death on this Quest would be obvious. That might attract the attention of the local Demon, Xanth, and cost her a point. She wouldn't like that. I'll stay. But perhaps the Princesses should return home."

"Oh no you don't!" Melody cried.

"We want a dangerous adventure," Harmony agreed.

"And if this is it, so much the better," Rhythm concluded.

"If you idiots are staying, count me in too," Metria said. "I can't let you be crazier than I am."

"Then I'm in too," Ryver said, glancing at her décolletage, which in her supposed distraction had drooped to the very verge of Too Low.

They looked at Drek. The dragon's right ear wiggled. He was in too.

Cube found herself halfway choked up. "Thanks, folks," she said. "I hope it all turns out well."

"Now we need to track our prospect," Karia said. "Girls?" Rhythm pointed into the cave-house.

Cube considered. "I think, in the circumstances, we had better go in. We'll apologize if we need to."

They entered cautiously. There was a smaller cave behind the front chamber. Karia was too large for this, so reluctantly went into the pouch. "But summon me if there is room, if I can help," she said as she slid out of sight.

The cave led back into the mountain. It soon lost the trappings of residence and became a winding tunnel. It became too tight for Ryver, so he too entered the pouch. Drek, however, had no trouble, though he was far more massive than the others, because his body was serpentine. He understood caves. Now he led the way, confident even in the looming darkness, with Metria following close after in the form of a small scudding cloud.

The Princesses made an incidental tune, and light formed around them, illuminating the passage so that Cube could see. That helped, though she remained not entirely easy about caves. She understood that they could be infested with goblins. Of course her nickelpedes could handle goblins, but might also gouge one of her Companions in the confusion.

At length the passage opened into a sizable nether cavern. The ceiling was a great dome, and there was a dark lake in the center. The air over the lake glowed, almost as if there were daylight, but the glow was from itself. "Who lives here?" Cube asked in a whisper, awed by the scene.

"It could be an old kraken retreat," Metria said, assuming human form. "There is probably access to the sea, down where we can't see."

"She can't see the sea," Melody said.

"Neither can we," Harmony agreed.

"So we'll let it be," Rhythm concluded. They giggled.

"A kraken?" Cube asked.

"A giant sea weed," the demoness clarified. "Carnivorous. I see no sign of one now, but if I were mortal I would not be inclined to enter this water." She dissolved back into her cloud, shuddering.

The Princesses went to the edge of the lake. They put their fingers in, and tasted them. "Boot rear!" Melody exclaimed, delighted.

"A whole lake of it," Harmony agreed.

"More than we can drink," Rhythm finished.

"Boot rear?" Cube asked.

The girls exchanged a look. Then a cup appeared in Melody's hand. She dipped it into the lake, filling it. "For you," she said. Harmony took it and brought it to Cube. "Try it," she continued. "You'll get a kick out of it," Rhythm concluded, without ever leaving the paragraph. That suggested they were up to something.

Cube took a careful sip—and got nudged in the back. Startled, she accidentally gulped a big mouthful—and got booted much harder. The three Princesses laughed merrily.

"You asked for it," Metria said from her cloud. "Boot rear."

"Boot rear," Cube agreed somewhat sourly. Too bad Karia had not been there to warn her with a groan for the pun.

There was a bleat from the side, and in a moment a hoofed animal came toward them. Cube's nervousness dissipated as she got a clear view if it. "It's only a goat."

The goat was tangled in vines that surrounded it and dragged behind. It must have been eating, and gotten caught, and now couldn't free itself. "Let me help you," Cube said compassionately. She reached for it.

"Nuh-uh," Metria's cloud murmured.

"But this poor animal needs help," Cube protested.

"Poor animal, my smoky fundament!"

"Your smoky what?"

"Posterior, behind, bottom, rump, seat—"

"Donkey?"

"Whatever," the demoness agreed crossly. "That's a scapegoat!"

"A what?"

"If you touch it, it will be fine and you'll be the one in trouble."

Oh. Cube withdrew her hand. The goat, disgusted that its ploy had not worked, walked away, dragging its vines.

Meanwhile the Princesses had done another Find, and pointed across the lake. The person they were looking for was that way.

"But how can we get across?" Cube asked. "If a sip of that stuff brings a kick in the, uh, donkey, how much worse would it be to try to swim in it?"

"Fortunately we can fly," Metria said.

That was right; she had forgotten the winged centaur. There was now plenty of space. She put her hand in the pouch. "Centaur."

A hand caught hers, and Karia slid out. "What a lovely subterranean lake!"

"It's boot rear," Cube told her.

"Ugh!"

"I'll check out beyond the lake," Metria said, vanishing.

Soon they were on the way, with Drek and the Princesses back in the pouch. Karia flew across the lake in the direction indicated. They came to a tiny island. Two women and a dog stood on it. There was barely room for them. One woman was remarkably tall, the other quite short.

Karia circled the island, as there was not room for her to land. "Are you the residents of the cave?" she called.

"Yes," the shorter woman answered. "We heard a bleat, so came back to check—"

"The scapegoat!" Cube said. "Now you're the ones in trouble."

"Yes. It was caught on a sort of raft. We threw a cord and drew it in, but the moment we touched it, we were on the raft instead, and it was kicking itself out across the lake."

"It was a boot rear float," the tall woman said.

"Ugh!"

"That was our sentiment," the short one said. "We had no

paddle and did not dare enter the, uh, water. It just kept going until it came here, where Diamond was stranded."

"Diamond?"

"The dog," the tall woman said. "She's a black Labrador from Mundania. We tried to pick her up, but instead the float tipped us off and kicked on, and we were stranded too."

"Diamond must have run afoul of the scapegoat here," Cube said. "Maybe it was on the island, and she tried to help. So it took the float."

"And then caught us," the short woman said. "Can you help us?"

"We can," Cube said. "But you may not like the method. You will have to enter this pouch." She held it up.

"We couldn't possibly fit in there!" the tall woman protested.

"It's magic. I'll bring you out as soon as we reach the shore. But first I need to know your names."

"Cory," the tall one said. "And this is my dear friend Tessa. And Diamond, of course." She patted the dog. Now Cube saw the white diamond on her chest, accounting for her name.

"I am Cube, and this is—is my centaur friend." That was a close call; if Karia had heard her name and drifted, they could have been dunked in boot rear. "Put your foot in this." She held forth the pouch.

"That looks like a dirty old sock," Tessa said as she got a closer look.

"Yes," Cube agreed. "But it's magic."

Hesitantly, tall Cory reached out with a foot and touched the pouch as Karia hovered close. "Oh!" she cried as she slid inside.

Then Tessa lifted her leg, but she was shorter and couldn't quite get there. Karia dropped lower, tilting, and then the woman's toe touched it and she slid in.

But the motion overbalanced them. Karia pumped her wings, jerking up, and Cube grabbed her mane with both hands, dropping the pouch.

"Oh, no!" she cried, seeing it fall into the lake. Already it was floating away from the island. How could she get it back?

Then the dog jumped into the water. The boot rear caught her, making her rise, and caught her again, propelling her forward. But she caught the pouch in her mouth, then turned and struggled valiantly back to the island. She dragged herself out, somewhat battered. But she had the pouch.

"Thank you, Diamond," Cube cried, relieved.

"Now I believe I can land, briefly," Karia said. "You take care of the rest."

"I will."

The centaur set her four hoofs carefully down on four sides of the dog. Then Cube reached down and took the pouch from the dog's mouth. "Now put your foot in, Diamond," she said.

The dog obeyed, and disappeared into the pouch. Karia took off, and winged rapidly back across the lake. She landed on the shore, and Cube slid off. She remained light from the flight, but could cope.

She held the pouch and put in her hand. "Cory." A hand caught hers, and she drew out the tall woman.

"Tessa." The short woman joined them.

"Diamond." The dog returned.

"We can't thank you enough," Cory said. "Normally we stay clear of the lake, but—"

"But we're soft hearted," Tessa said.

"I understand. I came to see you because I am recruiting for a special mission, a Quest. I can't tell you more unless you agree to join it, because it's supposed to be secret. But the Good Magician said that those who join will be rewarded."

The two exchanged a glance. "Why did you think we would be suitable?" Cory asked.

"We had a magic indication. It pointed to your cave-house, and then to here. One of you must have some talent or ability that we need."

"What we do, we do together," Tessa said.

"Perhaps it is both of them," Karia said. "Completing the roster."

"That might be," Cube agreed, surprised. "I can't really tell you more, unless you join, but maybe you could tell me whether you have any abilities that could help in a Quest."

"Does this by any chance involve travel to a strange region?" Cory asked.

"Yes!"

"Then we do have a talent that is relevant," Tessa said.

"Which of you has that talent?"

"Both of us," Cory said. "We share it, doing it together."

"Such a thing is known," Karia said. "Goblins and harpies share talents. What is the talent?"

"Sidestepping," Tessa said.

"What is that?"

"It's hard to explain," Cory said.

"Easier to demonstrate," Tessa said.

Cube pondered briefly. "Can you show me?"

Both women nodded. They linked hands. "Take my hand," Cory said, extending her free hand.

Cube took it. Then the two women stepped backward—into the wall of the cavern. Cube followed, drawn by Cory's hand.

Cube looked around, astonished and rather nervous. "What is this?"

"This is the other realm," Tessa explained. "You can let go now; once we are in, physical contact is not necessary. Only for getting in and out."

"But we're in the rock!"

"We're in the other realm," Cory said.

"I don't understand."

"Yes, this is why it is easier to demonstrate than to explain," Tessa said. "But you need to understand it, to determine whether it would be useful for your Quest."

Cube was pretty sure it was useful, because the Princesses had pointed the way here, and the two of them would complete the roster of nine Companions. But caution was best. "Yes, I want to understand."

"It is, as far as we can tell, an alternate realm with nothing in it," Cory said. "So what we see is regular Xanth, showing through. But it isn't real, in this realm. That's why we can walk through rock, or trees, or whatever."

"So I see," Cube agreed, peering through the rock surrounding her.

"Once we conducted a young man through a rainstorm," Tessa said. "He was amazed that we didn't get wet. That was fun."

"A young man?"

"His name was Umlaut, and he was handsome," Cory said.

"He kissed us," Tessa said, smiling reminiscently. "We didn't know that he didn't exist, then."

"He what?"

"He kissed us," Cory repeated. "He had to stand Tessa on a rock to do it with her, and had to stand on the rock himself to do it with me."

"Uh, that's nice," Cube said, wishing a handsome man would kiss her. "But what I meant was, he didn't exist?"

"Well, he *thought* he existed," Tessa said. "And now he does. He's dating Surprise, who is Grundy Golem and Rapunzel Elf's daughter. But back then he didn't."

"It's complicated," Cory said. "And incidental. We had better focus on clarifying sidestepping."

"Yes." Cube realized that it was best not to get sidetracked. "Your joint talent is to step to the, uh, side, and enter this empty realm. Can folk in regular Xanth see you when you do?"

"Oh, yes," Tessa agreed. "And hear us, a little. But they can't touch us. We seem like ghosts."

"Like ghosts?"

"We shall demonstrate," Cory said. "Step this way." She walked out of the rock.

Cube followed. Now she seemed to stand beside the dark lake. Karia and Diamond stood there. The centaur's mouth worked, but there was only the faintest of sounds. Cube nevertheless made it out, since there was no other noise. "Ah, there you are! Was it nice in the wall?"

"Observe," Cory said. She stepped right into the centaur—and through her, emerging on the other side.

Cube was almost as startled as Karia was. "Ghost," she said loudly. "We are like ghosts."

"Ghost!" Karia repeated loudly/faintly.

"Sidestepping," Cube shouted. "We're in a different realm."

"We'll bring them in now," Tessa said.

The two women linked hands and stepped forward together. Then Cory took Karia's hand, and Tessa rested her hand on the dog's back. They stepped back, drawing centaur and dog with them.

"Well hello again!" Karia shouted.

"Now sound's normal," Cube said. "We're both in the same realm again."

"Oh." Karia looked at the cave wall. "We can step into rock?"

"Follow me," Cube said, and walked back into the stone.

Centaur and dog followed, both looking bemused. "This is interesting," Karia said, evidently not one for overstatement.

"It's an—an alternate world, or something," Cube explained. "With nothing in it, so we see Xanth shining through."

"Without interacting physically with it," Karia agreed. "As if it is illusion. This could certainly simplify trekking through some of the natural hazards. I believe the Princesses are correct: we can use these people on the Quest."

"I agree. But maybe we should check with the others."

"Princesses?" Cory asked.

"Let's return to real Xanth, and I'll introduce you to the other members of our party."

They went back to the lake, and sidestepped out of the other realm. Then Cube brought the others out of the pouch, introducing each as she did. Cory and Tessa were duly awed by the presence of the Princesses and the dragon.

Demoness Metria popped into view. "Nothing much beyond the lake. Have I missed anything?"

"Very little," Karia said with half a smile.

"That's good. I would have hated to miss their smooching with Umlaut, because I knew him and smooched him some myself." She formed into a large floating candy kiss.

The centaur's half smile faded, becoming half a frown. Apparently she hadn't known that the demoness was not always as absent as she seemed.

Then they went through the sidestepping demonstration with the others. "Do these two women seem to be a worthy addition to the Quest?" Cube asked the group.

The others agreed that they were. So they explained the nature of the Quest and returned to the cave apartment, where Cory and Tessa made them all comfortable.

"How did the two of you get together?" Princess Melody asked as they relaxed on the couches and sipped boot rear diluted with tsoda popka.

"Since you must not have known your half talents before then," Harmony added, chewing on a mellow fragment of a sweet marsh—a marsh mellow that made the centaur wince.

"Or discovered the other realm," Rhythm concluded as she nibbled on assorted mints from a mint julep tree: hot pepper mints, delightful compli mints, and pointed spear mints.

"It's a dull story," Tessa said.

"Very dull," Cory agreed. "We're from Mundania."

"So we can skip it," Metria said. "Xanth is dull enough without even thinking about dreary Mundania."

"But you two have magic," Ryver said. "Everyone knows that Mundanes don't have magic talents."

"Everyone knows wrong," Cory said.

"We are the proof," Tessa agreed.

That got Metria's interest. "Are we about to puncture a common delusion? You must tell us all about it."

The two exchanged a glance. Then Cory spoke. "I was born in Mundania—"

"You were what?" Cube asked.

"The storks seldom deliver in Mundania," Cory said. "Instead there is a somewhat messy and painful process that—" She broke off as she noted the suddenly rapt attention of the three Princesses. "That we don't need to go into. I was part of a normal Mundane family, which is to say, dull. But even as a child I was tall. I had very long bones and loose joints. It is called Marfan syndrome, and it runs in families. You might call it a curse. Soon I was taller than any girl and most boys, and the other children made fun of me unmercifully. Women are not supposed to be that tall and clumsy. It did not abate as I reached maturity; others no longer teased me openly, but neither did they care to associate with me. Seeing all chance of a normal social life gone, let alone any prospect for romance, family, or success in life, I made a fateful decision. I announced that I was departing for a far country."

"Xanth!" Melody exclaimed.

Cory shook her head. "I did not know of Xanth. No, my words were a euphemism for a much darker denouement."

"A what for a what?" Harmony asked.

"A mild or vague expression substituting for something harsh or ugly," Karia clarified. "For a conclusion, outcome, or resolution."

"Death," Metria said.

"Whatever," Rhythm said, forcing a cute frown.

"Death," Cory agreed. "I needed only a private place to do it, where my body would not be found. I wanted others to believe that I had found satisfaction elsewhere. I wanted no further embarrassment. And so I sought the deepest, darkest forest I could find, that was reputed to be haunted, so most folk stayed well away from it. Within it I searched for the least accessible section, girt about by rough ground, brambles, and poisonous insects. I found a rushing river, with a brief level flow between two treacherous rapids, and it split, forming a tangled island. There was my place! It was all I could do to reach it, but I didn't want to drown, because my body might be carried out to some larger lake and discovered, ruining my secret. I struggled onto the island, and to the thickest brush at its center, and there I set about digging a grave. But a violent storm came up, and its wind and rain tore at me as if about to blow me away. I cowered down in my partial grave, clinging to the anonymous rock I intended as an unmarked headstone, and waited for the end."

"But that water didn't end you," Ryver said. "I know it wouldn't do that."

Cory nodded. "The river overflowed its banks and covered the island. I tried to hang on, but it carried me away. I feared I was about to drown, and be discovered. But it became oddly soft and warm, and bore me along like an encompassing cloak. Finally it left me on a distant bank. I was bruised and dizzy, but not dead, so I got to my feet and tried to organize to complete my mission. I had no idea where I was, but it was soon apparent that it was no place I had known before. I found a tree bearing pies."

"A pie tree!" Melody said.

"Yes. But they were not full pies. Instead they were slices. I picked and ate three slices, and when I had done that, I saw that it had grown one more slice. So I ate that, and then it produced four more. Suddenly I recognized a pattern I had learned in school: 3.14 was pi, the ratio of a circle to its diameter."

"A pi tree," Harmony agreed.

"Alerted by that, I soon saw other evidences of literalism. There was something that resembled a Mundane printer, but instead of paper, jam was oozing from it."

"Paper jam," Rhythm said.

"I saw a big dark bird, an owl, garbed with a helmet and sword."

"Ugh!" Karia said.

"A knight owl," Ryver said.

"At that point I was overcome by curiosity, so I started exploring this strange land. Then I encountered another person, a short one. I thought she would laugh at me, but she didn't."

"Which is where I pick up," Tessa said. "My journey to Xanth was far less traumatic. I had suffered some ridicule in

Mundania because I was too short. I pretended I didn't mind, but I did mind, and so I tried to find new friends who would accept me as I am. I drove to Florida, and down along the keys, which don't look like door keys in Mundania, but more like a string of islands, and I stopped at one called No Name Key. I had run out of money—that's something that is used a lot there—so I inquired at the first house I found for work. A nice man said he needed someone to carry a packet to another land, and he would pay me when I accomplished this. So I took the packet and went along the route he told me. But just as I got there, there was a horrible storm that pelted me with brightly colored hailstones. I tried to hide under a tree, but the hanging branches of the tree became tentacles and grabbed for me. I barely got away, terrified—but I had lost the packet. I knew I could not return and admit my failure, so I wandered on, dejected—and encountered a very tall woman."

"And so we met," Cory said. "We found this cave, and discovered that we liked each other's company, because each of us understood what it felt like to be teased for our height. We had no desire to associate with others, because the folk in Xanth consider us odd too. So when we happened to see other people, we hid."

"And one day after we had linked hands and fled desperately, we found ourselves in a really strange place," Tessa said. "Trees had become insubstantial; we could walk right through them. We were afraid we had died and become ghosts, but we were solid to each other. So we retraced our steps, and managed to return to regular Xanth. We had discovered sidestepping."

"A magic talent," Cory said. "Each of us had half of it, we could do it together but not alone."

"So it's not true that Mundanes in Xanth don't have magic," Tessa said. "It just takes time for them to achieve magic. They would discover their talents, if they ever thought to look for them."

"But they are so sure they have no magic, they never look," Cory concluded.

Cube was amazed. She had been one of the "everyone" who knew that Mundanes had no magic talents. But if the children of Mundanes in Xanth had talents, why shouldn't the Mundanes have them too, if they remained here long enough? She remembered how the Good Magician's sock had absorbed some of his magic; proximity did have its effect. Actually she wondered about that; he was the Magician of Information, while the sock was a transport mechanism, not his type of magic. So maybe Sofia Socksorter had confused the reason for the sock's magic. Not that it really mattered.

"So now you know our Quest, and we know your histories," Karia said to the two women. "I have no doubt of the usefulness of your talent, but there is another problem: we don't know exactly where we are going. We have been focusing on completing our roster of nine, and now that we have done that, we must orient on the mission."

"But you have more than nine," Tessa said.

"No, just nine Companions, including the two of you," Cube said. "Metria, Karia, Ryver, Melody, Harmony, Rhythm, Drek, Cory, Tessa. Nine."

"You didn't count yourself," Cory said.

"I'm not a Companion. I'm the one with the Quest."

"Is that what the Good Magician said?" Tessa asked. "Because it makes sense to me that your whole party be nine. That's the square of three, and you're looking for a new land, maybe the cube. Like your name."

"The twenty-seventh recorded adventure," Metria said. "I sneaked a peek at the Muse of History's list of titles."

"So there is three, squared and cubed," Karia said.

Cube turned her thought back to the Good Magician. "He said to limit my party to nine, no more, no less. So I did. And he said each person in it would be appropriately rewarded."

"Your party includes you," Karia said.

Cube realized that it was true. She was a member of her party; that must be what the Good Magician meant. She had one too many people. "But that means someone will have to go."

There was a silence. Then Cory spoke. "We are the last to join. We'll have to go."

"But then we'll be short one," Ryver pointed out.

"I'm the short one," Tessa said, smiling. "But we must be together; our talent won't work otherwise."

"We won't split up either," Melody said.

"Because we'd lose the cube of our talent," Harmony added.

"And we have to look out for each other," Rhythm concluded.

"I agree," Karia said. "They can't be separated. But perhaps I can be spared."

"You're the reason Mother let us go," Melody said.

"You have to stay," Harmony added.

"So *we* can stay," Rhythm concluded.

"Well, I could go," Metria said, looking uncharacteristically sad.

"I'm not sure that would be wise," Karia said. "We need the talents of a demon who can turn invisible or flit ahead. There's no telling what we will encounter along the way."

Drek wiggled an ear. "But we may need protection," Karia said. "We would be vulnerable without a dragon."

"That leaves me," Ryver said. "I'm sorry to go, but I guess I'd better."

That sent a pang through Cube. She wanted Ryver along, so he could be there when she got beautiful. "We need you too," she said quickly. "Your talent with water—we could need that any time."

"It is your decision, I think," Karia said. "It is your Quest."

Cube struggled with her conscience. "I don't think even the Good Magician knows exactly what's going to happen. Maybe he thinks nine is the right number, but maybe it's not. I want to keep our whole party together."

"I think keeping me is apt to bring more mischief than it's worth," Ryver said. "Betting that the Good Magician is wrong is foolish. He's never wrong."

"But he is seldom understood, either," Karia said. "Perhaps he *did* mean nine Companions, and a party of ten."

"I could pop back and ask him," Metria said.

"No," Cube said firmly. "Let's plow on, on our own, and see what happens."

The others nodded. They were committed, for good or ill.

7

THREAD

They rested that day, working out the details of their Quest for Counter Xanth. The three little Princesses tried to do a Find on it, but Rhythm's finger waved wildly, describing the contour of spilled spaghetti rather than any particular direction.

"This is frustrating," Melody said.

"Our magic is being balked," Harmony agreed.

"We don't like that," Rhythm concluded.

"This could be the work of the Demoness," Karia said. "Subtly interfering with the Quest."

Drek wiggled an ear. "You have an idea?" Cube asked him. He wiggled his right ear.

"This will be arid," Metria said impatiently.

"Be what?" Cube asked.

"Dry, sterile, aseptic, dull, irksome—"

"Tedious?"

"Whatever," she agreed crossly. "Why not have the Princesses make an illusion that can talk for him?"

Cube glanced at the three. "Can you do that?"

"Sure," Melody said.

"Now that someone thought of it," Harmony agreed.

"We'll make a talking picture tied to him," Rhythm concluded.

The three huddled, then sang, played, and beat, and the image of Drek appeared. It looked the real Drek in the snoot. "Hey, that's me!" the image said, surprised, while the real Drek wiggled both ears.

"That's you. You talk through the image," Karia told him. "To make it easier for those of us who don't speak Dragon."

Both the real and the image dragons looked confused, then thoughtful. Then the image spoke again. "How am I coming through?"

"Very well," Karia assured him. "Tell us your idea."

"It may not be the evil Demoness," the image said. "It may simply be that we have too many Companions, so the magic is fouled up. There may still be a Route, just more complicated than it might be. It may wind around and about, instead of being one straight direction. We can still follow it, if we make it visible."

A nod passed from Karia to Ryver, and through the three Princesses, the two sidesteppers, D. Metria, and finally ended with Cube. "Can you do that?" Cube asked the three again.

The three huddled, made music, and a silver thread appeared. It led out of the cave, wound around a nearby acorn tree, and headed away through the forest.

"And there we have it," the Drek image said, satisfied. "The winding route." There was perfume in the air.

"I'll follow it," Cube said. "And bring one of you out only when I have to, so as to keep the mission secret."

"What about Diamond?" Tessa asked. "We can't just leave her here."

Cube had almost forgotten about the dog they had rescued. "There must be a place for her. Maybe she could be a seeing-eye dog for Wira."

"Who?" Cory asked.

"The Good Magician's daughter-in-law. She's blind."

"Are you a guide dog?" Karia asked the dog.

Diamond looked down. Her tail drooped. She was not a guide dog.

Cube shrugged. "I suppose she can tag along with me, until she finds a place to stay."

Diamond wagged her tail.

In the morning, well rested and fed, the nine Companions slid into the pouch, leaving only Cube and Diamond. The dog tracked the thread by smelling it. Cube found that she was satisfied to have Diamond along, because it was suddenly lonely by herself, after being with the full group. She would have preferred to travel with all of them, openly, but that was not feasible or sensible. But who would notice a dog? They weren't common in Xanth, but neither were they unknown. So she had company after all.

The faint silver thread wound around the acorn tree, as they had seen before; Cube paused, considering, then decided that it was best to follow the trail exactly, so as to be sure not to lose it. So she didn't skip the loop, though she had to climb through brush, then returned to clear ground. She looked back, and the thread behind her was gone. It was like a one-way path, disappearing when used. What would have happened, had she skipped that loop? Would the whole thing have vanished? Of course she could bring out the Princesses and have them do it again, but that would be an admission of failure on her part and she didn't want to do it. She already felt guilty enough about getting the wrong number of Companions and complicating her route. She might have been there by now if she had been able to go straight. All because she wouldn't let handsome Ryver go. She knew appearance should not be that important—if she were judged by appearance, she'd be worthless—yet she was affected by it herself. She liked Ryver for his handsomeness, and wanted to win him, and to do that she had to have him there to see her get beautiful. So she had sacrificed her Quest for a selfish reason, which did not speak well for her quality of personality.

"Woof."

She came to with a start. She had been drifting, in much the way Karia did, except that her feet had not left the ground. Diamond had brought her out of it. Just as well, for someone was coming toward her, going the opposite way on the trail. It was a young woman, two and a half orders of magnitude more attractive than Cube, or par for the course.

"Hello," Cube said.

"Hi. I'm Heather. Would you like a flower?"

"A flower? All right."

The girl raised her hand, and there appeared in it a pretty little flower. Cube took it and put it to her nose. It smelled sweet. "Thank you."

"It's my talent," Heather said. "I conjure sweet-smelling flowers."

Belatedly, Cube introduced herself. "I'm Cube. I summon nickelpedes, but only when I have to."

"That must be awful."

"Oh, they don't gouge me, just whoever attacks me."

"May I pet your dog?"

"Oh, Diamond's not my—" Cube reconsidered. "Yes."

Heather petted Diamond, who wagged her tail. Then Heather conjured a sweet smelling dog-fennel bloom, gave it to Diamond, and walked on.

It had been a purely routine encounter, but Cube found it significant, because it was her first while she was officially on the route to Counter Xanth. If the rest of her journey went as well, she'd have no trouble.

She came to a furry creature that sat by the side of the path. It looked like an ape, but she wasn't sure.

"Have you been Saved?" the creature asked. "The key to salvation is to join my church."

Startled, Cube paused. "What are you?"

"I am a monk-key," it said proudly. "If you want to avoid damnation, you will heed my words."

A monk who preached a key. "I'll risk it," she said and moved on.

Now the thread cut to the side, skirting uncomfortably close to a tangle tree, and stopped at a set of parallel metal tracks running north and south. That was it: it went up to the first track and ended. So much for having no trouble.

Cube was wondering what to do, when she heard a tootle. It came from along the tracks to the south. Then something came rolling along them. It had metal wheels and looked like a carriage without a centaur to pull it. It made merry music as it moved, so it didn't seem dangerous. Diamond was not at all concerned about it, which was reassuring. As it came closer she saw words printed on its front: TUNEFUL TROLLEY.

The trolley drew to a stop right in front of her. Now the silver thread reappeared, going up the steps and into the vehicle. Did that mean she was supposed to enter this odd mechanical thing?

"All aboard!" a voice said loudly, startling her. It was an ugly troll (but that was redundant) sitting in the front. Suddenly it made sense; she could almost hear Karia exclaiming "Ugh!" Naturally the trolley was run by a troll.

Still, she hesitated to board it. The last time she had encountered a troll, it had carried her away, wanting to marry her. She didn't trust the species.

Then Diamond scrambled up the steps, following the thread into the trolley. Cube had to follow, not wanting to trust the dog to the troll.

There were halfway comfortable seats inside. Cube sat on one, because the thread led to it, and Diamond sat on the floor beside her. The troll turned a handle; the door closed, and the trolley resumed trundling along the tracks.

"Arf!"

Cube jumped and looked toward the sound. It was an animal with flippers, on the seat across from her. It wore a cap on which were the words STATE SEAL. Oh—one of the Mundane water creatures, perhaps traveling from one pool to another.

"Hello, maiden."

Cube jumped again, and turned to look. In the seat behind her was a cadaverous man with a small dark cloud hovering over his head. "Were you addressing me?" she asked.

"Of course. I don't often see such refreshing young flesh in my profession."

That sounded like a compliment, but for some reason Cube wasn't easy with it. "Uh, thank you. What is your profession?"

"Summoning zombies. It's my talent, so I travel from place to place to offer my services. I am surprised by how many otherwise adequate villages not only lack zombies, but claim not to need any. Would you like to have a zombie?"

"No thanks!" No wonder he considered her young flesh to be refreshing; most of the flesh he saw was rotten. The compliment was weaker than it had seemed. The man himself seemed not far removed from that state.

"They really make excellent servants," he said persuasively. "They are indefatigable, don't need to eat, and can be parked in any shallow trench when not in use."

"No, I'm traveling light."

Fortunately the trolley was creaking to another stop, and the thread led out of it. Cube lurched to her feet and stumbled for the opening door. She was relieved when the troll driver did not try to grab her and marry her.

Back on the ground with Diamond, she watched the tootling trolley roll on along its tracks. The thread was before her again.

"Hello."

Cube jumped again. She had been distracted by the trolley. There was another young woman, naturally far more attractive than Cube herself. "Hello."

"I'm Becca."

"I'm Cube."

"Nice dog."

"Thank you." Diamond wagged her tail.

"I could make her a mean guard dog, if you like. That's my talent: changing folks' personalities."

"No thank you. I like her the way she is." Then Cube thought of something else. "I met a young dragongirl named Becka. She caretakes a nice castle."

"Oh, I envy her!"

Cube realized that she had said too much. There was no point in making the girl unsatisfied with her lot. "But it has a dangerous chamber."

"Oh, I don't envy her."

Cube decided to move on before she said something clumsy again. "Well, I must be—"

"Have you seen my boyfriend?"

"Not unless he is a troll."

"No, he's half demon. His name is D. Cease. He can temporarily kill things."

"Temporarily?"

"They come back to life after a while. I'm just as glad. He killed me once. After that I changed his personality so he'd treat me better."

Cube was taken aback. "I should think you would leave him!"

"No, boyfriends aren't all that easy to get. But his sister D. Sist was jealous, so she stopped our relationship. That's her talent: stopping things."

Cube could almost hear Karia's groans. Decease and Desist—what a pair. "I'm sorry."

"But I'm hoping I can change him back to liking me, if I can just find him. Of course D. Sist may stop him again."

"Why don't you change *her* personality, so she likes you? Then you won't have to be concerned about her stopping your relationship with him."

"Oh, I never thought of that! Thank you." Becca ran off, looking for Sist.

Cube walked on with Diamond. Suddenly she came to the brink of a monstrous chasm. It seemed to drop down forever—and the thread led down into it. This must be the dread Gap Chasm, again. She hadn't known that it was this close; the trolley must have taken her farther north than she realized.

What was she to do now? She couldn't just step over the brink; she would fall to her death. But she had to follow the thread.

Maybe it was time to bring Karia out, so they could fly

across the chasm. But there were two problems with that: she wasn't sure the thread went all the way across, so they might lose it, and she didn't want to have to call on the flying centaur. She had already met several people along the way; there might be others, and if anyone saw her bring out Karia, they would either know or strongly suspect that something special was up. That could ruin the secret of the Quest. So she preferred to make it on her own, if she possibly could.

She got down on her knees and examined the edge of the cliff. Now she saw that the thread did not go straight down, but zigged and zagged. In fact it was following a precarious trail down the steep slope. There were little ledges and indents for handholds and footholds. She could climb down on her own, if she had the gumption.

But what about Diamond? The dog wouldn't be able to cling to those tiny crevices. "I don't know," she said.

Diamond sniffed the brink. Then she put her head over. "Look out!" Cube cried, grabbing for her. But she was too late; the dog had already gone over the edge.

Horrified, Cube peered down—and saw Diamond standing there, looking back at her. Standing on the face of the cliff, at right angles to the ground. Not falling.

What kind of magic was this? Cube felt the cliff by the thread, and felt her hand drawn against it, as if by gravity. She felt the cliff away from the thread, and got no such effect. So it was localized, and the thread knew where.

Well, maybe it would work for her too. If not, she could draw Karia out of the pouch and hang on while she flew. She clutched the pouch in one hand, and kept her other hand ready. Then she stepped over the brink, following the thread.

Her body swung around the corner and halted parallel to the ground. Her feet were set on the face of the cliff. She was standing normally, except for her orientation. "You're right, Diamond. This is the way down."

They walked down into the chasm, except that it seemed like walking level. Far ahead a hill rose, which was actually the floor of the chasm. They proceeded toward it, and made another turn when they reached it.

They were back to normal orientation. The thread had known the way.

They walked on across the base of the chasm. There were trees and bushes here, and even a small stream. In fact it was a rather pleasant scene.

Then Cube heard an odd whomping. Something was coming, but she wasn't sure what. She looked down the deep valley, between the bushes, and saw something green. It looked like a giant inchworm humping along, only it was steaming.

Then she remembered: there was supposed to be a dragon in the chasm—a steamer that hunted every creature that got stuck down here. How could she have forgotten? The Gap Dragon!

"Get beside me, Diamond!" she said. As the dog did so, she summoned a full slew of nickelpedes. They formed a thick ring around the two of them. She summoned a second slew. These formed a phalanx between her and the oncoming dragon.

The dragon whomped into view. It had six stout legs, small useless wings, and a horrendous head. It spied the nickelpedes and ground to a halt, as any sensible creature would. The nickelpedes waved their deadly little claws at it. Even the dragon should know that those claws could gouge out nickel-sized disks of flesh.

Then the dragon lowered its snoot and breathed out. A rush of steam bathed the nickelpedes. They fell over and died, cooked through. It was steaming them!

Cube realized that her talent was no defense against the Gap Dragon. Soon it would clear a path and reach her.

She cudgeled her stalling mind. What to do? Her first thought was to summon Karia, so they could fly away. But what about Diamond? She couldn't hold on to the dog and the centaur at the same time.

The dragon took a step forward, the better to steam the remaining nickelpedes.

Her second thought was to bring out the Princesses. But she didn't want to subject them to the risk. They might get steamed before they could make their magic music.

The nickelpedes were done for. The dragon raised its deadly snoot, pointing it at her.

Her third thought was to summon Drek Dragon. She didn't know whether it would do any good, but she didn't have time for a fourth thought. She reached into the pouch. "Drek!"

Drek slid out. He looked at the other dragon. Alarmed, he breathed out a truly ugly stench, reminiscent of rotten eggs, bloated gut, putrefied zombies, and worse.

Cube and Diamond gagged. What an awful smell! She was afraid her nose would fall off.

The Gap Dragon inhaled, the better to blow out more steam—and choked. It backed away, but the horrible odor followed. It couldn't breathe! Cube understood exactly how it was; she couldn't breathe either.

The Gap Dragon turned tail and fled. Drek saw that and was gratified. Strong perfume replaced the stench breath.

Cube and Diamond sucked in the sweet smell. What a relief! And what a proof of Drek's ability to protect them. Except that his weapon affected them too.

"Let's get out of here while we can," she gasped. She set out along the thread. "And thanks, Drek! You saved us."

The dragon wiggled an ear.

The thread led to the far cliff wall, and up it. Cube, Diamond, and Drek moved up it, the dragon surprised. In due course they reached the brink, turned the corner, and were back on regular land. Then Drek returned to the pouch, satisfied that the danger was over.

Cube and Diamond followed the thread north, away from the Gap Chasm. She was glad that they were on a regular path now, instead of plowing through brush or worse. The scenery was nice, and there seemed to be no immediate threats. In fact it was rather peaceful.

"Maybe this is a good place to rest," Cube remarked aloud. "We've been traveling much of the day, and my feet are tired."

They were not on an enchanted path, but Diamond sniffed out a pie tree. Cube had the supplies that Sofia had packed, but preferred to save them for dire need. The better she could forage for herself, the better off they would be. The tree had a nice meat pie for the dog, and a hot pot pie for Cube. Then they settled down to rest for a while.

"Wake up! Wake up!" Someone was shaking her shoulder, and shouting at her.

"What's the matter?" Cube demanded, vaguely irritated by this disturbance of her rest. "We were just resting a while."

"It would have been a long while," the annoying person said. "Don't you know where you are?"

"North of the Gap Chasm. Now if you will just let me finish my rest—"

"No! Don't go back to sleep. You must get up, get mad, walk around."

"Some other time," Cube said. "I feel rather peaceful now."

"That's the problem! You're in Peace Forest."

"That's nice." Cube relaxed.

But the person wouldn't let her be. Hands grasped her shoulders, three or four hands, hauling her to her feet. "Get awake! Get angry! Walk!"

Cube's irritation finally became solid. "What's the matter with you?" she demanded. "Why can't you leave me alone?"

"Because you'll die."

Cube opened her eyes. She saw a winged human girl bending over Diamond, trying to rouse the sleeping dog. The girl was so shapely as to stun men's minds just by the thought of looking at her, and even Cube was impressed. There was something about beauty that stirred the heart and imagination. Her wings were pure white, her hair was the same, and her gown matched. Only her huge eyes were different; they were pale electric violet. When she moved her head, her hair rippled in waves, and shone aqua.

This was no ordinary pedestrian. Cube, now fully awake, tried to suppress her burgeoning resentment of the girl's very existence, because no man would ever look once at Cube if he even suspected that such a creature existed. Then she looked to either side, to find out who was supporting her.

On her left was a pretty girl with long blue-green hair and black wistful-looking eyes. She was garbed in a black suit. On her right was an ordinary girl with brown hair and iridescent eyes. Even so, she was significantly better looking than Cube. But then, every young woman was.

"Who are you?" Cube asked. Then, realizing that she was being slightly churlish, she introduced herself: "I am Cube, traveling north at the moment, and the dog is Diamond, traveling with me. We were just resting briefly before going on."

"I am Oceanna," the black-clothed girl said. "I do things with water."

"I am Lucidia Feldspar," the brown-haired girl said. "I can change ordinary stones into gemstones, and vice versa."

"And I am Tala," the vision with Diamond said. "I sew enchanted clothing. Please help me rouse this dog; she's not responding."

"Why? Why can't you let her rest?"

"Because she'll rest forever. That's the nature of Peace Forest: folk caught in it become so peaceful they simply sink into oblivion."

Alarm was percolating through Cube's mind. They had told her that she herself would die, and Diamond would rest forever. "But we were just resting briefly."

"When did you start your rest?" Lucidia asked.

"Just a short while ago, as early evening was starting, and—" Cube paused, for the sun was high in the sky; it was now broad day. "Maybe—yesterday?"

"Or maybe several days," Oceanna said. "You are slightly off the beaten path; we discovered you only because we had to pause for a private function and saw the sleeping dog, and then you. So we acted, hoping we were not too late."

"It seems you weren't." Cube checked herself. Her clothing was rumpled and soiled with the green of crushed grass. Yes, she had been lying there for some time.

Cube went to the dog. "Wake, Diamond," she said. "Or I'll send a nickelpede to pinch you." A nickelpede appeared.

"You summon nickelpedes!" Tala exclaimed. "What a marvelous talent!"

Cube's resentment of the winged girl's beauty diminished. "It's useful at times."

Diamond's eye flickered halfway open. It spied the nickelpede and snapped all the way open. The dog struggled to her feet as the nickelpede scurried away.

Cube helped her. "We're in the Peace Forest," she said. "We've been sleeping for days. These nice girls roused me. We need to get out of here."

Diamond seemed to understand. She shook herself and gained steadiness.

They walked back to the path, and on north. Fortunately the thread continued that way, so Cube didn't have to say anything. "We travel together," Tala explained, "because it isn't safe for a single person."

"But can't you simply fly over the forest?" Cube asked.

"I can, but my friends can't."

"We tease each other and tell mean jokes," Oceanna said.

"And practice our talents," Lucidia said. She paused to pick up a pebble. "Would you like a gem?" She held it forth, and it was a sparkling diamond.

"Oh, I couldn't accept that," Cube said, though it drew her like a magnet. "I have nothing to exchange for it."

"Are your nickelpedes tame?"

"For me, or for someone I designate." Cube glanced at her, surprised. "You can't want a nickelpede!"

"One could be useful," Lucidia said. "Sometimes men bother us."

Cube could well imagine. "Have a nickelpede," she said, summoning one. "This is Lucidia," she told it. "Be her friend." Then she exchanged it for the diamond.

"Your clothing is spoiled," Tala said. "My talent is sewing enchanted clothing. I could make you a fresh outfit."

"Would it make me beautiful?" Cube asked wryly.

"It would fit you well, and keep you warm."

"Want to trade a nickelpede for it?"

"Yes. But it will take me a little while to make the clothing."

"That's fine. Here's your nickelpede." Cube summoned another, and attuned it to Tala.

They walked on. Tala brought out a length of cloth she had carried somewhere, and began adjusting it, forming a dress. The material shaped itself marvelously in her hands; she really was good at this.

Lucidia stumbled. "Oops, she's getting peaceful," Oceanna said. "I'll wake her." She ran to a nearby stream and scooped up a ball of water. She shaped it into a model of a waterfowl and set it on her friend's head. The moment her hand left it, the water dissolved, soaking the girl.

"Ooo!" Lucidia cried. "Why did you do that?"

"To make you mad," Oceanna said. "You were getting peaceful."

"Oh." The girl brushed herself off ineffectively. "You succeeded."

Cube thought of Ryver. He would like this girl. Probably a lot, as they had similar talents. But Oceanna was so much prettier than Cube, that Ryver would probably never consider her again after seeing Oceanna. But that was selfish, and Cube refused to be that way. "I know someone you should meet," she told Oceanna.

"Oh? Who?"

Cube put her hand in the pouch. "Ryver," she murmured.

He slid out. For a moment he seemed dazed, trying to take all the details of the three girls at once. So Cube helped him out.

"This is Oceanna. She's good with water. I thought you should meet her."

"Water!" he agreed. "How?"

Oceanna returned to the river and scooped up another ball of water. "Here," she said, tossing it to him.

"Great!" he said, catching it and throwing it back. Then he scooped up a water ball of his own and tossed it to Cube. "Thanks."

Cube caught it and held it. Meanwhile Oceanna was shaping her ball into the form of a miniature dragon. It looked very realistic, but it was translucent. She held it up to be admired. It turned its head and switched its tail as if alive.

"That's great," Ryver said. "I can't do that." Then he

stepped into the river and dissolved, disappearing into it. At the same time, the ball Cube held dissolved.

Oceanna stared. "And I can't do *that*," she breathed.

Ryver's head appeared from the water, followed by the rest of him, appropriately clothed. "So we have similar but different talents." He eyed her appraisingly.

"Yes. I can't wait to tell my boyfriend the ogre."

"The ogre," Ryver breathed.

"Yes. He thinks there's no one else like me. He'll be interested."

"Interested," Ryver agreed faintly. He approached Cube. "Maybe it's time for me to go back in."

Surprised, Cube held out the pouch. Ryver put in his foot and slid into it.

"That's a nice purse," Tala remarked.

"There's no point in us both walking when one can do it," Cube said, tucking the pouch away. "Why didn't he want to meet your boyfriend?"

"What boyfriend?" Oceanna asked.

"The ogre."

The others laughed. "That's just what she says to keep men polite," Tala explained. "Nobody wants to meet an ogre."

"Oh." Ryver had eyed her, but Cube had thought she would like it. Nobody ever eyed Cube that way.

Finally they left the forest. "We live in the North Village," Lucidia said. "That's another day's walk north. But maybe we can get a ride with a centaur. We're approaching their village."

Cube thought of Karia. She could get a faster centaur ride. But she didn't want to let that be known. She probably shouldn't have brought Ryver out, though that seemed to have been okay.

Tala finished the dress. "Try this on," she told Cube, giving it to her.

Cube pulled off her soiled clothing and tried on the dress. It fit marvelously well, and was supremely comfortable. It really did seem to be magic. "It's wonderful."

"I made it to keep you warm or cool," the winged woman said. "You won't have to worry about the weather."

"This is really much more than a nickelpede is worth," Cube said.

"I like making clothing. It's what I do. It was nice finding someone who was in need of a new dress."

"She made our dresses," Lucidia said.

"Then all I can say is thank you," Cube said gratefully. "I really like it."

"You're welcome."

Then the thread veered to the right, avoiding the centaur village. "Uh, it's been very nice meeting you," Cube said. "And I really appreciate the way you saved me from the Peace Forest. And the nice dress. But I'm not going to the centaur village. So I have to leave you now."

She was afraid they would ask where she was going, but they didn't. "That's fine," Tala said. "I have to fly now myself. Farewell, girls!" She spread her wings and took off.

"And farewell from me," Cube said.

"If you happen to pass the North Village, look us up," Oceanna said.

"Perhaps I will. I don't know whether it's on my route."

The two walked on toward the centaur village, while Cube and Diamond followed the thread east. It led to an enchanted path, and followed it to a camping site. Relieved, she settled in for the evening. She wasn't sure whether she had lost more than a day in the Peace Forest, but she wasn't on a fixed schedule. She and Diamond ate from the convenient pie tree, washed up, and prepared to sleep. She brought out the original water ball Ryver had given her and gazed into it reflectively. This ball survived, while the other he had tossed her had not. So he could do different types of balls.

Then Diamond's ears perked. She heard someone coming. Cube wasn't sure how she felt about that; she had met a number of nice people, but that wasn't guaranteed. She put away the ball, not caring to explain it to strangers.

It turned out to be a man and a woman of adult age. He had blond hair and golden eyes; she had aluminum hair and silver eyes. They turned in to the camp; they obviously planned to spend the night.

"Hello," Cube said. "I'm Cube, traveling generally north."

"I'm Trans Mitter," the blond man said. "This is my companion Ann Tenna. I can send message by projecting my image, and she can hear things from afar, when she focuses. So we work well together."

"I can imagine," Cube said. "My talent is summoning nickelpedes."

"No need of those here," Trans said.

"No need," Cube agreed.

They chatted amicably, then slept. Cube was glad there had been no problem. So far she had made it fairly well on her own. Still, there had been nervous occasions, such as the troll on the trolley, the Gap Dragon, and the Peace Forest. She had been lucky, but luck was fickle. She needed to do better at staying out of trouble.

In the morning Trans and Ann went their way, and Cube went hers, following the thread. Which now followed the path back the way it had come, west. Then north, toward the centaur village. Apparently it had made a detour to take her to the campsite. It seemed almost aware of her, which was strange. The Princesses had not said anything about that, and perhaps didn't know. Magic could have funny aspects.

She walked through the village, seeing the centaurs but not approaching any. They glanced at her only briefly, not noticing her any more than most men did.

The thread followed the enchanted path on north. Cube was glad of that, because it meant she would face no awkward problems. She marveled again at the virtuosity of the thread, showing her along a route that a person could follow, even if it didn't always seem so at a given moment. It was as if it had been spun from the future, after the Quest was done, so knew where she had been, and marked that route. Maybe if the Quest had been for Ryver, there would have been a Ryver Route, going to different places, or a Princess Route for the three, or even a Drek Route for the dragon. But it was the Cube Route. Maybe after this was done, and she had her beauty and her man, if she got bored (but how could beauty ever be bored?) she would make a study of magic threads and try to discover how they flowed. This might be the Cube Route, but it was probably also influenced by her Companions. A perfect route would be a straight line, while one with too many people would be distorted, yet have its relevance. As this one did.

All this walking was a bit tiring, but also invigorating. Cube had never liked to think of herself as chubby, but others had called her that; now she felt her body redistributing flesh to make more muscles for walking and less fat to carry. It would not make her beautiful, because she lacked the bones and the skin and the features, but it would make her healthy, and that was worth something. The journey was also taking her to new places, and she was glad to see them; it was evident that she did not know enough about Xanth, but could learn by seeing it.

Still, around midday she was ready to rest, so she sat on a convenient bench and got the weight off her feet. Diamond seemed satisfied to get off her feet too. "You're good company," Cube told her, patting her head. "You don't complain, you don't rush ahead or drag behind, you don't criticize my decisions." The dog's tail wagged.

Someone approached from the north. It was another woman, reasonably good looking. Cube's route seemed to be strewn with women who looked better than she ever had. "Oh, a bench," the woman said. "Just when I needed one. May I join you?"

"Of course," Cube said. She was about ready for human company, though a handsome and attentive man would have been better. "The enchanted paths seem to have facilities where they are needed, in contrast to the others."

"Which are the opposite," the woman agreed, laughing ruefully as she sat down. "And you have a Mundane dog. How nice."

"This is Diamond. She's not mine; we're just keeping

company for now. When she finds a place she likes, perhaps she'll stay there."

"That must be true for all of us."

Now Cube laughed, recognizing the truth of that. "I am Cube, on a private mission. My talent is to summon nickelpedes, but I don't do it unless there is need."

"I am Polly Graff. My talent is to detect lies."

"That must be useful."

"Sometimes. Not in this case; you haven't tried to lie to me."

"I'm not very good at it. The best I can do is to keep my thoughts mostly to myself."

"What did you think when you saw me coming?"

"Oh, that's not relevant."

"Yes it is. I'm trying to find out how well you lie."

Cube suppressed a sigh. "I half wished you were a man who would pay attention to me, instead of being yet another woman prettier than I am."

"You're right: you can't tell a lie. But you know, beauty isn't necessarily what you think."

"I think all my problems would be solved if I were beautiful."

"You do think that, but I just met a woman who would, if you'll excuse the expression, give the lie to that."

This was interesting. "A beautiful woman with problems?"

"I think so."

"But shouldn't you *know* so, since she couldn't lie to you?"

"Not in this case. She's a ghost."

"A ghost!"

"A lovely ghost. She has either just killed herself, or is about to."

This was more than interesting. "How could a beautiful woman ever want to die? She should be completely happy."

"I don't know. But I can tell you where she is. Maybe you can ask her."

"I'd like to, but—" Cube didn't want to say that she had to stick to the Route marked by the thread.

"She's in an inn south of the North Village. Right in your path, if you're going north. You'll arrive there around nightfall. That's where I stayed last night. The innkeeper tried to tell me all his rooms were taken, but I knew he was lying, and made him give me the one empty one. Then I found out why he was hiding it: because if others learned of the ghost, suddenly he'd have *all* his rooms empty. I saw the ghost, and felt her horrible unhappiness, but I couldn't learn more because my talent works on the living, not the dead. But you—you might have the inclination to get to know her, and find out who she is and what's the matter."

"Yes. I'm as wary of ghosts as the next person, but the mystery of a lovely woman who wants to die fascinates me. I'll check on her, if I possibly can."

"That's nice."

"But suppose I talk to her, and she lies to me? I don't have your talent."

Polly smiled. "I have discovered that often I don't actually need my talent. I can tell when a person is lying without it. Then I use it just to verify. Usually I am right. It's a kind of private game."

"How can you tell?"

"Well, an amateur liar will fidget. He'll avoid your gaze. There's a certain hollow sound when he talks."

"What about a professional liar?"

"He'll show none of those things. He'll be so smooth that you just naturally believe him. That's when you have to be wary: never believe a person just because he is convincing."

"But that means I can't believe either the clumsy ones or the smooth ones."

"That's right. Most folk are in between, and you can mostly trust them. It's the extremes that you must doubt."

"That may be too complicated for me."

"Well, it takes time to develop the touch. But give it a try; you might be surprised."

"Maybe I will."

"And pick up on the signals the dog gives. Dogs can smell lies. If you see her tail drop, beware."

"I'll do that."

"Well, I have to move on now, if I am to reach the centaur village by nightfall." Polly stood.

Cube stood too. "Same for me, going the other way. I left the centaur village this morning."

"Farewell."

"Same to you."

They parted, and Cube followed the thread north. "Was she right?" she asked.

Diamond's tail was high. That was encouraging.

By evening she saw the inn, and not only did the thread lead to it, it went inside. Could the ghost woman be part of her route? Ordinarily such a prospect would disturb her, but now she hoped for it.

She entered the inn. The innkeeper met her at the door. "Sorry, we're full," he said hollowly, fidgeting and looking away.

Cube glanced at Diamond. Her tail was low.

"What about the room with the ghost?" she demanded.

The man looked as if he had swallowed a bad prune. "Don't blab about that!"

"I won't," Cube promised truthfully.

The man became cunning, now that he had secured his secret. "What do you have in trade?"

"I can work for my board," Cube said. She was tired, but she knew inns were not free. "For me and the dog."

"Go to the kitchen. Do what the cook says. She'll show you the room when you're done."

"Done," Cube agreed. It was a fair bargain, considering.

The cook was a cheerful fat woman with a direct gaze and no fidgeting. "Good to have help. Here's food for you and the dog. Then you'll have to wash the pots and sweep the floor."

The food was good, the pots were greasy, and the floor was filthy. Cube did the best job she could, though she was really tired by the time it all was done. Diamond sniffed out a rat and growled it out of the kitchen, pleasing the cook. Then the cook showed her to the room. "You know it's haunted? The ghost won't hurt you, but she's sort of spooky."

"I know," Cube said. "We'll get along." She opened the door, and she and Diamond stepped into the room.

8

EXCHANGE

The ghost stood in the center of the chamber, facing them. She possessed unearthly beauty of face and form, and her dress was elegant. But tears streaked her classic face.

Cube suffered half a welter of emotions. She didn't know what to do. But Diamond didn't hesitate; she went up to the ghost.

"A dohg," the ghost said, surprised. She reached down to pat Diamond. Her delicate hand passed through the dog's head, but Diamond wagged her tail.

"Her name is Diamond," Cube said, seizing this opening. "Mine is Cube. We'd like to stay the night here, if it's all right with you."

"I'm so lohnely," the ghost said. Then she focused a little better. "Yes, if you wish. I have no escape. I am Silhouette."

Cube walked carefully around the ghost and sat on the bed. She was tired and wanted to clean up and sleep, but this ghost woman fascinated her. Certainly she was well named·

her figure was so shapely as to make any man who even heard about it drool. "Silhouette, are you alive or dead?"

"My body is alive, for now. My soul is dead."

"I don't understand."

"It is a long and dreary story. I took poison, but am not yet dead. I'm in a coma, and my soul is free to roam. But I have no way to leave this room, for this is where my body lies in my world."

"Your world?"

"I believe the last visitor called it Mundania. I gather this is an imaginary fantasy world, while my own is reality. So my spirit is in my imagination."

"This is Xanth," Cube said. "It is a magic place, and next to it is Mundania, where there is little or no magic. I am a traveler in Xanth."

"I think I'd like to travel in a fantasy realm," Silhouette said. "It would be so much nicer than what I know."

"You wouldn't want to exchange places with me," Cube said.

"Oh, but I would, if you can range freely amidst magic."

"But you're beautiful! How can you be unhappy?"

"How can I be otherwise? Appearance is nothing; my beauty has merely sealed my fate. You are far better off."

"Look at me! I am as plain as you are beautiful. My most ardent desire is to be beautiful."

"But you are free! That is what counts."

"How can I be free in a body like this? I can't get a man to look at me, let alone romance me. But if I were beautiful, I could be happy."

Silhouette gazed at her. "I wish we could exchange, so that you could discover what my life is like, and I could have the pleasure of yours."

"I wish so too! But—" Cube broke off, noticing something. The thread had led her to this inn and this room, but it hardly quit there. It went to Silhouette and stopped. It did not lead out of the room.

"You look as if you see a ghost," Silhouette said with sad humor. "Are you all right?"

"I think something—there is something—you may find this hard to believe, but—but maybe we *are* meant to exchange."

The woman shook her head. "I spoke foolishly. Even were it possible, I wouldn't care to do that to you. I am dying, and even if by some mischance I survive this siege, my life is not worth living. You would be locked in misery."

But the idea had taken hold. "Maybe. Silhouette, can you keep a secret?"

"I can do nothing else. It is the hard truths that should be revealed that are beyond me."

"I mean, if I tell you a secret, will you keep it?"

Silhouette met her gaze. She did not fidget, and her voice was firm. "Of course."

"I want to explain my business, so you can understand why I think we may need to exchange, at least for a while. Maybe just our souls. But you need to know what you would be getting into."

Silhouette laughed. "What *I* would be getting into! If you took my identity, you would be getting into hell!"

Still no sign of lying. She meant it. "Hell?"

"It is mostly of my own making, I confess. I simply lack the gumption to do what I know needs doing."

Something electric ran through Cube. "Gumption?"

"I am not a strong person. Until two years ago I never needed to be strong. My beauty and wealth safeguarded me, and so did my strong father. But when my father died, the vultures closed in. My aunt, my accountant, my boyfriend—"

"Vultures?"

"Oh, yes! They are feeding on my flesh and picking my bones, and I can't stand it, but neither can I stand up to them. So all I can do is escape by dying."

"But if you had—gumption—you could deal with them?"

Silhouette nodded. "Yes, I know exactly what is needed, if I just had the nerve to do it. But I don't, and they know it."

This aspect of Cube's mission was taking shape. "Then let me tell you my story, and you tell me yours, and we'll see."

"We'll see," Silhouette agreed.

They talked for two hours. Cube told of her secret mission, and the thread she followed, and how it led to Silhouette, even when she walked around the room. Then Silhouette told her of the horror of her own existence, and Cube realized that she had not been exaggerating. A beautiful woman could indeed be miserable.

But there were other aspects to consider. "You can't just walk around Xanth on your own," Cube said, "without knowing anything about it. There are many dangers we natives don't even think about; we just avoid them. You will need guidance and protection."

"Will your dog accompany me? She's a nice black Labrador, a good breed."

"I think so. But she's Mundane too; maybe she's staying with me so she won't get in more trouble in Xanth. I was thinking of more formidable assistance."

Silhouette shrugged. "Considering that I hardly care whether I live or die, anything should be sufficient."

"But you'll be living or dying in my body," Cube said. "I don't want anything bad to happen to it."

"Oh, of course. I apologize; I wasn't thinking. I've never been very good at thinking."

"Who told you that?"

"My domineering aunt, who runs our household since my father's death. She is surely correct."

Cube had not noticed any problem with Silhouette's mind, but saw that her self-esteem was even lower than Cube's own, if for a rather different reason. So she didn't argue the case. "I was thinking of a demoness."

Silhouette smiled. "You did mention something of the sort. You said this is a magic land."

She didn't truly believe. "Observe." Cube put her hand in the pouch. "Metria."

The demoness slid out. She looked at Silhouette, who stepped back nervously. "Well now! You're the prettiest ghost I've seen."

"And you are the most alluring demoness I have encountered," Silhouette said faintly. "I hope you're not going to do anything awful to me."

"The ghost is Silhouette Mundane," Cube said. "The demoness is D. Metria. Now you have been introduced."

"We have," Metria agreed, assuming the form of the ghost. "So why did you haul me out?"

"I think Silhouette and I are going to exchange places for a while. That is, my soul will go with her body, and her soul will be with mine. She would like to explore Xanth, but won't know much about it. I want you to stay with her, invisibly, and protect her from mischief."

The demoness considered. "The thread is sending you to Mundania?"

"It seems to being doing that, yes. It leads directly to Silhouette."

"Remember, there's no magic there. I've been there; you wouldn't like it. I remember when Willow Elf got together with Sean Mundane. She thought love would be enough, but she was isolated in a realm without magic. She didn't even speak their language. She got depressed. They finally had to move back to Xanth. Sean loved her, and of course Xanth is so much better than Mundania anyway, so it worked out. But you could get stuck there with no way to return."

"If the thread sends me there, I'll go there," Cube said. "When it brings me back, I'll return."

"*If* you return. If anything happens—if you can't make the rendezvous—"

"I just have to trust the thread. So I can accomplish the mission."

"To fulfill the Quest," Metria agreed. "You've got nerve, all right. Very well, I'll do it."

"One other thing," Cube said to the ghost. "Suppose I do something in your world? To change it? What will be the consequence?"

Silhouette made a wry smile. "Since just about everything in my world is bad, what harm can you do? I wouldn't mind if you entirely destroyed it."

"You're sure?"

"Oh, yes! Assuming that we exchange for a day or so, then return, my main objective will be to find a more effective way to kill myself. My father had a drawer full of weapons; I should be able to find one there to do the job. Obviously pills aren't sufficient, but perhaps a knife would be."

"This is one weird attitude," Metria said.

"She means it," Cube said. "You can talk to her while I'm gone. It should appeal to your demonic sense of humor."

"It should," the demoness agreed.

"Are we set?" Cube asked Silhouette.

"I believe so, assuming this works."

"If it works, just walking through each other should do it. And we should be able to exchange back the same way. Shall we make a date for exactly one day hence?"

The ghost looked at her watch. "Midnight. That seems appropriate. Yes, I will be here then."

Cube petted Diamond. "I'll be leaving you for a day, I think. But I hope you will help Silhouette while I'm gone."

The dog wagged her tail.

Then Cube, not nearly as confident as she pretended, nerved herself and approached the ghost. She walked through the form—

And found herself lying on a bed, woozy. A woman was leaning over her. "You're waking!"

"Ungh," she agreed, realizing as she spoke that it was a different language. Fortunately this body understood it, just as the ghost in Xanth had understood the Xanth human language. She recognized the woman as a hired nurse; Mundania had such things.

"We were afraid we had lost you. The stomach pump and counter-medication helped, but you were still fading until two hours ago. Then you began a remarkable recovery. The doctors can't explain it."

"I have unfinished business," Cube said through Silhouette's mouth. That was a serious understatement. She intended to turn Silhouette's world upside down, and make it worth enduring. The worst she could do was fail.

"We must get you up and about, for the circulation, and some food in you. You are not out of the woods yet."

That depended on perspective. Cube saw that beyond the window was another building. She checked Silhouette's memory and verified that this was a built-up area, all houses, stores, roads, and businesses. This was a private hospital unit, not marked as such, reserved for wealthy patrons. Rich folk did not mix much with the common herd; their illnesses were kept invisible. So Cube, in Silhouette's body, was definitely out of the woods.

"First I want to get a good night's sleep."

"But you have been unconscious for three days!"

"Not exactly. Come back in the morning."

The nurse, fazed by her tone, retreated. Cube relaxed, sleeping. She needed this body to be in decent shape for the coming day.

In the morning the nurse was back, more than eager to rouse her. Cube realized that the woman's position depended on the care she took of this important patient.

She sat up, assisted by the nurse. Her head threatened to spin off her neck; she was dangerously dizzy. But in a moment it passed. Not three quarters of a moment, not moment and two instants; here in Mundania such measurements were crude, rounded off to even moments.

She swung her legs from the bed to the floor. They were absolutely lovely legs; her illness had not damaged them. The feet were dainty, the knees were not knobby, and the thighs were thickening columns of delight. Her panties would not have magic, here in Mundania, but with legs like these, who needed panties? They would stun any man within range.

After another moment, she rose to her feet. The nurse steadied her again while her burgeoning head settled back into place. Then she walked carefully to the bathroom, checking Silhouette's mind to be sure she knew how it worked.

In the course of an hour, with the nurse's help, she got

herself cleaned, dressed, and combed. She stood before the full-length mirror. It wasn't magic, but it showed the loveliest creature she had encountered. She was ethereally beautiful. The Good Magician had said she would be, and she was, beyond her wildest dreams.

But this was not the end of the Quest. This was just an episode along the way, and this was Mundania. She could not keep this body—not unless she wanted to stay here. She did not. She wanted to be lovely in Xanth, so she could charm Ryver. So she would handle her business here, as she understood it, and return within the time limit. She did not want to miss her return connection.

She checked Silhouette's memory. Actually it was this body's reality; the memory was of Cube. Her soul was here, but the body and brain were Silhouette's, and therefore the memory too. She had exchanged limited life histories with Silhouette, not so that she would understand the woman's situation, but so the understanding of Cube herself would be firmly planted. Similarly, in Xanth, Silhouette's soul would be dependent on Cube's body and brain and memory. She would know who she was, but the details would be only what Cube had learned from their discussion. It was an interesting inversion.

She was feeling better now. The food had restored her, and limited strength was returning to her body. It was time to tackle Silhouette's problems. She had reviewed them in her mind while dressing, and saw that Silhouette knew what needed to be done, as she had said, but had lacked the gumption, as she had confessed. Cube had never been short of gumption. It was time to apply it. The thread had not, it seemed, brought her here randomly. This was the situation for her strongest character trait. She rehearsed it in her mind; she wanted to be sure not to muff it. A life was in the balance.

She dismissed the nurse and marched out of the unit to her expensive little car. She let Silhouette's familiarity with it take over, and drove to her plush gated estate. Once inside the mansion, she went directly to the aunt's office. She knocked peremptorily on the door, then pushed it open without waiting. The woman was seated at her desk, reviewing some papers. She looked up as Cube approached.

"Sil, I am glad to see you recovered, but you know I am not to be disturbed while working."

The aunt was formidable; Cube saw that immediately. That made her react in the way she did: the worse the challenge, the sharper she became. She was really a different person when under sufficient pressure. "Susan, we must talk," Cube said firmly, invoking the script in Silhouette's mind.

The woman's eyes widened. "I have told you not to be familiar. Have you forgotten your manners? Return to your room, Sil."

Which was just about exactly what Silhouette's mind had figured would be the response. The script was good. All she needed to do was activate it properly.

Cube leaned over the desk, putting her hands on the papers. Her heart was pounding, but she was in the gumption mode and it had but one direction: onward. This was the time to really make her point. "I have some concerns of my own about manners," she said firmly. "You will address me formally as Silhouette, Susan."

Anger flared in the woman's face. "I'll do nothing of the kind! What has possessed you, Sil?"

Now for the drama. She had to make the proper impact. Every nuance was important. No weakness must show.

Cube swept the papers from the desk. "Silhouette, Susan. You will not appreciate my reaction if you forget again." This was actually grim fun, because she knew the woman deserved it.

Now it was sheer outrage. "If I *forget*! You impertinent scamp! Go to your room this instant."

She had asked for it. "Susan, you have been leeching off my estate for the past two years since Father died. I am the legitimate heir; you are merely a temporary caretaker, actually an employee, remaining by my sufferance. You will treat me with the respect due me, and make yourself useful

in ways I shall define, or your sinecure will be terminated."
She fixed the woman with a steady glare. "Am I making my
position sufficiently clear?"

Aunt Susan's mouth worked for a moment before sound
emerged. "You—you—you impossible—"

Cube let the fire of her aroused nature burn in her gaze. A
different creature occupied this body. One with gumption to
spare. It was important not to shout, but to speak with absolute quiet conviction. "Now go to your room, Susan, before I lose my temper," Cube said evenly.

The woman stared at her as if seeing a ghost. Cube smiled
inwardly; if only she knew! "How can you possibly—?"

"You are my woman, Susan. Do not force me to punish
you more than you deserve. We shall talk later. Go to your
room and think about your situation. I suspect you will con-
clude that discretion is the better part of valor." That was a
nice phrase drawn verbatim from Silhouette's script.

Clearly stunned, Susan left the room. Cube breathed a
hidden sigh of relief. She had thought her animation of the
script should work, but hadn't been certain, and of course
her aroused gumption had forged onward regardless. Silhouette *was* the mistress of this estate, and her aunt knew it. She
merely had needed to have her face rubbed in it.

Cube let her passion subside somewhat. She wondered at
times whether it was related to her talent: nickelpedes were
among the fiercest creatures in Xanth. Maybe they took over
her mind when she was under pressure. Ordinarily she
would have faltered somewhere in the scene. She had been a
better actress than she expected.

Now for the second vulture: the accountant. This was a bit
trickier, because Cube knew nothing of money, finances, or
investments; all of them were Mundane concepts that Silhouette's mind wasn't fully clear on. She knew she was being cheated, but the details of it were beyond her grasp. But
she did have one key concept: auditing. If Cube understood
it correctly, it was like a magic word of power. That, and
gumption galore, should do the job. She hoped.

She sorted it through in her mind, lining up the concepts

and terms as well as she could. There wasn't as much of a script for this, so she would have to improvise. Then she drew on Silhouette's mind for another Mundane process: use of the telephone. She picked up the odd device and touched the button marked ACCOUNTANT.

"Yes," an unctuous voice said in the earpiece.

"James, this is Silhouette. Be here in half an hour with your figures."

"Sil, dear, is there a problem? I'll be glad to make a token advance from the account."

"There is a serious problem. Be here." She set the phone down, ending the connection.

Now she had half an hour to wait. She would use it to prepare for the third interview, which was likely to be the most difficult.

She went to the old den where Silhouette's kindly rich father had relaxed. It was untouched, in deference to a stipulation in his will (another complicated concept), and because there was nothing in it anybody wanted. She went to his desk. It was locked, but she knew where the key was hidden. Silhouette had been daddy's little girl, and he had shared secrets with her. She drew a loose brick from the fireplace, reached into the hole, and found the key. She took it to the desk and unlocked it.

The main drawer contained assorted old papers and pictures, including several of Silhouette as a child. She had always been pretty, and had soon grown into beauty. But as she had said, she had never had real strength of character. And would not, when she returned to this life. That was why Cube needed to do the whole job, and to secure it so that the vultures would not return. It was a lot to do in just one day, and would require hard measures.

Fortunately, as she had also said, Silhouette knew what those measures were. Now Cube was going to apply them.

She found what she was looking for in a lower drawer on the side: the collection of weapons. There was something called a Gun: it pushed out little bits of metal that would puncture flesh. It was a fearsome weapon, and Silhouette was afraid of it. She also had little notion how to use it. So that was out.

Another weapon was a Knife. Cube had seen similar in Xanth, and always been wary of them; they were dangerous enough just cutting vegetables. Also, she didn't want to shed blood here; that would lead to complications with the police, and Silhouette dreaded their involvement. Since it would be Silhouette handling the aftermath, that was out too.

A third weapon was odd. It was just an L-shaped piece of black plastic (a Mundane substance) with a hole at the top. All its edges were rounded; it was comfortable to handle because it couldn't scratch. It looked like useless junk; few folk ever recognized it for what it was. But Daddy had once shown the little girl how to use it, and, awed, she had remembered. Cube put her right forefinger through the hole, and closed her three remaining fingers around the shaft. The bottom of the L stuck forward below her small hand like a loose end. But it wasn't loose; it was the business end. She could use this.

She checked for pockets, and found that this gown-like dress didn't have any. She was expected to carry a purse. Cube knew of purses but had never used one herself, unless the pouch counted. But she didn't want to hide this weapon in a purse; she wanted it right on her body, where she could put her hand on it in a hurry.

She cast about. Finally she tucked it into her waistband under her blouse. That wasn't ideal, but her clothing left little choice. With luck the slight bulge over her tummy wouldn't be noticed.

She looked at Silhouette's watch. This was a gem-studded wristband with a small disk with two or three tiny sticks radiating out from its center, marking time. She had used up most of the time she had given the accountant.

She closed the desk, returned the key to its hiding place, replaced the brick, and strode for the main reception room. She just had time to settle herself in a fancy chair and cross her legs appealingly before the accountant arrived.

"Hello, Sil," he said with artificial joviality.

"Silhouette."

"Beg pardon?"

"You are my employee. You will address me formally."

He looked startled, then regrouped. "Of course, Silhouette," he said, humoring her. "Now what is this little problem? I am prepared to authorize any reasonable expense if there is a dress or item of jewelry you desire."

"James, I will cut to the chase. You have been embezzling from me for the past two years. This will not only stop, it will be reversed."

"Embezzling!" he said, astonished. "How can you say such a thing, Sil—Silhouette?"

"Do not attempt to play a game with me, James. I have known all along. Now it is time to correct it. I will give you one day to get your accounts in order before I have them audited." There was the magic word. If it did not work—

"Audited!" he exclaimed, his ruddy features paling. "You can't be serious! Your aunt would never authorize—"

So it had scored. "Susan will no longer be reviewing the estate accounts," Cube said. "I will do that personally, after the auditor is done." She fixed the man with a metallic gaze. "You have two choices, James: make prompt reparations and be allowed to resign from your position without adverse notice, or fail to do this and face termination and criminal charges."

The man stared at her with the expression that was becoming familiar. He couldn't understand how timid Silhouette could do this. He didn't know who was governing this body. "This—a joke, right?"

"An unfunny one," Cube agreed. "Now go to your office and get your accounts in order, because my next call is to the auditor. You have your instruction and your deadline. I suggest that you not waste further time."

Like a zombie, the man shambled out of the room. Cube nodded; the magic word had indeed been potent.

And no bluff. She drew on Silhouette's information to use the telephone book and check the Yellow Pages under Certified Public Accountants. Toward the end of the list was one called Xanadu. She liked that word; it sounded like Xanth. So that was the one she called. Soon she had an appointment with the auditor, Kubla. He would not arrive for two days, so Silhouette would have to handle it, but Cube had, as the Mundane idiom had it, greased the skids.

Now it was time for Yorick's afternoon visit. He was Silhouette's fiancé, an imposing and urbane man a decade her senior. He had the appearance of the ideal consort, and Silhouette's relatives approved of him. They didn't know he was a vulture.

For Yorick habitually brutalized Silhouette, carefully so as to leave no visible marks, and had raped her on occasion. At first she had been fascinated by him, but now she hated and feared him. He was like a hunting snake, to distort a metaphor, and she like a captive bird; she could neither resist nor escape him. He was the main reason for her decision to commit suicide.

Cube was not fascinated by the man, and she was no captive bird. Everything she knew about him from Silhouette's experience satisfied her that she wouldn't want him even if he came courting her in her real body. What use to exchange a manless life for a victim's fate? He, above all, had to be dealt with.

But mere words would not cow this brutal rogue. He was interested in Silhouette for three things: her money, her beauty, and her social status. He had a deal with the corrupt accountant to siphon her money, he ravished her beauty at will, and he would have her status when he married her. He would not lightly give up these things.

But there were measures that should be effective. Cube would invoke them. She had to prevail, because if she did not get this man permanently out of Silhouette's life, she would *have* no life. So she would address them in order, and with luck persuade him to look elsewhere for his gratifications. If she failed—well, it might get ugly.

Yorick arrived on schedule, for he was a punctual man, especially where his interests were concerned. "Hi, babe!" he said.

Cube froze for a moment. She had not made proper allowance for his appearance. He was a handsome man, the kind that could ordinarily make her swoon with frustrated longing. But handsome was as handsome did, she reminded herself with another Mundane aphorism. In any event, he was not for her. Even if he had been decent, he was a Mundane in Mundania.

Yorick swept her into his arms and kissed her, and she couldn't bring herself to resist. If only such a thing could be real, on its several levels!

Then she summoned her gumption. What she needed to do was cause him to break the engagement and go away forever. That would require some finesse and considerable ugly implication. First she had to undermine the foundations of their relationship. Then she had to provoke him into dumping her.

"Desist, dear," she said, gently pushing him away. "We have special business."

"Indeed we do, Sil!" His arms did not release her; instead one hand slid under her skirt to squeeze one firm buttock while the other quested for her breast. He liked the fullness thereof. "Let's get to the bedroom."

"Desist!" Cube said more sharply, twisting out of his grasp. "Sit down. We must talk."

"Sure we will, soon." He pursued her.

She found refuge behind a couch, where he couldn't conveniently reach. She had no script at all for this; Silhouette had never had the gumption even to try to avoid him. "There are matters relating to our marriage that must be settled. First, there will be a pre-nuptual agreement." That was another magic word or phrase.

"A what?" He was trying to figure out how to get to her.

"With teeth in it."

"A pre-nup!" he exclaimed, fidgeting and avoiding her gaze. "Whatever for?"

"In the event of the dissolution of our relationship, you will have a fair but modest stipend until such time as you marry elsewhere. You will have no claim on the estate, and there will be no cash settlement."

"What the hell are you talking about?" he demanded, out-raged. But there was a vacuity in his tone: he was bluffing. "You can't do that."

"There will be other details, of course, but that will be the essence. You will not get rich off me."

A cunning look replaced his incredulity. Then it was sup-pressed. He fidgeted and looked away again, apparently un-aware of the manner she was reading him. When he spoke, his voice was hollow. "Of course, dear. Whatever you say. All I want is your happiness."

"Excellent. I will have my lawyer draw it up soon. It will be absolutely tight."

"Not if I don't sign it," he muttered.

"What was that, Yorick?"

"Nothing, dear. Now let's get to the bedroom."

One support had been compromised. On to the second. "When we marry," she continued inexorably, "I will not be taking your surname. I will keep my own, so it will be quite clear that we are not social equals."

Anger clouded his countenance. "That's outrageous!"

She delivered the level gaze. "You do still wish to marry me?"

"Of course! But not this way."

She leaned forward so that the upper surfaces of her breasts were exposed and smiled, devastating him with her beauty. "What way did you have in mind, dear?"

"That's it!" he rasped. He lunged across the couch, catch-ing her by a long tress. "We'll have none of this crap! If you don't like the bedroom, we'll do it right here on the couch."

"Release my hair," Cube said firmly.

"The hell!" He yanked on it cruelly. "What's got into you, Sil? How come these sudden airs? You know you're nothing but a damned slut, nothing at all without me."

That did it. She had been foolishly half reluctant to de-stroy him, because of his handsomeness. Now she under-stood right through to the core that handsome truly was as handsome did, and he was fecal matter. Her gumption was converting to something like rage. "Release my hair," she repeated, her hand finding the plastic piece at her waistband.

"The hell!" he repeated, yanking so hard that she had to bend forward over the couch, showing twice as much breast as before. He reached over her back, caught her bottom, and heaved her up and over so that her head plowed into his thighs. His hands remained busy, catching her legs, hauling her the rest of the way onto the couch. She was unable to resist effectively at the moment, but the plastic was in her hand and her rage was burgeoning.

He turned her over, roughly, and ripped open her blouse. "You're just a piece of meat! Now spread your legs."

Cube tried to sit up, to get her feet on the floor. But he was holding her down as he continued to rip at her clothing, and she remained weak from her pill-induced illness. She could not get him off her, and could not get off the couch. The situation was out of control.

It was time to defend herself more effectively. Words had lost their power. She needed to temper her rage with effective action. She bent her right arm at the elbow and punched upward at his head. The L point of the weapon rammed into his left ear.

"Ooow!" he cried, lurching back. "What the hell?"

That was more like it. "Get away from me," Cube said.

"You bitch! You hit me! Well, now you're really going to get it!" He lifted his fist.

Cube's right hand was now beside her left jaw in the follow-through of her punch. She straightened her elbow, wielding the plastic like a hammer. It collided with Yorick's right eye. The force was not great, but the plastic was hard; that eye would be black tomorrow.

"Ooow!" he repeated. But still he did not desist. "I'll kill you!"

Her third strike had better aim and greater force. She flattened his nose. Blood welled out, dripping on her.

Now at last Yorick fell back, releasing her. Cube sat up.

Then she shoved him away from the couch. He sat on the floor, holding his face, groaning.

Time for the finale. The script for this was adapted from a dirty magazine that had shocked Silhouette when she read it. "Oh, this is fun," she said.

"Fun? What did you hit me with?"

He hadn't seen the plastic. Good. "Only my hand, dear. But I can get a knife if you prefer."

"A knife!"

"When we are married," she said sweetly, "this will be a regular thing. Violence turns me on. Now let's go to the bedroom."

"The bedroom!" he cried. "I'm bleeding to death!"

"This was an avenue you chose," she reminded him. "Sex with violence. I find I have developed a taste for it. Of course this level won't satisfy me long; it will have to escalate. I will order manacles for you, so that next time we can do it right. I have some delicious ideas."

"You're crazy! I'm getting out of here!" He scrambled to his feet.

"But dear—I thought you liked this! I thought you were a soul-mate. Now come to the bedroom, where I can make you really hurt."

"No way!" He stumbled toward the door.

"But we're engaged! It's all set."

"Not anymore it isn't! I'm gone!" And he was.

Cube smiled grimly. That had not played out quite the way she had hoped, but it was probably enough. Bullies didn't like to get bullied themselves. She had given him three excellent reasons to break up with her, and he would probably be too embarrassed to tell anyone else why.

But the job was not yet finished. Cube quelled her violent passion, for the next stage was of another nature. She went to her room, stripped away her ruined dress, stepped into the Mundane shower, and then changed to a new and more conservative outfit. No flexing surfaces of breast or thigh would show. She fixed her lovely hair, formulating her plan for the finale. Because she needed to secure Silhouette's situation, making sure the vultures would never return. Silhouette was not a strong-willed woman; she would need ongoing support. Cube would try to arrange for it.

She went to the aunt's room, tapped on the door, and opened it without waiting. The aunt looked up from her chair. "There is a small mess in the living room," Cube said. "See that it is properly cleaned up. I am going out." She departed, leaving the woman speechless. She would be worse than speechless when she saw the blood and understood that this time Silhouette had beaten up Yorick, rather than the other way around.

She went to the gardener's modest quarters behind the four-car garage. Silhouette's memory clarified him as a good man, a friend of her father's and still a loyal employee. Now she needed friendship and loyalty.

She knocked on his door and waited. After a moment the old man opened it. "Miss Silhouette!" he exclaimed. "So good to see you."

She stepped in to him and kissed him, startling him. "Filip, I need you."

"Miss Silhouette, I am always at your service. You know that." The startle was fading.

"This is not routine. Please, may I come in?"

"Oh, Miss Silhouette, this is not—"

"Sil."

He paused. "I think I do not understand."

"My aunt called me Sil, with contempt. Henceforth she will address me as Silhouette. You have always treated me with respect, even when I was a spoiled child. You may call me Sil."

"This is not proper."

"Because I need a friend I can trust."

Now understanding came. "Come in, Sil."

She entered the cramped chamber that was his kitchen, den, and bedroom. She sat on the bed, pretending not to notice that it had not been made. Filip sat in the one available chair. He was a portly man her father's age, in faded jeans and a worn plaid shirt, with nicely graying hair. He was an immigrant from central Europe and still spoke with an accent. He waited politely for her to state her business with him.

"I thought you had more space."

"Your aunt needed more storage space."

"My father would not have taken yours."

"Your father is not here."

Just so. "How is your son?"

"Phil's doing well in trade school. I see him every week."

"We were playmates as children. He was two years older than I, but he never talked down to me."

"He liked you, Sil."

"And I liked him. But I went to the fancy boarding school, and then to the fancier private college, and we grew apart. I regret that."

"So does he."

"But when we were young, and I had homework I couldn't handle, I would bring it to him. He wasn't in my school, and never had assignments like that, but he would tackle it and figure it out and ex'plain it to me. Then I understood it, and could keep up with my class."

Filip nodded. "He got a good education that way."

"The upper-class education not available to the children of immigrants."

"We are not complaining. Your father was always generous to us."

"When Father died, your situation deteriorated. So did mine."

"It pained me to see it, Sil. But it was not my place to comment. I'm only the gardener."

"My father's friend. And mine."

"And yours," he agreed.

Cube pondered briefly, not finding this as straightforward as she had hoped. This was not a man to put in his place, but a friend to enlist, and he might not appreciate what she meant to ask of him.

"Your son was smarter than I, and decent, like you."

"And homely, like me."

"Does he have a current relationship?"

"A girlfriend? No, he has never been interested."

Cube felt alarm. "He is not interested in women?"

Filip smiled. "It is not that, Sil. His heart is already taken."

Damn! "Who?"

"I think you know. But of course he knows it is futile."

Ah. "Not necessarily."

"I do not follow."

"Would he be amenable to a relationship with me other than as an employee?"

The man frowned. "Please, Sil, do not toy with my son. He has a life to make."

Cube wrestled with phrasing. "I think I am asking your permission to date your son."

"But you are engaged to marry Yorick!"

"Not anymore, I think."

"What happened?"

"I broke his nose."

He looked amazed. "How—?"

"With this." She brought out the plastic L.

He whistled. "That would do it! But why?"

"He would have broken more than my nose, in time, and my heart. The man's a cad."

"No argument! But I never thought you would take such action."

"Things have changed. I also put Aunt Susan in her place, and will fire Accountant James."

Filip shook his head with amazement. "I am not saying they do not deserve it, Sil. But I have a problem, no offense intended, in understanding how you could have done it."

"This is why I need a friend. I have a secret, and I need help."

"Anything, Sil."

"I hope this will not change your mind. You must keep the secret even if you do not approve."

"I will."

Cube told him of the exchange, and what she hoped to accomplish.

"That explains an enormous amount," Filip said. "I do not think Silhouette ever could have done the things you did. She was never emotionally strong."

"Yes. She lacks gumption, which happens to be a quality I have too much of. It was a struggle for her to get up the nerve to overdose on pills, and she didn't take quite enough."

"But you say you will exchange back at midnight. Then she will have the same problem."

"Yes. So she will need support. Someone who can be by her side without question, and who will not allow her to be bullied by others. Who will always love and respect her. As I remember—as Silhouette remembers—Phil is a strong man, and not given to timidity when his values are threatened."

"That is true. Except in the case of the woman. He would never have the nerve to approach Silhouette. She is not merely beautiful, she is rich. And his father's employer."

"That is why you must make him do it. Have him dress well, and come to the mansion. I will tell her to welcome him. I cannot speak for her follow-through, as she has had deplorable taste in men, but I know she always liked and respected him, and will be glad to have his strong support. Maybe it won't be a romance, but it can look like one, so that others will not question his presence. And if she does the sensible thing, and marries him, you will be her father-in-law, and she will listen to you. I know you will guide her well."

"This is almost more than I can imagine. It is so great a chance, so fast. But I will try. She is a nice girl, if she could just achieve stability."

"She can achieve it if she has by her side a man who will bristle if anyone, especially her aunt, tries to belittle or take advantage of her. If she knows he will always be there."

Filip nodded. "I think you are correct."

"I have a twenty-four-hour time limit," Cube said. "That's why I have to be brutally fast. I hope that this will not only save Silhouette from suicide, it will also straighten out the thread I follow and enable me to continue my Quest."

"You have been most forthright in that effort."

"It's gumption," she agreed. "Sometimes I annoy people. But I think what I am doing here is right. I hope it is."

"You are beautiful."

"Oh, no, I am worse than plain. It was been wonderful visiting this beautiful body." She stood, ready to return to the house.

Filip stood too, and approached her. "You are beautiful," he repeated, and kissed her. This time she understood what he meant, and appreciated it.

Cube returned to the mansion. She checked the living room and saw that the messed-up couch had been straightened, and the bloodstains were gone. Aunt Susan must have wondered about that! But perhaps she would also get the message: things had changed.

She spent the rest of the day absorbing Mundania. It was true that there was very little magic, but there were some interesting things, like a Mall stocked with all manner of wonders, any of which she could have by flashing her magic Credit Card. There were monstrous metal birds called airplanes that would take a person far beyond the boundaries of Xanth. And there was a box whose front flashed pictures ranging from things to buy, to couples endlessly summoning the stork. Overall, Mundania was fascinating to visit, but she wouldn't want to live here.

When evening came she retired for the night to her elaborate bedroom. But she didn't sleep. She donned conservative clothing, including a pair of the useful jeans, and left the house. She drove her car back to the hospital annex, and discovered that the room was now occupied by another patient. She hadn't thought of that; how was she to intersect Silhouette and change back?

She decided that boldness was best. She breezed by the desk clerk and went directly to the room. She entered, and found an old woman there. "Hello, Grandma," she said. "How are you doing?"

The woman stared at her, obviously not recognizing her. "Who are you?"

Cube hastily drew on Silhouette's memory of regulations. "They wouldn't let in anyone who wasn't a relative, so I became a relative. I'm actually a fellow patient. I was in this bed last night, in a coma."

"A coma!"

"But I recovered and went home. Now I'm visiting. How are they treating you—" she glanced at the nameplate at the foot of the bed. "Irma?"

"Wretchedly," the woman said, and commenced a litany of complaints. "The food is awful. They don't have the right brand of caviar, and they wouldn't allow me any champagne. Just because of my lacerated ulcer, they claim. It's outrageous."

"Outrageous," Cube agreed.

The woman talked until she fell asleep. Cube waited until midnight, then stood by the bed. She felt something overlapping her body. *Hello Silhouette,* she thought. *Check your memory. You have a new boyfriend and a new life.* She hoped that was true. It would be if Silhouette went along with it.

Then the presence was gone, and Cube was facing Demoness Metria.

9

THANKS

Hello, Metria," she said. "I'm back. How was it?"
"Let's make sure. Pull someone out of the pouch."
"There's a problem?"

"Silhouette couldn't do it. I want to be sure it's you."

"Diamond knows it's me." Indeed, the dog was licking her hand and wagging her tail.

"Diamond liked Silhouette too."

Cube shrugged and put her hand to the purse. "Ryver," she said.

The man caught her hand, then slid out. "Where are we?"

"In a dull haunted inn," Metria said, her dress abruptly covering anything interesting. "Go back in the pouch."

Ryver shrugged and put his foot to the pouch, then slid in. It seemed the demoness could turn it off as readily as she could turn it on, and she wasn't interested in fascinating any mortals at present.

"Now you know it's really me," Cube said. "What is going on?"

"You would hardly believe it! That woman got into more trouble! I'm accustomed to *making* trouble, not preventing it. What a chore."

"I want to know all about it," Cube said. "But can it wait until morning?"

"Yes, now that you're back. How did it go in Mundania?"

"I put her aunt in her place, fired her accountant, beat up her boyfriend, and set her up with a new one."

"Who?"

"Philip, son of Filip the gardener. He's in love with her."

"Odd. She didn't advert him."

"Didn't what him?"

"Allude, reference, touch on, bring up—"

"Mention?"

"Whatever," the demoness agreed crossly. "How can he be her boyfriend?"

"They were children together. He's a good man. She has execrable taste in men."

"Beautiful women do; it's in the Big Book of Rules."

"So I set her up with the one she needs. I just hope she has the wit to realize it."

"She was afraid you'd get raped."

Cube laughed. "Who'd ever rape *me*?"

"In her body."

That did make the difference. "He tried." Cube went to the bed and lay down. "Catch me up in the morning." She closed her eyes.

"You're a cool one." The demoness must have faded out, because she was silent thereafter. Cube lay for a while, reviewing the events of the past day, hoping she had done the right thing. But she knew it would take time to be sure she had. *If* she had. She sank slowly to sleep without resolution.

The mares brought her mixed dreams bordering good and bad without quite entering the territory of either. She woke in the night, thinking. Cube knew she had done things in Mundania she had never done in Xanth, and not just because she had wielded a beautiful body. Backing off Aunt Susan like that, putting pincers on the accountant, actually physically attacking boyfriend Yorick—this had been quite unlike Silhouette, but also unlike Cube herself. She had gumption to spare, but she had demonstrated more than that. It had bordered on cruelty. She had never been that way in real life.

And there, perhaps, was the key: Mundania had not been really real to her. It had been an alternate existence, like a game, where consequences weren't completely personal. So she had acted boldly. But now, done with it, she was reflecting on right and wrong. It had not been her life there, but it was Silhouette's life. Had she had the right to change it so substantially?

Yet Silhouette had been trying to commit suicide. Left to herself, she would have, literally, no life. Cube had acted to make it possible for her to have not only a life, but a good life. If she failed, the woman was no worse off than she had been. If she succeeded, Silhouette could forge on and perhaps accomplish worthwhile things. And make a good young man very happy.

Mostly satisfied, Cube returned to sleep. This time the mares brought her good dreams. Some daymares must have been moonlighting, because nightmares never brought good dreams.

In the morning Cube organized for the resumption of her trip. She saw that the thread now led out of the room. She must have accomplished her Mundane mission, apart from her personal satisfaction. She hoped so. She liked Silhouette despite her phenomenal beauty, and wanted her to succeed in life.

The innkeeper intercepted her, fidgeting and shifty with his eyes. "There's more pots to scrub. You owe me."

"I have paid you," Cube said evenly. She had had recent experience dealing with dishonest folk.

"How?" he demanded.

"I abolished your ghost."

"How can I believe that?" Naturally he, being untrustworthy, did not take the word of others.

"Go check the room. She's gone, and I don't think she'll return."

He lumbered off to check the room. Cube followed the thread out of the inn. Then it set off down a minor path into the deepest forest. Diamond followed it, evidently remembering the way.

"That's where Silhouette went," Metria said, appearing beside her.

"That's right: you were going to tell me how her day went. How did it go?"

"Mixed. First she didn't really believe this was a magic land. She wanted to see real live magic, and there wasn't any at the inn. She wasn't satisfied with my changes of form; she said I could be the only demon in an otherwise ordinary land. She wanted me to show her some real magic. So I guided her to the petrified forest."

"But she was already frightened enough."

"It's the forest that's frightened, not the person. I showed her some puns. And I kept an eye out for dragons; one of those would have impressed her."

They continued along the thread-marked path. "But she had all of my memory to draw on. She should have known Xanth is magic."

"She said it could be another hallucinogenic dream. In fact she wasn't sure she wasn't still in Mundania, with the pills she had eaten zonking out her mind."

"She must have been determined not to believe."

"Or afraid to believe. I'm a demon; I don't have many mortal emotions. But I was sorry for her."

"The thread led me into her life," Cube said. "I tried to clean it up by getting rid of the vultures. I must have done what was needed, because now the thread is moving on."

"But it's just showing you the way to Counter Xanth. Why should it care about Mundania?"

Cube wondered about that too. "It must be more than a line. There must be things I have to do or learn along the way, so it is making me do and learn them."

"What could you learn in *Mundania*?"

Cube considered. "That beauty is not necessarily enough,

by itself. Silhouette could attract men, but she didn't have the judgment to go with the right one or the strength to get rid of the wrong one." Cube had the judgment and strength, but of course lacked the beauty to make it count, here in real life.

"I tried to tell you that at the outset."

"I suppose I had to experience it myself before I could believe it." But now she wondered: she had thought the thread had been distorted because she had too many Companions, but now it seemed more sophisticated than that. Was it distorted at all, or merely devious? Reaching Counter Xanth seemed to be more than just a physical route.

A gentle wind ruffled Cube's dull hair. She thought of how attractively Silhouette's lustrous hair would flow with that wind. Yet the woman had been ready to die. Yes, beauty alone was not enough. But the lack of it was an overwhelming problem.

They came to a man with a bow. He was loosing arrows, but seemed to have no target. Some flew high, some flew low, and some disappeared into the forest. Diamond went to stand behind a tree, wary of this wild aim.

Cube paused. "What are you doing?"

He glanced at her. "I told you yesterday."

Of course he didn't know that was Silhouette. "Tell me again." She could surely research it from her body's memory, but lacked the patience at the moment.

"Just shooting the breeze."

This mystified her. "What is the point?"

"It passes the time."

Cube wasn't sure how much extra time she had to pass, so she moved on.

"Silhouette laughed when he told her that," Metria confided. "She said it was the first real laugh she'd had in a long time."

"What's funny about trying to hurt the wind? It can't be done, but if it could be, it wouldn't be nice."

"Maybe she finds painful things amusing." But the demoness was stifling most of a smirk. Cube concealed her annoyance. She had probably missed something that would have made Karia Centaur groan.

They came to a woman with an odd head. It seemed to be empty. Her hair framed eyebrows and mouth, but the skull was hollow. "Hello," Cube said uncertainly.

"That's fine," the woman said airily and went on by her.

"She's an air-head," Metria said. "Silhouette laughed when she met her, too."

"I see nothing funny about it. It's not nice to make fun of folk who are different from ourselves."

This time the demoness managed to stifle less of the smirk. "That reminds me of the next one we'll see, if she's still on this route."

"Maybe the thread was trying to cheer Silhouette up."

The next woman passed them. Her body was ordinary, but her head was that of a cat. A very severe looking one. Diamond gave her a wide berth.

"A sour puss," the demoness explained.

"And that is supposed to be funny?"

"Maybe you have to have the mind for it."

Metria was definitely amused about something, but it would be useless to inquire. Cube didn't like being on the outside of something others found amusing. Maybe her time in Mundania had made her too serious.

They came to a different kind of forest. The trees appeared to be frozen in positions of fear. Their trunks leaned away from the path as if trying to escape, and their branches were convoluted as if trying to protect the trees from attack. Cube had never before seen such frightened vegetation.

Then she caught on. "This is the petrified forest."

"Silhouette laughed so hard she cried. She said that forest was just like her. That mystifies me; she doesn't look anything like a tree, let alone a forest."

"At the time, she looked like me," Cube reminded her. "But I think I understand. She was girt about by fears. The vultures could never have picked at her bones if she hadn't been so weak. Every which way she turned, there was another horror. Just like this forest."

"What's so eccentric about that?"

"So what?"

"Bizarre, freakish, weird, quirky, idiosyncratic—"

"Funny?"

"Whatever," the demoness agreed crossly.

"It's not funny hee-hee, but funny realization. Silhouette saw an analogy of herself. That amused her."

"I don't see what's funny about that. Not one of these trees slipped on a banana peel or got a pie in the face."

"Maybe you have to have the mind for it," Cube said smugly.

The thread led on through the frightened forest and back to more natural vegetation. Here there was a man with a collection of wood fragments. He was putting his hands on them and concentrating so hard that little clouds were forming and dissipating over his head.

Diamond went up to him, wagging her tail. "Hi, Di," he said, smiling.

So Silhouette had met this man too, and must have learned what he was doing. This time Cube did what she should have done before, and checked her memory. For whatever the woman had experienced was in Cube's memory, just as her day in Mundania was in Silhouette's memory. "Hello, Mike. Still changing regular wood into reverse wood?"

"Still doing it," he agreed. "There's a lot of demand."

Evidently so. They moved on. "So did that make Silhouette laugh?" Cube asked.

"No. She didn't know what reverse wood was."

"But it's in my memory."

"She didn't think to look there, and I didn't tell her. I just explained that it reversed magic in what it touched. Since she still wasn't sure she believed in magic, she didn't react."

"Maybe that was just as well."

The forest opened into a large glade. Here there was a class of some kind in progress. Children were walking carefully, sometimes losing their balance and falling. "What—?" Cube started, then remembered to check her own memory.

"They're walking on air!" For the children's feet were not quite touching the ground.

"They're happy children," Metria agreed. "Their folks don't want them to get hurt, so they're learning how to do it right."

"That must have interested Silhouette."

"Yes. She finally believed that there is magic here. She was sorry she couldn't walk on air herself, but was pleased that Diamond managed it."

"But she's a Mundane dog. She couldn't—" Cube broke off, because there was Diamond with the children, walking on air. She wasn't good at it, and occasionally a foot slipped through to the ground, but she was definitely doing it. "Then again, maybe she can."

"It's not a talent so much as a state of mind," Metria said. "Children do it naturally, but adults usually forget how."

"Adults get serious about life," Cube agreed.

"Next stop is a sad Magician."

Cube decided not to check her memory, preferring to be surprised. They intersected an enchanted path and followed it a short distance to its end.

Its end? How could an enchanted path have an end? They all went to important places.

There was an old man there, facing the brush ahead. He looked tired. "Oh, hello Diamond," he said as the dog joined him. "I'm sorry I haven't finished this section yet. I can't do it as fast as I used to in youth."

Cube decided to check her memory after all. There it was: this was Patxi, the Magician who made the enchanted paths. Silhouette had talked with him for some time, learning that he labored continually because of a curse. She had sympathy, regarding herself as being cursed in another manner. They had, in their fashion, hit it off. And Metria had been totally bored, fading out as much as possible until evening came and it was time for Silhouette to return to the inn, lest she miss the return rendezvous. But the woman had, in her fashion, enjoyed the day. "I wish I could stay here, or at least visit when not a ghost," she said sadly. "But of course I can't."

The thread led right to Patxi and not beyond him. He, like the ghost, was another problem to be handled before she could move on. Cube sighed inwardly.

Now she reviewed the story Patxi had told Silhouette about his curse. She suspected that this related to the thread's interest in him, and that she would have to find some clue therein to her destination. What she had thought would be a simple way to find her destination was instead turning out to be on ongoing challenge of understanding and performance.

Patxi had been a rather wild child and youth. His talent, once he discovered it, was to make an invisible and unfeelable barrier that would stop anyone or any creature from passing. No one knew his talent, and he decided not to tell them. He simply went around setting up barriers in awkward places, then hiding and watching the mischief they made. He made one by the village playground so that the other children couldn't reach it. They didn't bang into it, they merely found themselves unable to get there, no matter how hard they tried. It was as if they suddenly couldn't find the way. They got very upset, and some cried, and Patxi had to stifle his laughter lest he give himself away.

He set one up by the pie tree grove, so that the village women could not harvest pies for meals. They could see the pies, and smell them, but not reach them. They were most annoyed. It was hilarious.

He set one up by the village spring, so that no one could get a drink of water. The men had to go to a neighboring village and carry heavy jars of it back. What a great prank!

But it was when he put a wall around the village sanitary trench that the fun really began. No one could dump their slops there. The waste piled up in the houses, and soon an awful stench suffused the village. Patxi found the joke so funny that he rolled on the ground laughing helplessly. That was when he gave himself away, for no one else found the situation remotely humorous.

They asked him nicely to remove the walls. He said no. They explained that he was seriously disrupting village life and causing distress for many people. He said that was their tough luck. They said he would be punished if he did not reform. He formed a wall around himself and no one could touch him. He capered and made rude noises at them, laughing so hard his sides hurt.

That was when they held a village council and decided to take a stronger measure. They sent an emissary to the notorious curse fiends and asked them to put a curse on Patxi that would fix the problem and make him a good citizen instead of a bad one. The curse fiends obliged. They could not take away his magic, but they could govern him through the curse.

They cursed him to use his talent only for good, and to continue until he was formally thanked. After that he would be released, having expiated his obligation.

That was when his laughter stopped. He found himself compelled to remove all the walls he had erected, and to seek ways of using his talent to help others. But the villagers did not need or want any invisible walls on their premises. They just wanted to be left alone so they could get on with their dull lives. Since he could do them no good—and he had to keep doing good until he was thanked—and no one thanked him—he had to leave the village and quest elsewhere. But other villages had heard about him, and wanted none of his help, fearing it would turn to mischief. In that period came the Time of No Magic, which was a horrible disruption for all Xanth, and folk were suspicious that he might have had something to do with it, so they were even more wary of him.

Finally he had gone to the king of Xanth, one Magician Trent, and begged for some assignment that would enable him to do good indefinitely, at least until someone thanked him. And the king pondered and consulted with the Good Magician, and assigned him the chore of making safe paths between all the major places of Xanth. They gave him a map of the places to connect and the various minor obstacles between them, such as the Gap Chasm, and let him be.

He worked diligently, making all the paths on the map, and constantly improving them and making protected camps and way stops too, but no one ever thanked him. The king changed, and it seemed no one even remembered him or his job, but he kept working, because he couldn't quit until thanked. Now it was nigh sixty years later, and he wanted very much to retire, but could not.

Silhouette had wanted to thank him, but she was not a citizen of Xanth, so she kissed him instead. He stared at her, amazed. "For an instant it seemed I was being kissed by the loveliest woman I ever saw," he said. "But—"

"I may be prettier inside than outside," she said. Then she had left him, regretting that she could do nothing for him. But his plight had moved her, for she knew that every youth had indiscretions, and did not deserve a lifelong punishment for them. She knew from Cube's memory that the enchanted paths had been well done, and were a real service to all of Xanth, because people could travel along them with safety and comfort and not get lost. Surely he had more than repaid his debt. How was it that he had never been thanked?

Now Cube was here in the same body, and she wondered too. But this was simply remedied. She opened her mouth to thank him—and could not speak.

"That curse," she said after a moment. "It stops people from thanking you."

"Yes. I think some might have been inclined, but they can't do it. So I'm stuck."

"I think I need to try to abate that curse," she said.

He viewed her with faint hope worn down by decades of disappointment. "I think others have tried, without success."

"I may have greater resources," she said. "I can't promise success, but I'll try."

"I wish you well," he said dully, and returned to his work. It seemed he had to clear the way by hand, then establish the invisible walls to keep all hostile creatures out. It was good work, but tedious.

She retreated a short distance, until she was alone except for Diamond and Metria. Then she put her hand to the pouch and drew out the three Princesses. "I think I need some help," she said. Then she explained the situation.

"This should be child's play," Melody said.

"Which is fine for us," Harmony agreed.

"Because we're children," Rhythm concluded.

They focused on the problem, making their music. Soon they had a report:

"This is a complicated curse," Melody said.

"It was made a long time ago, by many curse fiends," Harmony added.

"Most of whom have now faded out," Rhythm said.

"Don't curses quit when the ones who make them are gone?" Cube asked.

"Some do," Melody said.

"Some don't," Harmony added.

"This one didn't," Rhythm concluded.

"But don't you have the power to break it? You are Sorceresses."

"We would if we could understand it completely," Melody said.

"But there are so many nuances in the programming that we can't fathom them all," Harmony said.

"It's old programming," Rhythm said. "They don't make spells like this anymore."

"But you three together have so much power! Can't you just destroy it without understanding all its nuances?"

The three shook their heads. "That would be dangerous," Melody said.

"It could have roots in some of the vital functions of Xanth," Harmony added.

"Like our share of the magic of gravity," Rhythm concluded.

Oh. "Well, can you do something partial, that doesn't risk disaster?"

"Yes," Melody said.

"We can fathom its key points," Harmony agreed.

"And reveal how they may be handled," Rhythm concluded.

They labored, and in due course came up with three key aspects of one point:

"The curse channels through a secret name assigned to Patxi," Melody said.

"Nullify that name, and the curse will not get through," Harmony added.

"And that name is Unthank," Rhythm finished.

Well, that was progress. "How do we nullify that name?"

"This is tricky," Melody said.

"It's not just a name, it's a magic channel," Harmony clarified.

"If we abolish it, the curse might pollute all Xanth," Rhythm concluded.

"But if we leave it, we can't help him," Cube protested.

"Maybe not," Metria said, appearing. "You folk aren't devious enough. You don't have to abolish it, just change it a little, so that it becomes a block instead of a conduit."

"Change it?" Cube asked.

"Erase the Un."

Cube and the three Princesses exchanged a tangle of glances. "Can you do that?" Cube asked them.

Melody shook her head. "This is delicate surgery."

"We might destroy it when trying to destroy part of it," Harmony said.

"We're not good at tinkering with other folks' magic," Rhythm said.

"But if you can't, who can?" Cube asked, frustrated.

"I know someone who might," Metria said. "Kim Mundane. She has the talent of erasure. She can erase anything, in whole or in part."

"Erase part of a name?"

The three Princesses nodded. It might work.

"Where is this Kim Mundane?" Then Cube realized the implication of the name. "Mundania!"

"I can't go there," Metria said. "But I can tell you where she lives. You'll have to go and bring her here."

"But I can't just go there! I have no one to switch places with this time."

"Physically."

"Physically," Cube echoed.

"You will have to use the portal at No Name Key," the demoness said. "Then travel through Mundania to where she lives."

"But I can't do that alone! I have no real knowledge of Mundania. I'd get lost."

The other four, and the dog, merely looked at her.

Cube knew she was stuck for it.

She returned to Patxi. "I will try to help you," she told him. "But it may take a while. I have to make a trip to Mundania first."

"There's no need," he said. "It's not a bad curse, as curses go."

"I think that I am—not cursed, but obliged—to help you. So I will make the effort. I hope it works out."

"That would be nice," he said.

Then she saw the thread, leading away from him. It had appeared when she made her commitment. Diamond saw it too, or perhaps smelled it.

She followed it back along the path he was making. When she was out of his sight, the thread abruptly stopped.

She stared at its end. What did this mean?

"It means it jumps, bird," Metria said, reappearing.

"It jumps what?"

"Ignorant, stupid, idiot, moron, dumbbell—"

"Dodo?"

"Whatever," the demoness agreed, for once not crossly.

Cube realized that she had indeed been stupid, and not just for forgetting that the thread could seem discontinuous at times. She hadn't needed to ferret out the precise insult when she already had the meaning of the main comment. "Very well. Get in the pouch."

Metria slid into the pouch. "You too, Diamond," she said,

holding it down for the dog. Diamond slid in paw-first. Then she put her hand in. "Centaur."

Karia emerged. "I need to go to the portal to Mundania," Cube said.

"Readily accomplished," the centaur agreed. "Mount."

Cube got on her back, and soon they were in the air. Cube admired the clouds and landscape, as she had before; this was too novel an experience to ignore. She saw the huge Gap Chasm, not looking nearly as formidable from this height. While they flew, she caught Karia up on recent developments.

"That is remarkable," the centaur said. "A ghost, an exchange, and now a physical visit to Mundania."

"It is where the thread leads me. It seems to be a good deal more sophisticated than I first thought."

"I wonder. I don't think the Princesses were trying for anything fancy. It must be that their magic enables them to do a magic thing right even if they don't fully understand it."

"That must be it. When I think of it, I realize that generating a full-size castle from air requires a great deal more knowledge of detail than seven-year-olds can be expected to have. Maybe there is a store of information they draw on without realizing it. So the thread may have similar sophistication. But I dread going out into Mundania on my own, and not just because I'm no Sorceress—and it will have to be alone."

"I see no real problem. Get Turn Key to help you."

"Who?"

"He's the gatekeeper there, a nice older man, I have heard. Ask him how to proceed, and he will surely give you good advice."

"I'll do that," Cube agreed, somewhat relieved.

Soon they came to the southeast shore of Xanth. "It looks golden!" Cube exclaimed.

"That's the Gold Coast. No Name Key is not far from it."

"Why didn't you groan?"

"Groan?"

"You hate the puns."

"What puns? The Gold Coast is called that because that's its nature, and they must simply never have figured a name for the key."

"I suppose that's right. I suppose not everything in Xanth is built on puns."

"Fortunately," Karia agreed.

They glided down to the string of keys. These were shaped like the keys to assorted locks, but were of course considerably larger. They were rather pretty. "What's that huge one?" Cube asked looking south.

"That is Centaur Isle, where the centaurs live," Karia said.

"Oh, you must like to visit there."

"No."

"But—"

"They are all grounded centaurs," Karia explained. "No wings. It requires magic for a creature our size to fly, but ground-bound centaurs don't approve of magic for themselves. In fact they consider it obscene. So they don't associate with the winged monster branch of the centaur family."

"But you're no monster!"

Karia turned her head back, smiling. "It is a broad classification that unites all winged creatures. We regard it as a signal of unity, not as an affront. No winged monster is supposed to attack another, outside of the normal predator/prey activity. I am proud to be a winged monster."

"That's nice," Cube said, taken aback. "You mean a dragon wouldn't attack you if it came by now?"

"Not normally. Of course if I were intruding on its nest, trying to steal its treasure, that would be a different matter. Still, it is best not to take chances. I have my bow, and the threat of a well-aimed arrow can be persuasive even to a hungry dragon."

"Sort of the way my nickelpedes discourage robbers," Cube said.

"Yes. When you are beautiful, you may find them even more useful as protection against aggressive men."

Cube laughed. "I think I would find it hard to object to a man who found me attractive." But she remembered Yorick.

"Perhaps," the centaur said. "Ah, there's Big Pine Key."

Cube looked down. Sure enough, there was a towering pine tree rising from one of the larger keys. It was amazing that the giant tree had enough room for its roots. Perhaps they extended down more than out.

Karia avoided the tree and glided down to land on a largely featureless isle. "And here is No Name Key."

"But there's nothing on it! Where is the gateway?"

"On the Mundane side. They set larger store by buildings than we do. There should be a picture here. Ah, there it is."

They walked to a picture on an easel. It showed the interior of a fair-sized building. That was all. "But there has to be more than a picture."

Karia smiled. "Just step through it. But perhaps I should return to the pouch first; that way I'll be with you when you need me again. I would not be comfortable in Mundania."

That made Cube think of something worrisome. "Magic things can't exist in Mundania. What about this magic pouch?"

"I suspect it is crafted to endure. After all, it was fashioned by a Mundane, Sofia Socksorter. But you will not be able to bring any of us out of it there. Take care that you do not mislay it."

"Mislay it!" Cube said in horror. But the centaur was already sliding into it. It had been humor. She hoped.

Now she stood alone before the painting. Step through it? How could she do that? Well, if it was similar to the pouch, or the Phaze picture, it might work.

She put forth a hand to touch the picture. The hand found no resistance; it entered the scene. She pushed her arm in, and then lifted a foot to climb on in.

Suddenly she was standing in the building. She turned around. Sure enough, there was a picture of No Name Key behind her, hanging on a wall.

She heard footsteps. A portly man entered the chamber. "What may I do for you, sir?" he inquired.

"Uh, I'm a woman. My name is Cube."

He looked again. "Why so you are. I apologize. I am Turn

Key, the gatekeeper for this portal. What may I do for you, miss?"

"I am on a—a private mission. I need to reach a Mundane person and bring her back to Xanth."

"Naturally. What is her identity?"

"Kim Mundane. She—"

"Of course. She won the game contest and a fine magic talent. She is allowed to visit Xanth at any time, but has elected to make her home in Mundania, incredible as that may seem."

"Yes," Cube said, somewhat off-balanced by his ready understanding. "How can I reach her?"

"The readiest way is via Com Pewter's Xanth Xone connection."

"Who? What?"

Turn Key frowned. "Perhaps another time. I suppose you could telephone her, but she has an unlisted number."

"Do what?"

The man took visible stock of the situation. "You have no idea of the protocols of Mundania?"

"Well, I visited there recently, but only—" Cube remembered using the phone when she was in Silhouette's body. Numbers were magical, but she had none. "Yes, I have no idea."

"You will need the help of a native. Do you know any Mundane?"

"Only Silhouette."

The man fetched a big bendy book. He opened it and turned the pages. "Tampa Bay area?"

"I don't know. I was near the North Village when—"

"That's confirmation. Let me see if I can reach her." He took a phone—now she recognized it, having seen it in her memory of Mundania—and punched some little buttons on it. He listened, then spoke into its mouthpiece. "Miss Silhouette? Do you know a woman named Cube?" He listened, then handed the instrument to Cube. "She remembers you."

"Uh, hello," Cube said.

"Cube! Where are you calling from?"

"No Name Key. It—"

"I know where it is. I will come and pick you up in an hour. I want very much to meet you."

"Uh, thanks. I—I need a favor. Someone I have to find in Mundania."

"Have no fear. Keep an eye out for our helicopter."

"Your what?"

But the woman had already hung up.

Cube returned the phone to Turn Key. "She says to keep an eye out in an hour for their he—hel—"

"Helicopter," Turn Key said. "Obviously she is eager to meet you. May I inquire the nature of your prior encounter?"

Cube decided it was safe to explain about the ghostly exchange. "So I was able to do her a favor," she concluded.

"A considerable one," he agreed. "No wonder she wants to meet you physically."

"I hope she can help me find Kim."

"I will give her the address, which I do have. She is, it seems, a rather wealthy woman. She should have no trouble."

"Yes, she lives in a mansion, and people work for her."

"And you have an hour to relax. I am glad it is going well. Let me show you around our station while you wait."

The hour passed swiftly. Then they were waiting outside the house. A huge noisy whirling machine came chugging through the air and landed on the lawn. A woman emerged.

Turn Key stared. "You did not exaggerate about her appearance! That is the most beautiful woman I have seen in a decade."

Then Silhouette spied Cube and came to her. "I am so glad to meet you in person, Cube! I owe you everything."

"All I did was—"

"I trust you have the number or address of your party?"

"Here," Turn Key said, giving her a piece of paper.

"Thank you so much." She gave him a kiss on the cheek. Then, leaving him stunned, she took Cube by the arm and led her to the whirling machine. "Phil is piloting it. You met his father."

"You did decide to—"

"You were right, Cube! He is the man for me. He is strong and capable and kind, and he loves me. I'm sure I will love him soon. I simply lacked the wit to orient on him. I was horribly foolish."

Cube was amazed at the change in Silhouette. She had been unable to assert herself; now she was assertiveness itself. "You have changed."

"Because of you, Cube! You showed me how to do it, and how well it worked. I explored my memory of that day—was it only yesterday?—and simply continued in that mode. All because of you! You completely changed my life. I'm still in euphoria."

A man stepped out of the machine. He looked like a younger version of Filip the gardener. "Welcome aboard, Cube!" he said.

They climbed into the machine, which was somewhat like a small house, and then it was airborne. Silhouette gave Philip the paper, and he piloted the the craft north and west while the two women talked. Again, time passed swiftly.

The helicopter landed on a bare paved space known as a parking lot. They got out and approached the house of the address. A woman came to the door. She was ordinary rather than pretty, which gave Cube secret relief; she liked Silhouette, but hated the extreme contrast between them. "Yes?"

Now was the time. "I am Cube, from Xanth. I must talk to Kim."

"I am she. The last time I visited Xanth, it was to serve jury duty. Has something else come up?"

Cube explained about the need for her talent of erasure. "So if you could possibly come with me—"

"I'll have to clear it with my husband Dug," Kim said. "And I'll have to take my son along, because I can't be sure how long I'll be. He'll love Xanth!"

She had a child. Somehow that possibility hadn't occurred to Cube. "These are my friends Silhouette and Philip. They have a helicopter to take us to No Name Key."

Kim was surprisingly amenable, and soon she had made

arrangements for Dug to hold the fort, and joined them in the helicopter, holding her three-year-old son. "This is Knut," she said, introducing him. "In Xanth, men generally have sons and women have daughters, as signaled by the first letters of their names, but we're in Mundania, so he's mine, a K."

"He's darling," Silhouette said, smiling at the boy. Her beauty smote him like an ocean wave, and he fell back against his mother, suddenly shy.

"We're thrilled with him," Kim said brightly. "We thought we couldn't have a child, but Nimby fixed that."

"Nimby?" Silhouette asked. Cube wondered too.

"He's a donkey-headed dragon who can assume man-form. He and Chlorine go around doing favors for folk. They live in the Nameless Castle, built on a cloud, floating over Xanth. That's about all I can say."

That was interesting. Cube got the impression that there was a good deal more that Kim could have said, but wasn't free to, like Cube with her Quest. She would have to learn more about this odd dragon.

"Here in Mundania," Silhouette said, "NIMBY stands for Not In My Back Yard."

"Yes," Kim agreed. "That's the idea. Who would want to be near a donkey-headed dragon?" She seemed amused. That made Cube wonder further. What was it about Nimby?

The dialogue went on to other things. Silhouette was eager to learn more about Xanth, as most of what she had experienced in Cube's body remained in Cube's memory, just as most of Cube's experience in Silhouette's body remained in Silhouette's memory. This physical visit to Mundania was strengthening memories that would otherwise have been fleeting. But mainly she was relieved and pleased to see how well Silhouette was doing. Her life really had been transformed.

They arrived at No Name Key as dusk was approaching from the east. They landed on the back lawn. "I haven't used this route before," Kim said. "But I know of it."

"Turn Key gave us your address," Cube said. "He knows of you too. There he is now."

They went to the picture inside the house. "This must be where we part company," Silhouette said with regret. "I'm so glad we got to meet, Cube. You truly have changed my life."

"Knut and I will be returning," Kim said.

"We will make arrangements to get you back to your home," Turn Key said.

"No need," Silhouette said. "Phil and I will wait."

"There's no need to inconvenience you," Kim said. "We can manage."

"I want to learn more of Xanth."

"Oh. Then thank you. It will certainly help."

Cube stepped through the painting, and found herself back on the empty key-shaped island. Kim and Knut appeared behind her. "Now I'll bring out Karia," Cube said.

Kim opened her mouth to speak—and stared in astonishment. So did Cube. For Silhouette had just appeared.

"Oh, I'm sorry," Silhouette said. "I just touched the picture, curious about its nature. I didn't mean to interfere. I'll go back."

"You're in Xanth!" Cube said.

"We didn't think you could cross," Kim said. "Usually only those who have been here before, or who have special dispensation, are able to cross."

"Well, I was in Xanth before," Silhouette said. "But not in my own body."

Kim exchanged a look with Cube. "It must count," she said. "Well, then, come on, Silhouette. We're glad to have you with us."

"I can explore Xanth personally?" Silhouette asked.

"So it seems," Cube said.

"Then let me tell Phil." She poked her head through the picture, but not the rest of her body. After a moment she withdrew it. "He understands. He'll wait."

"Then I think you'll have to ride in the pouch," Cube said. "I don't think Karia can handle three of us."

"Karia?" Silhouette asked.

"She's a winged centaur." Cube put her hand in the pouch,

and in a half a moment Karia had joined them. There was a quick round of introductions, and the usual warning about speaking the centaur's name.

Then Silhouette, Kim, and Knut made ready to enter the pouch. But Karia stopped them. "Weight is not a factor. If you can hold on, I can carry you. I think the little boy might like to see the sights."

"Oh, yes," Kim breathed.

So Silhouette mounted first, then Kim with Knut, then Cube at the rear. Karia flicked them all with her tail, making them so light they almost floated away. Then she took off.

"Ooooo!" Knut and Silhouette cried together, putting five O's into it. It was hard to tell who was more thrilled. They continued to be thrilled as they looked down at the pattern of Xanth.

"This is better than the helicopter," Silhouette said.

"Yeah," Knut agreed. The two were getting along well.

But evening arrived before they got to the site. "I will have to put down at an intermediate station," Karia said. "We'll resume travel in the morning."

"That's fine," Kim said. "All the more time in Xanth."

They landed at a campsite on an enchanted path. "This is safe," Cube told Silhouette. "But don't leave the marked area. There really are dragons out there, and other things."

"Dragon!" Knut cried joyfully.

Cube wrestled with her judgment and lost. She brought out Drek Dragon for a brief visit. Soon Knut was climbing all over him, and the dragon loved it. The perfume was almost too strong.

In the morning they resumed travel, the four of them on the centaur. This time a mischievous little cloud loomed near, darkening. "Oops, that's Fray," Karia said.

"Who?" Kim asked.

"Several years ago Fracto Cloud helped confine the invading storm, Gladys. He put her in the region of Air, and evidently tamed her, because now they have a baby cloud, Fray. She's only five years old and mischievous when she gets loose. Usually she'll back off when told."

"A cloud!" Silhouette exclaimed. "A cloud has sentience?"

"Oh, yes, in Xanth," Kim said. "Just about everything has some awareness and feeling, so you have to be careful what you say."

"Fascinating. And they have a child? Gladys must be a sexy lady cloud."

"Yes, in Xanth she became Hurricane Happy Bottom."

"Ugh!" the centaur said.

"She doesn't like puns," Cube explained.

"Oops. I suppose it is. I apologize."

Karia flew toward the cloud. "Fray!" she called. "Move aside!"

But the cloud moved ahead of them, blocking their way. "And sometimes she doesn't back off," Karia said grimly. "I'll have to fly around her." She veered to the side.

But the cloud moved to intercept her again, playing a game. Little jags of lightning zipped across her face.

"I can erase part of her if I have to," Kim said. "But I'll need my hands free."

"I'll take Knut," Silhouette said. Kim passed the boy forward, and Silhouette held him before her, standing on the centaur's mane. Then she caught on to another aspect. "How can you erase a cloud?"

"That's my talent," Kim explained. "If I can see it, I can erase it magically with a sweep of my hand. Normally I use it to eliminate obstacles in my path. I'll try to be careful not to hurt Fray, just brush her back a bit so we can pass." She moved her hand, and a swath of outlying vapor disappeared.

"Nice cloud," Knut said admiringly.

Fray reacted. A vague smile formed across her substance.

"Well well," Silhouette murmured. Then she smiled at the cloud. "Nice cloud," she echoed.

Fray turned pink and floated back. She was blushing! Because a truly beautiful woman had smiled at her. Cube wished she could do that. Maybe once she got beautiful herself . . .

Karia flew past the cloud without molestation. Knut and Silhouette waved as they passed. They were still hitting it off.

"That was a better way," Kim said. "The last thing I want to do is hurt a child."

Cube was nevertheless impressed with the bit of erasure she had seen. That was a dangerously powerful talent.

Karia glided down for a landing on the path, out of sight of its end. "I'll wait here," she said as they dismounted.

"Perhaps I should wait also," Silhouette said uncertainly.

"No, I think it's all right," Cube said. "I'll introduce you as a Mundane I know. That's all that needs to be said."

"Very well." Silhouette was still holding Knut's hand. He obviously liked her. It was yet another demonstration of the power of beauty. They walked together, following Cube and Kim.

They came to the end of the path, which was farther along than it had been the day before. There was Patxi, laboring diligently to clear brush by hand. It was obvious that his job was tedious, with his magic applying only when he had the path set. Cube had used the enchanted paths without ever thinking about their construction; that would never be the case again.

Patxi paused when he saw them. "Hello a third time," he said to Cube. "I don't believe I know your friends."

"This is Kim, who I hope will abate your curse," Cube said. "And this is Silhouette Mundane, with Kim's boy Knut."

The man nodded to Kim, then started to nod to Silhouette, and froze. He too was smitten by her beauty.

"Hello," Silhouette said, smiling. That made it worse.

"That's something," Kim murmured. "Usually a man has to see bra or panties to freak out. She does it fully clothed."

"Beauty does as beauty is," Cube agreed. "I'm so envious."

"Me too. But there are other things than beauty. After all, I managed to marry Dug." Then she got more serious. "Now what's the curse name?"

"Unthank," Cube said. "My idea is for you to erase the first two letters. Can you do that?"

"I'm not sure, but it's worth a try. With a computer, if you erase the name of a file, you lose that file. There are ways magic is similar to computing. Let's see what we can do." She smoothed a place on the path, then took a stick and wrote UNTHANK. "Is that it?"

"That's what the Princesses said," Cube agreed.

Kim brushed her hand across the first two letters, erasing them.

Nothing happened.

"I was afraid of that," Kim said. "You have to know how to address a spell."

"Maybe if we made it clearer that it relates to him," Cube said.

They went to the man, who was still gazing raptly at Silhouette. Cube put some dirt on her finger and wrote UNTHANK across his back. "This is your secret name," she said to him, though he seemed to be beyond hearing. "This is the word that enchants you." She felt a small shudder of power. "I think that connected."

Kim brushed away the first two letters, using her magic. It was a bit strong, and his shirt disappeared in that region too. But nothing else happened.

They looked at each other. "We need a better instruction manual," Cube said. Unfortunately magic seldom came with instructions. They were stumped.

Then Knut walked up to Patxi. "You made this nice path? Thank you."

And something dissipated around them, like a fire going out. Magic was fading.

"It worked!" Kim said. "We did it! We just didn't think to complete it. To thank him."

Patxi stirred and looked around. "It's gone!" he said. "The curse is gone."

"It's gone," Cube said. "Now you can retire."

"But this path isn't finished."

"You don't have to finish it. Your curse is no more."

"But it wouldn't be right to leave it incomplete. Folk might get lost."

Cube exchanged a look with Kim. Had they really abated the curse?

Then Silhouette stepped in. "This path was, in a manner, my salvation. I was here before, though you did not see me. I kissed you."

"Oh, I think I would remember if—"

"Like this." She kissed him.

Patxi reeled, almost falling. "That *was* you!" he exclaimed.

"In Cube's body," she agreed. "She saved my life. I think it would be nice if you completed this one path, so that it does go somewhere, as my life is doing now. It is symbolic. I would consider it a personal favor. Then you may retire if you wish to."

"I'll do that!" he agreed gladly.

She smiled at him, then turned away so that he could recover. She caught Knut's hand and walked back down the path. Her effort not to leave him stunned was not entirely successful, because her backside was as esthetic as her frontside, even fully clothed, but then she rounded a turn and was out of sight. Then he blinked, getting his eyeballs realigned, and returned to work, not even noticing Kim and Cube.

Cube was almost sick with longing for a figure like that. Would she really have one, after the Quest?

"Beauty has power," Kim said as if reading her thoughts. "But there are other things."

"For men?"

Kim shrugged. "Sometimes."

The thread led back the way Silhouette had gone. "I think we're done here," Cube said.

"Yes. It has been nice visiting, but Dug's waiting for me."

They rejoined Karia, finding Silhouette and Knut already mounted. The thread stopped there. They mounted too, and soon were flying south.

They landed at No Name Key and went to the picture. They saw Turn Key and Phil there, looking out.

"We will take you home," Silhouette said to Kim. "I hope we can be friends hereafter."

"Surely so," Kim said. "We've been to Xanth together."

Silhouette turned to Cube. "I owe you everything," she said. "I fear we'll never see each other again. I hope you finish your Quest and gain your desire." Then she embraced Cube and kissed her on the mouth.

Such was the power of her beauty that Cube, too, was stunned. By the time she recovered, Kim, Knut, and Silhouette were in the picture. They waved to her, then walked out of sight.

"Charming folk," Karia said.

"Yes." Cube felt as if she had just lost lifelong friends.

10

NIMBY

I believe I see the thread," Karia said.

Cube looked. There it was, proceeding to the edge of the key, and on across the surface of the water. "I can't walk on water!"

"But I can fly over it, and follow the line," Karia said. "That's no problem. I'm glad the landbound centaurs separated No Name from Centaur Isle; it would have been awkward for me otherwise."

"They separated it?"

"Originally they had bound it in with their main isle. But there was too much traffic through the portal. Once, I understand, an entire Mundane vehicle came through, with a Mundane family. The centaurs were courteous to them, but thereafter decided that this was not the sort of intrusion they preferred. So they cut it loose. That means that magic centaurs like myself are not barred."

"That is convenient," Cube agreed. "I don't know how I would have come here without your help."

"That's why I am on this Quest. Now you have been rather

busy, and had emotional experiences. Why don't you relax in the pouch while I follow the thread? I assure you I will notify you when your presence is required."

Cube remained slightly faint headed from the kiss. She had never had any romantic interest in women, yet that kiss had stunned her in much the way it had stunned Patxi. She needed to sort that out. "That would be nice," she agreed.

So Cube slid into the pouch, and Karia put it in her quiver. Cube was aware when she took off, then turned her thoughts inward. She had been in Silhouette's body, and used the power of that beauty herself, braced by her own gumption. Then she had met the woman, and seen how she affected others, including the old man and the young boy. Then she had experienced it herself. Beauty was power: that was all there was to it. The old man hadn't wanted to romance Silhouette, and neither had the young boy; it was merely a social effect. Now she understood that it worked on women too.

And that was the kind of power Cube craved for herself. She had seen it in action, and felt it. Now she wanted to wield it. And perhaps, once the Quest was done, she would.

Satisfied, she sank into sleep.

She woke when Karia landed. She slid herself out of the pouch. They were at one of the enchanted rest stops. She appreciated those twice as much as she had before meeting Patxi. "There is a problem?" she asked.

"Just that the thread seems to terminate here," the centaur replied. "So I thought it was time to stop for the night."

"The night! How long have I been sleeping?"

"All day. I flew across the strait separating Xanth from the keys, then across the Gold Coast and southern Xanth, past Lake OgreChobee, and within sight of Mount Pinatuba, as you can see." She gestured.

Cube looked. There in the sunset was a towering conical mountain. "Isn't that the bad-tempered one?"

"Yes. Once it blew its stack so hard that it cooled all

Xanth by one degree. We all hope it won't blow again. I understand it is very sensitive to disparaging remarks."

"As are so many inanimate things," Cube agreed. "Well, I will have no problem. I think it's a magnificent peak."

"As do I. Nevertheless, I hope the thread does not take us there."

"Agreed. Though I am curious where the thread *is* taking us. It seems to have a mind of its own."

"Yes. It is a most remarkable effect."

They picked pies for supper, washed up at the local stream, and settled in for the night.

Then someone came. It was a flying creature. In fact it turned out to be a winged mermaid, innocent of clothing like all her kind.

"Now that's interesting," Karia murmured. "Another complicated crossbreed, like me."

"Hello," the mermaid called, hovering outside the shelter. "Is everything all right?"

"Of course it is, thank you," Karia said. "This is an enchanted campsite."

"It is, but it still requires upkeep," the mermaid said. "That's my job: to check it regularly and make sure everything is in place. I am Nepherina."

"I am Karia Centaur. We are both winged monsters."

"Yes," Nepherina said, giggling.

"I am Cube," Cube said.

"I see you have four wings," Karia said. "Like a dragonfly."

"Yes, it enables me to hover or fly backwards. But your feathery wings are prettier."

"That depends on whether the viewer is an insect or a bird. Any style of wing is fine as long as it does the job."

"There is one thing," Nepherina said. "This is an enchanted site, so it is protected. But there may be danger close by."

"We can handle ordinary dangers," Cube said. "We can repel aggressive creatures."

"This is not that type. The stream derives from Mount Pinatuba, and it can be as mean tempered as the mountain. There is a great lake that formed in the cone after the last eruption, and we fear that one day that lake will burst out and inundate everything below. So please don't dally long if you go outside the protected perimeter. If the lake burst right then—"

"We understand," Cube said. "Thank you for the warning. We will stay clear of the base of the cone if we possibly can."

"That's good. Have a good night." The mermaid flew toward the river, and in a moment they heard a splash as she plunged into it.

"I wonder what she does with her wings in the water?" Karia mused. "They seem very delicate."

"They probably fold down behind her," Cube said. "Maybe she even flies in the water."

"If that lake let go and a torrent came down, she'd probably have to take to the air to escape."

"Which perhaps makes it safe for her to use that river," Cube said. "She is not bound to it."

"So she can tend to this campsite," Karia agreed. "Which in turn suggests that the threat is real. They wouldn't assign someone who could be washed away by the flood."

"I wonder how the enchantment protects against a flood."

"It must divert it. I hope."

On that slightly nervous note they slept. Cube had no trouble sleeping despite her long nap of the day. Maybe she had been affected to some extent by the time-stopping effect the others experienced, so hadn't really been sleeping long.

In the morning the thread resumed. It left the enchanted path and plunged into the thickest brush. "I can't go there," Karia said.

"You have been on duty a long time, and done a lot of flying. It's time for you to rest. Go in the pouch, and I'll tackle this. It probably won't last long."

The centaur nodded. "It was a fair flight yesterday, and my wings have not yet fully rested. I kept myself light, but it still requires energy for the forward motion. Don't hesitate to call me out if you need me again."

"I won't hesitate to bring any or all of you out if I need you," Cube agreed. "But since I'm not supposed to make my Quest obvious, I hope to travel by myself as much as I can, between emergencies."

"By all means." Karia put her forefoot to the pouch, and slid in.

Cube was on her own. She plunged into the thicket, forging determinedly onward. The brush caught at her body, trying to hinder her, but she kept going. Then she paused, distrusting a bush just ahead. It didn't look quite right. But she had to pass it to get past the brush.

"Well, let's test it," she murmured to herself. She conjured several nickelpedes. "Go check," she told them.

The bugs scuttled to the bush, and under it. In a moment three bad boys leaped out, exclaiming. The nickelpedes had gouged them in the pants, just below their BAD BOYS shirts. They fled and soon disappeared.

Just as she had suspected: that had been an am-bush. Her talent had broken it up, but common sense had been perhaps more important. She was able to make her talent work for her better than otherwise, by applying that sense.

She brushed by the bush, which was now harmless; it would take it a while to reset for the next victim. She passed a moderate cave, with a neatly printed label: COM. Suddenly something hurtled out from the dark hole: a plane, a bird, no, a bat. A very aggressive bat. It swooped at her, chittering.

"I'm not trying to invade your cave," she protested, ducking. "Just let me be, and I'll soon be far from it."

But the bat continued to attack. Finally she conjured a really big nickelpede and held it over her head, its claw waving menacingly. That made the bat keep its distance. But it did not give up; it circled, looking for an opening.

What made it so aggressive? Had she stepped on its child? She looked back at the cave, seeing nothing but the label.

Then she thought she heard Karia's groan. "A bat from the COM cave," she said. "Com-Bat. You like to fight."

"Aw, you figured it out," the bat chittered, disgusted. "Now where's the fun?"

"You can talk!"

"You figured that out too, genius?"

"I didn't know bats could talk human."

"Well, most can't, but we guardians of Mount 'Tuba are smarter than average as well as fiercer. My pal Pete's just as smart as I am, and he's a serpent. Likes to race."

Cube looked at the cave again. It was almost perfectly round, as if fitted for a snake whose torso was as thick as the height of a man. "Com-Pete," she said.

"Right. And if you think I'm bad, you should see him. He'd gulp you in one bite."

"I'll pass up that pleasure," she said.

"Aw, I thought if I kept you talking long enough, Pete'd wake from his nap and come out."

"Some other time, thanks all the same."

"You have a sarcastic streak. I like that."

"You're welcome." She plunged on, holding the nickel-pede aloft, and finally the combative bat left off, maybe getting too far from its cave. It was probably hard to be aggressive when half of your nature was out of sight.

Now she came to a small but deep and rushing stream. It was probably another section of the mean-tempered river the winged mermaid Nepherina had warned them about, that flowed from the lake that stopped up Mount Pinatuba. She would have to be careful of it.

The thread went right across the stream. The footing on the banks seemed good, so Cube made a good jump across.

Too good. Her effort caused the pouch to be dislodged from her waistband. She grabbed for it, but missed, and it fell into the water as she landed on the far bank. She turned around and threw herself down, reaching for it, but it was already being carried away by the swift current.

Cube scrambled to her feet and along the bank, trying to get in position to catch the pouch. But the thick brush held her back, and she couldn't quite keep pace. What a situation! She had to recover that pouch.

Then she saw something worse ahead. The river disappeared. It sucked down into the ground, looking like a reverse-flowing spring. The pouch was circling, descending into the small whirlpool. Cube flung herself down, making a final desperate grab. Her hand splashed in the chill water, but didn't catch the pouch. It vanished into the ground.

Cube sat there, for the moment stunned by the enormity of the disaster. She had lost the pouch! All her Companions were there. She couldn't summon any of them to help, because they were completely out of reach.

She thought about crying. But she was not the crying type. She knew she had fouled up. She might have forfeited her Quest by this blunder. But worse, she had put all her friends into oblivion. They could not get out unless she brought them out. Their fate was her fault.

She sat with her head in her hands, suffering for a good three moments. Then she summoned her gumption. What could she do? There had to be something.

Maybe the stream emerged from the ground farther along, and would carry the pouch there, so she could recover it. But if so, where? She had no idea. Karia might have carried her high enough so she could see where, but Karia was in the pouch. And even if the stream did emerge, there was no guarantee that the pouch would be with it; it could get stuck anywhere below, or simply sink to the bottom of some unknown and inaccessible underground pool.

Cube realized that she was not competent to recover the pouch by herself. She needed help. But who could—or would—help her, when she wasn't supposed to let the nature of her Quest be generally known? No one, she feared.

But there had to be something. She couldn't just give up. So she made her way back to where she had crossed the stream—and saw the thread, leading on. The thread didn't know she had lost the pouch! What point to follow it now?

Or *did* it? It had seemed remarkably savvy so far, even when it had led her to seemingly irrelevant places, like Mundania. Was it possible that it still had something for her?

Well, there was one way to find out. She would follow it.

If it didn't lead anywhere, what would she lose? No more than she already had. And if by chance it took her to someone who could help, then maybe she could salvage this Quest after all.

She followed the thread around and about, o'er hill and dale, avoiding dragons, pitfalls, and tangle trees. As it skirted a village she saw a man wandering somewhat uncertainly, as if lost. She knew the feeling, so she paused, leaving the thread briefly to check on him. If he turned out to be a bad man, well, a few nickelpedes would distract him.

"Hello," she said. "You look confused."

"I am," he said. "My name is Bruce, and my talent is finger writing in stone."

"I'm Cube, and I can summon nickelpedes. You write in stone?"

"Yes." He demonstrated by lifting a rock and using one finger to make a smiley-face. The surface seemed to be like malleable clay. Then he handed it to her.

Cube touched the stone, expecting it to be soft, but it was rock-hard. "That's impressive. What's confusing?"

"That is just about all I remember. I don't know how I got here, or where I'm going."

Oh. "Did something happen to you?"

"I don't know," Bruce said. "I just suddenly found myself walking here."

"Maybe you live in that village."

"Maybe. I don't remember."

This was curious. "Maybe we can retrace your steps, and find out where it happened, whatever it was."

He turned around. "See, there are my footprints in the dirt."

They followed the prints back along the trail. In the distance Cube saw another person coming from the same direction. This was a young woman, small, dark-haired, and cute. Naturally she was cute; just about every woman Cube encountered looked much better than Cube did.

Then the woman paused, looking confused. Cube saw that Bruce's footprints hesitated there too; they had been going straight, then wavered as if the maker was distracted. Cube and Bruce paused as the woman came hesitantly up to them.

"Hello," the woman said. Her hair closed in under her chin, wreathing her cute face. "I am Angela, and my talent is conjuring Mundane objects. Do you happen to know why I am here?"

"We are Cube and Bruce," Cube said. "With talents of summoning nickelpedes and writing in stone. Bruce doesn't know why he is here either."

"Maybe you live in that village," Bruce suggested.

"I don't remember."

Then Cube caught on. "A forget whorl!" she said. "There must be one there, and you both walked through it. It took most of your memories, except what is most important: your names and talents."

The two looked at each other. "That must be it," Bruce said. "Maybe we do live at the village, because we were walking toward it."

"Maybe people there will know us," Angela said.

"Maybe we know each other," Bruce said, reacting to her the way men tended to in the presence of cute girls.

"You do now," Cube said. "Why don't you walk on to that village and inquire? And warn them of the forget whorl on the trail, so others don't pass through it. It must have drifted there today."

"All right," Angela said. "Thank you for your insight, Cube; that must be what happened."

"I know what it is like to feel lost," Cube said sincerely.

"Still, we'd like to thank you," Bruce said. "Here is a name stone for you." He picked up a small flat chip of stone and finger painted CUBE on it. He gave it to her.

"And here is a Mundane purse," Angela said as one appeared in her hand. "Since I see you don't have one." She glanced at it. "I think this is from the Philippines, home crafted." She presented it to Cube.

"Uh, thank you both," Cube said, not wanting to admit that she had no idea what part of Mundania that might be. "I don't suppose you want some nickelpedes?"

Both shook their heads no, laughing. Then they walked on toward the village, holding hands.

Cube considered the gifts, then put the name stone in the purse and tucked the purse in her waistband where the pouch had been. She would try not to lose this one.

She returned to the thread and began to follow it. Then she stopped. The thread led right to the forget whorl!

She sat on a small boulder, feeling perplexed, then frightened, then angry. If she had followed the thread any farther, she would have lost all memory of her mission, remembering only her name and talent. Then she would have been completely unable to rescue her Companions in the pouch, or to complete her Quest. That thread had tried to wipe her out—and in such a way that no one else would know what happened. They might think she had wandered into a tangle tree and gotten eaten, or perhaps simply given up and gone home.

But the Princesses would never have set it up to do anything like that, and not just because it would cost them perpetual imprisonment in the pouch. So what had happened?

The Demoness Fornax, who didn't want Counter Xanth to be colonized: this could be her mischief. A series of seeming accidents that stopped the Quest. She must have jogged the pouch loose, so that it would be lost, then changed the thread to make Cube forget her mission. What a dastardly deed!

Well, if that was the way it was, Cube would just have to rescue her friends and complete her mission anyway. But how? She had avoided one trap, but still lost her Companions. What could she possibly do alone?

But if she was so helpless, why had the Demoness bothered to set another trap for her? There must be something she could do. Like return to the Good Magician and tell him what happened. Then he would send someone else on the Quest, trying to get it done, and maybe have a way to locate the lost pouch, so that it could be recovered and Cube could let the others out. So Fornax had tried to prevent that too.

She could hardly be faulted for being balked by a Demoness. Still, it galled Cube to fail. She wanted to succeed, and to become beautiful, and win Ryver for her man. Failure, even with her memory intact, would leave her as she was now: a woman no man noticed with favor, if at all. She had started out well enough, gathering her Companions, and must have been on the way to success, because otherwise the Demoness would not have bothered to interfere.

So was there any way to prevail despite the loss of the pouch? Yet if there was, she wouldn't want to do it while her Companions remained in limbo. First she had to rescue them, even at the expense of the Quest. She would rather save them than be beautiful, if that was her choice.

It was pretty clear that she wasn't able to save them on her own. She had to have help. But what help could there be, that wouldn't mess up the Quest by exposing its nature?

Then it came to her: What about that mysterious couple Kim Mundane had mentioned, Nimby and Chlorine? The donkey-headed dragon and the beautiful woman, who liked to do favors? Maybe they would do Cube a favor. At least she could ask.

They lived in the Nameless Castle, floating on a cloud. What a weird place for a castle! But some folk had weird tastes. It did suggest that they had more than incidental powers of magic. Maybe not Magician or Sorceress level, but maybe enough to enable her to find and recover the pouch. Then she would be able to carry on, on her own. With luck they wouldn't tell anyone else about her Quest. How could she get to that castle?

She stared at the sky—and saw a cloud. Something sparkled above it, like light glinting from a shiny turret. Could that be it? The cloud seemed to be moving slowly toward the tall cone of Mount Pinatuba. It might even touch that peak before it moved on.

If she could just get up there before the cloud passed, she might be able to jump onto that cloud and reach the castle. It was a long shot, but what else was there?

She ran back toward Mount Pinatuba, but quickly realized that she did not have a hope of the ghost of a chance to reach it in time, because of the thickets at its base, and as for climbing it—parts of its cone were sheer smooth rock, too steep to climb. She had to have help just to get up it, let alone in time.

What to do? She was desperate. She knew that no ordinary expedient would do, like locating climbing boots or circling the mountain to find a better route. If only she could bring Karia centaur out! But of course if she could do that, she wouldn't need to make that climb.

What could make it up that mountain in a hurry? Goaded by that question, she looked around her with a new awareness—and spied a hole in the base of the mountain. Com-Bat's cave!

Did she dare? She had to. If she could speak their language, she might make a deal. She put her hands to her mouth, forming a magic funnel, and yelled through it. "Hey, Com-Bat, you handsome rascal! Come here, and bring Pete."

In a moment she saw the small flying figure. "What the #### are you up to, you moronic idiot?" he chittered. "You trying to wake my friend?"

"That's what I'm trying to do, you winged chit." She put her cupped hands up again. "Hey Pete! I've got a deal for you!"

"You're crazy! You can't outrun Pete. He's the fastest thing in the thicket."

"That's what I'm counting on. Does he talk the way you do?"

"No, he can't chitter. But he understands."

"Then you can translate for me."

"What, after he's eaten you?"

"Tell him to listen to me first."

"You're almost as nervy as you are crazy!"

"Thanks." She raised her hands a third time. **"PETE!"**

In no more than a moment and a half there was a faint shudder in the ground, as if something heavy were approaching. Then the huge head of the serpent appeared. The mouth opened and a horrendous hiss issued, like steam from a mountain vent.

"I tried to stop her, Pete!" the bat chittered. "Honest! I tried to protect your sleep."

Cube was terrified. Therefore she performed as if nerveless. "You don't want to eat me, Pete," Cube said. "I'm not pretty enough to taste good; you can see that. You want to hear my deal."

The huge serpent gazed at her with the sort of look she had seen before: part amazement, part dawning respect. He hissed.

"He says this better be good, human," the bat chittered.

She knew it. "I need to get up that mountain in a hurry. Before that cloud gets there."

If there had been doubt that the serpent understood her, it would have faded as Pete turned his head to view the cloud, then the mountain. There was a hiss.

"Pete says he can make it," the bat chittered. "What's your deal?"

"My talent is summoning nickelpedes. You've seen it, Bat. I'll summon some to go after the nits and lice and things that bother every big creature. Life will be more comfortable then."

"He'd like that," the bat chittered. "But what's in it for me, for translating?"

"Some to keep you company in the cave, too, if you like. They're not tame, but if I tell them to treat a person or creature well, they will."

Pete hissed. "I travel a lot; I can't carry them with me," the bat chittered for him.

"Yes you can. You can carry them in a purse in your mouth, and let them out when you're ready for them." She brought out the Mundane purse Angela had given her; this was a good use for it. "And here are the nickelpedes." They were clustering by her feet. She picked up five. "Go with Pete, here, and tackle his vermin when he wants you to. Meanwhile, stay in this purse." They obediently climbed into the purse, and Cube held it up for the serpent. "Try them out, if you wish."

"No, he felt your magic," the bat chittered. "He knows they'll do it."

The serpent took the purse between his teeth, surprisingly delicately. His long tongue came out, wrapped around the purse, and hauled it into his cheek.

"You'll have to take me to the cave, so I can leave some for you," Cube told the bat.

Pete hissed. "Get on," Com-Bat chittered.

Cube approached the huge body. She jumped, sprawling across it, then scrambled to get astride. "I'm not sure how I'll hold on," she said.

"Hold on to the skin," the bat chittered.

She tried, and found there was a halfway loose patch before her. She caught a double handful of it.

Then Pete moved. One moment he was still, the next sliding through the brush with astonishing velocity. Cube had to draw up her legs to avoid getting scraped by the branches. In barely three quarters of a moment they were at the cave.

She dismounted and summoned several more nickel-pedes. "This is Com-Bat," she told them. "He is your associate. Help him guard the cave, and do not bother him or the serpent." They waved their claws, capable of gouging out nickel-sized disks of flesh, and scuttled into the cave.

Pete hissed. "Get aboard," the bat chittered. "That cloud is getting close."

Cube looked up and saw that the cloud was almost to the cone. That was too close; could they make it? She scrambled onto the serpent's back and grabbed skin.

"This way," Com-Bat chittered, flying ahead. Pete slithered after him, forging through the thicket, then up the steep slope of the mountain.

Cube hung on. She had a good hold, but now the serpent was really moving, and his undulations flung her from side to side. They were traveling *up*, and this made her handhold the only secure contact. She clutched it desperately.

The mountain shuddered. Pinatuba was aware of them, and not pleased. Of course nothing pleased this mountain, but this made her nervous. Suppose it decided to throw them off?

"You know us!" the bat chittered at the mountain. "Com-Bat and Com-Pete! We are coming to admire your peak."

The shuddering eased. Pinatuba was satisfied that these weren't intruders. Did it know about Cube? How would it react if it caught on? She had heard that it was a pretty ornery mountain.

The climb became steeper. How could the serpent stay on without sliding down? She was virtually hanging by her hands. She saw into the sky, and the cloud was already touching the top of the mountain. Were they too late?

"Here!" the bat chittered. The serpent followed him into a vertical crevasse in the side of the mountain, wedged his sides against the sides of the crevasse, and powered on upward. Now they *were* traveling straight up, and Cube *was* hanging. She felt her grip slowly slipping.

Then they emerged at the top—and there was the interior of the crater, filled with water. Cube had forgotten about that; Nepherina had explained about the cone filling with water, and the stream originating from that. This was a huge lake.

On the far side of the crater, the cloud was just passing the rim. They were too late!

But Pete launched from the rim and dived into the lake. Horrified, Cube hung on; she knew she'd drown if she lost her grip. The water surged around them, tearing at her body. She tried to scream, but water filled her mouth.

Then the serpent rose to the surface, and was undulating smoothly across the lake. Cube choked and coughed, clearing her lungs. Was the cloud still there? She couldn't tell; her eyes were too teary.

Pete reached the far side and slithered up the rim. He crested it and stopped at last. Cube looked, blinking.

There was the cloud, just below, moving away from the peak. It was the right one; she saw the castle on it. "Thank you, boys!" she cried, and flung herself off the peak.

For two instants she fell through the air. Then she landed on the rear fringe of the cloud, and bounced. She was falling off the edge! She reached out, and her fingers caught fluff. She grabbed handfuls, swinging in closer, and in a moment was buried in cloud stuff. She scrambled up, and soon lay panting on the surface. She had made it.

She sat up, facing toward the mountain. There were the serpent and bat, poised at the rim. She waved. "Thanks," she repeated. The serpent flicked his tail, then slithered over the rim and out of sight inside the cone.

"Hello, Cube."

Cube jumped, but managed to stay on the cloud. There was a lovely woman with greenish-yellow hair and perfectly fitting blue dress standing behind her. "Who—?" she asked somewhat stupidly.

"I am Chlorine," the woman said. Naturally her voice was dulcet. She made Cube seem absolutely drab in comparison. "You seem to have made some effort to reach us. Now you can make your case to Nimby."

"Nimby," Cube agreed blankly. "I—"

"Of course. This way, please." Chlorine led the way toward the castle. It wasn't far, because this was not a large cloud.

Cube looked down at herself. Her clothing was a grimy mess, and her face and hair were surely no better. "But I'm not—"

"Yes you are," Chlorine said. And suddenly Cube was exquisitely garbed in a sparkling red gown that strove valiantly to make even her dull body esthetic. She felt clean, and her hair was fresh and fluffy.

"Uh, thank you," she said, not questioning her condition further. It was evident that these folk did have magic, plenty of it.

They came to the moat. Cube didn't make the effort to question how a water-filled moat could be on the top of a cloud. Obviously it could be, at least in this instance.

She gazed into the water and saw her reflection. Her dress was lovely, of course, and she wore a matching tiara. If only her face weren't so plain, and her body so dull. Chlorine's dress enhanced her notable curves, while Cube's dress lacked anything to work with.

"Before we meet Nimby," Chlorine said, "let me tell you something about him. I presume you don't know his nature."

"I don't," Cube agreed, embarrassed. "I met a Mundane woman, Kim, and she mentioned you and Nimby, saying that you liked to go around doing favors. I need a favor really badly, so—"

"Of course. Nimby is a donkey-headed dragon who has the power to make himself or his companion be anything that companion wants. When I first met him I was, well, like this." Suddenly a rather dull and bitter-looking woman stood there, and the dress hung on her awkwardly. Cube remembered Fluorine, who had said she was Chlorine's sister. That seemed likely. Then the original woman returned, filling the dress with deserved pride. "And my talent was poisoning water," Chlorine continued. "So you can understand that when I say I appreciate your situation, I truly do. I asked Nimby to make me beautiful, and he did. I asked him to make me smart, and he did. When I was smart I had much better ideas for self-improvement, and became a better person in every way I could think of. Later I married Nimby—"

"You married a dragon?" Cube had thought it was a prince, or something similar.

Chlorine smiled. "I asked him to make himself into a princely handsome man, and he did. But I still rather liked the ugly form he had first had, so usually he remains that way. Appearance isn't everything."

"But it's a lot," Cube said somewhat bitterly.

"Yes. Which is why I prefer to keep my enhanced form. But I don't require it of Nimby, and he doesn't require it of me. Sometimes we, well, relate when he is handsome and I am my old way, just for the variety. We know each other, you see, so it makes less difference. Once you have it, you don't need it as much."

"Could he make me beautiful?"

"He could. But that would interfere with your Quest."

Cube realized it was true. She was good for the Quest because no one noticed her. If she looked like Silhouette or Chlorine, everyone would notice her, women included. Also, assuming that Nimby would help her once, she could not take the aid for herself while her Companions were lost. Anyway, the Good Magician had already promised her beauty when she completed the Quest. "Yes, I must complete my Quest."

"Nimby doesn't talk," Chlorine continued. "But he understands, the way many animals do."

"Yes, a big serpent helped me get up the mountain so I could catch this cloud. He could not talk human, but he understood, so we were able to deal."

"We saw. You really struggled to reach us."

"Yes. I'm desperate."

"Nimby will help, I'm sure. Just explain to him what favor you want, and if he is inclined, he will grant it. If he has a question, I will ask it. I understand him."

"That's wonderful," Cube said gladly. "I don't know what I would do otherwise."

"You may find Nimby somewhat strange, but don't be concerned. He will not hurt you."

"I know dragons can be friends," Cube agreed. "When you get to know them."

"Exactly. You can trust him. Tell him anything you think he might need to know. Now we shall meet him." Chlorine led the way to the small drawbridge, and they crossed.

The castle was huge. Cube was amazed that such a massive edifice could perch on so small a cloud without sinking it. There was chamber after chamber inside; this building could house an army if it wanted to. How had it come to be used for just a woman and a dragon? Was this another situation like that of Castle MaiDragon, with caretakers? That seemed to make the most sense.

They came to the main reception chamber. Just then there was the sound of a child's cry. "Oh, that's Nimbus," Chlorine said. "He's gotten into trouble again. I must fetch him.

Just go on in; Nimby is expecting you." She hurried away, and in a moment turned a corner and was gone.

Cube entered the chamber. There was Nimby—and he was indeed strange. He was a dragon ass, with a donkey head and a dragon body striped diagonally with pastel pink and bilious green. He was big enough to be dangerous, but that stupid head and coloration made him seem laughable. She was glad Chlorine had warned her; she would not have wanted to offend Nimby by her initial reaction.

"Uh, hello," she said. "I'm Cube. Chlorine told me to tell you my situation. I have a favor to ask."

The dragon gazed at her. When their eyes met, she suffered sudden vertigo. It seemed as if she were falling into a whirlpool, spinning around, and seeing everything and nothing all at once. It also felt as if Nimby had drawn out half her soul. This was no ordinary dragon!

Then things stabilized. Their eye contact had broken, and she was not eager to renew it. So she plunged in. "I am on a—a Quest for the Good Magician Humfrey. I have nine Companions. They are in a pouch the Magician gave me, and I lost the pouch. I—"

Suddenly the enormity of her problem overcame her, choking off her words. Cube had not really allowed herself to consider it before, being intent on doing something about it. But now that she was telling it, it overcame her.

Chlorine entered the room, leading a three-year-old boy by the hand. That was evidently Nimbus, who would be her son. She took in the situation at a glance. "What do you need, Cube?"

"The pouch," Cube said. "I lost it. I—" She choked off again.

Nimby wiggled an ear. "Let's go for a ride," Chlorine said.

The little boy charged the dragon and scrambled onto his back. Chlorine followed more sedately, leading Cube. There was a saddle Cube hadn't seen before; in fact there were three of them, lined up along the dragon's back. Nimbus took the first, Chlorine the second, and Cube the third.

Nimby moved. He walked through the wall, which seemed illusory. Cube reached out to touch it as she passed—and it was solid. So the dragon could walk through walls as well as grant favors. What else could he do? Cube's surprise was building into awe.

They emerged on the surface of the cloud. Then Nimby spread his small wings, which Cube also hadn't noticed before; it was as if they had simply sprouted when needed. He lurched off the edge of the cloud and sailed through the air, spiraling grandly down toward the forest below.

"Nimbus loves to ride," Chlorine said conversationally, as if this were routine—as perhaps it was, for them. "Any excuse will do."

They glided toward Mount Pinatuba. The mountain reacted, sending up a warning puff of steam. How it did that with a water-filled crater Cube wasn't sure. Nimby turned his donkey head and glanced at the mountain—and the steam dissipated and was no more. It was almost as if the silly-looking dragon had cowed the terrible mountain, surely not the case. *Nothing* cowed Pinatuba. Maybe they were friends, as was the case with Com-Pete the serpent.

They circled the mountain and found the stream that coursed down its slope. How did Nimby know where to go? Cube hadn't told him where she lost the pouch. Maybe he had gotten it from her when their eyes met. Chlorine had rather understated the case when she said Nimby was strange. Cube had never heard of a dragon with the odd powers this one was demonstrating. The ability to make a person beautiful; to grant favors; to walk through solid walls; to fathom folk by a glance; to find a lost pouch. Maybe even to make an ornery mountain back off.

They came in for a landing in the thick forest. "Look out!" Cube cried as the dragon was about to crash into a tree. But then they passed through the tree, and others beyond it, and came to the ground below. The boy was chortling. Oh—that phasing through solids ability, again.

"Nimby always does that," Chlorine explained. "Nimbus likes to crash."

They did not land on the ground. They sank into it. In most of a moment they were gliding under the ground as if it were so much fog. Yet Cube was sure that if she reached out, she would feel its solidity. This time she did not reach.

Finally the dragon came to rest in what seemed to be a glowing cave. Nimbus jumped off and ran around it, picking pieces of glow fungus from the wall. "Don't bother with that," Chlorine called to him. "Fetch the lady's pouch."

The boy veered to a glowing river that, as usual, Cube hadn't noticed before. He plunged a hand into it, fished around for half a moment, and pulled out—the pouch. He shook it off, and brought it to Cube.

"Thank you, Nimbus," she said, unable to think of anything else. It was plainly the right one. Just like that, she had it back!

The boy remounted, and they moved through the ground again. They looped around and came to the surface. "This I think is where you get off," Chlorine said. "It has been a pleasure. We wish you well."

"Uh, thanks," Cube said as she got down. "I—"

But the dragon was already moving away, and then was gone. She was standing alone beside the stream, exactly where she had been when she lost the pouch.

There was nothing to do but go on. She jumped over the stream again, this time holding the pouch firmly in her hand.

She saw the thread, as before. But she didn't trust it. It had tried to lead her into a forget whorl. She had better consult with the others, and catch them up on what had happened.

She paused at a reasonably open glade and put her hand in the pouch. "Everyone," she said.

Hands grabbed all of her fingers. They all slid out, landing in a circle around her. Metria was the first to catch her balance. "This must be some stretch," she said.

"Some what?" Ryver asked.

"Reach, length, range, extent, scope—"

"Extremity?" Karia asked.

"Whatever!" the three Princesses said together, laughing as they tried unsuccessfully to make cross faces.

"I have a problem with the thread," Cube said. "And that's hardly the beginning."

Diamond Dog and Drek Dragon sniffed the thread. There was a bad smell.

"It has gone bad," Cory said. "They can tell, and so can we." Tessa nodded.

The three Princesses inspected it. "There's that magic again," Melody said.

"The magic we saw at Castle MaiDragon," Harmony agreed.

"Demoness Fornax," Rhythm concluded.

"You caught on then?" Karia asked them. "Why didn't you say something?"

"We didn't want to worry you," Melody said.

"Or anyone else," Harmony agreed.

"And Mother might not have let us go on the Quest," Rhythm concluded.

That was surely the real reason, Cube thought. "Can you fix it?"

"Sure," the three said together. They sang and played and beat, and the thread quivered, vanished, and reappeared.

"Why did you summon all of us?" Karia asked. "Instead of just the Princesses?"

"It's a long story, but you had better hear it," Cube said. She launched into it, telling of her loss of the pouch, her trip to the Nameless Castle, and Nimby's rescue of the purse. "So you see, I almost got all of you into serious trouble," she concluded. "You may want to reconsider whether you want to continue with this Quest."

"One question," Karia said. "Did it occur to you that you could have summoned the Princesses, gotten the thread fixed, and continued on the mission without saying anything about the intervening loss of the pouch?"

"No, I never thought of that. It wouldn't have been honest."

A glance circled around the group.

"Two questions," Ryver said. "Did you think of giving

up the Quest and going home, instead of struggling to recover it?"

"No, I just couldn't do that."

A second glance circulated.

"Three questions," Melody said.

"Do you know who Nimby really is?" Harmony asked.

"Or why he helped you?" Rhythm concluded.

"No, though I think he is more than he appears to be. I'm really very curious."

A third glance went around.

"I think we are agreed that we wish to continue with the Quest," the centaur said, and the others nodded.

Just like that? "What's so significant about these questions?" Cube asked.

"The first shows your integrity," Karia said.

"But it's the only way I know." Actually she had lied to Yorick in Mundania, but that was following a script while dealing with an unscrupulous man. On her own, truth was best.

"Precisely," the centaur said. "We like that, and know we can trust you."

"The second shows your determination and courage," Ryver said.

"Well, I always had gumption; that's just the way I am." But she certainly hadn't felt very brave during the crisis.

"Precisely," he agreed. "If you had been some other way, we would still be underground."

"The third shows that you found the right course when you were on your own, despite the bad thread," Melody said, seeming unusually adult for her age.

"By remembering Nimby, and the Nameless Castle, and figuring out how to get there," Harmony agreed, just as seriously.

"And without knowing that Nimby is actually the Demon Xanth," Rhythm concluded.

"Who?" Cube asked, astonished.

"And of course the Demon Xanth does not like having the Demoness Fornax poking around his territory," Tessa said.

"Demons don't," Metria agreed. "I should know, having irritated countless demons. Capital D Demons are worse."

"You told him something he wanted to know," Cory added. "So of course he helped you. And I suspect there will be no more interference from Fornax, for each Demon is supreme in his own territory."

"The Demon Xanth?" Cube asked, grasping a thin straw of understanding. Now that weird power of the dragon gaze was becoming intelligible, and the manner he did things.

"He knew you didn't know," Karia said. "He doesn't do favors for folk who know."

"I—I—" But Cube couldn't formulate any coherent thought.

"Put us back in the pouch and continue the Quest," Ryver said.

"But—" Cube paused and tried again, this time getting it out. "But all of you shouldn't go in. I might lose it again."

"Keep Diamond out," Metria suggested.

"And you," Cube said. "Because you could catch it if it fell into another stream."

The demoness shrugged, her shoulders and bosom rising off her body, then settling back. "This Quest does seem to be getting interesting enough to be worth my attention." She faded out.

"Very well," Cube agreed, enormously relieved and flattered. "If that's the way the rest of you feel." She held out the pouch.

"We do," Karia said, sliding into it. Then the others did the same, until only Ryver was left. "You're a lot of woman," he said as he approached.

"But not beautiful," Cube said ruefully.

"Not yet," he agreed, and slid into the pouch.

Oddly exhilarated, Cube turned to the dog. "Are you ready to continue?" she asked.

Diamond wagged her tail.

11

MOONING

They followed the revived thread onward. Soon it diverged from the route the prior thread had taken, and Cube was glad to see it. It picked up an enchanted path, which she was especially glad to see, and went northeast.

It was late in the day, so she stopped at a convenient camp. Diamond was good company, but that made her wonder. "You're a Mundane dog," Cube said. "You shouldn't have to wander around Xanth indefinitely. In time my Quest will be over, one way or another, and I'll go home or get into romance, depending. You need to find someone who needs a dog like you permanently."

Diamond wagged her tail sadly. She knew.

As usual, someone else came to spend the night at the same camp. Cube realized that though the paths might not seem crowded, there were only so many camps, so that was where travelers were most likely to meet. This was a nondescript woman, somewhat dusty and tired from a day of walking.

"Hi, I'm Brenn," she said. "My talent is to change into a brick wall, but since this camp is convenient, I won't bother tonight."

"I am Cube. I can summon and control nickelpedes, but I never do it mischievously. This is Diamond."

"That's good." Brenn patted the dog. "Where are you going?"

Cube hesitated. She didn't know where she was going; she was following the thread. She didn't want to say that, because it would suggest her Quest. Yet it was a reasonable question.

"What have we here?" a voice inquired as a small black cloud formed between them. "A gold brick?" The cloud became a shining yellow brick, still floating.

"What are you?" Brenn demanded.

The brick expanded into human form. "Demoness Metria, not at your service. I'm keeping an eye on Cube so she doesn't get lost."

Cube realized that Metria had been doing exactly that, and appeared in time to distract Brenn from her question. She appreciated that. "Thank you, Metria. I was just talking with Brenn, here, before we settle for the night."

"Don't settle yet. There's another mortal coming."

And there was: another young woman, who of course looked significantly better than Cube. "Hello, I'm Kelsey," she said. As she spoke, her hair seemed to change color.

The other two introduced themselves, and so did Metria. "A demoness?" Kelsey asked, surprised. Her hair turned purple.

"She's watching over Cube," Brenn said.

"But demons don't care about mortal people."

"Of course I don't care," Metria said. "But I promised someone I'd see her safely home, so I'm doing it. What is with your hair?"

"Oh, that." Kelsey hair turned light blue. "That's my magic. My hair changes color with my emotions. I can't control it; it just happens."

"It's lovely," Brenn said.

Kelsey's hair turned deep red, blushing. "It's embarrassing," she said.

"Another coming," the demoness announced.

It was another young woman. "Hello. Is there room for one more?"

"I think so," Cube said, smiling.

They went through another round of introductions. The new one was Seren, who didn't know whether she had a magic talent, but was disgusted with her name.

"What's wrong with it?" Brenn asked. "It seems nice."

"My last name is Ity. People always say it as one word: Serenity. Then they pretend they are being very serene."

"That's doesn't seem too bad," Kelsey said.

"And my middle name is Dip. I tried to get it changed, but it's locked in."

"Serendipity," Cube said.

"Yes. Others find that funny, but I don't."

"But that could relate to your talent," Cube said. "Do you find things?"

"Sure, all the time, but never what I'm looking for. For example I was looking for a camp with several attentive handsome men."

"Instead you found us!" Kelsey laughed, her hair flickering yellow.

"Yes. I'm sure you're nice people, but—"

"How old are you?" Brenn asked.

"Fourteen, I think. I was a foundling, about two when found in a cabbage patch."

"That's why," Cube said. "You aren't old enough to join the Adult Conspiracy. Those men would have betrayed it. So you found something else."

"If that's my magic, I don't like it."

Metria appeared. "If you're a foundling, how do you know your name?"

"It was on the only thing I had, a broken pacifier." She held it up. Sure enough, on it was printed SEREN DIP ITY.

"I wouldn't mind having a talent like that," Cube said. "Mine is summoning nickelpedes."

The girl looked at her. "That's not very feminine."

"Exactly. It's useful when I encounter a wild beast, but I'd rather have some other talent."

"Will, if mine is finding things I'm not looking for, I'd gladly trade it for yours."

"Too bad talents can't be traded," Kelsey said.

"Or names," Brenn said.

Cube got the hint of a weird idea. "I wonder. Maybe the talent is associated with your possession."

"The pacifier? I've tried to get rid of it, but it always comes back."

Cube's idea got weirder. "I have something like that." She brought out the mirror. "I have tried to give this away several times, but it returns. Let's see if we can trade."

"All right. I wasn't looking for a mirror, but I wouldn't mind seeing my face when I do my hair."

They traded items. Cube put the pacifier in a pocket, wondering how long it would stay there. "About the mirror—"

"What is this?" Seren demanded.

"It's a rear-view mirror," Cube explained. "What you weren't looking for."

"Actually this is okay," the girl said, admiring her rear, which was a pert one.

"Let's see how long we can keep each other's things," Cube said. "They may both be magic, and will probably revert soon."

"Okay."

But the two objects did not revert that evening. In the morning Cube still had the pacifier, and Seren still had the mirror. "Maybe they can't be given away, but can be exchanged," Cube said. "If your talent really is connected, you won't find what you aren't looking for while you have the mirror."

"Does that mean I'll lose the name?"

"Maybe. I don't know how these things work."

"What else could I call myself?"

"Mirror," Kelsey suggested, her hair turning green.

"Mirror. I like it," the girl said.

They went their separate ways. Cube wondered whether her wild idea could be right: that the name and talent went with the pacifier. If so, they both might be hers now.

Ridiculous! Her imagination had made her believe something that couldn't be. Still, she wondered.

Metria appeared. "You know, Seren, this path is heading toward Castle Roogna. But you've already been there."

"What did you call me?"

"Seren." Then the demoness looked startled. Little startle lines radiated out from her, making the air wiggle. "What are you doing with that name?"

"Nothing. My name is Seren." Cube bit her tongue. "I mean Seren." She halted abruptly, causing Diamond to look askance at her. "I can't say my real name!"

"That pacifier," Metria said. "It really *is* magic."

"I wonder." Cube focused her mind. "Nickelpedes: come here."

Nothing happened.

"Maybe you can't summon them on the enchanted path."

Cube stepped off the path and tried again, with no better success. "What have I done?" she asked. "I was just curious about whether the mirror and the pacifier related. I didn't really mean to trade names and talents."

"You found something you weren't looking for," Metria agreed. "That's your talent, now."

"It must be," Cube agreed ruefully. "Maybe I should go back and trade back."

"You'd never find that girl if you look for her."

Cube realized that was likely to be true. "So I'd better just keep following the thread, and hope it doesn't lead me anywhere I need my nickelpedes."

"That works for me," the demoness agreed.

Then Cube had another idea. "Diamond—how would you like to have this pacifier?"

The dog looked at her and wagged her tail, not quite understanding.

"I'll take it back if it messes you up," she said. "I promise. I just need to see how this works."

She found a thread and used it to tie the pacifier to the dog's collar. Then she stepped back. "My name is—Cube," she said. Then realized the significance. "It worked!"

Seren wagged her tail agreeably.

"Now you can find the girl and trade back," Metria said.

"Now I don't need to."

"Sometimes we demons have trouble understanding mortals."

"Sometimes we have trouble understanding ourselves."

They continued along the path, following the thread. They stopped at a conveniently situated garden at noon, where Cube harvested and ate a peanut pie and Diamond discovered a biscuit tree with assorted dog biscuits. The dog was obviously surprised, but pleased, and feasted on them.

Cube pondered that as they resumed their walk. Diamond had found something nice that she wasn't looking for. Could that be coincidence?

As evening loomed, they came to another camp. It was already occupied. Cube suddenly realized that she liked traveling like this, meeting fellow travelers, then moving on. Little was required except an exchange of amenities and a bit of tolerance for individuality. She knew that here on the enchanted path there would be no dangers, and that included other travelers. She appreciated the paths much more since meeting Patxi, who had labored so long and hard to make them. She would be sorry when the Quest was done, and she would have to return home.

Of course she would be beautiful. That would make all the difference, wouldn't it?

The campers were a man and a horse. Diamond seemed surprised; she had not been looking for folk like this. That was indeed interesting, because there were few straight horses in Xanth, and not many unicorns. "Hello!" she called as she approached. "I am Cube, and this is Seren."

"Hello," the man said. He had a vaguely horsy face, and his voice sounded somewhat like a neigh. The horse, in contrast, had a vaguely human countenance. "I am Bert, and this is Lam. We are the two parts of a centaur."

Cube couldn't help showing her surprise. "But centaurs are—"

"Merged," Bert agreed. "We made the mistake of trotting into Mundania, where we split into these two parts. We hurried back into Xanth, but the damage was done. We remain a split personality."

"Oh." For the moment Cube couldn't think of anything appropriate to say.

"We plan to visit the Good Magician, and ask how we can be unified again."

"That seems good," Cube agreed, somewhat blankly.

The pair turned out to be fair company for the night. They remained close together, and the horse seemed to understand everything that was said. But it was plain that neither was whole alone; they needed to be restored. Cube hoped the Good Magician enabled them to do that.

In the morning Bert and Lam took the fork marked for the Good Magician's Castle, while Cube and Diamond took the one marked for Castle Roogna. Soon they hove into sight of it. Cube had never tried to hove before; it had just come naturally.

"I'd better get back into the pouch," Metria said, appearing. "The denizens here have been known to get annoyed with me."

Cube wondered what the demoness had done to deserve it, but didn't argue. Surely she would need no protection here. She held out the pouch, and Metria lifted her lovely leg in that annoyingly suggestive way she had, almost but not quite showing panty, and slid into it. Then Cube glanced at Diamond. "You too?" But the dog decided to stay outside. That was fine.

They advanced on the castle, following the thread. It took them right to the moat and drawbridge.

A huge green head rose from the water. Diamond shrank back nervously. "That's just Soufflé, the moat monster," Cube said reassuringly. "He doesn't bother anyone who means no harm." Evincing more certainty than she felt, she lifted one hand to the monster. "You remember me, don't you? I'm Cube. I was here a few days ago with the Princesses."

Soufflé moved forward to sniff her hand. Then she patted him on the nose, exactly as the Princesses had done. He accepted this, showing that he did remember her. He surely had a good memory for visitors, or he wouldn't have this important position guarding the castle.

Reassured, Diamond stepped forward. Soufflé's head went down to meet her. They sniffed noses. Diamond wagged her tail. The monster wagged his tail; it lifted from the water and swished back and forth. Then he sank back under the water.

"We're approved," Cube said. But her knees felt a bit rubbery. She could have brought the Princesses out to reassure the monster, but that would have publicized the way she was transporting her Companions, so she preferred to avoid it. Of course, if the monster had gobbled her down, the Princesses would be just as lost as they had been in the underground cave, for no one would know where the pouch was. So maybe she had been foolish. She would have to watch that; she was responsible for more than herself.

Princess Ivy met them at the front gate. "Your Quest is done?"

"Not yet. I'm—I'm following a thread the Princesses made. It shows me my route. It led me here."

"That's a new kind of magic," Ivy said, petting Diamond. Everybody liked the dog. "They keep discovering new things."

"I need to tell you that I put the Princesses in danger. It was a stupid mistake, and maybe you won't want them to continue with me. I—"

"You lost the pouch."

"You know!"

Ivy smiled. "Chlorine told me. She's a mother herself now, and has become sensitive to mothers' concerns. She also said that you tried very hard to recover it, doing what you needed to."

"Of course I did! But I shouldn't have lost it."

"Chlorine said you didn't have a choice. But now Nimby knows about Fornax's interference, and will make sure there is no more. You should be all right."

"You're very understanding."

"It comes with the territory."

"Of Princesshood?"

"Of motherhood. One day you will discover it for yourself."

"Oh, I don't think so. I'm not beautiful."

Princess Ivy paused for half a moment before speaking. "Not yet, perhaps."

Cube glanced at the thread, which led on down the hall. That surprised her, because she had thought it would depart the castle after she had cleared things with the Princesses' mother. Where was it going? "I suppose I should go where I'm going, though I have no idea where that is."

"None of us really know where we are going," Ivy said. "But I'm sure my daughters' thread will not lead you astray."

"But it's not leaving the castle."

"Then let's discover what it is up to. I can't see it, but of course I don't have the need-to-know."

"It's going that way," Cube said, pointing. "To—to the stairs."

"This is interesting," Ivy said. "The only person upstairs at the moment is my sister Ida."

They walked down the hall, then up the stairs. "I didn't know you had a sister."

"That may be just as well."

"There—there's something wrong with her?"

"By no means! She has an extraordinary talent. But we prefer not to advertise it."

Cube took the hint and did not ask what that talent was, though she was quite curious. Why should the thread take her to the Princesses' aunt?

The thread took them to a door and passed through it. The plaque on the door said PRINCESS IDA. "This is where," Cube said.

Ivy knocked. "A visitor for you, Ida," she called.

"Come in." The voice sounded just like Ivy's.

Ivy opened the door, and ushered Cube in ahead of her. It was amazing how unpretentious she was. Inside stood—another Ivy. No, not quite the same; the features differed subtly. But the height, form, aspect, and crown were so similar that it was obvious they were sisters. Yet there was one strikingly different thing: Ida had a moon. It was a small ball that orbited her head. Cube had never imagined such a thing.

"This is Cube," Ivy said. "She knows nothing of you, Ida, but is led to you by a thread my daughters crafted to guide her on her mission."

"Hello, Cube," Ida said politely.

Cube recovered some of her composure. "Uh, thank you," she said. "I mean—"

"You are taken aback by my moon," Ida said. "Many folk are. It is called Ptero, and is a world in itself where all folk exist, past, future, and possible."

"Uh, yes." Now Cube saw that the thread went to the moon. There was no doubt about it; the thread moved to track the moon as it orbited.

"I will leave you two to talk," Ivy said, and was gone.

"I see you have a companion," Ida said.

"Oh. Yes. This is Seren. I mean Seren. I—oh, the pacifier."

"I am not certain I understand."

"She—I think she's lost, but we have been keeping company. Then we got a magic pacifier, that causes folk to find what they aren't looking for, and I—I gave it to her. Now I can't call her by her real name."

"What did you call her before?"

"Diamond." Cube paused half an instant. She had said it! "And will again, I think, once I take back the pacifier. But right now it's too awkward for me to carry it, because when I do, I am Seren and my talent is serendipity. I—does this make any sense to you?"

"Yes. Did the thread lead you to the pacifier?"

"I'm not sure. I met the girl who had it, and we traded

things. The thread put us together, I suppose—yes, I guess it did. Because when I learned of it, I wanted it."

"Then I'm sure it was destined for your use."

"Maybe so. Actually the thread has been leading me all over Xanth, and even into Mundania. I think it is taking me places I need to be, to learn what I need to learn, so I can complete my Quest."

"I'm sure it is," Ida agreed.

"But it's such a convoluted route! I thought I'd just go directly to—" She paused. "Is it all right to tell you of my Quest? It's supposed to be private, but if I need your help—"

"What do you think?"

Cube pondered. "I think it must be all right, because the thread leads right to your moon, and I have no idea how to go there. So I must need your help, and that means you should know what I'm trying to do."

"I'm sure that's the case," Ida agreed. She seemed very agreeable.

So Cube told her about the Quest, and the Companions, and how she might have fouled it up by choosing too many of them, so that the thread was stretched all out of shape. So maybe she could have had a simple, direct route, instead of this devious one, but actually she was coming to like this one, because of all the places she was seeing and the interesting people she was meeting. So maybe she was as well off this way, because she had always wanted to have a life of adventure instead of being a dull stay-at-home girl.

"I'm sure that's true," Ida agreed.

"And the Good Magician said I would be beautiful, when I finish," Cube concluded.

"I'm sure you will be."

This was weird: things that had seemed speculative now seemed certain. Princess Ida was a very reassuring person. "I long for it."

"Has it occurred to you that your Route might be one of personal discovery, rather than mere geography?"

Cube was surprised. "No, I never thought of that. I

thought I was just paying for a stupid mistake, and messing this up for the others."

"Would the others be needed, if it were not for the deviousness of the Route?"

"I don't think so. I need them only when there is trouble."

"Is it possible that what you need is not physical beauty so much as self-knowledge?"

"Why should anyone care what I know about myself? I'm supposed to be doing a job for the Good Magician."

"Is it possible that you were not the person to accomplish that task when you started, but that you are in the processes of becoming such a person as you handle the challenges of the Route?"

Cube considered that with dawning wonder. "You know, I think it *is* possible! The things I have seen, the people I have met, the experiences I have been having—even if I fail to complete the Quest, I'll be a better person. That's worth a lot."

"I'm sure it is," Ida agreed.

"But I think I *can* complete the Quest, because what I can't do, my Companions can, and it is worth accomplishing."

"I'm sure you can complete it."

However, Princess Ida's automatic certainty was becoming wearing. Cube had never been much for unsupported belief; she preferred to prove herself in whatever way she had to. "So will you help me find the way to your moon? I don't think I'll fit on it as I am."

Ida became businesslike. "You are correct. My worlds are very small. Your physical body can't go there, but your soul can. You will have to rest here, while your soul proceeds to Ptero."

"My soul goes alone?" Cube wasn't comfortable with this. "Doesn't a person's body die when it loses its soul?"

"Not entirely. A portion of your soul remains, but not enough to animate your body, so your body slumbers. Your full soul will return to it when your mission on Ptero is done. If there is some mishap, your soul will revert immediately.

And there is no need to be concerned about the safety of your body; your canine friend will be here to guard it."

Diamond whined, her tail dropping.

"Can she come too?" Cube asked. "She doesn't want to stay here alone. I mean, without me."

"Of course. She can soul travel the same way you do." Ida went to a shelf and fetched a small vial. "You must each lie down and sniff this elixir. Then focus on Ptero and float toward it. You'll get the hang of it soon enough. When you are there, remember that geography is time; your age will change as you travel east or west. East is From and is yellow; west is To and is green; north is blue and south is red, so you'll always know your directions. Beware of the Comic Strips! But I trust the thread to guide you safely through the perplexities so you can reach whatever your destination is."

Time as geography? This was different! But she'd figure that out when she got there. She lay on the couch in Ida's room, and Diamond lay on the floor beside her. "We're ready, I think."

Ida leaned down and held the vial to the dog's nose. Diamond sniffed. Nothing happened. She did not go to sleep.

"That's odd," Princess Ida said. "I wonder." She reached down to pat Diamond on the back. Her hand passed through the dog's body. "It's true! She's already a soul!"

"But she's physical!" Cube protested. "Many people have patted her."

"I suspect they patted her form, and thought they felt flesh, but it was just expectation," Ida said. "Expectation is most of reality. This dog lacks substance. She's here, but not physically."

Astonished, Cube reached down to touch Diamond. Her hand passed through the dog's body without resistance. "But then how can she carry the pacifier? It's physical."

"Is it?"

Cube felt for the pacifier. Her fingers passed through it too. "I guess I just thought I touched it, before."

"I'm sure you're right. At any rate, this dog will have no problem accompanying you."

"That's nice," Cube said faintly.

Ida brought the vial, and she sniffed. Then she found herself clambering up out of a somewhat cloying muck. She got on top of it, then floated above it. She formed an eyeball and peered down.

There was her sleeping body, plain as plain could be. Other girls might sleep pretty, but Cube was never pretty, always plain. She looked away—and saw Diamond. The dog was floating up to join her. She really was a soul.

"Hi, friend," Cube said, patting her—and now the dog seemed solid. She realized it was because they were in the same soul state; she had no more substance than the dog did. "Let's go to Ptero."

The dog wagged her tail and led the way, walking on air toward the tiny moon. As she went she shrank, and Cube shrank with her. The closer they got, the bigger the moon seemed, until it was a full planet, massive and variegated. Then they were falling toward it, but able to slow in the air, flying without wings.

They landed on verdant ground beside a great sea. The air was pleasantly warm, and there was the smell of salt water. It was pleasant, and seemed quite physical. Cube stamped her foot on the ground, and it thunked solidly. The dog sniffed the pebbles of the beach and seemed satisfied. Souls they might be, but they were definitely here.

The atmosphere was colored, just as Ida had said. She saw blue in one direction, and red the opposite way: north and south. To one side was a blue haze; that would be west, where folk got older.

The thread led to the east, where the haze was yellow. As they moved, she felt a weird shifting of her body, not pleasant, and realized that this was her change of age. They were both getting younger, as Ida had warned. She hoped they didn't get too young before reaching their destination.

But that was only part of it. She looked at her hands and saw that they were not the same as they had been. They looked—older. And the dog looked ancient.

They must have landed in a time where they were both significantly older. This was alarming.

A castle loomed ahead. It looked just like Castle Roogna. How could that be here? It must be a copy.

A Princess came out to meet her. She looked vaguely familiar, but not quite. She wore a green dress and green hair ribbon, matching her green/blonde hair, and her eyes were blue. "Hello, Cube!" she said.

"Uh, hello." Cube was trying to place this woman, who obviously knew her.

The Princess laughed. "You're visiting!" she said.

"Visiting this world, yes. But I don't think I know anyone here."

"Yes you do; you just don't know our ages. I'm Princess Melody."

Cube laughed. "You can't be; she's seven years old."

"In your time, yes. But this is the year 2118, I'm twenty-two, and Anomie and I have a baby girl, Melanoma, whose talent is growing or reversing tumors on anything. Of course she's too young to know it yet, but soon we'll take her into the future so she can try it out."

Cube's head was spinning. "How can you be there, when I have you here in my pouch?"

Melody laughed. "Age seven is the year we can't overlap. We can be any age we want to be, merely by traveling From or To. But we have to bypass that one. I remember our adventure with you, but none of us can come out to meet our other selves, because that would be a paradox."

"You can't come out? What happens if I bring you out?"

Melody shrugged. "Try it; it won't work."

Cube tried it. She put her hand in the pouch. "Melody." Nothing happened.

"I find this hard to believe, but you seem to be right."

"Here on Ptero we are not limited by belief."

"How is it that your sisters aren't with you? I thought you were always a threesome."

Melody frowned. "We were. But then I married Anomie,

and summoned the stork, and that set me apart. There were those who thought it wouldn't work out with Anomie, because his talent was having bad ideas, but now he carries a piece of reverse wood with him and he has good ideas. Now Harmony and Rhythm are a twosome."

"I don't know whether to express congratulation or regret."

Melody frowned briefly, then smiled. "Life is mixed, and there is a price to pay for everything. I wouldn't trade. We can't be children forever."

"Maybe when the others marry and communicate with the stork, they'll rejoin you."

"Yes, that would be nice." Then she changed the subject. "You need to follow the thread east. You'll get there."

Something else registered. "This is 2118? That's fifteen years in my future! I'm thirty-five!"

"Indeed. And the dog is too old to live long. This is really outside her range. So you need to move From quickly, for her sake."

"From. That's east?" Now she remembered that Princess Ida had told her that.

"Yes. Toward the past, and youth. You'll get used to it."

"I hope so. Thank you for clarifying things."

"I knew you would need it, so I intercepted you. You both will be fine, as you get younger. Just beware the Comic Strips."

Princess Ida had said that. "Just what is a Comic Strip?"

"It's a boundary between sections, jammed with egregious puns. That's why we don't cross the Strips unless we really have to; nobody can stand them."

"I'll be careful," Cube agreed. Now she had another belated memory: she had encountered a Comic Strip at the Good Magician's castle. She hadn't had to ask at all. Some savvy traveler she was proving to be! "Thanks again."

"Oh, I almost forgot. You must meet Mother."

"Princess Ivy?"

"King Ivy. She wanted to talk with you."

Cube was taken aback. "Not Queen Ivy?"

"Xanth is ruled by kings, and Ptero echoes it. Come."

Cube followed her to the throne room. There sat Ivy, about fifteen years older, with a more substantial crown. "Hello, Cube!" she said immediately, rising to join her. "I'm so glad you could come."

What was the protocol to meet a king? Cube had no idea. "Uh, hello," she said faintly.

Ivy hugged her. "The girls' adventure with you was one of the defining experiences of their childhood. They learned some of the limits of their powers of magic. I think it helped them grow up. I just wanted to thank you again."

"Uh, you're welcome. They were—are—a big help."

"That's right—this is part of your Quest. Then I won't keep you longer. It wouldn't be kind to Seren; she has to get younger quickly."

Cube had evidently been dismissed. Melody guided her out. "Mother really worried when we were gone," she confided. "We didn't realize how much, at the time. But it certainly was a great adventure with a surprising conclusion. Ah, here is the thread."

She was right: the thread led out the back door of the castle and across the moat. But there was no bridge at this location. "Uh—"

"Don't be concerned; Soufflé will take you across."

The moat monster's head rose from the water. He set it at the edge before her, and Cube climbed on. She held the dog on her lap. Then he carried them smoothly across and deposited them beyond the moat. "Thank you," she said.

Soufflé nodded and sank out of sight.

"Hi." It was a seven-year-old boy standing by the bank. Cube had been too distracted by the ride to notice him before. "I'm Vice."

"Hello, Vice. I'm Cube, from Xanth."

"Hi." It was a seven-year-old girl. "I'm Versa." She petted Diamond.

"Our talent is to change anything to its opposite," Vice said proudly.

"And back again," Versa said.

"That's nice for a brother and sister," Cube said.

Both laughed. "We're not siblings," Vice said.

"We're cousins," Versa said.

"But you look like twins."

"That's because we're the children of twins," Vice said.

"Dawn and Eve," Versa said.

Cube remembered that the Princesses Dawn and Eve were the older cousins of the three little Princesses, so it was natural that they be in the vicinity. But they were only about twelve years old. How could they have children?

Then she remembered that this was fifteen years in her future. Plenty of time to grow up, marry, and summon storks.

"I am going east," Cube said. "You are welcome to come along if you wish."

"We mustn't," Vice said.

"We'd get too young," Versa said.

Oh. Of course, here where time was geography. "Then it has been nice meeting you," Cube said.

"Bye," the two said together.

They followed the path beyond Castle Roogna, and sure enough, the dog got visibly younger, and Cube felt better. But her initial pleasure in this world had changed; now she just wanted to do what she was here to do, and return to normal.

As they walked, some things occurred to her. She was here in soul form, and so was the dog—but what about her Companions? They must still be in the pouch, back with her body. That had to be why she couldn't call them out; this was an empty ghost pouch.

And she was not beautiful. She didn't need to see her face; she could see her body. She was the same way she had always been, only older. What did that suggest for her future? Was she going to fail the Quest after all? That was a disquieting notion.

They came to a changed scene. It was not exactly a wall, but it wasn't forest either. The thread led right through it.

Then she remembered the Comic Strips: this must be one. She gazed at it for half a while. It didn't look bad. Why were people so wary of these Strips? So they had egregious puns; that wasn't like death or dismemberment. She could handle puns. This seemed to be a perfectly pleasant small valley with flowers and browsing deer beside a trickling streamlet. Except that at its near fringe was a row of prickly plants she knew better than to touch. Fortunately there was an avenue through them, between two tall trees.

Maybe this was a punless section of the Strip. Or maybe it took time for the puns to collect, like biting flies, when someone stepped into it.

"Let's go," she said to the dog. "We'll just go straight across, and it should be all right."

Diamond wagged her tail.

They stepped between the trees. Cube felt something touch her body, causing her to start with alarm. It was a cobweb she hadn't seen in the shadow. She tried to scrape it off, but it clung to her like a film of paint. It had caught Diamond too; she was trying to brush it off with a paw, but not succeeding.

"Well, a web is harmless, as long as there's no big spider. We'll cross first, then take time to get it off."

They forged on. But now the scene had changed. The valley was darker, and the stream had become a rushing torrent. The deer were now rather more sinister creatures with red eyes and big horns. "We can't cross that! How did it change so fast?"

Even as she watched, the scene changed again, becoming lighter but stranger. Now the creatures were alien, not threatening but not reassuring either, and the river was odd. In fact it looked like mercury flowing down a metallic channel. But mercury was deadly; she didn't want to breathe its fumes. She stepped back in fright, but found she couldn't retreat; the prickly plants had closed in behind them. That intensified her fear.

The dog whined. Cube saw why: the valley had become a graveyard, with walking skeletons beside a sickly flow of pus. This just kept getting worse! Every time she looked, it was different.

Then she reconsidered. Could she be responsible for the changes? They seemed to vary with her mood. So if she could make herself feel good—

The lovely valley returned, with the clear stream and browsing deer. So she was right; all she needed was a good mood. But this was supposed to be a Comic Strip, so there must be a pun. What pun?

Then she saw a little sign: LANDS CAPE. Suddenly it fitted together. She had inadvertently donned a cape, thinking it a cobweb, and so had the dog. It changed her view of the land. Landscape. That was the pun. She had assumed that the puns would be silly or humorous. This one was not.

"Come on, Seren," she said briskly. "We can get through this, if we just keep our minds clear."

But how were they to have clear minds, while shrouded by the capes? She realized she had to get rid of the mood effect, because any little thing could set off a mood change and then the phenomenon would feed on itself. But the cape was invisible and largely intangible.

Well, there was one way. Cube took off her clothing, carrying the cloak with it. She stuffed her things in the pouch for safekeeping. Of course she wouldn't want to be seen bare by any other person; she was no voluptuous nymph. As soon as they got out of the Comic Strip, she'd brush off her clothing and put it back on.

She paused, realizing that she had fallen into another pun: Comic *Strip*, and she had stripped. Well, it couldn't be helped.

Now the valley was neither pleasant nor horrible; it was purely routine. Just a dip with a bit of water and a few rocks that had seemed like animals before. She was seeing it clearly for the first time.

She used her spread fingers to comb the cloak from Diamond, and soon the dog was seeing clearly too. But why had she seen it differently before she walked into the cloak? She must have been looking through the cloak, so that it distorted her perception.

But then a group of goblins charged along the valley.

They surrounded Cube and Diamond, reaching for them. They started pinching bare flesh. Diamond yelped.

"Hey!" she cried. "What are you doing?"

"We're the vice squad," a goblin answered. "We pinch bare people for no reason."

It was another pun. "Well stop it! The dog isn't bare, she's wearing her fur, and I'm not worth it."

The goblin looked at her. "Good point." They moved on.

Cube was not entirely pleased. She knew that had she had the lush figure of a nymph, the goblin would not have agreed. Which suggested that there *was* reason for the pinching, but not one the pinchers admitted to.

Meanwhile she had a scratch on her bottom where she had been pinched. How sanitary were those goblins? Could she be infected? She'd like to have a magic medicine.

And there it was: a big jar labeled PENICILLIN. She should be able to smear some of that on the scratch, and it would get rid of any infection. She reached into the jar and pulled out—a pen. She tried again, and got a pencil. Then a piece of white chalk.

"This isn't medicine," she said, annoyed.

Then she got the pun: penicillin made writing utensils like pens and pencils. In the jar.

"Now I understand why folk can't stand the Comic Strips," she said. "Come on, Seren; we're getting out of here."

They forged on across the river and up the far slope, and soon were back in regular territory. Cube brought her clothing out of the pouch and used the same technique she had used on the dog to clear the invisible cloak from it. She donned it, and the terrain did not change with her mood, so she was all right.

As they continued east, or "From," the years peeled away, until Cube realized she was in her teens again, and the dog was quite lively. But how far was the thread taking them? Cube could get younger, but the dog would soon reach her limit.

The thread led to a pleasant house in a pleasant garden.

Maybe this was their destination. Cube hoped so; she found she was not getting tired, in soul form, but she was getting bored.

They came to the door of the house. Cube knocked. In a moment it opened.

"Oh, there you are!" It was a young woman of ordinary aspect, which was of course better than Cube's aspect. She was about twenty years old. "Right on time." But of course Cube was about sixteen years old now, so was four years younger.

"On time?" Cube asked, bemused.

"Yes. I suppose I should introduce myself. I'm Lacky, a might-be daughter of Vernon and Lacuna, and my talent is writing things true. That is, what I write comes true, though not always in the way I expect."

Who were Vernon and Lacuna? Cube found the names vaguely familiar, but couldn't place them. She had met so many folk recently that it was hard to keep them all straight. Probably it didn't matter. Evidently they hadn't had this daughter in Xanth, so she was confined here as one they might have had. "I'm Cube, on a private Quest. This is Seren." The dog wagged her tail.

"Oh, that can't be right. I needed a name for a dog, so I wrote 'Diamond.' You see, my companion Boss needs company of his own kind, so I thought maybe a nice female dog."

Cube reached down and removed the pacifier from the dog's collar. "I—I misspoke. This is Diamond."

"Wonderful!" Lacky turned her head. "Boss! You have company!"

A big male black Labrador dog appeared beside her. Diamond looked surprised.

"You were wearing the pacifier," Cube explained to her. "It made you serendipitous. You found what you didn't expect."

"And of course you'll stay," Lacky said. "Oh, Prince Dolin will be so pleased. He likes dogs."

"Prince Dolin?" Cube asked blankly.

"The son of Prince Dolph and Princess Taplin. He's a child; he died early. It's a long story. I take Boss to visit him regularly. Now I'll take both dogs."

"I think you have also found a home," Cube said to Diamond. "By surprise, of course. Are you satisfied to stay here?"

Diamond wagged her tail.

Cube found a tear in her eye that she hadn't expected. She had gotten used to Diamond's company. But this was best. "Then I'll go now," she said, turning away before her tears embarrassed her.

"But you must stay and visit," Lacky protested.

"No thank you," Cube said tightly. "I have an urgent mission." She hurried on, following the thread. It was best this way. She realized that she had the pacifier now, so was finding what she wasn't looking for—such as the loss of Diamond. Yet of course this was best for the dog. She couldn't begrudge that.

There was a sound behind her. She turned to look, and saw the two dogs racing after her. In a moment they caught up, and of course she had to pet them both. They made a fine couple.

Lacky approached. "You have to meet Prince Dolin. Boss thinks he has something for you."

How did she know what the dog thought? "But I don't even know Prince Dolin, and I have to be on my way." She refrained from saying that she had used up more than enough time traveling here, apparently just to find a home for Diamond. Of course that was worth doing, but surely wasn't on the way to Counter Xanth. She suspected she had a long lonely trek back the way she had come. She needed to get moving.

"It's not far," Lacky said. "Just a little way north."

Diamond caught Cube's left hand gently in her mouth, and Boss caught her right hand, tugging her north. But the thread went west.

She blinked. The thread made an abrupt turn north. She was sure it hadn't done that before. It was telling her to go with the dogs.

What could she do? "Then I suppose I'd better meet the Prince," she agreed.

"His castle is right this way." Lacky walked briskly north, and the dogs bounded after her.

Cube caught up to the young woman. "Why would a Prince have anything for me? I have nothing for him, and I can't stay here."

"He knows that. He likes Boss, but thought that Boss needed some company of his own kind. So I wrote my note, and you brought Diamond. It must have been some trouble for you; I know this isn't an easy place to reach, from real-time Xanth. He must have told Boss that he would have a reward for whoever brought him company."

"I'm not looking for any reward! We—I found Diamond, who seemed to be lost, and she was good company, and we didn't even know she would find a home here. It was serendipitous." Then she explained about the pacifier's magic. After that, Lacky explained how her mother Lacuna, daughter of the original Zombie Master and Millie the Ghost, whose talent was to cause print to form anywhere she chose, had lived a dull life until she got the chance to go back in time, to the year 1078, and propose marriage to the man she liked. It seemed that he had been too shy to propose to her. That had ushered in her retroactive change of life in the year 1090, and suddenly she had three children. Lacky was delivered in 1079.

Cube had heard this story before, but still couldn't quite connect it to her prior experience. "But then you were a legitimate—I mean regular person," she said. "Why are you here?"

The woman shook her head sadly. "I was the result of Vernon's proposing to Lacuna."

"But you said he didn't—" Then it came together. "If he had, then the stork would have delivered you. But because she did it retroactively, and proposed herself, that didn't count."

"So I was a might-be," Lacky agreed. "Like so many others. Of course there's not room in Xanth for all of us. It's not a bad existence. But enough about me; how did you come to be traveling so widely?"

Cube gave an edited account, not mentioning Counter Xanth or the nine Companions. By the time that was done, they had come to a low hill.

"Here we are," Lacky said. "The Prince's castle. Isn't it beautiful?" Both dogs wagged their tails.

"But this is just a rounded hill," Cube said. "Or maybe a huge fallen tree." For the slope resembled bark. There was a curlycue pattern of grooves in it, as if some ogre had scraped his fingernails there.

"Well, let's see." Lacky put her hands to her face, forming a magic funnel, and called "Prince Dolin! Company!" And Boss added a loud "Woof!"

After a generous moment a wooden column rose from the slope. Its sides were smooth and polished. It became a small tower about the height of a man, dark on top where the bark was and with lines showing the growth rings of a tree. But it was hardly a castle.

"It gets better," Lacky said.

A second section rose, around the first, bearing it upward. This was similar to the first, only larger in diameter. When it stopped it was about man-high, with the first column rising another length higher. But it still wasn't a castle.

Then a third segment lifted, bearing the other two upward, followed by a fourth that raised all the others. Several sub-sections also rose to buttress the formation. Now it was indeed a castle, albeit not a big one.

"This way," Lacky said, walking around to the side. Behind was a door, and beyond the door was a flight of steps leading down. Most of the castle was underground. They all trooped down, the dogs leading, and came upon an eight-year-old boy wearing a small crown. Prince Dolin, embracing the dogs.

"The new one is Diamond," Lacky said. "And this is Cube, who brought her here. Cube, this is Prince Dolin."

The boy stood up so quickly his crown fell askew, and he had to straighten it. "Thank you, Cube! Boss is great, but he needed canine company, and now he's got it. I have a present for you."

"There's no need," Cube demurred.

"This whisk broom." He presented it to her.

Oh—a token gift. She could accept that. "Thank you."

He glanced at her cannily. "It's magic."

"It is?" The little broom seemed ordinary.

"It sweeps away distance."

"I don't think I understand."

"When you have a long way to go, it makes it short. You'll see when you use it. I know you came a long way to bring Diamond; this will make it shorter."

"That's nice," Cube said, not sure he was serious.

"You'll see." Then he returned to playing with the dogs.

"He's a child," Lacky murmured. "He has a short attention span. We'll go now." Then, louder: "Bye, Prince!"

"Bye," he said, not looking up.

They exited the castle. "It was really the Prince who needed more company," Lacky said outside. "But I pretended it was Boss. I'm so glad you came."

"So am I," Cube said. This had turned out to be worth it after all, making two dogs and a Prince happy. "Now I should be on my way."

"Of course. If you see my brother, back in real Xanth, give him my regards."

"Your brother?"

"His name is Ryver. He has a wonderful talent with water."

"Ryver!" Cube echoed, stunned. "I know him!" Vernon and Lacuna were his parents. He had told her. That was why she remembered them.

"You do? That's wonderful! I know his Ptero self, of course, but I've never met the real one. Real folk seldom come here."

Acting impulsively, Cube put her hand in the pouch. "Ryver," she murmured. Then she remembered that this wasn't the real pouch, but just her soul emulation of it. So her Companions weren't in there.

A hand caught hers. Then Ryver slid out and stood beside her. He spied the woman. "Sis!" he cried, and stepped forward to embrace her.

"Oh, it's so good to see you, Ryver," Lacky said. "But what are you doing here? You didn't die, did you?"

"No, I'm traveling with Seren." He turned to face Cube, who was tongue-tied. "She's on a Quest, and I'm a Companion. I had no idea she was coming to see you."

Cube finally untied her tongue. "Neither did I. It was serendipitous." As she said it, she realized that this was the work of the pacifier. It had renamed her, again, and was causing her to find more unexpected things.

"Do we have time to visit, Seren?" Ryver asked. "I'd really like to be with my sister a while. I never see her in Xanth."

How could she say no? It wasn't as if she had a real schedule, and she liked being able to do something for Ryver, however unexpectedly. "Of course."

"No, she's just being nice," Lacky said. "She has a Quest she has to return to."

"She *is* nice," Ryver said. "Just not beautiful, yet."

Lacky's eyebrow lifted. "You have an interest?"

"She's going to be beautiful when she finishes the Quest. Then I'll be interested."

"If you associate only with beauty, what about me?"

"You're my sister. You don't count."

Lacky glanced again at Cube. "My brother is male," she said. "He sees better than he thinks."

"What's your point?" Ryver asked.

Both Cube and Lacky laughed, while Ryver was mystified.

Then, to distract herself from the unfunny aspect, Cube tested the whisk broom the Prince had given her. How did it work? She made a little sweeping motion in front of her—and suddenly she stood alone. What had happened to the others?

She looked back, and there they were, about a hundred paces behind. She looked at the broom. Had it really swept away that distance?

She faced back and swept again. And almost collided with Ryver and Lacky.

"I see the whisk broom works," Lacky remarked.

"Yes," Cube agreed, amazed. "This will make traveling much faster, if I don't bang into things." In fact, it would allow her to visit for some time, and still make faster progress than before.

They continued on toward Lacky's house. "How did you recognize me, since we haven't met before?" Lacky asked Ryver. "I know you, because your non-Xanth aspect is here, but you shouldn't know me."

"I dreamed of you," Ryver said. "You're the big sister I never had. I'm sorry you didn't get to be delivered in Xanth."

They had a nice visit at Lacky's house. Then the dogs returned. "That's our signal," Ryver said. "I wouldn't want Seren to go without me." He put his foot to the pouch and slid in.

"I can't thank you enough for bringing my brother," Lacky said. "He's really not a bad sort, when you make allowances. I hope you do manage to get beautiful. Then maybe you can tell me how."

"Maybe," Cube agreed. "I'm not sure I quite believe it yet. This trek is more of a challenge than I expected."

"That's the way it is, when you're real."

And Cube realized that whatever her appearance, she was better off than this nice woman, because she was indeed real. That was another serendipitous lesson of life.

12

TESSERACT

S he went outside, stood with the thread extending ahead into the blue mist, and made a little sweep with the whisk broom. Nothing happened. She took a step forward and tried again—and found herself well away from the house. It was motion that did it! So she tried running along the line, and sweeping—and suddenly she was almost to the Comic Strip.

She paused to consider. Could she whisk right through that Strip without suffering its effect, or was that dangerous? She had been whisking past largely empty terrain, but she probably did pass through it, very fast. Suppose she collided with a pun? It might explode, soaking her in pun ichor. Then nobody would want to be near her.

It was better not to risk it. She would have to navigate the Comic Strip on her own, then resume speed beyond it. She braced herself and stepped into it.

She found herself facing a giant eyeball. It was lapping up some dark liquid with a strong smell. She wasn't sure how an eyeball could lap up anything, but it was doing it. "What are you doing?" she demanded, not sure whether this thing was dangerous.

"I'm dining, of course," the Eye observed.

She thought she heard a groan from the pouch. She was imagining Karia reacting to a pun. Then she got it: "Eye-o-dine!"

"What else?" the Eye squinted.

She dodged around it, and almost collided with a small person, resembling a goblin but different. It was female, and was swinging back and forth across the path with a clicking sound, blocking the way. "Who are you?"

"Metra Gnome, of course."

Now Cube was almost sure she heard a groan from the pouch. She timed her move, and dashed through while Metra was swung over to one side.

Ahead was a sign: PASSING WIND. Cube hardly had time to ponder that before the foul-smelling wind gusted through, catching her and blowing her into the river, which had become a lake. Well, the sign had warned her that a wind was passing; she had foolishly supposed it meant something else.

Her feet splashed in the water, which was only knee deep. But the bottom was mucky and she wanted to get back to land, so she strode toward a small island just ahead. Just as she caught up to it, it zipped away from her so that her foot splashed back into water. Now it was just ahead of her again. Maybe she had misjudged its distance.

She forged on toward it, and lifted a foot to step on it, when the island moved again. This time she was watching closely and saw it happen; it had just jumped to another location.

Annoyed, she gave up on the isle and walked on across the lake, no longer caring that it was mucking up her legs. At least the shore did not move as she stepped on it. She stood on it, dripping sludge, and looked back.

Now she saw the sign: BEWARE THE MISS-ISLES. This time she didn't need to imagine Karia groaning; she groaned herself. Isles that were hard to catch.

A group of dishes on spindly legs ran past. The last one was small and unsteady, and it almost collided with her. She put her hand on it to steady it, and sent it on to catch up with the grown dishes. Across its face was printed the word CHILD. Did she hear a groan? This was a child dish.

"What are you doing?" a woman's sharp voice came.

"Just setting the child dish straight," Cube said.

"That's bad."

Bad? "Why?"

"Because children should be abused."

If this was a pun, Cube did not find it funny. "Who are you?" she demanded angrily.

"I am the wife of Uncle Nym."

That would make her Aunt Nym. Was that another groan? Cube focused, and put it together: Auntie Nym. Antonym. The opposite of a given word. So when she said something was bad, she meant good, and children should not be abused, but pampered. "You're a loathsome hag," Cube told her.

"You're worse," Auntie said, obviously flattered, and moved on.

Tired and wet, Cube sat on a handy ledge by the lake so she could remove her shoes and wash off her legs. She splashed the water on herself, getting her feet, ankles, shins, calves, and knees clean. Suddenly her mind seemed to expand. "Why, I know everything!" she exclaimed. "The origin of puns, the secrets of the Stork Works, the meaning of ultimate reality—all the information of the universe is cramming into my head and threatening to explode it." Nervous about this, she stood and glanced back at the ledge. On it was printed KNOW LEDGE. Oh.

But one advantage of having sat on this seat of learning was that now she knew the best way out of this Comic Strip. She marched past a shelf of beer bottles, knowing better than to drink from any, because they were bottles of ail. She went to a nearby plant with many identical leaves, picked one leaf, and ate it. This was the re-done-dent plant that made for repetition; that was one of the things she had learned. "Out," she said. "Out out out out out out—"

Then she stopped: she was out. She had used the pun against the Comic Strip, forcing it to eject her.

But now she was back on regular land without her shoes, and she still had a fair distance to go. Well, it couldn't be helped; she was not going back into the Comic Strip to retrieve them. She took a step and swept with the broom, and moved rapidly forward. Soon she came in sight of Castle Roogna, and felt her age: she was back in her mid-thirties, because she had been traveling To, into the future. She could appreciate the advantage in being any age one chose, but overall she preferred to live through all her ages slowly, as she did in Xanth proper.

The thread led her back into Castle Roogna. This time no one intercepted her. She followed the thread across the drawbridge, into the castle, down the central hall, and up the stairs. Suddenly she recognized where it was going: to Princess Ida's chamber. Was there another Ida here on Ptero? This was weird even on a world whose weirdness she had been getting used to.

She came to the Princess's door and knocked. Ida opened it. She was about fifteen years older than the one Cube had met before. Around her head orbited a pyramidal-shaped moon. "Why hello, Seren. Is there a problem?"

"I, uh, I'm the one from Xanth, here on a mission. I met your Xanth counterpart, and she sent me on to Ptero. I—do you know anything about my Quest?"

"I remember that you had one about fifteen years ago. I believe it came out all right."

"That's the one I'm on now," Cube said uncomfortably. "Will it change it if you tell me what happened?"

"Probably not. Fate can be devious. Sometimes a person is supposed to know how something finishes, in order to ensure that it does. You discovered Counter Xanth."

"Well, I didn't discover it, but I'm trying to find a good route to it. I'm following a thread the three Princesses made, and it led me here."

"That means you must go to my moon Pyramid, or beyond. That is quite in order."

Cube quailed. "I'm already on one moon. You mean there's another?" But obviously there was, and the thread led right to it. "Is it possible for a person not of Ptero to—to go to your moon?"

"Oh, yes. There is a seemingly endless chain of moons; no one has explored them all."

"But Pyramid is so small! Ptero is just a little ball, and Pyramid is just as tiny. How can it be a whole world?"

Ida smiled. "Magic is marvelous stuff. Each moon is a full-size planet, with its own rules of magic unlike any others. They just seem small from our perspective."

"But I'm here only in soul form. To go to Pyramid, wouldn't I have to leave most of my soul behind?"

"Yes, but that is no problem; it will rejoin you when you return. You will be perfectly normal, as you are here."

Cube looked down at her bare feet. "I feel more like a barefoot girl. I lost my shoes in a Comic Strip."

"Those are horrible, I know. But you will have no trouble on that score on Pyramid. When you get there, simply mold some of your surplus soul stuff into a new pair of shoes. You will be able to do that with a thought, merely by concentrating."

Cube thought of something else. "You say there are many moons. Is there any chance that I will have to go beyond Pyramid, to yet another moon?"

"There is certainly that chance."

"And it will seem just as big as Ptero does?"

"Not only as big. It has its own obstacles and dangers."

"That's what I was afraid of. This tour is threatening to take forever."

"Perhaps I can help. Some time ago I was given a dogsled. I do not travel enough to use it sufficiently, so I shall lend it to you. That will take you rapidly and safely to your destination, wherever it may be."

"A dogsled?"

"I will show you." Ida opened a door to the outside wall. She put her head out and whistled. In a moment there was the sound of barking. Then something slid into the chamber.

Cube stared. It was a sled, or a dog; she wasn't sure which. It had runners or legs, and a canine head or a prow. "A dog sled," she said, catching on.

"A very good one," Ida agreed. "Simply tell it where you want to go, and it will take you safely there."

"But I don't know where I'm going. I'm following the thread."

"It can do that too. Go ahead, get in. This should greatly facilitate your traveling."

Bemused, Cube climbed into the sled. It was comfortable, with furry pillows inside, and strong handholds. "Uh, follow the thread," she said.

Instantly the sled was in motion. It slid along the thread toward Pyramid, and the moon quickly expanded into a planet and then into a world, each side colored with a different hue. Cube saw blue, red, green, and gray as it rotated. Each side was a triangle, and she thought there should be three of them, but somehow there were four, with the gray one at the bottom.

Meanwhile, she felt her age diminishing. She was reverting to her natural age of twenty. That was a relief.

The dogsled came in for a landing on the blue face and followed the thread rapidly across it. Cube remembered to concentrate on shoes, and they formed around her feet, very nice ones. She must have been shedding soul stuff without realizing it.

She looked around. Everything was shades of blue. The mountains were blue, the plains were blue, the trees were blue. Even the occasionally glimpsed animals and people were blue. She and the sled were the only ones in other colors. That made them stand out as alien; blue heads were turning. She was glad they were moving rapidly so she didn't have to try to explain.

And the magic here was different? Ptero had been tricky enough to adjust to, with its timed geography and Comic Strips; what might she encounter here? Why was the thread taking her here? She no longer had a dog to deliver to a good home; the dogsled belonged to Princess Ida and should be returned to her when Cube left the moons.

But she did still have the serendipity pacifier. There was no telling what further surprises it had in store for her. This dogsled must be one of them. Meanwhile she hoped Mirror, the former Screen, was doing well. That trade seemed to be permanent.

The weirdness of traveling moons in soul form was fading; her body seemed as solid and sensitive as always, and not half a whit prettier. Could she reshape herself, as she had her shoes, to be better looking? She wasn't sure, and was wary of trying, lest she mess herself up. She was, as far as she could tell, herself, and that was good enough for now.

The thread came to a lake, and crossed it to an island. The dogsled zoomed along the thread like a track, heedless of the water. Cube was increasingly glad to have it; she wasn't sure how she would have crossed the lake on her own. For all she knew, there could be dangerous monsters in it. Maybe the whisk broom would have whisked her across—and maybe not. Of course she could summon her nickelpedes—or could she?

She set aside the pacifier, then made the effort, and a blue nickelpede appeared on her hand. Relieved, she banished it. She could still protect herself if she had to. She took back the pacifier.

The thread brought them to the door of a nice little house. This must be her destination. The sled stopped and Cube got out. "Wait here," she told it. "I'd be lost without you." The sled woofed and sank into a snooze.

She knocked on the door. It opened, and there was Princess Ida, all in blue, with a small blue doughnut circling her head. Cube wasn't sure what she had expected, but it wasn't this. She was speechless.

"I see by your color that you are from one of the other worlds," Ida said. "How may I help you?"

"I—I am Seren, from Xanth proper. I'm on a Quest, following a thread, and it led me here. I have no idea why."

Ida smiled. "Come in, Seren, and we'll discuss it."

Bemused, Cube entered the house, and sat on one of the blue chairs therein. Everything was in shades of blue here too. She was beginning to get used to it.

Ida brought a plate of blue cookies, and a glass of blue drink. Cube tasted and sipped, and found that they tasted normal: blue chocolate and blue lemonade.

"I should explain that my name is not really Seren," she said. "But I carry a magic amulet, and it changes my name and causes me to find things I'm not looking for."

"That is intriguing. May I see it?"

"Of course." Cube handed her the pacifier. "I traded a rear-view mirror for it. My name is really Cube."

"And my name is Seren," Ida said. "Oh, I see what you mean; now it has changed mine."

Cube smiled. "And it may cause you to find something you are not looking for. I should take it back before there's any mischief."

"Oh I have no fear of mischief. My life is dull; some mischief would enliven it."

"But you're a lovely Sorceress!" Cube protested. "How can your life be dull?"

"My talent is the idea. What I believe is true, becomes true, even if it wasn't before, as long as someone who doesn't know my talent says it. That means I can't improve my own reality, and so I remain unmarried and alone. That is dull."

"Your talent is the idea? I didn't know."

"My Xanth self would not have told you, because then she could not have helped you as much."

"She did help me. She believes that my Quest will be successful, and I will become beautiful."

"Then you surely will succeed, and be beautiful. But what man, knowing my talent, would be interested in me? He wouldn't dare get any ideas. I'm so blue."

Cube was amazed. Here was a Princess and a Sorceress—they did go together—who was alone and lonely, in much the way Cube had been before starting this Quest. "Maybe if he didn't know your talent, it would work."

"I would not deceive him. My talent is too strong to allow him to be ignorant. In fact, I think no one but a Magician would care to associate with me at all, and he would surely know."

Cube wondered if the thread had brought her here to help solve Ida's problem. Yet how could she, a mere ordinary person, presume to try to solve the problem of a Sorceress? "I wish I could help," she said. "But I have no idea how."

Ida smiled ruefully. "I wish you had had an idea, because then I could have agreed with it. So now we know you can't help me. But I thank you for the thought."

"Maybe that pacifier could help you. It can bring about some remarkable coincidences."

"Oh, I wouldn't keep it. I am merely looking at it. On this world, anyone who gives a gift gains stature, while anyone who receives it loses stature."

"This is a social thing?"

"No, a physical one. If you gave me this charm, you would become larger and I smaller, unless I gave you something of equivalent value in return."

Physical size change! That was indeed different from Cube's experience. The folk of this world would have to be very careful about gifts. She was glad she had learned of this before accepting anything from anyone. Except—

"You gave me refreshments. Does that change our sizes?"

"No, that is ordinary hospitality. My refreshments for your company; it balances. Balance is important."

Obviously true. Still this situation bothered Cube. The thread had taken her to remarkable places, and did not seem to be done yet. She suspected she could not continue until she did help Ida. There had to be something else. "How is it you have the moons? Aren't they like a talent?"

"They relate to my talent. The moons are filled with all the ideas that haven't made it to Xanth proper. They have nowhere else to go, you see, so they exist on their own worlds."

A dim bulb flashed over Cube's head. "All the might-be folk—they're ideas! Until they make it to Xanth proper."

"Exactly. And I'm an idea too, a derivative of my Xanth-proper self. That way she doesn't have to hold all the ideas in her own head; she can store them in the moons."

"I'm astounded that there can be so many worlds and ideas and people. Each one seems as big as all Xanth. Is there any end to them?"

"None we know of. Perhaps someday someone will explore all the way to the last world. There used to be travelers back and forth, but recently there haven't been. That's another reason it has become dull. You are the first in some time."

"I hope nothing has happened to the others."

"I hope so too." Ida got up and walked to the fireplace. "It is cool here; I'll light a log."

"There's no need just for me. I don't mean to be a burden."

"You're not a burden, dear, you're a visitor. You are alleviating the dullness. I will be sorry when you go on your way." She fished a small knot of wood from a wood bin, set it in the fireplace, and snapped her fingers. A fire formed, igniting the knot. It blazed up vigorously, and she carefully set sticks of wood over it to burn.

There was a knock on the door. "Another visitor!" Ida said. "Would you answer that, dear? I'm afraid the fire will go out if I leave it too soon."

"Yes, certainly." Cube got up and went to the door and opened it.

A handsome red man stood there. "Would not," he said.

"Excuse me?"

"You misunderstand. That's wood as in a tree, and knot as in tied string. Wood knot. I smelled the wood smoke, and came immediately."

"Came for what?" Cube asked, confused.

"To marry you, of course. It is fated that I marry the one I would not, I mean wood knot." He gazed at her more closely. "Perhaps a small spell can improve your appearance."

Cube began to get a glimmer. "Oh, I'm not the mistress of this house. I didn't burn the knot. You are looking for Seren."

He looked relieved. "I do not know this name."

"She's really a Princess, but there's a spell—"

"Say no more. I understand. May I come in?"

"I—"

"Who is it, Cube?" Ida called.

"What a lovely voice," the man said. "We must be properly introduced. I am Magician Jaycn."

"Uh, yes, I will introduce you," Cube said. "Do come in." She led him inside.

Ida was just rising from the fire. "Hello," she said, surprised.

"This is Seren," Cube said, finding that she still was unable to speak Ida's real identity. "A very fine person with remarkable magic." Then, to Ida: "This is Magician Jaycn. He has come to marry you."

"Marry me!" Ida exclaimed. "But first I have to tell him—"

Jaycn held up a hand in a powerful stop signal. "Tell me nothing, Seren, before you hear this. I am under a curse that I may have no relations with any woman whose magic I know. I see you are beautiful and I know this is my only chance, so I must ask you to swear that you will never tell me the nature of your magic."

"But—" Ida protested, nonplussed.

"My only chance was to come to the wood knot when it was invoked," Jaycn continued. "Because it is an unusual variant of reverse wood. When it is burned, it changes reality to what might have happened but did not. You might have married me, but did not, because we did not know of each other. I lived on the red face, and you on the blue face. But I smelled the smoke and came at once. Swear never to tell me your magic, and we can confirm this reality, which frankly promises to be better than that lonely life I have known hitherto."

Still Ida hesitated, not wanting to deceive anyone.

"He has a point," Cube said. "His curse prevents him from

marrying any woman whose magic talent he knows, so it would be unkind of you to spoil it by telling him."

"I suppose it would," Ida agreed. She looked at Jaycn. "If you really do not want to know."

"I really do not," Jaycn said. "What is that orbiting your head?"

"That's a small affliction she has," Cube said quickly. "She can't get rid of it, because it relates deviously to her magic. But it's harmless if ignored."

Jaycn caught on immediately. "I shall ignore it, of course."

"Have something to eat," Ida said, handing him a glass of blue drink. Evidently she was somewhat flustered, understandably. The appearance of the Magician had been entirely serendipitous. Because she had the pacifier, Cube realized. It had struck again, perhaps changing her life.

"I must give you something in return," Jacyn said, and Cube understood why.

"No need," Ida said quickly. "You are giving me the pleasure of your company."

But awkwardness remained. "Tell us about yourself," Cube said. "You are a Magician? What is your magic?"

"I am the Magician of Matter. I can convert liquid to gas." He demonstrated by glancing at the blue drink, which fizzled into a cloud that floated out of the glass. "And gas to solid." The cloud shrank into a blue block. "And solid to liquid." He caught the blue liquid in the glass as the block dissolved. "And vice versa, of course." He sipped the drink. "Very good, I must say. Reminiscent of our red lemonade." He looked at Ida. "Now tell me more about you. Everything except your magic. You are of course single?"

"Oh, yes," Ida agreed. "Come sit down. We have much to catch up on."

Cube saw that the thread now extended to the doughnut orbiting Ida's head. So her journey wasn't done yet. "I think I should be on my way," she said. "Seren, may I speak with you privately for a moment?"

At this point Ida was surely eager to be alone with the Magician. "Certainly."

The two of them stepped out the door. "I think I should take back the charm," she said, reaching for the pacifier. "You have no further need of it, I suspect."

"Yes! I can tell him my real name, now that I won't tell him my magic." She returned it.

"And I need to follow the thread on to your moon."

"Torus. Do you have a way?"

"Yes." Cube got into the dogsled. "Farewell, Princess!" And to the sled: "Go."

The dogsled took off, zooming along the thread toward Ida's head. But it did not collide; the doughnut-shaped moon loomed larger, and soon Ida disappeared in largeness. Cube was coming down for a landing on the inner side of Torus. She was sure that Princess Ida would be able to carry on, now that her life had been serendipitously changed. That wood knot must have been there all the time, but never burned before the pacifier caused it to happen. What a devious interaction of spells!

So what would it be like on this weird-shaped world, and what kind of magic did it have? This was certainly a tour to remember.

They landed and zoomed across the rounded surface. At least this world was normally colored, so Cube was not obviously alien. But after the time magic of Ptero, and the size magic of Pyramid, she was nervous about this new world. What mischief might come of her ignorance?

Another thing that was weird was the fact that this world made an enormous curve, passing right over her head as she crossed the inside of the doughnut. She could see its mountains, rivers, and lakes, and marveled that none of them fell across the empty center to land on her head. But with enough magic, anything was possible.

She came to another lake. No, it was larger, a sea, for there was a sign saying SARAH SEA, and again the thread went right across it. The thread must have known that she would have a way to follow it unflinchingly.

There was an island on the sea, and it bore a sign saying ISLE OF NIFFEN. It seemed nice enough, but the thread didn't pause until it came to another house and stopped. Why did she think this would belong to another Princess Ida?

She got out and knocked on the door. Sure enough, it was answered by Ida, this time with an orbiting cone. It seemed that each moon was a different shape as well as having different magic.

Cube plunged right in. "I'm Seren, from Xanth proper. I'm following a thread that took me to your door. There must be something I'm supposed to do or learn here before I go on, and I hope you will help me do or learn it."

"This is a problem," Ida said. "On this world, favors rendered incur burdens of love. If I did you a favor, you would love me, and I suspect you would prefer not to do that."

So that was the local magic. "Is there any favor I can do you in return, to equalize it?"

"I am aware of none."

But Cube was already thinking of something. "I have a charm that generates serendipity. It makes good things happen by surprise. If I lent it to you, it might do you some good."

"I am already well enough off, thank you."

"Such as maybe finding you a good man."

Ida paused. "Come in."

"Thank you." Cube entered the house.

"How did you know I would like to locate a good man?"

"I discussed it with the Ida on Pyramid. The charm found one for her. Of course I can't guarantee what it will do; the results are always unexpected."

"I understand. May I see it?"

Cube presented the pacifier. "But I must warn you, it assigns you its name when you have it."

"That is hard to believe." Ida took the pacifier. "What is your name?"

"Seren, of course." She paused. "Oh, I see."

"You will have your own name back when it leaves you."

"This alarms me," Ida said. "Please take back your charm." She returned it to Cube.

"I'm not sure what else I have to offer."

"We have been assuming that we have to exchange favors. But it may be that you are merely traveling through, and this constitutes no favor."

"I suppose that is possible," Cube agreed dubiously.

"Where does your thread lead?"

Now Cube saw it. "To your moon."

"That confirms it. Go on to Cone, unhampered."

"Thank you." Cube went out, got in the dogsled, and urged it onward. It zoomed along the thread toward Ida's head, and soon was arriving at the growing cone-shaped world.

Thereafter, things blurred as Cube followed the thread through world after world, seeking the Ida on each and going to her moon. Cone was filled with water, and Ida lived at the bottom of the pointed sea; somehow breathing wasn't a problem. Her moon was Dumbbell, where everyone constantly exercised. Then Pincushion, where everyone lived on huge long pins, and Spiral, like a little galaxy, Tangle, like knots in spaghetti, Motes, which seemed to be a swarm of particles, Trapezoid, which was not exactly cubic, and Shoe. Every old woman lived in Shoe, with myriads of children, so that none of them knew what to do. Then Implosion, Puzzle, and Octopus, which had to be seen to be believed. Then Tesseract—and the thread stopped.

The dogsled came to a halt inside a hollow cube the size of a world. The mountains, forests, lakes, and houses were all on the six great walls of it. And there was no way out.

Cube looked around. The dogsled rested on the floor of the giant box, beside a river and a hill, near a wall. Everything seemed normal, except that the thread stopped. That was why she knew there was no way out; the thread ended.

Well, not exactly. As she peered more closely, she saw that the thread actually turned and went into the wall to the right. But the wall was a picture, a painting, a mural, and the thread became a diminishing line on it, until it disappeared behind a painted house.

She got out of the dogsled. "Wait here," she told it, and the dog eyes closed for another snooze. It was a very obliging sled. Not the company Diamond was, but useful. As an afterthought she set the pacifier on the seat, so that it would not affect her exploration of this situation.

She walked up to the wall and tapped its surface. It was rock hard. She rubbed a finger across it, and it was mirror smooth. She squatted and traced the ground up to the wall; there was a faint path there, that became part of the picture so neatly that it looked real from any distance. She stood and reached high, verifying that the sky was painted too, and the clouds.

This was one giant picture, with only the square ground being real. But what was the point of it?

She traced the thread back the way they had come. She discovered that she was in a corner, and the thread came from another wall. She had come from another mural.

She walked out of the corner, toward a house that seemed to be in the real section. There was a man hoeing his garden beside it. But as she approached him, she discovered that he was frozen in place. This was odd in more than one way: not only was he absolutely still, not even breathing, he was off-balance, and should have fallen. But he remained as he was, slightly tilted.

"Hello," she said. But of course there was no answer. She touched his elbow, and it was as hard as stone. She pushed him, at first lightly, then strongly. He remained fixed in place.

She realized that the man must be a realistic statue, fastened to the ground at a slight angle, immobile. All the vegetables growing in the garden were fixed too; she could not bend so much as a lettuce leaf. All part of the crafted scene.

She went to a nearby tree. All its leaves were fixed in place. There was no breath of wind. She checked the farmstead's pitcher pump. A drop of water was falling from the spout. It was in mid air, frozen too, but not cold, just locked in place. All part of the scene.

Cube was beginning to feel nervous. She had thought this was a world inside a huge cube, but it was actually a lifeless model. She was the only thing moving within it. The only thing alive.

She explored further, using the whisk broom to get around faster, but only confirmed what she had discovered. All the trees, rivers, houses, and people were statuary, part of one encompassing artificial scene, marvelously made. She was alone in a three-dimensional picture.

"I think I need help," she murmured to herself.

She returned to the dogsled. Then she reached into the pouch. "Metria."

The demoness caught her hand and slid out. She looked around. "Oh, my! What fine mess have you gotten us into this time?"

"A three-dimensional painting," Cube said. "I was riding the dogsled along the thread, into the world of Tesseract, and found myself alone in this cube."

"Cube! That's fitting," the demoness laughed. "Cube in a cube."

Cube hadn't thought of that. "Names are seldom entirely coincidental, in Xanth. Could I have been drawn to this world for a reason?"

Metria got serious. "But you said the world was Tesseract."

"Yes. But it seems to be a cube."

"Let me check this out. I'll just pop off for a moment." The demoness disappeared with a sharp pop, leaving a dissipating wisp of smoke behind.

Cube, alone again, tried something else. She summoned a nickelpede. The creature appeared, looked around, and glanced curiously at her.

"I don't understand it any better than you do," she said, and banished it. She had merely been verifying her talent. She felt safer, knowing that she still had her nickelpedes.

Metria reappeared. "It's a cube, all right. Outside it's a cubic moon in orbit about Ida's head, featureless. Inside it's just this decorated shell. Could this be the end of the line?"

"I don't think so. The thread goes into the wall. I just can't follow it."

"Maybe the thread has given out. How many moons has it traversed?"

"I believe this is the fifteenth. But if it's the end, what am I supposed to do here?"

"I just remembered: it's not the end, because there's Zombie World on down the line. So it must be a tired thread."

"I'll bring out the Princesses," Cube said. She put her hand into the pouch. "Princesses."

Three hands caught hers. The three slid out together, and landed before her. "Wow!" Melody said, looking around.

"A square world," Harmony added, looking asquare.

"A *cubic* world," Rhythm said, looking acube.

"Cube's world," Metria said.

"But it's supposed to be Tesseract," Cube said. "Whatever that is."

"We'd better look it up," Melody said.

"I'll get the big dictionary," Harmony agreed.

"Ooof!" Rhythm grunted as a huge tome landed in her arms.

They put the dictionary on the ground and turned the pages, poring over it.

"Tesseract," Melody said, finding the word.

"A cube generalized to four dimensions," Harmony read.

"A four-dimensional hypercube," Rhythm read.

"A structure consisting of eighty-one identical cubes occupying the same space," Metria read over their shoulders. "That's three to the fourth power."

"We're only three to the third power," Melody said.

"You mean three cubed," Harmony said.

"That's wrong," Rhythm said. "We are really only one Sorceress cubed."

Cube was having difficulty following this, but doubted that the little Princesses knew exactly what they were talking about. "Do you mean that however you figure it, the tesseract is beyond your power?"

"That's what they mean," Metria said. "They can't fix it."

"Then who can fix it?"

"Maybe one of the others," Melody said hopefully.

"Like Karia," Harmony said. "She's smart."

"All centaurs are," Rhythm said.

Cube brought out the centaur, and explained the situation. "Do you know what a tesseract is?"

"Of course. It's a hypercube. A four-dimensional structure."

Cube's head was thickening. "Can you explain that from the ground up?"

The centaur smiled. "I'll go into didactic mode." She reached behind her to draw an arrow from her quiver. She used the tip to make a dent in the sand before her. "A dimension is a measurement. This is a point—a no-dimensional object." She scratched a line. "This is a line, a one-dimensional object. It has length, nothing else." She scratched a square. "This is a two-dimensional figure, length and breadth. Infinitely greater than the prior figure, but still limited." She glanced at the Princesses. "Eight sticks, please." They appeared in a bundle, and she continued her lesson. She stood four sticks at the corners of the square, and connected them with four more. "This is a cube, a three-dimensional figure, with length, breadth, and height. Now if we extend it another dimension, we'll have a hypercube. A tesseract. It's elementary."

Metria and the three Princesses looked as blank as Cube felt. "How do you extend it?" Cube asked. "I mean, what other dimension is there?"

"The fourth dimension is time, of course. Backwards, forward, sidewise, above, and below. It increases the volume of the figure enormously, without adding to any of the three spacial dimensions. A tesseract would be a perfect four-dimensional square: eighty-one similar cubes in the same space."

"Time," Cube said, clinging to that sliver she could understand. "You mean a cube before this one is another cube, and one after this one is still another?"

"That depends on how you see it, but that is approximately it. The fourth dimension can add infinitely to the three spacial dimensions."

"But it still looks like a cube," Cube said.

"Yes, just as any even cross section of a cube looks like a square. Of course if you get into tilted slices, like conic sections—"

"So this world-sized cube we're inside of is a cross section of a world-sized tesseract."

"Yes. Wasn't that obvious?"

"Not at first. What do you make of the walls?"

Karia inspected the nearest wall. "I believe this shows one of the other aspects of the hypercube. Unfortunately it has been imploded, so is not serviceable at the moment. See, it is not a picture; it has perspective."

"It has what?" Cube asked.

"This is a special kind of magic that makes distant objects change position with respect to close ones," the centaur explained. "See, if you walk along the wall, you can see things shift behind others."

Cube and the others walked along the wall, looking. It was true; distant mountains seemed to shift, so as to be behind different trees or houses. Yet when she touched the wall, it remained impenetrable.

"You mean that everything in the walls is real, too?" Cube asked. "Just flattened?"

"Because of the compression of the tesseract into a simple cube," Karia agreed. "It is not functioning, any more than we would be if we were squeezed into two dimensions."

"What would make this cube serviceable?" Cube asked.

"Restoration of the proper tesseract. Then the inhabitants could resume motion."

"The statues are real people?" Metria asked. "Frozen in time?"

"Yes. A population with no temporal dimension is unable to function properly."

"So we need to restore time," Cube said carefully. "Then they'll return to life, and the world of Tesseract will be whole again."

"Who could implode a tesseract?" Metria asked.

"A Demon," Karia said.

"Fornax!" the three Princesses said together.

"She's still trying to mess up the Quest," Cube said, as the fog in her head cleared.

"Figuring the Demon Xanth wouldn't notice a tiny spot like this," Metria agreed. "The fifteenth derivative of Ida's little moon."

"She must have been right," Cube said. "Because she got away with it."

"And now we have to fix it," Karia said.

"If we just can figure out how," Cube said.

There was half a silence. None of them knew how.

"Maybe one of the others will know," Karia said, timing her comment to come exactly as the half silence ended.

"Who?" Cube asked, her hand poised near the pouch.

"Maybe Ryver," Melody said. "He's handsome."

"Or Drek," Harmony added. "He's big."

"Or Cory and Tessa," Rhythm concluded. "They sidestep."

Cube put her hand in. "All remaining Companions," she said. The four of them slid out.

There was a tangle of explanations. Then Cory spoke. "Tessa must hold the key, because her full name is Tesseract."

Cube's jaw dropped. "The same as this world!"

"Well, it's too big a name for me," Tessa said. "It's downright ungainly, so I don't use it."

"Still, you must be the key. I came here, and it's a cube; maybe you can make it return to tesseract form. Names relate."

Tessa smiled. "I wonder how Cory's relates? Her full name is Corybant. It means a wild dancing spirit."

"I'm too awkward to dance," Cory said, embarrassed.

"But you know, names do relate," Ryver said. "Cube found this cube, and she had to gather nine Companions. There must be some reason for all of us. Tessa must be part of the key, but she can't do it alone. Maybe Cory is another part of the key."

"Wild dancing won't help," Cory said sourly.

"How do you know?"

There was most of another silence, which Karia again managed to catch just as it ended. "Perhaps it is so. We don't know the rules of magic here; they could be anything. Maybe dancing would cause the tesseract to be restored."

"Maybe by all of us," Ryver said. "Maybe that's why all of us are here. To be part of the magic dance."

"I can't dance," Cory said. "I ruin any dance I try."

"So do I," Ryver said. "I'm all feet."

"We don't know any dances," Melody said.

"We haven't learned the steps," Harmony agreed.

"So we just make the music," Rhythm concluded.

"Nobody ever wants to dance with me," Cube said.

"And how is Drek supposed to dance?" Metria asked. "He doesn't have any feet."

"So that's out," Ryver said.

"Perhaps not," Karia said. "There is a kind of dance that does not require intricate or beautiful body motions, or memory of patterns. All it needs is following directives as they come. It's called square dancing."

"Square—as in cube?" Ryver asked. "As in tesseract?"

The centaur nodded. "Perhaps that does relate." She sent a glance around to the others. "Shall we try it?"

Cube shrugged. She wasn't at all sure this would work, but she had no better idea.

"A square dance requires four couples," Karia said. "Four men and four women. Since we have eight females and only two males, and one of the latter can't dance, we shall have to make do with some substitutions. Shall I make assignments?"

"Girls have to play boys?" Melody demanded.

"Some will," the centaur agreed.

"Not us!" Harmony protested.

"But for the purpose of the dance—"

"Yuck!" Harmony concluded.

Karia rolled her eyes so sweepingly they almost fell out of her head. "You three will be girls," she conceded. Then she turned to the others. "You are amenable?"

The others nodded.

"Cube, you will be a male," Karia said. "Dance with Melody. Metria, dance with Harmony. Ryver, dance with Rhythm. She will enchant your feet just enough to enable you to do it." She sent the little Princess a look that required agreement. "Cory, dance with Tessa. Form your couples."

The three Princesses ran to join their partners, and Cory and Tessa were already together. Cube had known she would not be cast as a woman and was resigned. She suspected that Cory was similarly resigned; she was the tallest member of their party, and not pretty. Metria seemed to be handling it well enough; maybe her sense of mischief sufficed. She had assumed the aspect of a portly middle-aged gentleman.

"I will direct the dance," Karia said. "Drek will watch the thread and seek to follow it. The moment he makes it, we will follow, for the way will be open. The rest of you must focus on the dance, for if it is to be effective, it must be accurate. Keep dancing, whatever happens, until I say it has ended."

The centaur did seem to know what she was doing. Cube almost found a modicum of confidence. Half a modicum, anyway.

"Couples form a square, facing each other," Karia said, and made spot adjustments so that they got it right. Cube and Melody faced Metria and Harmony, with the other couples forming the sides of the square.

"Now there are certain basic actions, which we will rehearse first," the centaur continued. "When the dance starts, you will do them when I call them out. The important thing is that they be done together; a square dance is a pattern, most esthetic when performed precisely. You need have no concern for what is past or what is coming; it is ongoing. Simply listen to my calls and it will go well. Now the first action is 'swing your partner.' " She directed them in that, and soon Cube was swinging Melody competently. Other actions were do-si-do, promenade, and balancing. When they had these straight, Karia asked for music. The Princesses got together and generated loud square dance music from a spot in the air above the square. Now they were ready to dance.

"Set in order," Karia said. "Balance to your corner." Cube turned and did the leg swinging motion facing her corner, who was Rhythm. As they finished, she faced the girl's partner Ryver briefly. He was dancing competently, his partner having enchanted his clumsy feet as directed. Cube smiled at him, beginning to enjoy this. To her surprise, he smiled back. Then she really enjoyed it.

"Swing your partner." Cube turned back to swing Melody.

"Gee this is fun," the girl said.

"Promenade." Cube and Melody linked arms the prescribed way and stepped around in a circle, in time with the others. She could see that it did form a pattern, an artistic whole. There was pleasure in that too.

Meanwhile she saw that Drek was elongating along the nearby thread, getting close to it, facing its entry into the wall. If, somehow, this dance made it possible to enter the realm of that wall, he would be ready.

The dance intensified. Not only was Cube getting into it, she saw that the others were too. There was something about the music, the beat, the pattern, and the participation that was exhilarating. She had never been a great dancer, but she could follow directions, and the basic forms were easy. She saw that this was true for Ryver, who did not need fancy footwork, and Cory, who did not need to be short, and of course the girls. Even Metria in her jolly coachman guise was smiling. There was pleasure in unity, and doing things together, making the patterns. They were being melded into an artistic whole. Too bad they didn't have an audience!

Something happened. At first Cube thought it was merely her joy of the dance; she was feeling giddy as she moved through the forms. For one thing, she even got to do-si-do with Ryver on occasion, though both had male parts; not everything was male-female. The dance seemed to be transcending itself, becoming something larger, more significant. But soon she realized that it was something beyond it. The very air seemed to be coming alive.

Drek was disappearing into the wall.

"Promenade!" Karia cried. "Along the thread!"

They followed the thread—right through the wall and into the adjacent cube. Along a path, until they came to a broader section. They formed the square again, bowed to their partners, and ended it.

There was a burst of applause. Startled, Cube looked. People were all around them. The folk of this realm had come alive! The bad spell had been broken, and the tesseract had been restored. All through the magic of the dance.

They broke it up, breathlessly congratulating each other. Suddenly Cube was being hugged—and realized with amazement that it was by Ryver. "We did it!" he said. "We danced and won."

They had indeed. But for the moment all Cube could think of was being held by Ryver. What absolute joy!

13

AMBER DAWN

Of course the good folk of Tesseract World insisted on feting them all with a great party, and they insisted on learning how this marvelous magic square dance was performed. It turned out that they had been aware of their predicament, but unable to do anything about it. The collapse of their four-dimensional reality into three dimensions had happened in less than an instant, rendering them helplessly timeless. Until they were restored by the dance troupe, and they were duly grateful.

First the group repeated the dance they had done, which was easy, because Karia remembered the calls. Then they became instructors, each taking a Tesseract partner to guide through it, forming two squares. The natives were good at multiplying squares; it was their nature. Cube got to dance as a woman, with a handsome male partner; she loved that. Even Drek Dragon got to dance with a slinky lady dragon, in their fashion, and she loved his perfume.

At last they were able to proceed. The others slid into the pouch, and Cube followed the thread to Princess Ida, whose moon looked like a stylized bug. It seemed that the tour of the moons was not over, because the thread led to it.

"This is Fractal," Ida said. "Much of it is invisible from here, but when you go to it you will find that it is surrounded by one or two myriads of threadlike patterns, leading to ever-smaller similar worlds. My next self resides on one of those worlds. I'm sure she will help you."

"Is there no limit to these moons?" Cube asked. "Is every one different?"

"The answer seems to be no and yes. We have discovered no limit, and no two worlds similar in shape. Perhaps it is your destiny to reach the end of the line, as it were, and fathom the last of the chain."

"I don't know," Cube said doubtfully.

"Neither do I," Ida agreed.

Cube thanked her, and rode the dogsled to Fractal World. It was as described, replete with many sprouting threads, twisting into intricate diminishing patterns. Her own thread followed the fractal thread from the nose-point and came to a tiny bug-world hidden there. But of course it seemed full world size when she got there. The Ida there was hospitable, and helped her on her way to the next moon.

And the next, and the next. It became a blur, and Cube regretted that she could not linger to admire the truly different worlds she saw in passing. But she had somewhere to go, and she wanted to get there.

Then she came to Zombie World. It looked like a moldy apple, and she hoped she would not remain there long. But as fate would have it, this was the one she had to explore.

The thread did not lead her to a zombie Princess Ida, but past rotten trees and decaying people to a crumbling castle surrounded by a stinking moat. "Oh, no!" Cube breathed. "Castle Zombie."

So it was. Cube knew that most of the zombies had retired to their own world, along with the original Zombie Master, and that there was now a replacement couple in Xanth proper. That was all she knew; she had not been curious about the affairs of zombies, preferring only that they be elsewhere. Now it seemed she would be learning more, though not by choice.

The dogsled stopped at the moat. The drawbridge was down, but looked too decrepit to sustain the weight of even one loaded sled. Yet the thread continued on into the sagging castle.

Cube sighed. "You stay here," she told the dogsled. "Maybe my weight won't be too much for it."

The dogsled looked relieved. She wondered how there could be danger, here on the tiniest part of the tiniest world, but it did seem like full size, and she felt as solid as she had on Xanth. Magic didn't have to make sense except on its own terms.

Now what about the pacifier? This time she put it into the pouch. That should stop it from doing anything weird while she was dealing with the Zombie Master.

She put a tentative foot on the derelict bridge. The wood looked rotten, but was actually firm under a squishy surface. She let her weight come down on it, and it held. She took another step, and then walked on out over the moat. It seemed that the rot was mostly for show. If the rest of the castle was that way, it was safe.

Just when she was halfway across, a bilious dripping head rose out of the green soup that was the moat. The moat monster! It opened its festering mouth. It was going to eat her!

Almost without thinking, she put her hand to the pouch. "Drek!" she said.

The dragon emerged so quickly he missed the bridge and dropped down into the moat with a great gooey splash. He wasn't pleased; an absolutely putrid stench wafted up.

The moat monster sniffed, sneezed, and recoiled. It seemed that even a zombie had limits.

Cube held her breath and hurried on across. "I'm okay, Drek!" she called. "Come on back."

The dragon shook his head. She knew why: he didn't want to stink up the pouch.

"Very well; I'll return for you when I'm done in the castle. See if you can find a place to clean up."

Drek nodded. She turned to face the castle, musing how the folk in the pouch always emerged in proper scale for the world they were in. Maybe her soul management, as she shucked off most of it each time she went to a smaller world, applied to the pouch and its contents, so that the process was automatic. She was just glad that her Companions were still with her, when at one point she had feared they weren't. Their souls had after all come along in the soul pouch. Again, magic was wonderful.

She knocked on the great sagging door, hoping a zombie wouldn't answer. She was in luck: a lovely elderly woman was there. Even old women looked better than Cube did, of course. "Yes?"

"I'm Cube, from Xanth proper. I—I'm here on a Quest, and it led me here."

"Why come in, dear," the woman said. "I am Millie the Ghost."

"A ghost!"

Millie laughed. "So-called because I was a ghost for eight hundred years. I was a restored-to-living woman for more than fifty years before retiring here to Zombie World with my husband, the Zombie Master. I'm so very glad to see you; you're just in time."

"In time?" Cube asked blankly.

"I will fetch her. Meanwhile make yourself comfortable." Millie hurried off.

Fetch who? Cube wasn't sure there wasn't a misunderstanding of some sort. But she saw the thread moving on down the castle hall, so she made herself comfortable by following it. It led to a stairway, which was in good order, as was the hall; there was no trace of zombie rot here.

At the top of the stair was a raised alcove, and in it was a mass of fur or wild hair. The thread stopped at the fur.

Cube picked it up. It seemed to be a cap, or perhaps a wig. She set it on her head, and felt a strange surge of emotion. She had been entirely too nice; it was past time to do something for herself, and to hell with the consequences.

Alarmed by the unaccustomed thought, she swept the wig

off her head. It landed back in the alcove, askew. "What is that thing?" she demanded, flustered.

"That is the Hell Toupee," a man's voice answered. "It makes its wearer evil."

That explained it. Cube turned to face the man, who had come along a side hall. He looked cadaverously old, but otherwise healthy. "Hello. I'm, uh, Cube."

"And I am the Zombie Master. My wife said you were here. She is fetching the baby."

"The baby!"

"Isn't that why you are here?"

"I know nothing about any baby. I'm on a—a private Quest, which just led me to—to the Hell Toupee."

"I see. But I am not at all sure why you would wish to have that artifact. Even the zombies won't touch it. We have left it alone, pending some decision on its disposition."

"I don't know why either, but it seems I'm supposed to take it. Maybe I don't have to wear it."

"Perhaps it is your destiny to deliver it where it belongs."

"Maybe that's it." She put the toupee into the pouch.

"Cube!" Millie called from downstairs. "Where are you?"

"That's my wife," the Zombie Master said. "We must discuss this matter of the baby."

"I think so," Cube agreed.

They walked down the steps to the lower hall. There was Millie, holding a swaddled baby.

"There seems to have been another misunderstanding, dear," the Zombie Master said. "This young woman is not here for the baby."

"Oh," Millie said faintly. "Then what are we to do with her?" She held up the baby.

"You see, the stork got confused," the Zombie Master explained. "It delivered the baby to the wrong Castle Zombie. This one was obviously intended for Breanna of the Black Wave, and Justin Tree. But by the time we realized the error, the stork was gone; it did not seem to like the environment."

Cube looked at the baby. She was the color of amber, with

a full head of hair that resembled waves of grain. She was the loveliest baby Cube had ever seen.

"She has to be delivered to the right castle," Millie said. "I assumed—we don't get many visitors from Xanth—that you were here to do that."

Now Cube saw that the thread went to the baby. "I—maybe that's the case. I—I didn't know what I was here for. I just never thought of a baby." And it seemed that the paci-fier was still having some serendipitous effect.

"That must be it," Millie said, relieved. "We are really too old for that now, and this is not the ideal world for new life." She handed the baby to Cube. "She has a nice talent." She went on to describe it.

"But I don't know anything about caring for a baby," Cube protested belatedly. "It was a long way, coming here, and will be a long way back. I don't have the right kind of food or clothing or anything."

"That should be no problem," Millie said. "You can re-turn to Xanth must faster than you came, simply by expand-ing back to normal size; your soul remnants will find you as you do."

"But I'll be in Castle Roogna! I'll have to travel to Castle Zombie. That will take at least a day."

"You can put the baby into that magic pouch," the Zombie Master said. "No time will pass for her, and she won't need to be fed or clothed or changed." It seemed he had seen that kind of item before.

"So I can," Cube said. "What's her name? I need that to bring her out."

"We don't know," Millie said.

"She has a point," the Zombie Master said. "We shall have to give the baby a name, so she isn't lost in the pouch."

"She has such lovely amber skin," Millie said.

"And she was delivered at dawn," the Zombie Master said.

"Then let's call her Amber Dawn," Cube said. She didn't mention her confusion about how there could be dawn here on a world that derived from an endless chain of worlds orbiting Princess Ida's head in Castle Roogna on Xanth, so saw no sunlight.

They nodded. "It's a nice name," Millie said.

Cube spoke to the baby. "We hereby name you Amber Dawn," she said. "Do you understand?"

There was no response. "She's too young to understand," the Zombie Master said.

"Besides, she's asleep," Millie said.

So she was. "I will bring you out soon, Amber Dawn," Cube said. Then she slid the baby into the pouch.

"Oh, my, I just remembered," Millie said. "Now that the baby has been named, she has to rejoin her body within a day, or her soul will perish. Normally the storks keep their schedule, and soul and body don't get separated."

"Separated?" Cube asked.

"This is Amber Dawn's soul, of course. Her body remains in Xanth proper."

"Of course," Cube said faintly. So she had a deadline, regardless of how time seemed to the baby in the pouch.

"So that means dawn at Castle Zombie," Millie said.

Cube realized that she had better get moving. "Now I'll just—you say I can expand my way back?"

"Aren't you forgetting something?" the Zombie Master inquired gravely.

"Forgetting?" Cube repeated blankly. Then she remembered. "Drek! Drek Dragon! I can't leave him here."

"Of course you can't," Millie agreed.

Cube bid them both farewell and went outside. "Drek!" she called. "Where are you?"

There was a honk. Cube looked across the moat to a nearby pond that looked reasonably clean. Drek had found it and washed himself. He came sliding to meet her as she crossed the drawbridge. He no longer smelled of moat or stench. Cube hugged his neck, relieved that she hadn't left him behind. Soon he was back in the pouch.

Now what about the dogsled? "Can you find your own way back if I leave you now?" she asked it.

The dogsled wagged its tail. She hadn't known it had a tail. "Okay, go home now, with my thanks."

The dogsled puffed into smoke and disappeared. Actually it was returning the same way as she was about to, just not as far. It would be hard to get lost, since everything was circling Ida's head. But would that have worked for Drek, who had come here in the pouch?

Cube checked for the thread. It led ahead, but not the usual way. It was growing larger, thicker, and higher. In fact it was a huge cone, its apex just before her. It was expanding into infinity. Which was exactly what she should do.

"On my way," she said, and concentrated on expansion. Immediately she felt herself growing larger, puffing out, becoming as big as the castle, and as big as the world. As big as the universe! She saw Ida's head, as Zombie World orbited it, but she was still growing, expanding to the next stage, to the next Ida, and the next and the next, too rapidly for her to count.

Suddenly she was lying on a bed in a small chamber. What had happened? Why had the expansion been interrupted?

Then she saw Princess Ida, with the little globe of Ptero orbiting her head. She was back to Xanth proper! "I'm back," she said, half in wonder.

"That's nice," Ida said. "Did you accomplish your mission?"

"Some of it, I think." She sat up, feeling rather massive in her original body. "I have a baby to deliver to Castle Zombie."

"A baby!" Ida said, as surprised as Cube had been.

Quickly Cube explained what had happened. "So I'll need to hurry there, but I don't know the way."

"Perhaps one of your Companions does."

"Karia! She can take me there."

"Unfortunately it is now night," Ida said. "Flying is not safe at this time."

"But I need to get there by dawn!"

"Perhaps your centaur can take you on the ground. The enchanted path should be safe even at night."

"Yes, that will have to do," Cube said. "Uh, thank you, Princess Ida. There turned out to be a lot for me to do on the moons."

"When you are done with your Quest, you must return and tell me about it."

"I will!" Cube hurried out of the chamber, and out of the castle.

When she was beyond the moat, she put her hand to the pouch. "Centaur."

Karia grasped her hand and slid out. "I see we are back at Castle Roogna, at night."

"Yes, and we need to get to Castle Zombie by dawn. Do you know the way? I understand that you won't fly at night, but if you know the enchanted paths—"

"I do. Will you tell me why the sudden urgency?"

"Yes. As we travel."

And while they traveled rapidly along the dark path, Cube told the centaur about Zombie Planet and the Hell Toupee and the baby girl with her deadline for delivery.

"That is remarkable," Karia agreed. "I wasn't aware that the storks made errors like that."

"They must have had an address, Castle Zombie, and not realized there were two of them."

"Perhaps. Yet I remember that Breanna of the Black Wave was active in the notorious case of the Swell Foop that won Counter Xanth from Demoness Fornax."

"Another trick by Fornax?" Cube asked. "But how would that interfere with my Quest?"

"Perhaps you were not the target, this time. She might have been trying to punish Breanna."

"But hurting a little baby? I can't believe that."

"It may be that you lack the necessary evil mind."

That gave Cube an idea. "I can consider it with an evil mind." She explained about the Hell Toupee. "Make sure I take it off again, just in case."

"I will."

Cube brought out the toupee and put it on her head. The nicety of the ploy was immediately apparent. "Oh, yes, that is the most effective punishment," she said. "To deny Breanna what she most wants: a wonderful baby. Naturally I won't deliver Amber Dawn to her."

Karia's arm swung back and knocked the toupee off her head. It fell on the ground. "Leave it there," the centaur said. "You're right: it is evil."

Cube shuddered. "Thanks—I needed that. But I'd better recover it. The thread led me to it, so there must be a reason for me to have it."

"That must be true," Karia agreed reluctantly. She turned and trotted back. Cube dismounted, picked up the fallen toupee, put it in the pouch, and remounted.

"When will we reach Castle Zombie?" Cube asked.

"Two hours after midnight. You should get some sleep."

"I should," Cube agreed. "But wake me if there is any trouble."

"I will do that."

Cube relaxed, lulled by the steady beat of the centaur's hooves. Soon she slept.

Then Karia woke her. "Cube. Wake quietly."

Cube looked around. The centaur had stopped moving. Darkness was all around. "What's the problem?" she murmured low.

"I seem to have lost the path. I don't know how it happened."

There was a burst of demonic laughter. "Ho ho ho! I did it, centaur! I tricked you from the enchanted path."

"Who are you?" Karia demanded.

"I am Demon Viate."

"Ugh!"

Cube realized there was a pun, as there often was in demons' names. D. Viate—deviate. Demons did not exactly have talents, but they did have specialties, and evidently this one's specialty was to cause travelers to lose their way.

"Maybe we need a demon on our side," Cube murmured. She put her hand to the pouch. "Metria."

The demoness emerged. She caught on instantly. "Viate, get your obscure posterior out of here!"

"What are *you* doing here, Metria? Go make your own mischief."

"This *is* my mischief. Now put us back on the right path before I get annoyed."

"And what if I don't?"

"I'll smack you on the kisser."

"How could you do that?" he demanded contemptuously, raising his fists.

"Like this." Metria popped across and caught the demon with a loud smack.

"Ooooo!" Viate wailed, and vanished.

"Darn!" Metria swore. "Maybe I kissed him too hard."

"We need to get back to the enchanted path," Cube said, trying to stifle a smirk. "Can you find it?"

"Let me look," the demoness said, and popped off again.

"You'll never find it," another voice said.

Cube couldn't see who spoke, but it sounded like a demon. Her nickelpedes wouldn't have any effect against a demon. So she tackled it forthrightly. "Who are you?"

A glowing manlike shape appeared. "Demon Vious, not at your service."

"Ugh!" Karia exclaimed.

That would be D. Vious. Devious. There was unlikely to be any help there. But Cube had a notion: maybe he could be made to help if she used his own nature against him. So she got devious. "Let me talk to your awful girlfriend."

"Why would you want her?"

"Why would you want to know?"

Evidently perplexed, he yielded, probably curious about the point of her deviousness. "Cent!" he called.

"Ugh!"

A shimmeringly lovely outline appeared. "What is supposed to be so awful about me?" the demoness asked, sounding hurt.

"Nothing," Cube said quickly, giving the centaur a warning nudge with her knee. D. Cent was exactly whom they needed, a decent demoness. Naturally opposites attracted. "It's your boyfriend we don't like. You are Demoness Cent?"

"I am. Is there any way I can help you?"

"We have lost our way, and would like to return to the enchanted path. Will you show us?"

"I regret I am unable."

This was one demon who would be unlikely to deceive them. "Why is that?"

"Because this is the Isle of the Goles. It relates to Xanth only once a day, actually night, at midnight, and has no connection at other times. So there is no way to the enchanted path. Not until next midnight."

"But we can't wait that long!"

"I am extremely regretful," Cent said sincerely. "Perhaps my former boyfriend Termined can help you.

"Ugh!" But at least the centaur had the wit to muffle it this time.

Demon Termined—D. Termined. That sounded promising. "Yes, we would like to talk with him."

"Termined!" she called.

"Demon Termined here," a new voice said. "I happen to be busy at the moment, but if you really want to make up—"

"No," Cent said. "I want you to help these nice folk get off the isle. Viate led them astray, and they need to leave immediately."

"But they must wait until midnight."

"We know that," Cube said. "But we thought that if anyone could help us leave sooner, you are the one. You have such—"

Karia tried to stifle her ugh but some of it leaked out anyway.

"Resoluteness," Cube said firmly. "Surely there is some way, for a person like you."

"Hm. What kind of deal do you offer?"

This was progress, of a sort. "Maybe there is something we can do for you in return."

"Maybe there is. I am trying to train a surly mortal horse. How are you at horses?"

Cube knew nothing about horses, but did not feel it would be expedient to say that. "Perhaps if I saw the horse."

"This way. The corral is nearby." The demon lighted the way along another path. Karia followed, with Cube still riding.

Metria reappeared. "There's no path back," she said, frustrated. "This island has no connection to Xanth."

"Not until midnight," Karia informed her. "It seems we were led here at the one time it was possible."

"That's a suspicious coincidence."

"Fornax, again," Cube muttered. "She must have enlisted Demon Viate to do it."

Metria glowed purple. "I could get annoyed, if I tried."

"Our best course is to find our way through despite her," Karia said. "Not only will that enable us to complete the Quest, it will make her madder than ever."

Cube and Metria laughed together.

They arrived at the corral. Within it stood a bold warrior horse with a glittering harness and saddle. "What a magnificent creature!" Cube exclaimed.

"He's an ornery brute," Termined said. "I can't do a thing with him." He threatened the horse with a whip that appeared in his hand.

"Don't you dare!" Cent cried, outraged.

The horse's ears laid back. Suddenly the demon groaned and fell to the ground. "$$$$!" he swore villainously, puffing into smoke. "He did it again!"

"Now this is interesting," Karia murmured approvingly. "This is obviously a highly trained horse, and he has some kind of power."

"He may not like demons," Metria said.

"He may not like being disparaged or abused," Cube said. "I appreciate that."

The horse's head turned toward her. He evidently understood what they were saying.

"Let me see what I can do," Cube said, dismounting. "Termined, what is his name?"

"Charles."

Cube approached the horse. "Hello, Charles. I've probably forgotten more than I ever knew about horses, but you strike me as a remarkable specimen. I hope you will talk with me."

The horse nodded.

"Do you like demons?"

Charles shook his head.

"Do you like being called an ornery brute?"

He shook his head.

"Do you like girls?"

The horse nodded.

"What about me?"

Charles hesitated.

"I'm a mortal girl," Cube clarified. "Even if I'm not beautiful."

The horse looked embarrassed. He sniffed her hair. Then he nodded, recognizing her as a girl.

"You evidently have a magic talent. You can make a person hurt."

Charles nodded.

"Ugh!"

Karia had just caught on to a pun. Cube cudgeled her balky brain, and managed to get it. "Is your nickname Charlie? Charlie Horse?"

He nodded.

"So you can give muscle spasms to folk that bother you."

He nodded.

"I like you, Charles. I have a talent like yours, in a way. I can conjure and control nickelpedes." A nickelpede appeared in her hand. "It's unladylike but useful."

Charles nuzzled her cheek. He liked her.

Cube banished the bug. "I considered making a deal to make you manageable, in return for being shown a way off this island. I can't make that deal, because you're not unmanageable, you just don't like being treated like dirt. I know the feeling. You have the right of the case."

The horse gazed at her soulfully.

Cube faced Demon Termined. "No deal. I can't make this horse treat you with a respect you don't deserve."

"I can't get you off the isle before midnight, either," the demon responded.

"Why you bundle of stinkweed!" Metria exclaimed. "I ought to smack you one, like this." She puffed across and have him a lip-smacking kiss.

"Ungh! Keep the #### horse; he's your problem now." The demon disappeared. Demoness Cent also faded out, and Vious was already gone.

"It seems the horse is yours," Karia murmured.

"He's not mine! I don't own him." Could this be another unlooked for discovery? No, because she wasn't carrying the pacifier, so that she could use her own name and summon nickelpedes. Just to be sure, she put her hand to the pouch and found it there.

"Yours because he chooses to be," the centaur clarified. "He likes you."

"Oh—like a Companion." She faced Charles. "You want to come along with us?"

The horse nodded. He nibbled at Cube's pocket where she had just absent-mindedly put the magic pacifier.

"Hey, you don't want that!" Cube protested.

"Yes he does," the demoness said.

Cube sighed. "Okay, I'll fasten it to your saddle. But it will change your name and your luck." She took the pacifier and fastened it.

"Not that we know where we're going," Metria said.

"Maybe the goles can help us," Karia said.

"The whats?"

"Don't you remember? This is Gole Isle.

"Oh. Yes. You have a sharper memory than I do."

"Centaurs do. Why don't you ride Seren? He'd like that."

Cube turned to the horse. "Would you?"

Seren nodded.

She put her foot in the stirrup and climbed into the saddle. It was surprisingly comfortable. "Do I have to use the reins? I don't know reins."

The horse shrugged. The reins disappeared.

Cube considered that for half a moment, and decided not

to say anything. Obviously Seren had always been his own horse, when he chose to be.

"I think you don't need me now," Karia said. "Since there is nothing I can do to return us to the path, I'll return to the pouch." She did so.

"Me too," Metria said, and slid in also, with another naughty display of thigh. Apparently she couldn't help being seductive, even when there were no men to freak out.

"We need to find the goles," Cube said to the horse. She felt uncomfortably alone, but refused to give up hope.

Seren set off at a trot. Cube grabbed the saddle horn, not used to the gait. Somehow Karia had always managed to walk or fly in a way that made Cube secure, but of course she was not a horse.

Soon they came to a lighted village. As they did, two creatures came to meet them. They were about as strange as Cube had seen. They were humanoid in shape, but their heads were those of horses and they had the hoofs and tails of horses. They also had wings. They looked like winged centaurs gone wrong.

"Uh, hello," Cube said to the creatures.

"Hello," the taller horsehead said, speaking perfect human. He had a fine brown mane. "I see that you have tamed Seren." Then he looked surprised, having thought to use a different name.

"He's a good horse."

"Evidently so. He did not seem happy here, so the demons said they would take him."

"That's over. Seren is my companion now. I am Cube, and I would like to get off this island."

"I am Gomer Gole, and this is my friend Goldie Gole."

"Hello," Goldie said. Her mane was bright golden yellow. "We can give you housing for the night, and show you the isle in the day, and conduct you to the connection with Xanth at midnight."

"But we need to be on our way immediately! We can't wait a day and night."

"We regret that," Gomer said apologetically. "But that is

the only time our isle relates to Xanth. All the islands are like that; they phase in to Xanth at different times, and are otherwise separate."

Cube was feeling desperate, but knew that hysterics would accomplish nothing. There had to be a way! She simply needed to find it.

"Will you tell me more about yourselves and your island now?" she asked, hoping that there would be some hint there.

"Gladly," Gomer said. "We two are the night watch, and it does get quiet. Our kind lives peacefully and in harmony with each other. We fight only when we absolutely have to. Because we found ourselves surrounded by neighbors who did not share our values, we finally moved to this isolated island."

"He is putting it politely," Goldie said. "Our neighbors regarded us as freaks. We are not freaks, we are an established crossbreed species, similar to the centaurs."

"Well, there is the matter of the healing and the reverse healing," Gomer reminded her.

"Reverse healing?" Cube asked.

"We have natural healing powers," Goldie said. "If one of us is cut, we regenerate swiftly. But if one of us is killed, that healing is reversed, and our bodies become poison. That developed, we think, to stop predators from killing us for meat. But we don't want to poison predators, we want to be left alone."

"I can appreciate why," Cube said. "I think you're right to be isolated. But this does interfere with my Quest and my immediate mission. If only there were some way to depart without waiting—"

Then a bulb flashed over Cube's head, so bright in the darkness that both horse and goles blinked. "We can get off the isle on our own. Sidestepping."

Both goles were perplexed. "We are not familiar with this term," Gomer said.

Cube realized that she shouldn't have spoken aloud. "It's

a special talent two of my friends have. They can go anywhere without normal limitation."

"But your friends aren't here," Goldie said.

"Not at the moment," Cube said. "I'll go look for them."

"They could not have reached the island unless they came
when you did," Gomer said.

"Maybe not," Cube said. "I'll check anyway."

The two goles exchanged a glance, evidently suspecting
that she was overtired. Cube nudged Charles (she found she
could think of him by his correct name, as long as she didn't
speak it), and the horse turned and walked back the way they
had come.

When they were alone in the darkness, Cube explained it
quietly to Charles. "I have several Companions with me. I
keep them in a magic pouch. So don't be alarmed when they
appear. Don't knot up their muscles."

She dismounted and put her hand to the pouch. "Cory.
Tessa."

The two women slid out and stood beside her. "It's dark,"
Cory said. "Is there a problem?"

"There is, but I think you can handle it." Then she realized
that they were looking at the horse, surprised. "This is
Seren, with the ability to give muscle spasms to folk he
doesn't like. He—he was in a bad situation, so now he's
with me."

"He's beautiful," Tessa said.

"We're on Gole Isle. The goles are nice folk, but their island touches Xanth only at midnight. I have a baby to deliver, and—"

"What have you been doing?" Cory asked sharply.

Cube felt herself blushing. "Not my baby! I couldn't—
there hasn't been time—this is a baby soul that the stork left
at the wrong address. I have to get it to the right place. I have
it in the pouch. It was due yesterday."

"The worlds of Ida," Tessa said, catching on. "They have
places very similar to those of Xanth."

"Yes. This one was delivered to Castle Zombie on Zombie

World. So I'm bringing it to the Xanth Zombie Castle. Before dawn tomorrow, if possible."

"That's urgent," Cory agreed. "We don't know the side-stepping route to Castle Zombie, however."

"If you can just get me back to the enchanted path, I'll be fine."

"To do that, we'll have to know exactly where we are," Tessa said.

"Then maybe just to the Xanth mainland," Cube said, beginning to get nervous.

"That we can do," Cory said. "Xanth is easy to find. It will be just across the water."

"Let's do it," Cube said. Then, to the horse: "Maybe I should ride you, for this, Seren. It will be strange, but don't be concerned; it's safe."

The horse nodded. Cube climbed back on the saddle.

Cory and Tessa linked hands and took a step backwards. They shimmered like ghosts in the darkness. Then they stepped forward again.

"Take my hand," Cory said to Cube. Meanwhile Tessa put her hand on Charles's neck, so that he was in contact too.

"Stay with them," Cube told the horse. "Small steps."

They took small steps, and followed the two women into the sidestepping aisle. Then they walked along it, Tessa leading, Charles following, Cory trailing. They walked through trees, startling the horse, but Cube reassured him.

They came to the water and walked across it. Again the horse was surprised, but discovered that his hooves were able to cross the waves. "I told you it would be strange," Cube reminded him.

It got stranger. Something came lunging through the water toward them. It looked like a bull, but it was under the water. It had hooves, but also a fish tail.

"Well well, a bull shark," Tessa said.

"It looks dangerous," Cube said nervously.

"Don't be concerned; it can't gore us. We are displaced in time."

The bull charged them, leaping right into the sidestepping aisle. Charles looked at it, then started to shy back.

"It can't touch us," Cube said reassuringly, hoping she was right.

The bull came at them—and through them without contact. It was a ghost.

"We can see out, they can see in," Tessa explained. "But there can be no physical contact."

That was a relief. But the bull wasn't satisfied. It turned around and ran back, trying even harder. In fact it tried so hard that it did a somersault and landed on its back with a great splash. Little stars and planets clustered about it.

Another creature arrived on the scene. This one wore a hospital uniform—Cube had never seen a hospital, and didn't know of any in Xanth, but she still recognized the uniform—and seemed very attentive. It went to the bull and tended to it, helping it recover.

"Nurse shark," Tessa said.

Cube fancied she could hear Karia groan.

They came to the beach and stopped. "We could sidestep farther," Tessa said. "But we might just lead you astray."

"We need to know a region physically before we can craft a good sidestepping path across it," Cory said.

"We'll get there," Cube said a bit more confidently than she felt. "If I get in trouble, I'll bring someone out to help."

Cory and Tessa returned to the pouch. "Now we need to find the enchanted path to Castle Zombie," Cube told Charles. "I think if we simply cut inland we should intercept it at some point."

The horse nodded and set off. He did seem to have a general idea of the lay of the land.

The crude trail the horse was following through the darkness came to mountainous country. It passed through a narrow cleft which suddenly opened out into a fissure with vertical stone sides. Carved into one side was an illuminated sign: PETRA. Cube had no idea what it meant.

Then she found out. There were buildings carved into the

cliff, with columns and steps leading into the mountain. A city of stone.

Well, that was all right, as long as this path led to the enchanted path. There was just enough light radiating from the rock to clarify the path so that Charles could follow it without stumbling.

The way opened out into a central court. Within it was a dais, and on it was a collection of tea kettles. The stone beneath them seemed to be hot, because the kettles were steaming merrily. Beside them was a collection of tea bags. A neatly printed sign said DRINK ME.

Suddenly Cube was thirsty for tea. It had been one of the few things she enjoyed at home, and she missed it. A drink of tea would be very good at this point.

She urged the horse on toward the dais, but he abruptly balked, his nostrils flaring. He smelled something.

That made Cube nervous. "What do you smell, Seren? Is there some danger?" She looked around, but didn't see anything.

But the horse still balked. After a moment she dismounted and walked toward the dais. She could have some tea while she waited to see what was bothering Charles.

A muscle in her leg tightened up painfully. She stumbled, then recovered her balance. And realized something.

"Seren!" she said indignantly. "You gave me a Charlie horse!" Obviously the horse had kept his own magic.

The horse nodded apologetically.

What was going on here? "You don't want me to drink any of this tea? Why not?"

But of course the horse couldn't explain.

Cube pondered. It might be that Charles smelled something in the tea or the water that he knew was dangerous. She didn't dare ignore that.

"Okay," she said after a bit or two. "I won't drink the tea. But I do want to look at it."

Charles nodded.

She approached the dais and bent down to read the labels on the tea bags. One said PARTEA. Cube didn't recognize that type. Another said SPONTANEITEA. What flavor could that be?

Then she thought she heard a groan. That would be Karia, in her mind's ear. There must be a pun in the neighborhood. It generally paid to fathom puns, because of course they were not just verbal, in Xanth. So she concentrated.

And got it. "Party! Spontaneity. These teas must make a person want to celebrate, or to do something unanticipated. They are magic." She read the other labels: CONFETEA, which might cause a person to shred paper. NOTORI-ETEA, which might make a person well known, for good or ill. IDENTITEA, which might make a person find herself. AMBIGUITEA, which seemed somewhat vague. SOFTEA, which might make a person readily give in to the wishes of others. POSSIBILITEA, which might arouse hope for new prospects.

These should not be dangerous, but might be awkward. Suppose she drank CASUALTEA or DEBILITEA? What about ADVERSITEA, or worse, CALAMITEA? Charles had been right to warn her.

She searched through the bags and finally found one that seemed suitable: MODESTEA. She held it up. "There's no harm in modesty, is there?"

She got a muscle twinge in her arm, causing her to drop the bag. Ouch! What was the matter with that horse?

Rather than make an issue, she gave up on the teas. She walked back toward Charles.

Suddenly goblins appeared in the arches and doorways of the surrounding stone houses. They were big-headed and big-footed little men, ugly and scowling in the goblin manner. Goblins were almost always trouble; they didn't like human folk. They must be the inhabitants of this odd city.

Still, it was best to assume the best, until she knew otherwise. "Hello, goblins," she called. "We are just passing through your citea, I mean city. We mean no mischief and will be on our way."

But the goblins scowled worse, closing in on them from all directions. Not only were they hostile, they seemed to be somewhat woozy, as if they had been imbibing something intoxicating. In fact a number of them looked downright crazy.

Was that a groan?

Then Cube thought of something. This was a stone city, so it was possible that the denizens could be stoned. There was the pun. But what were they stoned on? Surely the tea. The labels might not mean anything; it could all be insanitea. And they wanted her to drink it too.

Cube vaulted onto the horse, which was a good trick as she didn't know how to vault. Maybe she had sniffed some alacritea. "Let's get out of here. Seren!"

The horse moved, but the goblins clustered to shut off the main trail. He turned to go back, but they were clustering there too.

"Maybe a surprise move to the side," Cube murmured, taking a good double handful of saddlehorn.

Charles lurched to the side, finding a path there guarded by only two goblins. Those two abruptly dropped to the ground, clutching their legs. They had muscle cramps, of course. The horse charged through.

But they were still in the stone city, with the cliff-buildings closing in on both sides. They had no choice but to follow the single narrowing alley between them, with the goblins in pursuit.

Charles snorted. Cube sniffed. There was an unkind odor. They seemed to be heading into a bad section of town.

The alley ended in a dead end. Truly dead, by the smell. At its termination was a pedestal with a jar of some kind of food. It stank to high heaven. Cube was sure of that, because the very constellations above were averting their faces. The stench was so thick she had to breathe through her teeth to strain it out.

The words on the pedestal were GAME PRESERVE. That was no understatement; it was truly game. "Talk of all the things I wasn't looking for," Cube muttered. "Spoiled preserves."

And the crazy goblins were charging in from behind.

Then a bulb flashed, reflecting off the facades of the buildings. "Serendipitea!" she exclaimed. "I mean,—ty. You weren't looking for this, we don't want it, but it's what we need. Shut your nose, Seren; we're going to take this with us."

The horse glanced back at her, horrified. But then he stepped close to the pedestal so that she could pick up the jar. The putrid aura of it surrounded them.

"Back!" Cube rasped, unscrewing the lid. "And out." She got the lid off. The fetor intensified. She was out of breath, because her chest didn't want to inhale. This stuff must have been spoiling for centuries!

Charles oriented on the alley and charged. Cube held the jar out front, fogging the air with its miasma. The goblins turned green, which was something normally impossible for them, and fell to either side, gagging. The game preserve was defeating even their madness.

The goblins thinned out, and they galloped back the way they had come, toward the center of the city. They reached the court with the quantitea—Cube groaned mentally and corrected herself—quantity of teas—and swerved around to proceed forward out of the city. But the turn was too sharp for her; she started to fall out of the saddle, and had to drop the jar and grab the horn. The jar smashed on the ground behind them.

"Oh, no!" Cube wailed. "I lost our defense!" For the horrible odor was rising and spreading out like an evil cloud, preventing any pursuit from behind, but more goblins were appearing in front.

Then another bulb flashed in the darkness, making the goblins blink. She had an idea!

She put her hand to the pouch. "Drek," she said.

The dragon slid out and came to rest on the ground beside the horse. "It's okay, Seren," she said quickly. "Drek Dragon is a friend. He'll help us escape. Drek, this is Seren Horse, another friend. We're surrounded by crazy goblins and need to clear them out so we can escape this city. We need to clear the way with a bad smell."

There was the odor of perfume. Drek was pleased to be asked.

Cube was desperate. "Touch him, Seren," she said.

Drek flinched, his tail knotting up. The perfume faded, to be replaced by a smell not unlike the game preserve.

"Onward!" Cube cried. "We've got to get out of here!"

The horse leaped forward. Cube hung on to the horn. They galloped down the street past the tea dais.

"Come on, Drek!" Cube cried. "Follow us!"

The dragon followed—and the goblins did not follow him. In fact the goblins ahead of them got an early whiff of stench and tumbled over themselves to escape it. The way cleared.

Soon they escaped the stone city and were back in the forest. Charles slowed to a walk, breathing hard, and Drek came up behind.

"I'm sorry I had to do that," Cube called to the dragon. "We needed a stench to brush back the goblins, and you weren't making it. Charles's talent is to give folk painful muscle spasms."

Drek assimilated that. For a moment the stench got worse. Then it faded to perfume. He understood the necessity.

"Now we're going to Castle Zombie to make a delivery," Cube said. "You might as well ride; you have helped enough."

Drek nodded, and soon slid back into the pouch.

They moved on through the night, and finally found the enchanted path. They were safe, and should be able to make it by dawn.

Indeed, as the darkness slowly faded in the east, they came into sight of the decrepit castle. "One thing about this," Cube said. "They won't be remarking on our smell."

They stopped at the drawbridge. They had found the thread again, but hadn't been able to see it in the darkness; now it showed the way across the moat.

A zombie came out to intercept them. "Halsh!" it said.

"I am Cube," Cube called. "I have a delivery for Breanna of the Black Wave. It's urgent."

"Breanna'sh nosh seeing anyone," the zombie said.

"She'll see me." Cube urged the horse forward across the bridge. He hesitated, tested it with his hoof, concluded it would hold despite its appearance, and trod across.

"Noo," the zombie protested.

The sun was getting ready to rise; they could not afford to get hung up here. "Do it," Cube murmured.

The zombie fell, grabbing a leg. They moved on into the castle.

The thread led upstairs. "Maybe I'd better go alone, from here," Cube said. "But don't go away, Seren; I'll be back soon." She dismounted. Then as an afterthought she summoned Metria. "Will you keep Seren company?" she asked as the demoness emerged. "I don't think he's fully comfortable in Castle Zombie."

"Who else is?" Metria asked. "Come on, you handsome beast; we'll tour the premises."

Cube followed the thread up the stairs. It led to a closed door. Cube knocked. There was no answer.

She had half a notion what the problem was, so she opened the door and entered the room.

It was a nursery. A dark young woman was sitting in a rocking chair, holding a still bundle. Tears were running down her face and puddling on the floor.

"Hello," Cube said. "I have a delivery to make."

The woman's eyes opened. "Go away. I'm in hopeless grief."

"You must be Breanna. I am Cube. Here is my delivery." She put her hand into the pouch. "Amber," she murmured.

Baby fingers grasped her forefinger. The infant came out. She floated up into the air, a tenuous soul gathering in its nebulous substance. Very little of the soul had been on Zombie World; the rest had to be drawn in from the remnants left along the way.

Breanna's eyes focused on the soul. "You're delivering a ghost?" she asked bleakly. "The ghost of my dead baby?"

"Not exactly. This is the soul of your live baby."

"My—!"

The soul, now complete, oriented and floated to the bundle in Breanna's arms. It overlapped it, then infused it.

The bundle stirred. The baby cried.

"For sure!" Breanna said in glad wonder.

"The stork got confused," Cube explained. "Somehow it delivered the body here, and the soul to Castle Zombie on Zombie World. I happened to be passing through, so I brought it here." As she spoke, the first light of the rising sun showed, sending a beam slanting through the window. "Her name is Amber Dawn, because of her color and the time of her delivery. Her magic talent is to produce a sticky resin that can trap debris, insects, enemies, or whatever else it contacts, hardening and preserving them for later use. I understand her father was a tree, so that relates."

"Amber Dawn," Breanna repeated blissfully. "Oh, I'm so glad! I thought she was dead."

"I made it in time," Cube said. "It had to be by dawn."

"By dawn," Breanna agreed.

"I'll be on my way now," Cube said. "I'm sorry I had to break in on you, but the delivery just couldn't wait."

"I understand," Breanna said. "Don't go yet; we have a celebration to make."

"Really, I don't—"

But Breanna, now fully recovered from her grief, insisted. Soon they were with Justin Tree, who was as surprised and pleased as his wife. He had been out walking in the forest, finding some solace among the familiar trees. They had suffered a night of horror, knowing no way to fix the problem.

In the end, all of the Companions had to come out and join the celebration. Charles Horse was invited too; after all, he had enabled Cube to make it in time.

"I'm a demon," Metria murmured to Cube. "But I do have half a soul, and a child of my own. I know how it is." She wiped away a tear.

That about covered it.

14

INVERSION

Next morning Cube really had to move on, and now Breanna let her. She and Justin Tree gathered with Amber Dawn to see Cube and Charles off, with the other Companions back in the sack, as they put it. "I couldn't let you go yesterday," Breanna said. "There was too much grief and too much joy. Now there is only joy, and I can return to wondering about zombies and talents."

"Zombies and talents?"

"Some zombies keep the magic talents they have in life. Others lose them. I've been trying to figure out the rule. It doesn't relate to how healthy they were when zombied, or how long they are zombies, or whether they are male or female, or person or animal. I just can't figure it out, and it drives me crazy in off moments. Millie and the Zombie Master surely know, but I never remembered to ask them while they were here."

"Do zombies keep their souls?"

"Yes, though these tend to be somewhat battered. They

need some soul to remain the people they were, to the extent possible."

"Do talents connect to the body or the soul?"

"That varies," Justin said. "Some relate to the body, and others to the soul. There seems to be no consistent rule for that."

"Could that account for the difference in zombie talents?"

Breanna stared at her. "The difference in connections," she breathed. "That must be it!"

"That must be it," Justin agreed. "If a talent is tied to the body, it is lost when the body dies. But if it is tied to the soul, then it is retained, since the soul doesn't die."

"You're amazing," Breanna said. "You ask one question, and you solve the riddle that's been bugging us for years."

Cube shook her head. "I can't take credit. I have a magic pacifier that is serendipitous. Actually Seren has it now, but it affects us both. I wasn't looking for an answer for you, I was just curious—and found what I wasn't looking for."

"The answer," Breanna agreed.

"That would be a useful item," Justin remarked.

Cube had a bright idea. "If you would like to have it, I'll give it to you. But there's a problem: whoever has it is called Seren, short for serendipity."

"I find that hard to believe," Breanna said. "No offense."

Cube removed the pacifier from the saddle and handed it to her. "Say your name."

"Seren." Then the woman looked surprised. "You're right."

"Yes. So it's awkward to have, if your name makes a difference. But its surprises are usually nice ones. It helped me a lot."

Amber Dawn's little hand came out and grabbed the pacifier. She put it in her mouth and sucked contentedly on it.

"Seren," Breanna said reprovingly to the baby. "We don't know if that's sanitary." Then she looked surprised again. "Oh, no!"

"The name returns when the pacifier goes. It's not lost, just superseded for a while."

Breanna caught the loop in the pacifier and pulled it from the baby's mouth. "I don't care if it does return, I want to be able to say my baby's name."

The baby opened her mouth and bawled.

"Oh, no," Breanna repeated. "She likes it." She winced, and gave it back. The baby settled down contentedly.

"Maybe when she's older, she won't need it for its quieting magic," Cube said.

"Let's hope."

"Perhaps the pacifier itself was seeking a baby," Justin said. "So that it could perform its primary function."

Cube and Breanna stared at him, and at the baby. That made sudden sense. The pacifier's original baby had grown up.

At last Charles (with his own name back) and Cube (with hers) resumed their journey.

The thread led north along an enchanted path. They didn't hurry, as Cube found she just wanted to be on her Quest, not rushing through any part of it. In fact this Route had already made her understand that she liked going places and meeting people, even if only briefly. She had thought she wanted to be beautiful and have fantastic adventures; she still wanted to be beautiful, but now she had had some reasonably fantastic adventures, and some routine ones, and it seemed that the routine ones had their points too.

Near noon they came to a wayside stop. A girl was already there, sitting at a table. "Will you join me?" she called. "I have lots of incidentals."

"Well, I don't know," Cube said, uncertain what mischief there might be in unnamed incidentals. Also, the girl was prettier than Cube, as all girls were, and that nagged her.

"Oh, what a handsome horse!"

That decided Charles. He veered to the table, and Cube didn't argue. "Yes, we'll join you. I'm Cube, and this is Charles."

"I'm Etcetera. What does Charles prefer to eat?"

Cube realized that she hadn't been with Charles long enough to see him eat. "I think some nice grain, or fresh hay."

"Etcetera," the girl said, and a pan of grain appeared along with a bale of hay and a salt block and bucket of clear water.

Charles sniffed the collection, and started in, satisfied.

"And what would you like?" the girl inquired.

She was evidently a conjurer. "Oh, a sweet roll, some boot rear—"

"Etcetera." And on the table were not only sweet rolls and glasses of drink, but several cookies and pastries, together with assorted apples, bananas, and other fruits.

"Your talent!" Cube exclaimed. "Et Cetera!"

"Exactly," the girl agreed. "Someone else has to start it, then I can add on to it. I can't do it purely on my own."

"Talents often do have limits," Cube agreed. "Mine is summoning nickelpedes. I would rather have a more feminine talent."

"Why?"

Oh. "I'm a girl."

Etcetera looked at her more closely, then blushed fetchingly. "Oh. I thought—never mind."

Cube knew she just *had* to get beautiful.

As they ate, a white rabbit hopped close. "Oh, what a lovely bunny!" the girl exclaimed.

The rabbit's ears blushed flattered pink.

"He's probably just looking for scraps," Cube said.

The rabbit's ears turned angry red.

Could it be? Cube decided to experiment. "You're a pretty sorry example of your kind," she said to the rabbit.

The rabbit's ears turned black with mortification. It was true: they changed color with the creature's mood.

"I'm sorry," she said. "I didn't mean that. I just wanted to see your ears change."

The rabbit gazed at her, his ears slowly fading to neutral gray.

"Let's get him some nice cabbage," Cube said.

"Etcetera!" And cabbage appeared, along with lettuce, carrots, and parsley.

The rabbit's ears turned happy white. He started eating the lettuce.

A wolf appeared at the edge of the forest. The rabbit's ears turned fearful yellow.

"A dangerous creature can't come onto the enchanted section," Cube said. "He can't get you."

The rabbit's ears returned to white. He resumed eating. But then he paused, his ears turning green.

"Oh, some broccoli or asparagus must have gotten in there," Etcetera said, chagrined. "I'm so sorry."

"Have a bite of apple," Cube said, putting one down for the rabbit. That soon put the ears right.

When they finished their meal, Cube thanked Etcetera and mounted Charles to travel on. The rabbit's ears turned sad blue; he was sorry to see them go.

Then Cube saw another woman coming from the other direction. There was something odd about her. Her hair was moving in an unnatural manner. As she walked under a low-hanging mass of foliage, her hair lifted up to push it away. She had prehensile hair!

As Cube rode on, she saw the woman pause by the rabbit, then squat down. Her hair reached out to stroke him. The rabbit's ears turned white. He wasn't blue anymore. That made Cube feel better.

They continued north. Suddenly a cloud formed before Cube's face. "My, you're an ugly one," it said.

At first Cube thought it was Metria, but then remembered that the demoness was in the pouch. "Look who's talking."

The cloud formed into a handsome man. "How do you like me now? Demon Lete, just drifting by."

Cube thought she heard a groan. "D. Lete," she said. "Why don't you subtract your presence?"

"I can't," he said. "I gave up my talent to be the prize that Kim Mundane won."

Cube remembered that Kim had the talent of erasure. "You didn't do that voluntarily."

Lete looked abashed. "I was in one of Demon Professor

Grossclout's classes, and I sassed him. Then he taught me a lesson I wouldn't forget. He deleted my talent."

That was a pretty stringent punishment. Cube had some sympathy. "I'm sorry."

"Oh, I'm sure I deserved it." The demon faded.

Cube made a mental note never to cross Demon Professor Grossclout.

In the evening they came to another campsite. This time there were two men there. Cube was slightly wary, but reminded herself that no hostile folk could get on the enchanted paths, and anyway, she had her nickelpedes, which she could surely use if she jumped off the path and summoned them. So she put a positive face on it. "Is there room for one more?" she called.

"Certainly," the older man replied. He looked to be about forty-seven. "I'm Terry Tamagni. My son Jerry and I were about to swim in the pool. You're welcome to join us."

Cube dismounted. "I'm a girl." She hated having to say that so often.

"Oh," Terry said, embarrassed. "I—we're rather new here. Still finding our way."

"In fact we're Mundane," Jerry said.

That meant they were here without magic. They were worse off than she was.

"Nice horse," Terry said.

"I changed my mind," Cube said. "I'll swim with you, if you don't mind."

The two men exchanged a glance. "No problem," Jerry said. He looked to be about twenty-four, a nice age.

So they stripped and swam, and splashed each other, and it was fun. Then they dried and harvested assorted pies for dinner, and talked about this and that. Cube found that she enjoyed socializing with men as well as women, when it was just companionship. These ones were nice enough. She had never actually played with men before; there had always been the problem that they saw her as a woman—or didn't. With Mundanes it didn't seem to be a question. She was happy to answer their questions about Xanth, reassuring them that it was a nice enough place to be.

In the morning the men continued on south, and Cube and Charles went north. In due course they came to the Gap Chasm. This time the thread led directly across it, straight from one side to the other, though the air.

Cube contemplated that. Then she put her hand to the pouch. "Metria."

The demoness appeared. "No problem," she said. "It's the invisible bridge. Just walk on across." She slid back into the pouch.

Invisible bridge. Cube nerved herself and reached tentatively forward over the emptiness with one foot. And found solidity. In fact there was a walkway there, and a rail for her hand. That helped.

She walked out over the dizzily deep chasm, leading Charles, who was as nervous about it as she was. The bridge was strong; it supported them both.

When they were halfway across, they encountered a column of people going the other way. Oh, no! The bridge was wide enough only for one, and Charles would not be able to turn around. She might summon Karia to take her on across, but that wouldn't do for Charles.

The lead man spied them and halted. "We have a problem," he said.

"Hello. I'm Cube, and this is Charles. I don't think he can turn around."

"We're on a schedule; we can't afford to back off and wait for you to clear the bridge. We'll have to pass each other. But there's a problem."

"Not enough room," Cube agreed.

"I think there is room, if we squeeze. But we are blessed, or cursed, with magic that prevents any person from passing us without guessing our first names. We're not allowed to tell others what they are."

"It could take me all day to guess all your names!" Cube protested.

"Not necessari—lee," he said.

Was that a groan in the back of her mind? Cube pondered half a moment, and got it: pun names. He had given her the hint.

She looked more closely at the first Lee. He was tall and thin. "Thin," she said.

"ThinLee. You catch on quickly," he agreed, angling to slide by her and then the horse. There was after all room, with a squeeze. Cube didn't mind squeezing by a man like that, innocent as it was; she could pretend it *wasn't* innocent.

The second Lee was a plump smiling woman. "Cheerful," Cube said.

"CheerfulLee," the woman agreed, pushing past her. Cube's pretending turned off.

The next was a frowning man. "I ought to just push you off the bridge," he said angrily.

"Angry," she said.

Angrily he shoved by her. She pretended he was afraid she would seduce him.

Soon enough she and Charles made it by all the Lees, and she never had to summon a nickelpede and Charles never needed to knot a muscle. Her mind had done the job. That pleased her.

But the travail of passage across the gulf had not ended. A cloud appeared, low and small and wild. "Fracto?" Cube inquired. "I'm not looking for any trouble."

A fuzzy face formed on the cloud. "Die!" it breathed. Then it blew out such a stiff gust of chill wind that Cube had to grab on to the invisible rail to keep her place.

"What are you doing?" she cried, alarmed.

"Keeping my own," the cloud said windily. Then it blew a harder and colder gust right at Cube and the horse. There was snow in it, and ice formed on the rail, making it slippery. The force of wind made the bridge swing and start to turn over.

"Fornax!" Cube cried, catching on. But it did her no good; she and Charles were already falling off the bridge, down toward the awful bottom of the chasm. They were doomed. No one would know why they had fallen from the bridge and perished.

Then something strange happened. Time froze around them. Cube and the horse stopped falling, remaining in stasis at weird angles. So did the cloud, which now looked horrified. There was an awesome scintillating environment of magic power much greater than anything the little Princesses had worked.

GOTCHA!

Cube looked where she sensed the exclamation. There on the frozen bridge stood a ludicrous striped donkey-headed dragon. He winked at her.

Then cloud and dragon vanished. The amazing plasma of magic faded. Cube and Charles were back on the bridge, exactly as they had been before the cloud appeared. The air was calm. They proceeded somewhat numbly on to the end of the bridge.

Cube realized that the Demon Xanth had been waiting to catch the Demoness Fornax in the act of interfering with the Quest, and finally nailed her. This was the Land of Xanth, where he had supreme power. Fornax would have an awful time getting out of this mess. She had been caught meddling in Xanth's business, a no-no for Demons.

There would be no more interference of that nature.

Cube's knees were weak, but she was exhilarated. She realized that the Demon Xanth hardly cared what happened to a lone mortal woman or horse, but perhaps his consort Chlorine did, and he had been looking out for them for his own reasons. She had seen Demons in action, opposing each other, and survived the experience. That alone was mind blowing.

But she still had her Quest to finish. She quelled her galloping heart and focused on that. She was back on her own.

The thread did not continue north beyond the Gap. Instead it turned east and angled down the face of the cliff. She stood at the brink, daunted. How was she going to go there? She didn't have the ability to walk down the cliff as if it were level. That applied to only certain parts of the Gap Chasm, and this wasn't such a part.

"You look as if you have a problem," a voice said from just below her. Cube was so startled she almost jumped, which could have been disastrous.

In most of a moment she saw that there was a man on the cliff below her. He had been in shadow so that she had missed him. "Why don't you fall?" she asked.

"I have sticky hands and feet," he explained. "It's my talent." He pulled a hand away from the stone, and there was a faint snapping sound as it unstuck.

She nodded. "I could use that."

He climbed up to the top and stepped over, joining her. His hands and feet looked normal, but she had seen them in action. "You have to go down there?"

"Yes."

"And your horse?"

"Yes, of course."

"I can show you a way."

Could he really? "Can we make a deal?"

"What do you offer?"

A pretty woman would have only one acceptable answer, but Cube didn't have that problem. "I can summon nickel-pedes. I could give you some tame ones."

"Tame nickelpedes? I never heard of that."

"I never heard of someone with sticky hands and feet. It's my talent."

"Let's see."

She summoned a nickelpede. It perched on her hand, looking around. "What's your name?" she asked.

"Ray."

She addressed the nickelpede. "This is Ray. He is a friend. Go with him and protect him." Then she proffered the bug.

Ray, understandably hesitant, slowly put out his hand. The nickelpede crossed over and perched there, not attacking. The man stroked it with a finger, very gingerly. It still did not attack. "Maybe it's in a stupor," he said suspiciously.

"Threaten it with a stick," Cube suggested.

Ray bent down to pick up a small stick from the ground. He struck at the nickelpede. The nickelpede's claw whipped across and cut the stick in two by gouging out a nickel-sized section of its center.

Ray nodded. "How many?"

"Three."

"Done."

She summoned two more nickelpedes, attuned them to the man and gave them to him. They perched amicably on his shoulders and head. "Now where's the way?"

"This way," he said, stepping over the brink. But this time his feet did not stick to the visible surface; they sank into it. Knee-deep in rock, he turned back to face her. "There is a broad ledge here, leading down, masked by illusion. Try it."

She tried it, and found it was true. The way had been there all along—right where the thread was. She should have had more faith in the thread.

She walked down the gradually sloping ledge, scuffing with her feet to ascertain its extent. It was indeed broad enough for the horse. "Come on, Charles," she called.

The horse followed. She saw his front legs disappear into the seeming stone, then his rear ones.

"It goes down to an old deserted building," Ray said. "It's a good place to hide."

"I'm sure it will do. Thank you."

"Thank you for the bugs." He scampered away across the face of the cliff.

Soon they were entirely covered by the illusion, and could see the stone ledge as it was. It tracked down the cliff, covered by what looked from below like a tarpaulin. This was really interesting; who had set it up, and why?

They came to a building set into the vertical stone, reminiscent of the city of Petra. There were a number of cubic chambers, all empty. Cubic—as if waiting for her, Cube. Was this coincidence?

The thread led into the center of the main chamber and stopped. It didn't go into the rock, it simply ended in mid air. That suggested that it truly ended here.

But this was obviously not Counter Xanth. Her route had not ended. So what did this mean?

"Time for a consultation," she said aloud. She put her hand to the pouch. "All."

All her Companions slid out and stood around her. "Don't go outside yet," Cube warned them. "This is a house on the wall of the Gap Chasm."

"Wow!" Metria said, sailing out to look.

"But it is not Counter Xanth," Cube continued. "The thread ends here."

The three little Princesses investigated. "She's right," Melody said.

"It stops here," Harmony agreed.

"And goes directly to Counter Xanth," Rhythm concluded.

"So how do we get there?" Karia asked.

"Sidestepping," Cory said.

"This must be the proper avenue for it," Tessa agreed. "The most feasible route between the two lands."

"Before we blithely go there," Karia said, "there's a matter that disturbs me. I understand that this land was won from Demoness Fornax, who is the mistress of contraterrene matter. So Counter Xanth is surely of that nature. As I understand it, normal matter is incompatible with contraterrene matter. So how can we go there, regardless of the Route?"

"It must be possible," Ryver said, "or the Good Magician would never have set up this Quest."

"And Mother would never have let us go," Melody said.

Metria popped back in. "That's why there's no direct land route between the two," she said. "They'd both go up in a quasar."

"A what?" Harmony asked.

"Explosion, detonation, ka-boom, blast, eruption—"

"Total conversion of matter to energy?" Rhythm asked.

"Whatever," Metria agreed crossly. "Hey—how can a little tyke like you come up with such language?"

"A little what?" Melody asked.

"Child, tot, kid, juvenile, brat—"

"Princess?" Harmony suggested.

"Whatever. How—"

"I made it up," Rhythm said smugly.

"Nevertheless," Karia said firmly, "She has a point. There can be no direct contact between the two, lest mutual destruction result. Sidestepping must enable us to transfer from one to the other without suffering that fate."

"Are you sure?" Ryver asked.

"No."

Silence settled in about them as they pondered that. This time Cube broke it. "I'll go alone. If I am destroyed, no one else need follow."

For a space between an instant and a moment, all eyes focused on her. Then Karia spoke. "Are we agreed?"

There was a chorus of nods, including even Charles Horse. "Then we'll all return to the pouch," Ryver said. "Except for Cory, Tessa, and Cube."

"But I don't want to leave the pouch behind," Cube protested. "I never want to risk losing it again."

"We're going with you," Metria clarified. "Except for Charles Horse, who will guard this important site."

Charles nodded.

"With something to eat," Melody said. A bale of hay appeared.

"And drink," Harmony agreed. A bucket of water appeared.

"And something for comfort," Rhythm concluded. A pile of pillows appeared.

"There's something else," Cube said. "The Demoness Fornax tried to blow us off the bridge over the Gap Chasm, but the Demon Xanth stopped her. I don't think Demon Xanth would let us go to destruction after that."

They were obviously impressed. "Tell us about it," Karia said. So Cube did.

"So we were right," Ryver concluded. "It was Fornax."

"And she would not have needed to act, if Counter Xanth was going to annihilate us anyway," Karia said. "That is reassuring." The others nodded.

Then they entered the pouch, leaving only Cory, Tessa,

and Cube. It was time to go on to Counter Xanth, whatever happened there.

Cube was both nervous and proud. "We'll return soon, Charles," she said.

"This is new territory, in more than one sense," Cory said. "We shall have to go slowly and carefully."

"I wouldn't have it otherwise," Cube said, dry-mouthed. The new land might not destroy them, but it was bound to be different from their experience.

The two women linked hands and stepped backward, setting up the route. Then Tessa caught Cube's hand, bringing her in. There was the thread, leading out of the chamber and back up the ramp to the surface. That was a relief; at least they knew they were going the right way.

They reached the brink of the cliff, with Xanth stretching out before them to the north. It looked subtly odd. "Is this really the same?" Cube asked, as they stepped out of the sidestepping channel.

"It's empty," Cory said. "Except for plants."

"Because Xanth will get to colonize it," Tessa said. "There are no people."

"That must be it. It was an easier crossing than I expected, after the deviousness of the thread's prior route. I'll bring out the others."

Cory and Tessa didn't answer. Cube didn't notice for a moment; she was busy bringing out the others. In a moment they all stood around her.

"What is that?" Karia asked, staring south.

"The Msahc Pag, of course," Cube replied. Then she paused, startled. "What did I say?"

"Look south, Ebuc," Ryver said.

Cube turned around. And stared. The chasm was gone; in its place was a towering mountain range. The peaks reached so high they scraped the clouds and were white with snow. "But—the Pag was here a moment ago," she protested somewhat inanely.

"Perhaps not," Cory said. "When we reached the surface,

we emerged in Counter Xanth. The mountains are where the Gap Chasm is in Xanth."

"The Gap Chasm," Cube echoed. "But I said something else."

"What is your name?" Karia asked.

"Ebuc."

"Which is Cube spelled backwards," the centaur said. "I believe we are experiencing the effects of reversal. My name is now Airak, not Karia. And the great gulf has become a great ridge. I suspect the mountains of Xanth will be depressions here, perhaps lakes."

Cube realized that it must be true. "Demoness Fornax is the Demon of contra-terrene matter," she said. "Antimatter. The opposite of what we have, though I understand it looks the same. So things are similar but opposite."

"Which could be fun," Metria said. "At least we didn't detonate."

"Didn't what?" Melody asked.

"We covered this ground before," Karia said sharply.

"Awww," Harmony said.

"And we do have more important things to do," Ryver agreed.

"True," Rhythm concluded. All their names were all right as long as no one tried to say them.

Cube looked around. "I think we have found what we sought. But I'd like to explore it enough to be able to make a competent report. There could be other surprises."

"Agreed," Karia said. "Lead; we shall follow."

Cube stepped north, walking toward one of the odd trees. The others followed in single file. The air smelled pleasantly clean.

The tree turned out to be a fruit tree, but of no kind Cube knew of. The leaves were brown and rolled up. The fruits were large and blue, with pale pink stripes. She picked one and bit into it. The flavor was different too, but not unpleasant.

"There's something really weird about this," Metria said. "Something's missing."

"This land seems quite nice," Karia said. "It doesn't irritate me."

"That's it!" Ryver said. "No puns!"

"That *is* it," the centaur agreed. "Strange geography, strange fruit, but no puns, egregious or otherwise."

"If that's the worst of it," Ryver said, "I'm sure there will be folk willing to colonize." Then he stared past Cube to one of the other members of their party. "Who are you?"

"I am Asset, of course," the woman replied.

"But you're taller than I am!"

The others looked. It did look like Tessa, but she was now the tallest member of their party. Beside her stood a much shorter woman. "Yroc?" Cube asked her.

"I'm short," Cory replied, astonished.

Now it was apparent: the two had exchanged heights. "It's another reversal," Karia said. "But why didn't it affect the rest of us?"

But it had. When they looked more carefully, they discovered that Cube was now taller than Ryver, and the three little Princesses were now three big Princesses, though they looked just as young as usual. The centaur seemed to be a bit taller, and Drek Dragon was shorter. Tall had become short, and short had become tall, with those in the middle changing less.

"It affects the extremes more than the middle," Ryver concluded. "Which maybe makes sense. The question is, is it permanent?"

"Xanth magic fades when we leave Xanth," Metria said. "So maybe this will fade when we leave Counter Xanth."

"Let's hope so," Tessa said. "I don't like being Tall Asset."

Cube made a note on a pad. "We'll warn the folk back home. Now I'm sure we need to explore farther."

They walked on, and the terrain was interesting, but there were no further changes.

"Can we go faster?" Melody asked plaintively.

"We're getting bored," Harmony agreed.

"We can make a fast carpet," Rhythm said.

They had a point. "Make your carpet," Cube said.

In a moment the Princesses conjured a large carpet, and the humans sat on it. The centaur and dragon preferred to move on their own.

The carpet lifted, carrying them to tree-top height. Karia flicked herself and flew up beside it, while Drek moved sinuously below it.

They moved rapidly east, parallel to the mountains. Suddenly things changed again. Karia, flying beside them, changed colors. Now her wings were brown instead of white, and her flank was white.

"Airak!" Cube called. "Your colors just reversed!"

The centaur did not reply. Instead she folded her wings and floated aimlessly.

"Oh, no!" Cube cried. "She's carried away! I forgot."

"We can guide her gently to the ground," Ryver said. "Then snap her out of it."

Cube looked at him. He had been white. Now he was black.

In fact, all of them had reversed their colors, body and clothing. White became black, red became green, blue became yellow, with shades in between.

"And it's cumulous," Metria said.

"It's what?" Ryver asked.

"Cloudy, vague, nebulous, confusing, misty—"

"You're on the wrong track," Cube snapped. "You mean cumulative."

"Whatever," the demoness agreed crossly.

"Well, *I'm* confused," Ryver said.

"Wonderful!" Metria said, and kissed him so hard that her face sank part way into his face. He looked a quarter stunned.

That irritated Cube, but she didn't say so. Instead she focused on the problem. "We need to guide the centaur down."

They did so, flying close and nudging Karia until she touched ground. Then Cube snapped her fingers. "Wake!"

The centaur's eyes opened. "Oh—did it happen again?"

"My fault," Cube said. "I called your name when you changed color."

Karia looked at herself. "Oh, my!"

"Now we have had two reversals, and they're cumulative," Cube said. "I think we need to be sure we can eliminate them."

"Sidestepping should do it, as we surmised," Karia said. "I doubt the local magic extends beyond Counter Xanth."

"We hope so," tall Tessa said.

Cory and Tessa formed their sidestepping aisle, then brought the others in. As each entered it, he or she reverted to normal. They hugged each other in gladness; it seemed that the changes had bothered them more than they had indicated.

"So now we know we can reverse the reversals," Karia said. "So it doesn't matter if they are permanent and cumulative; we can escape them. But colonists will have to keep them. This rather limits the field, I suspect."

"And we'd better find out what other reversals are here," Ryver said. "So we can warn colonists."

"And take them via sidestepping to only the particular reversals they want to have," Cube said. "Some short folk may want to be tall, some may prefer to change colors."

They set about exploring methodically, flying the carpet in a squared-off pattern across the width of the land. It seemed to be the same general shape as Xanth, but the vegetation and animals were different. They saw what looked like six-legged cows grazing, and four-winged birds flying, and twin-hulled fish swimming. There were occasional clouds of sparkling insects. Nothing seemed friendly or hostile; some looked at the carpet, but without much curiosity. It seemed that they had not seen Xanth folk before, so did not recognize them as friends or enemies. That suggested in turn that it was safe to colonize, especially if the colonists treated the native creatures with respect.

They did encounter other reversals, which they nullified as soon as they understood them, and marked their territories. One section made a smart person stupid, and vice versa; another made nice folk mean, and the opposite; another made happy folk depressed, and the other way around. Strong-weak, big-small, fat-thin, honest-dishonest, healthy-sickly. Most of the effects were moderate, because the members of the exploratory party were in the middle range of most things, but they were able to tell by the shifts in their members. They landed at each site, analyzed them, and Cube made a note. Then they retreated to sidestepping to nullify the change, and emerged to fly on to the next. Thus they were generally affected by one reversal, but not by the prior ones.

Even so, some of the reversals were startling. At one site the people started quarreling violently. Cube felt it too; she hated all the Companions. But she realized that this was not natural. "Our feelings are changed," she said. "Friends have become enemies."

They hastily returned to the sidestepping aisle, and were friends again. Judging by the power of their mutual dislike before, they had to be excellent friends now.

But there was worse. On another site Cube felt a strange change in her body. She looked around, and found herself surrounded mostly by men, including one floating demon. There was just one woman, a rather pretty one. "Ryver!" she exclaimed. "You're a woman!"

"And you're a man," he/she retorted.

Cube looked at herself. She was male. They had all changed gender.

"You know, you're not bad looking as a man," the male centaur said. "Evenness and delicacy of feature doesn't matter as much for a man."

"I don't want to be a man!" Cube said.

The others laughed. They understood perfectly. They retreated again to the aisle and were restored. Drek had become a female dragon, but the genders of dragons weren't as obvious to human folk.

"But there may be some folk in Xanth who do want such a change," Metria said.

Cube marked the spot on her map. "They are welcome."

Another change was trickier to fathom. The humans didn't change, but there was a fine male centaur who wasn't Karia. "Who are you?" Cube asked.

"I am Kerd," he replied.

That would be Drek, backwards. He had changed form. "Then who is the dragon?"

"She is Airak," the centaur said. "Oops." For the dragon was drifting away. He ran after her. "Snap out of it, female," he said.

That was Karia all right; she had been carried away at the sound of her name.

"I apologize, gourd style," Drek said. He caught her serpentine head in his hands and kissed her snoot.

"That's how they do it, in the gourd," Metria explained, spying Cube's blank look. Metria now appeared to be a mortal human being—and Ryver was a demon.

They returned to the aisle. "Thank you for rescuing me," Karia said to Drek. "Perhaps someday I'll return the favor."

"But what was the reversal?" Cube asked, still somewhat mystified.

"I believe it is that different creatures exchange forms, not genders, with those they happen to be closest to at the moment," Metria said. "I was next to Ryver, so we switched. Karia and Drek were close. The rest of you were all humans, so the change didn't make any difference."

"This is remarkable," Cube said, her appreciation of the wonders of this realm growing.

At another spot, good became evil. Cube brought out the Hell Toupee and became good again; its effect reversed also. That made it potentially very useful.

As the day faded, it seemed they had done enough. "We know the general nature of this land," Karia said. "We can continue mapping it in the future, but probably it is time to wrap up here and return to Xanth for the night." The others agreed.

They checked one more section—and the change was dramatic. The others were suddenly staring at Cube.

"What is it?" she asked uneasily. "Have I turned into a frog?"

"Here is a pond," Karia said. "Look at your reflection."

Cube did—and saw a woman who could have been Silhouette's sister in beauty. Where had she come from? She looked at the others, and saw that they had changed; Karia was now a hag of a centaur with shaggy wings, standing beside three ugly children and a homely man.

Slowly it came to her: the lovely woman was herself.

Amazed, she tried the only thing she could think of at the moment: she summoned a nickelpede. It was the most beautiful creature she had seen. This region really did convert ugliness to beauty, and vice versa.

"We'll retreat to the sidestepping aisle," Karia said. "You may wish to remain here."

Cory and Tessa set up the aisle, and the others entered it. Cube lingered, staring at her reflection. The Good Magician had said she would be beautiful when she completed her Quest; this was the proof of that. Now at last she had her desire.

"It's true," Ryver said. "You are transformed. Now at last your appearance matches your character."

"All I have to do is stay here," she breathed.

"Yes. You are beautiful and I love you. But—" He shrugged.

"But what?" she asked.

"What would you want with me, now? I have lost my looks."

"But I don't judge by appearance," she protested. "I know better."

"Do you? Why were you interested in me? I'm not smart, I'm not strong, I'm not deep. My talent is way below Magician caliber. I'm just an ordinary guy. What did I have, besides my appearance?"

Cube realized that he was right. She had been foolishly attracted to his handsome face. Now that was gone. She had objected to being judged by her appearance, but she had been doing the same. She was a hypocrite.

"So there's no point in my staying here," Ryver said. "You can do better, now."

Had she been in Xanth, a bulb would have flashed. But there were no punnish effects in this new land. Still, she understood that the place and time to abolish her hypocrisy was here and now.

She brought out her water ball, which she had never forgotten. It had been her link to him. "I love you too," she said.

"You kept the ball!"

"Always. It was my memory of you." She put away the ball, put her hands on his arms and drew him in to her. She kissed him and let him go.

He stood for a moment, then spoke. "In Xanth I'd be freaked out," he said. "As it is, I am merely dazzled."

"Stay here with me, and I'll dazzle you constantly." She found that she loved having this power of beauty.

"But I'm ugly!" he protested.

"You're still you."

He gazed at her with the sheer adoration reserved for sheer beauty. "You mean that?"

"Yes. I of all people know that appearance is only one aspect of a person, and beauty fades with age. I am happy to be beautiful for you, because I want to please you. You don't have to be handsome for me."

Still he protested. "But you know that I didn't love you until you were beautiful. I knew your qualities, but love wouldn't come before that. I'm shallow."

"You're a man. That's not quite the same. You were upfront about that. You never deceived me. Now I have it, and I'm glad it enabled me to gain your love."

He nodded. "I rather thought you would say that. You know I can recover my appearance by stepping into the sidestep aisle. But I can't be handsome here, where you are beautiful."

"But since the effect is cumulative, I can go from here to another section, and suffer a change, but I'll remain beautiful. So if it is important for you to be handsome, I can join you there."

"We'll see. But we'll both have to remain here in Counter Xanth. I don't mind, as long as I'm with you."

But that reminded her of something else. "I can't remain here. I have to complete my Quest, establishing a safe route to this realm. I have to return the Princesses to Castle Roogna, and Drek Dragon to his home in the Purple Mountains. I can't leave the others in the lurch."

"But you will lose your beauty if you leave."

Cube knew it was true. She suffered a siege of grief, then marshaled her gumption. "And that means I will lose you too. I hate that. Still, I have to do what I came to do. But at least I have had beauty and your love for this wonderful moment. That memory will last the rest of my life."

Ryver nodded. "We will return to Xanth."

She hoped he would ask to kiss her again, but he didn't. "Yes, we'll return and get the job finished." She hoped no tear was showing. This was one time she almost wished her gumption would fail her, but it didn't; she would do what she had to do, regardless of the cost.

They stepped into the aisle. Cube felt the reversion as they did; her beauty was gone. "We're going back," she said. "I have to—"

"We know," Karia said. "We've worked it out."

"But you have spent most of the time in the pouch. How can you have the larger picture already?"

All of them looked at her knowingly. Something was up.

"Let me tell her," Metria said.

"Tell me what?" Cube asked, nettled. Losing her dream was bad enough, without some other complication.

"You put a gourd in the pouch," Metria said.

Cube remembered. "So I did. I never had to use it."

"But we used it."

"How could you? You were in stasis."

"Not quite. We were asleep. That's different. We dreamed."

"But demons don't dream."

"I have half a soul," the demoness said. "Now I can dream. We couldn't leave the pouch, even in our dreams, but we found we could share a dream. So we had a dialogue—a number of dialogues, actually, there in a pleasant dream setting. We compared notes, we argued points, we hashed things out. We got to know each other really well." She glanced at Karia, then at Drek, and smiled almost tenderly. "We concluded several things. One is that we like each other and want to remain as a group, even if we separate physically at times. Another is that you are a truly worthy person, and deserve your reward. We helped you get it."

"But I can't keep my beauty," Cube said. "I've already lost it."

"Was it really beauty you wanted—or the love of a good man?"

Cube stood there, emotionally stunned. "The man," she confessed. "The beauty was just the means to that end."

"Let me," Ryver said. He approached Cube, so handsome she was smitten all over again, despite cursing her own foolishness. He took her in his arms, and she yielded, loving his touch for whatever reason. He kissed her, and she felt as if she were floating.

After a timeless time she found herself standing, recovering her speech. "You didn't have to do that. I know that—"

"I love you," he said. "I no longer mind what you look like. Love doesn't turn off like that."

"But—"

"You're still you. You didn't dump me when I was ugly. Why did you think I would dump you when you lost your beauty?"

Cube fumbled for words. "Well, men are affected by, everyone knows—a woman's appearance is all that really counts. I have to be beautiful, if—"

"You had to be beautiful to win my love. Because of my male nature. You won it. Now it remains. Our magic talents don't change in Counter Xanth, and neither does the magic of love. And it isn't as if you won't be beautiful again. We'll return to Counter Xanth many times, and stay as long as we want, after we wrap up the Quest."

Cube began to understand that he meant it. She gazed at the others. "You—the rest of you—knew?"

"They knew," Ryver said. "They told me in the dream that I would never find a better woman than you, and finally I believed. I was just waiting for the beauty to clinch it. I already knew you were the one for me."

"And you aren't the only one," Metria said. "Drek and the centaur are getting together."

"But—"

"We found affinity in our minds, in the dream dialogue," Karia said. "And we found that we can change our forms, in the right section of Counter Xanth, as you saw. With a little management we can both be dragons for a while, or both winged centaurs. We'll be staying there, after the quest is done, to help colonists find their way around a perplexing realm." She smiled briefly. "And nobody need know my name."

Cube realized that that solved the problem that had originally brought Karia to the Good Magician, though not in the anticipated manner.

"And Tessa and I will move to the Gap building," Cory said, "to be there to sidestep colonists to Counter Xanth. We have found our mission in life."

"We'll be in touch too," Melody said.

"We can't stay, because we're still children and Mother won't allow it," Harmony added.

"But we'll be there when we're needed," Rhythm concluded.

"And so will I," Metria said. "I'll pop back and forth to keep the rest of you in touch. This will be a continuing project. We have each found what we truly wanted, though not all of us understood our true desires at the outset. We have all received our rewards."

"Your rewards?"

"Some of us sought a useful mission in life." The demoness glanced at Cory and Tessa, then at herself. "Some sought true love with a worthy other." She glanced at Karia and

Drek, then at Ryver and Cube. "Or a better understanding of the nature of magic." She glanced at the three Princesses.

"But they are already Sorceresses," Cube said.

"With more power of magic than we know how to control," Melody said.

"For example, the thread," Harmony added.

"We made it, but didn't know how it worked," Rythm concluded.

"It led me all over Xanth!" Cube said. "Instead of straight to Counter Xanth."

"We struggled with that for some time," Ryver said. "Finally we concluded that it was like water." He formed a water ball. Cube smiled and brought out hers again. "It forms marvelous contours, sinuous rivers, round lakes, and dramatic waterfalls, but it has no intelligence or artistic sense. It merely seeks the lowest level it can find without ever running uphill, unless there's a spell on it. The thread sought Counter Xanth, but had to align with the needs of the person it was made for."

"That was me," Cube said. "I just wanted to go to Counter Xanth."

He smiled at her, and she melted. "You were not ready, when you started. So it took you to the experiences you needed to become the kind of person who could handle Counter Xanth. It had no intelligence of its own, it just oriented on the need, with all the power of Sorceress magic cubed." He smiled at the Princesses, who giggled. "It was a learning route."

"A learning route! Some of the things that happened—"

He silenced her with a spot kiss. "For all of us. I needed to broaden my own outlook, so as not to be completely dominated by appearances. To be worthy of you. You had gumption, but lacked experience with people, so it enabled you to meet many. You needed to learn more about Mundanes, because you will be guiding some of them to Counter Xanth, so it took you to Silhouette. You needed to appreciate the role Nimby plays in Xanth, so it took you to him. You also needed experience with realms whose magic is fundamentally different from that of Xanth, so it took you to Ida's moons. When you were ready, it took you to Counter Xanth."

Cube wanted to argue, but realized it was true. She had fleshed out considerably, in understanding and appreciation of the variety and wonder of Xanth. She was not the frustrated woman she had been. The thread had done it. "You have it all worked out," Cube said, awed.

"We do," the demoness agreed. "You did your part; now we'll do ours."

"But you have done yours. You all helped me get through at key spots. Karia flew me places, the Princesses made the thread, Cory and Tessa did the sidestepping, Metria helped me deal with difficult people and demons, Drek drove off attackers, Ryver—" She paused. What had Ryver done?

Karia smiled. "Ryver found the gourd in the pouch, and used it to contact the rest of us. He made our dream dialogues possible. We would have been far less effective, otherwise, and not gotten to know each other as well."

And they had been remarkably savvy when she brought them from the pouch. So Ryver had been a key player too. "But—"

"Methinks she protests too much," Karia said.

"I'll stop it," Ryver said. He embraced Cube again and kissed her. Repeatedly.

"Show her," Metria advised him.

"Show me what?" Cube asked, bemused.

He took her into the pouch and showed her the dream setting that the gourd enabled. It was a lovely chamber with romantic pictures on the wall and pillows piled high on the floor. "This is now our bower of love," he said. This time he did not stop at kissing.

By the time her wits returned, in and out of the dream, they were back in the Gap Chasm building in Xanth. She remembered none of their trip there; someone else must have carried the pouch. She was still floating on an inner sea of love.

* * *

"There's someone at the brink," Metria said, appearing in the chamber where Ryver had been keeping Cube in chronic bliss, no longer using the dream setting. "I think you need to see to it in a hurry."

Cube had little idea how much time had passed, but she suspected several days. The stone house had been provisioned with furniture and food and other nice things. Cory and Tessa had one room, Ryver and Cube had another, Charles Horse had a nice stone stall, and the Princesses, Karia, and Drek were gone. She hurried out and up the ramp to the surface of Xanth. Because the stone house was near the invisible bridge and the enchanted path to the north, it was easy for them to intercept travelers.

There was a young woman. She looked extremely ill, and there was something wrong with one foot. She also looked as if she was about to jump into the Gap Chasm.

"Hello," Cube said. "Have you lost your way? I am Cube; maybe I can help you."

"I don't think so," the woman said. "I am Sarah Spirlock, from Mundania. I—came to Xanth because they said I could be made well by a healing elixir. But I seem to be immune to it. All I face in life is more pain. So there is nothing left but to end it quickly."

Cube remembered the section of Counter Xanth where healthy folk became sickly, and vice versa, the most extreme cases changing the most. Here was the first colonist, who would become radiantly healthy. They would have to have her ride on Charles, because she couldn't walk along the sidestepping route, but that was easy enough. Cube remembered how dramatically Silhouette's life had changed after she had tried suicide, then gained what she needed. Cube knew exactly how to handle this; she had been there before, as it were. "Oh, Sarah, you are going to like where I will take you."

"I don't understand."

"None of us do, at first." Cube took her hand.

AUTHOR'S NOTE

Of course the novel's title relates punnishly to the content and the series. This is the twenty-seventh Xanth novel, and thus is the completion of the magical trilogy: three cubed. Three is the cube root of twenty-seven, and it has been a long and devious route to get here. The Cube Route. Back when I wrote the fourth novel in the Xanth trilogy, critics sneered at my supposed mathematical ignorance. Never mind that I had been a math instructor in the U.S. Army; they figured I didn't know what was what. Then Arthur Clarke had a fourth novel in a trilogy, and suddenly it wasn't fit for ridicule anymore; he was a Critically Approved Writer, so what he did could not be ignorant. My relations with critics have been like that, which is why I parody them in Xanth as loathsome, mean-spirited bugs, the cri-ticks. Many of my readers don't see that as parody so much as accurate description. In fact Janie Lee Dawe E-mailed me to advise that when a critic cuts me off at the knees to shorten my stature, I should tell him to take a long walk off a shortened Piers. Shortened by one letter: a pier. Okay, critics, all together now: GROOOAN!! Meanwhile, don't be alarmed; Xanth is not ending. I am already making notes for the first novel of the second trilogy. I have titles and a contract for several more, but am not yet sure of their order. Like quantum physics, Xanth doesn't get defined until I actually look at it.

As usual, there is strong reader input here. Some readers, perhaps discerning the paucity of my imagination, strain their brains to generate pages of puns for me. Others express deep respect for my time, and also send pages of puns. Others tell me there are too many puns in Xanth—and send more puns. I do try to exercise some discrimination in accepting reader notions, and reject many, but still they squeeze under the door like roaches. I have used so many over the years that I can't remember them all, and it may be that some get reused. Actually they aren't all puns; I get many suggestions for talents and characters. Which brings up a problem: I have been trying to use all the suggestions on hand at the time I complete a novel. This time some seemingly incidental ideas became significant, like Diamond Dog or Charles Horse; I never can tell what will happen. But some would have to be given incidental treatment in one novel, while deserving of fuller treatment in another. So if there are readers who expected to see their ideas here, and don't, chances are that I marked them for subsequent use. I have a list, and I check off each notion as I use it, so it doesn't get lost. Some may get lost anyway, but I think not many. Individual novels have particular themes, and it's better to group ideas that relate. For example, there are several relating to the storks that I am saving for a Xanth novel a couple of numbers down the magic path, about the storks. I don't like to waste good ideas on stories that don't relate well. Contrary to appearances, there is a certain amount of artistry in the organization of Xanth adventures. So the ideas that have been postponed will get better treatment in the hereafter. As it is, there are about 135 reader notions in this novel, and a number did not receive the treatment they deserve. There just wasn't room.

There are other mishaps. Sometimes I have a note for a reader idea, and can't find the reader's name. I *always* list the names—yet somehow they can turn up missing. That happened with the revelation that adult Mundanes do develop magic talents in Xanth, in time. I'm expecting a deserved rebuke on that one, from the omitted reader. The opposite can happen, too: I have a note that Tim Bruening had a number of odd "teas," and I wanted to add them to the teas another reader sent—but can't find them. He does have others in the novel, however. Sometimes I make a note of an idea, expecting to use it, then find I can't. For example, Liam Thompson suggested quintuplets with the talents of summoning, controlling, enhancing any thing, enhancing any action, and changing moods. But then the three little Princesses entered the picture, and made the quintuplets seem redundant, so I couldn't use them. Then there are those who send so many pages of puns and suggestions that I can't keep up with them, and they get lost. A single suggestion that I like gets my notice; pages of them tend to get filed in the Xanth folder, which is like the magic pouch, and they can get lost in there.

Readers may have noticed how I parodied a certain software company in *Xone of Contention*: Macrohard Doors. I wanted to gain more control over my computer destiny, so changed to Linux, an "open-source" operating system, and the StarOffice Writer word processor. These programs are essentially free for the price of the disks they come on and postage, or completely free for downloading. But I didn't do it for money, and in fact it cost me a good deal more in related charges than Macrohard would have, because I'm not a computer geek, merely a writer. It was a struggle that took most of a year, because the local shops didn't want to tackle Linux, and its conventions are different. I broke in the new system on a short children's novel, *Tortoise Reform*, then got serious with this Xanth novel. At this writing there remain problems, such as balky printing and file sizes double what they are in Doors, but overall I like it. In time it will surely be a viable system for folk who want more choice, but at present, the year 2001, it really isn't. So if this novel seems better or worse than the others, maybe that's why.

Personally, things remain okay. At this writing I am sixty-seven years old (I'll be sixty-nine when the novel is published) and on Medicare, but have no intention of retiring. Writing is my life, and what the regular publishers don't want, I'll put on the Internet in due course. I am already putting my old out-of-print novels there, as electronic files or print-on-demand books, so that collectors can get them. I maintain an ongoing survey of Internet publishers as a service to readers who are aspiring writers; you can find it and my ornery bi-monthly column at *www.hipiers.com.* My wife and I have been married forty-five years and have one grand-daughter; pictures are also at the Web site. I still practice archery, right- and left-handed, for exercise, and ride a recumbent bicycle. We live on our small tree farm, and a recent drought killed a number of our slash pines, and then storms felled some of them across our long driveway. So I have to wield ax, clippers (the trees can be tangled with voluminous grapevines), and long crowbar to get them clear. Apart from such things, my life is conveniently dull. I watch video movies on my system when not actually writing, but since I'm a workaholic, that's not a great deal.

Now here are the credits for reader notions, in approximate order of appearance in the novel, except when a person has more than one. Some were suggested by E-mail, without full names, so I put as much as I have: bubble gum tree, gum drop tree—Morgan Williams; rear-view mirror—Mary Martell; hay—Isaac Sherman; romants—Tyler Hylen; hydra ant, sarcas-stick—Alexandra C.; talent of summoning nick-elpedes—David Wallace; talent of negativity—Brecil D. Durano; Demons Port, Volve, Louse, Mystify—René Blaise; Demoness Va—Dylon Mantin; bathtub jinn, bull shark, nurse shark—Kyle Johnson; stick-hers, stick-hims—Chris Eddy and Sylvia Worley; boy who sees girls' panties, mermaids' aisle—Jessica; headline—Richard Kern; cottonwood tree—John H. Frey; door becomes a jar—Taqvaec; Karia getting carried away—Karia Lanken; talent of making an animal friendly—Terry Young; laughing stalk, changing one kind of plant to another—Amanda Wainman; ash tree—Saiya-jin Raditsu; filing cabinet—Keith Byron; weeping willow—W. Hugh Callen; tangle trees have dryads—Katrina Ludvig-Turner; change in rules about demons giving their souls to their babies—Einstein X. Mystery; Dupli Kate—Mark Phillips; Chlorine's sister Fluorine—Jim Loy; point of vision, Jacyn, Magician of matter, opposites—Jason Chierello; rainbow trout, wood knot—Bryan Punyon; winds of change—Jessica Halper; D. Pression—Joyce Collar; poultry, gallantry, sentry, elementary, entry—Avi Ornstein; the Cookie Lady—Penny West; fortune cookies—Patty Smith; talent of commanding—Promise and Rebecca Lambert; talent of making things appear like quartz—Sarah Luddy; realm of the Mixed Metaphor—Victoria Jones; mango, woman-go fruits—Ginger and Richard Kern; pig pen, pocket watch, water moccasin, L-bow, dazey flower—Ginger Kern; books as portals to their worlds, boot rear float—Robbie Price; scapegoat—Isaac Sherman; Diamond—Marie Boyette; marsh mellow—John Starkie; mint julep tree—Kelly Campbell; pi tree—Hugh Callen; paper jam—Nick Barrington; knight owl—Mike Zavitz; Mundanes do develop magic in Xanth—anonymous for now; a guide dog for Wira—Roger Brannon; Heather with sweet-smelling flowers—Heather Clark; monk-key—Elizabeth Nunley; trolley run by trolls, state seal, talent of summoning zombies—Francis Gradijan; talent of changing folks' personalities—Becca Blake; D. Cease, D. Sist—Roxanne Gill; Taia Taylor winged girl, Oceanna water girl, Lucidia Feldspar—Lisa Rufer; Trans Mitter, Ann Tenna, lands cape—Bruce Durano; Polly Graff—Sheila LeMaster; Willow Elf's need to return to Xanth—Thomas Richardson; shooting the breeze, airhead, petrified forest, talent of reversing wood, walking on air, who enchants paths?—Mike Otten; Nepherina—Sara Grzovic; am-bush, Com-Bat, know ledge, childish,

antonym—Tim Bruening; talent of finger writing in stone—
Bruce Atchison; talent of conjuring Mundane objects—Ben
Allan, Angela Pineda; Brenn, becoming a brick wall, Petra—Brenn Ritchie; hair changes color with emotions—
Kelsey Collins; Seren Dip Ity—Filia24; split centaur—P
and R Lambert; Melanoma—Hannah M. Reff; Anomie with
reverse wood—Shane; Vice and Versa—Victoria; vice
squad—Kenneth Brooks; penicillin—Robbie Price; wooden
castle—given to author by Alan and Peg Riggs for Christ-
mas 2000; whisk broom—Cheri E. Newman; Eye-o-dine,
Metra Gnome, passing wind, miss-isles—Arlen Phillips and
Lars Neufeld; bottle of ail—Dianne Stambaugh and Beth
Johnson; re-done-dent—Milli Jo Hutt; dog sled—Katie
Berning; Hell Toupee—Kirk; Amber Dawn—Amber Baker;
D. Viate, D. Vious, D. Cent—Allen Hamilton; D. Termined—Mike Zavitz, Patricia K. Curl; Charles Horse—
Chris Grohs; goles—David "Zochmen" Buck; assorted
teas—Peter Shanedling; game preserve—Wil Manning;
zombie talents tied to souls—Elena Greenberg; Etcetera—
Sarah Jackson; ears change color with mood—Rose Forrest;
prehensile hair—Thomas Thomas; Demon Lete gave up talent for Kim—Sylvia Navato; Terry and Jerry Tamagni—
Michael Tamagni; Lee characters—Zachary Yerian; sticky
hands and feet—Ray Bryan; Sarah Spirlock—Tonja Cox.

And that's it for this year. There is more in the pipeline.

A preview of
CURRANT EVENTS

I

CLIO

Clio was tidying up her office, as she did every century or so even if it didn't really need it. Dust did tend to collect, along with dried bugs, apple seeds, and lost wisps of fog. Then she paused, which was easy to do during a dull chore like this. There was a volume on the shelf she didn't remember. That was odd, because she had an excellent memory. She had to, to be a competent Muse of History.

She lifted it up, noting the clean spot of shelf beneath it. She blew off the dust and looked at the title. She couldn't quite make it out, so she opened the volume to the title page. That was written in her handwriting, but was somehow blurred. It might be *CURRENT EVENTS,* but could also be *GETTING EVEN.* Neither one made much sense, as she did not handle either contemporary news or revenge plots. Her specialty was history, past and future. The present bored her.

She turned the pages. They had all been filled out, and definitely in her handwriting, but she couldn't read a word of it. She blinked to clear her vision, but it didn't help; every word was fuzzed. The pages might as well have been blank.

She stood there, bemused. How could she have written a volume of history that she herself couldn't read? It didn't make sense. Was she losing her sight?

Alarmed, she set the volume down and picked up the one next to it. That one was clear enough: *PET PEEVE*, with a picture of a disgruntled bird. That was incomplete, because it hadn't happened yet; she was working on it. So she checked the prior volume: *CUBE ROUTE*, which was complete. That was the story of a girl with gumption, and the text was quite clear.

So it wasn't her eyes, which was a relief. It was the volume. What was wrong with it? And why couldn't she remember writing it? How could she be writing the following volume, and remember its details, while being fuzzy on this one?

Fuzzy: her memory of it was as fuzzy as its print. There was definitely something strange here.

She considered for a good three and a half moments. She seemed to have two or more unenviable choices: principally to let the riddle be, or go to Good Magician Humfrey for advice. Humfrey could surely unravel the enigma, but would take obscene pleasure in her predicament. She hated giving him that satisfaction. But she knew the mystery would bug her until it became a downright nuisance.

She sighed. She would stuff her pride into her nonexistent handbag and go to see the Good Magician.

Humfrey's castle was some distance away from the home of the Muses, so Clio got transportation. She walked down Mount Parnassus and out to a babbling brook and spoke to it. "May I have your attention for a moment?"

The brook ceased babbling and formed a swirling eye. It looked at her, recognized her, and formed a mouth. "So good to see you, Muse," it bubbled.

"I need to pay a call on the Good Magician. Do you suppose I could prevail on you to transport me there swiftly?"

"Gladly, Muse. I owe you favors from way back."

That was true, but she hadn't cared to put it that way.

"Then I should be obliged if you would run me there now."

The water humped up into a shape like that of a centaur without a human forepart, standing in the riverbed. "Immediately," it agreed. "If I can make it past the fish."

"The fish?"

"Recently there have been so many fish they clog my channel. It has never been this bad before; normally the water dragons eat them."

"The dragons must be off their feed," she said. That was humor; dragons were never off their feed. Still, it was an oddity.

Clio stepped close to the bank, glanced around to be sure no one was watching, then lifted one leg and swung it over the centaur's back. Skirts were not the most convenient clothing for riding, but they were required for her gender and age. She caught hold of the liquid creature's flowing mane and drew herself fully onto it. "I am ready."

The legs of the water horse went into instant motion. It galloped down the riverbed, following its twisting channel. It had to, because it was unable to run anywhere else. But the running water was so swift that it would soon reach the Good Magician's castle regardless of the indirectness of the route.

She looked down through the horse's translucent substance. Sure enough, the channel was packed with fish so thick it was almost solid. She looked across the landscape around the river channel, and saw rabbits in similar number; in places they were like a gray blanket covering the ground. That was another oddity; were the land dragons similarly off their feed?

She looked in the sky, and saw clouds of crows harassing the other flying creatures. Where were the flying dragons? Normally crows were hardly in evidence, because dragons toasted them on sight. Only in Mundania did they really flourish, normally.

Soon they were in sight of the castle. There was a stream access to the moat that enabled the water horse to reach it. In hardly more time than it took to see it, they were there, splashing to a halt.

The moat monster was snoozing, hardly expecting any intrusion from this direction. It lifted its head and gaped menacingly. Then it recognized the visitors, nodded, and returned to its snooze.

"I thank you kindly," Clio said, dismounting. The water horse had stopped beside a steep bank so that her foot could readily reach it. "Your swiftness was a real pleasure."

The horse nodded, dripping with pleasure. Then it galloped back the way it had come. Running water could never pause long, or it lost its definition.

A sad young woman was walking away from the castle, staring at the ground. "What's the matter?" Clio asked. "I'm Clio; maybe I can help."

"I'm Cayla. I came to ask the Good Magician what my talent is, because I haven't found it yet." She twiddled nervously with a wooden twig she carried.

"That's something you usually just have to find out on your own," Clio said. "It's almost impossible to guess."

"Yes, I've tried guessing," Cayla said. "It doesn't work." She twiddled some more; the twig was taking a beating. In fact there were two twigs getting intertwined.

"So did the Good Magician have the Answer for you?"

Cayla burst into tears. "No! I never got to see him. In fact I flunked the first Challenge."

Clio was morbidly curious. "What was it?"

"It was a big square park set on its end. That is, one corner was toward me as I came to it. I thought the challenge was to get in, but when I got in nothing happened. There was a ball flying around in there, but I had no idea what to do with it. I finally gave up." She blew her nose into a handkerchief, then returned to twiddling the twigs.

A square park, set on its end. "A diamond!" Clio said. "A baseball diamond. You weren't supposed to get 'in,' you needed to get an 'out.' By catching the ball."

Cayla looked at her. "I don't understand."

Clio realized that this would be complicated to explain. "It's only a guess." Then she noticed something. The two twigs were not just intertwined, they were knitted together. "Do you knit?"

"Yes, when I have wool."

"Have you tried knitting other things?"

"Of course not. Why would I do that?"

"Look at those twigs."

"Oh, these are nothing. I'm just frustrated and nervous."

"They are knitted together."

Cayla looked. "Why so they are. But I don't have knitting needles."

"Try something else," Clio said. She looked around and found several bricks. She picked two up. "Try these."

"Bricks? That's crazy!" But the girl took them and put them together.

The bricks twisted and merged. They were getting knitted together. "That's your talent," Clio said. "You can knit wood and bricks. Maybe other things. Maybe anything. You'll have to experiment and find out."

"Oh!" Cayla said, thrilled. "So I don't need the Good Magician after all!"

"You don't," Clio agreed, pleased. This was her first personal interaction with a human person in regular Xanth in some time, and she was glad it had been positive.

"Thank you so much! I was so sad; now I'm so happy." Cayla ran on along the path.

Clio walked toward the drawbridge. This was the obvious way to cross the moat, as she didn't wish to get her feet or skirt wet. But as she approached it, it lifted off the bank, being drawn up by its chains.

"Halt!" she cried. "I wish to use you."

The bridge halted.

She arrived at its resting spot. "Now if you will just drop back down to the bank, I shall be happy to set foot on your sturdy surface," she said.

The bridge started to drop, but a chain snarled and it got hung up. It was stuck a small but inconvenient distance above the ground.

Clio considered it, an unbecoming suspicion hovering at the fringe of her awareness. It wasn't like the Good Magician to have flawed mechanisms. Was it possible that this was not a malfunction? That she was being subjected to a Challenge for entry?

No, of course not; she couldn't believe that of her old friend Humfrey. So it must be a rare glitch in the mechanism.

"Hello the castle!" she called. "You appear to have a problem. The drawbridge is stuck."

There was a little shed associated with the near side of the drawbridge. Now the bridge tender emerged. "Harold the Handyman here. What can I do for you?"

"I am Clio, the Muse of History. I wish to confer with the Good Magician Humfrey, but am unable to cross the moat. Can you fix the connection?"

"Sure, I'll be glad to lend a hand," Handy said, extending his right hand.

She took it. "Excellent. The lines seem to be snarled, so— EEEEEK!" Her scream was a full five E's, and would have been six, had she not run out of breath.

For the man's left hand had just reached around and goosed her right through her skirt.

"Oh, I'm so sorry," Harold said, hastily retreating. "I forgot to warn you. I have two hands."

"I appreciate that," she said somewhat coldly as she rubbed her indignant bottom.

"I mean, they're different. My right hand helps others, but my wrong hand roves. I can't stop them."

She saw his problem. "Perhaps the Good Magician can help you with that problem."

"Maybe, after I complete my year of service."

"I should think he would fix the problem first, to better enable you to perform your service effectively."

"Not exactly. This *is* my service."

"Tending the drawbridge," she agreed.

"No. Being a Challenge."

She gazed at him. "You are a Challenge?"

"That's right. Any querent has to navigate three Challenges before getting into the castle to query the Good Magician. He doesn't like to be bothered by folk who aren't serious."

"I know that. But I'm not a querent; I'm his friend!"

"You're coming to ask his advice."

The hovering suspicion abruptly landed. She was indeed being subjected to the Challenges. That was as outrageous to her mind as was the goose to her bottom. "Well, I never!"

"My right hand should be able to fix the drawbridge," Handy said. "But my wrong hand will interfere. So I have to deal with my hands before I can deal with the problem."

"And I am expected to fathom how to resolve your problem of hands," Clio said. "As the first of my Challenges."

"You catch on quickly," the man agreed.

She was tempted to think an unkind thought about Humfrey, who was definitely not acting in a friendly manner. The very idea that she should be subjected to this process! He deserved to receive a sour piece of her mind. But unkindness was not in her nature, so she realized in half a moment that this was probably a confusion on Humfrey's part, an error. He used water from the Fountain of Youth to prevent himself from aging beyond a hundred years, and perhaps needed to set the mark a bit younger, to prevent senility. She would suggest that to him, as he surely did not want to be confusing his friends with querents.

But first she had to get in to see him. Well, then, there was no help for it but to tackle the three Challenges, preposterous as the situation was.

She looked at Harold the Handyman. So he had a right hand and a wrong hand. Her challenge was to discover a way to nullify the wrong one, so that he could let the right one function. She doubted that any permanent solution was within her power, as she was a Historian, not a Magician, but perhaps there could be a temporary expedient. One that would enable him to function during the interim of his Service to the good Magician.

"I am neither a Magician nor a Doctor," she said. "So I am

unable to offer a cure for your condition. But I may have a way to negate enough of its effect to enable you to perform satisfactorily."

"That would be great," Handy said.

"I believe you should identify your hands. The right one can be called Dexter, and the wrong one can be called Sinister. Put labels on them so that all who encounter you will know them well enough to be able to avoid mischief."

"That sounds great," he said. "Forewarned is foreordained."

"Forearmed," she said.

"Whatever." He fetched some sticky labels and a pen. But when his right hand tried to write on them, his wrong hand jerked the paper out from under the pen.

"Let me see if I can do that," Clio said, smiling. She took pen and paper and neatly printed DEXTER and SINISTER. "Now hold out your hands."

Handy's right hand cooperated, and she fastened its label to the back of it. But the wrong hand jerked away, raising a middle finger. A cloudlet of smoke formed around it, suggesting that this was not a nice gesture. It didn't want to be labeled.

She tried to catch it, but it dodged aside, avoiding her. Then she had a naughty idea. She stood straight, half turning away. "Very well, if I can't label you, I will go elsewhere."

The wrong hand couldn't resist. It dived in for another goose. But as it touched her skirt, she slapped the label against it. Now the hand was marked despite itself.

"You got it!" Handy exclaimed.

"Well, I should hope to be able to outsmart a mere hand." She was privately pleased despite the embarrassing touch. She had, as it were, gotten to the bottom of the problem.

The hand was so ashamed of being tricked that it hid behind the man's back. That allowed the right hand to reach up and unsnarl the lines, and the drawbridge dropped to its proper landing. She had navigated the first Challenge.

At the far end of the bridge was a gate with an oddly

folded turnstile. In fact it was shaped like the letter W. Clio paused to examine it. If this was a Challenge, its operation was obscure. It was mounted on a post that allowed it to rotate, so that it should be possible to step into one of the indents and circle through to the other side. What was supposed to be so difficult about that? She was not a suspicious woman, but she distrusted this.

Still, there seemed to be no other way to proceed. She stepped into it, put her hand on an end, and pushed. It turned, briefly enclosing her as she passed through the gate, then releasing her on the other side. No problem at all.

She turned to glance back—and saw another woman right behind her. She looked rather familiar. In fact she looked exactly like Clio herself in the mirror. Where had she come from? She had not been on the bridge.

"Get out of my way, witch," the woman snapped.

Clio stepped out of her way, affronted. "Who, if I may be so bold as to ask, are you?"

"Who do you think I am, idiot? I'm your double, Oilc."

"My double! How can that be?"

"Didn't you just pass through the Double-You? What did you think it was going to do, cut you in half? Have you no wit at all?"

There was something about this woman that annoyed Clio, but she restrained her temper lest there be some misunderstanding. "The Double-You? It doubles you?"

"What else, dullard? Why'd you go through it if you didn't want to be doubled?"

This was evidently another Challenge. How was she supposed to deal with this abrasive copy of herself? Now she realized that the woman's name was her own name, backward. And the woman's character was the opposite of her own, in the ways that showed so far. Clio tried always to be polite, moderate, and helpful, while this creature was unpleasant, aggressive, and sarcastic. Still, maybe she was merely on edge because she had suddenly been created. It was best to give her every reasonable chance.

"What is your purpose here?" Clio asked.

"You need to ask, stupid? You've overstayed your visa. I'll be taking over now."

This set Clio back again. "You'll be what?"

Oilc favored her with a withering stare. "I'd better put you out of your misery." She looked around, and saw a stick of wood lying on the ground nearby. She picked it up and advanced on Clio threateningly, brandishing her improvised club.

Clio stepped back. "What in Xanth are you doing?"

Oilc swung the club at her head. Clio ducked aside just in time. Should she use her talent? No, it was probably blocked here, and if not, the other woman might have the same talent, which would greatly complicate things. So she ran to the side and fetched a stick of her own.

Oilc came at her again, swinging. Clio managed to block the blow with her stick, but it was a physical as well as an emotional shock. How could she be engaging in physical combat? That was not her style at all!

"I really don't understand," she said as she retreated. "Why are you attacking me?"

"You really don't get it, do you, moron," Oilc said as she swung again. "There can't be two of us; people would notice. So one of us has to go. So I'll just eliminate you, and then your life is mine. No one will know the difference, and I'll be able to do whatever I want."

"But you have no positive agenda," Clio protested as she awkwardly fended off the attack. "You would quickly make enemies, and leave my reputation in ruins."

"More fun," Oilc agreed, this time aiming for the knees.

"Who would write the Histories of Xanth?" Clio asked, jerking her knees back.

"Who needs to? They're dull, boring, repetitive, and uninteresting, with egregious puns."

That generated some ire. "Who makes any such claim?"

"The critics, jerk. Who else?"

"Nobody else," Clio said with some asperity.

"Anyway, I won't bother writing anything. It'll be a lot

more fun to go around messing people up. They deserve it."

Clio realized that she really had to do something about this double. But how could she get rid of the woman without being unconscionably violent? That just wasn't her nature. Which, it seemed, was why it *was* Oilc's nature, she being opposite in everything but appearance.

Now Clio was backed up against the bank of the moat. One more step and she would fall in, and she rather suspected that this would represent a failure to navigate the Challenge. Whatever was she to do?

Oilc swung again, trying to knock her into the moat. Clio tried to avoid her, but lost her balance and started to fall. She flung her arms out, losing her stick, and happened to catch Oilc by the arm. She hauled on it, trying to recover her balance.

"Let go, imbecile!" Oilc snapped. "I don't even want to touch you, you emotional jellyfish."

Then Clio got a wild idea. She flung both arms around Oilc and hugged her close. "You're my other half," she said. "I love you and want you with me always!"

"Stop it, you mealymouthed disaster!" Oilc cried. "I want no part of you!"

But Clio clung close. She brought her face to the other face and kissed it.

Oilc screamed in sheer anguish. Then suddenly she was gone. Clio was left standing holding nothing, shaking with reaction.

She had done it. She had solved the riddle. She had realized that the only way to be rid of the ugly facet of herself was not to fight it but to take it back into herself and suppress it with her conscience. In this manner she had destroyed Oilc before Oilc destroyed her. She hoped she would never have to go through anything like that again.

She brushed herself off and walked through the main portal into the castle. The entry wasn't straight; it made a right angle turn to the right, then to the left. The wall to the right was carved in the shape of a huge human face.

As she stood there, a panel slid across the passage she had

just passed through. She was blocked in; she could not retreat. Well, she hadn't intended to go back that way anyway; her business was forward into the castle.

She looked down the left side passage. It led to a ramp that rose to about head height, then evidently descended beyond. The ceiling rose accordingly, so there was room to walk up and over the ramp to reach whatever was on the other side. It was an odd layout, but maybe there was something beneath that couldn't be moved or altered, so the passage simply had to go over it. Just about anything was possible, here in the Good Magician's castle.

Could this be the next Challenge? The fact that she was closed in here suggested that it was. She had solved one man's problem of wrong-handedness, and abated her doubled alternate self, so this must be some other type of endeavor. Like the drawbridge and the W turnstile, it looked innocuous and probably wasn't.

She would find out. She marched down the hall and started up the ramp. It was steep but not too steep; she could handle it for this short distance.

Suddenly she felt heavy. Very heavy. Something was weighing her down horribly. It wasn't her imagination; her feet were pressing into the ramp and sliding down it as if shoved by a giant hand. She barely kept her footing as she landed back on the flat portion of the floor.

The weight left her. It must have been magic, because there was no evidence of any natural force. This did seem to be the Challenge: to mount to the top of the ramp, when it made her so heavy that she got pushed back down.

She tried it again, bracing herself against the extra weight. And ran right up the ramp as if she were featherlight. In fact her feet left the surface and she floated, drifting back, unable to gain any purchase to push her forward.

Now this was interesting, in an annoying sort of way. The first time she had grown heavy; the second time, light. Both balked her; what she needed was a compromise, her normal weight. How could she keep that?

She tried again, treading carefully up the slope. The heaviness came, increasing until she was unable to drag herself up farther, and had to let herself slide back down. She tried a fourth time immediately, moving slowly, and the higher she went, the lighter she became, until she could no longer maintain contact with the ramp, and drifted back in the slight wash of air coming from its far end.

Well, she had defined the problem. It alternated between heavy and light, and neither suited her purpose. It seemed simple, yet she had no idea how to handle it. Obviously she had to *get* an idea, or she would be stuck here indefinitely.

She walked back down the passage. The huge carved face was still there, gazing at her. The enormous eyes blinked.

Blinked? The face was alive!

"Now I recognize you," she informed it. "You're a sphinx, serving your year of Service."

"Congratulations, Muse," the sphinx replied. "You have solved the first riddle. Do you care for the second?"

"Does it relate to my Challenge?"

"No, it is merely a diversion to entertain you while you remain balked."

"I already know what walks on four legs, then two legs, then three legs," she said with some asperity. She was good at asperity. "A woman, when she's a baby, grown, and old with a cane."

"Unfortunate. I trust you will forgive me if I don't throw myself off a cliff and perish."

"Considering that there's no cliff here, I seem to have no choice but to forgive you."

The sphinx smiled. "So good to encounter a trace of humor. I haven't had a good laugh in centuries."

"Neither have I," she agreed. "Shall we exchange introductions? I am Clio, the Muse of History."

"I am Gravis the Sphinx."

"Gravis. Would that have something to do with gravity?"

"It would."

"In fact, that would be your magic talent: to increase or

decrease gravity in a region. That is what is balking my passage."

"Congratulations. You have solved another riddle."

"I am curious: how far does your ability extend? Could it bring a flying bird down from the sky, or raise a fish from the sea, should they happen to traverse the region you affected?"

"It could. In fact I used to make sport of passing birds and fish who did not understand why they could not fly or swim past a given region."

"It is certainly a significant talent."

One eye squinted. "You would not by any chance be seeking to flatter me into allowing you to pass?"

"I would not have the temerity to attempt any such thing." She was not good at temerity.

"That is fortunate, because it would only annoy me."

"I surely would not want to do anything like that."

"That is good to know."

They understood each other. She had of course been trying to flatter him, and he had rebuked her for it.

That left the original problem: how to get past the ramp while the sphinx guarded it. She had no magic to oppose his; she saw no way to counter the unbearable heaviness or lightness of being.

Then she got a notion. Gravis had not had a good laugh in centuries. Maybe she could provide him one.

"I regret I must leave you now," she said, "as I have business within the castle."

"Must we part already? I had thought we would have more time for dialogue."

"Another time, perhaps."

She oriented on the ramp, then lifted up her skirt and charged toward it as fast as she could. Obviously she hoped to run up it at such speed as to get over the hump before the heavy gravity stopped her.

She made it up several strides before the increasing weight caught her. "Oh!" she cried, and toppled back, somersaulting to the base head over heels, her panties surely showing. She landed on the floor with a thump.

"Ho ho ho!" Gravis roared, thrilled by her humiliation. Young women flashed panties deliberately; mature ones concealed them at all costs. He took a breath and laughed twice as hard. The force of his breath made a blast of air down the passage.

Clio clambered to her feet and charged up the ramp again. This time the lightness struck, as it was its turn. In a moment she was floating—and the moving air carried her on up the ramp to the top. It stopped abruptly as the sphinx realized how he had been tricked, but too late; she had passed over the hump.

She recovered her normal weight and touched down on the far side of the ramp, running. She was through. She had navigated the third Challenge. Now to tackle Humfrey.

"So nice to meet you again, Clio." It was a young woman approaching her from the far side of the hall, which debouched into a larger chamber.

"Nice to see you also, Wira." Wira was Humfrey's daughter-in-law, one of the few people he really liked. She was blind, and had seemed useless to her family, so they had put her to sleep. Later Humfrey and the Gorgon's son, Hugo, had awoken her and married her after she had taken a dose of youth water to reduce her age to his. Now she mostly ran the castle, with the help of the Good Magician's designated wives.

"Can you tell me why I was subjected to this querent business?" Clio asked. "I thought I came as a friend."

"I am not sure, but I believe Dara knows."

"She is this month's Designated Wife?"

"Yes, it is her turn. I understand she was after all Humfrey's first wife."

"She was," Clio agreed. "She had half a soul, but gave it up and left him, then regretted it."

"Well, souls are awkward," Dara said, for they were just arriving at the main room. "Can't live with them, can't live without them."

"We mortals can't live without them," Wira agreed. "I will see if he is ready." She departed quietly.

Clio hugged Dara. "It has been a while," Dara said.

"A hundred and fifty-two years since we first met," Clio agreed. "I left after you married Humfrey the first time, and we have encountered each other only passingly since. Did he ever get your name straight?"

"Never. He still calls me Dana. I'm getting used to it."

"Well, he's a slow learner."

They both laughed; it was a private joke. The Good Magician had made it a point to learn everything he could, so he could put it in his Book of Answers. That was just as well, because later he had taken Lethe water and forgotten some things, and now needed the Book to remind him of them.

"What brings you here?" Dara inquired.

"My 28th Volume of the *History of Xanth* is illegible. I evidently wrote it, but now can't read it or remember it."

"Just like Humfrey with his Book!" They laughed again.

"So I came to ask him if he knows of this matter. But I had to go through the querent Challenges, which were a nuisance; I can't say I'm pleased. Do you know why he put me through that?"

"I'm sorry, I don't. I didn't realize it was you until Wira told me. But you know, he has some weird ways. When the Gorgon came and asked him if he would marry her, he made her do a year's Service before he answered."

"I remember. Then she became Wife #5. But there was a reason: he's such a difficult old man that she needed to have that year's experience with him before she could be truly sure she wanted to marry him."

"I don't think 'difficult old man' quite covers it. How about 'irascible ancient gnome'?"

"At present I'm not sure that covers it either. He is going to have to have an excellent reason for treating me this way, or I shall be annoyed."

"You might write him out of Xanth history!"

They laughed again. It was humor; Clio wouldn't actually do that. They both knew she was too nice a person.

"How is it, being his wife for just one month in six?"

"It takes the first week to get used to his grumpiness, and

another week to seduce him away from his musty tome, and by the last week his stinky socks are piling up and I'm quite ready to disappear back into demonly oblivion."

"You don't pick up his socks?"

"I'm a demoness! How could I even focus on a dirty job like that? Have you ever smelled one of them?" They laughed again. "Fortunately Sofia Socksorter handles that, in her month. Without her, this castle would melt from the accumulated stench."

"She's a sturdy woman. Of course that's why he married her: to catch up on his old socks."

"She knows. She calls him 'Himself,' because that's what he's full of."

"Does anyone really like him?" Clio asked. It was humor; liking was hardly the point, with the Good Magician.

"Wira does."

"Wira's an angel in human form."

Wira reappeared as if summoned. "Humfrey will see you now, Muse Clio," she said.

"And I shall see *him*," Clio said grimly. But her dialog with Dara Demoness had taken the edge off her irk.